PRAISE

"Hold on tight when you read *Hold Still*, for the Lisa Regan roller coaster has taken thrill rides to a whole new level! She sends you up that first hill and then just drops you into a twisting, turning maelstrom of breathtaking suspense! *Hold Still* is one of the most captivating books I've ever read!"
—Michael Infinito, author of *12:19* and *In Blog We Trust*

"Tense, harrowing, and chillingly real, Regan weaves yet another engagingly sinister tale that will leave your nerves on edge right up to the frightening end."
—Nancy S. Thompson, author of *The Mistaken*

FINDING CLAIRE FLETCHER

"Readers should drop what they're reading and pick up a copy of *Finding Claire Fletcher*."
—Gregg Olsen, *New York Times* bestselling author

"Author Regan keeps the tension alive from the first page. Her psychological insight into her characters make the story as intriguing as it is real as today's headlines. This is a well-written and thought-provoking novel that will keep you riveted until the conclusion."
—*Suspense* Magazine

ABERRATION

"*Aberration* is a sophisticated and compelling suspense novel. Just when you think you know what's next, the story whips you around a corner into shocking new territory and you discover nothing is quite what it seems. Lisa Regan has also created that rarity, a wonderfully original and complex heroine in Kassidy Bishop, who is a tough and bright FBI agent but also refreshingly human."
—Mark Pryor, author of *The Bookseller* (Hugo Marston series)

HOLD STILL

HOLD STILL

LISA REGAN

THOMAS & MERCER

This is a work of fiction. Names, characters, organizations, places, events, and incidents are either products of the author's imagination or are used fictitiously.

Published by Thomas & Mercer, Seattle

www.apub.com

ISBN-13: 9781477826416
ISBN-10: 1477826416

Cover design by theBookDesigners

Library of Congress Control Number: 2014941744

Printed in the United States of America

For Melissia McKittrick and Kerry Graham, my real-life heroes.

ONE

October 4th

Secrets and lies—even the most innocent of lives spring from secrets and lies. Jocelyn Rush's blood froze in her veins when three-year-old Olivia asked, "Mommy, do I have a daddy?"

Jocelyn was grateful to be driving. Olivia couldn't see her face from her car seat in the back. She couldn't see the pallor and the hollow look that came over Jocelyn's features. To buy time, Jocelyn said, "What did you say, baby?"

She glanced in the rearview mirror. Olivia's gaze was turned toward the scenery passing by. Her eyelids were heavy, drifting closed and snapping back open every few seconds. Jocelyn was surprised she wasn't already asleep. They had spent the entire day at Smith Playground, where the two of them had slid down the giant wooden slide so many times, Jocelyn's ass hurt. Olivia called it "the Whee" because Jocelyn yelled, "Whee!" every time they slid down.

With its indoor playrooms and extensive outdoor playground for children of all ages, Smith was one of Olivia's favorite places to go on Jocelyn's days off. Jocelyn liked it too because it was free. She worked full-time as a detective for the Philadelphia Police Department, but raising a child alone was costly. She had to cut corners where she could, and free was always good.

"Do I have a daddy?" Olivia inquired again.

"Everyone has a daddy," Jocelyn mumbled.

From the day Jocelyn had taken Olivia in, she'd known there would be questions about Olivia's parentage. Why hadn't Jocelyn's sister, Camille, been able to raise her own daughter? Who was Olivia's father? Why couldn't she meet him—ever? Jocelyn hadn't expected the questions to start so soon. She thought she'd have more time. She had imagined a teenager—or a tween, at least—demanding to know who her real parents were. She had envisioned a child old enough to understand violence and junkies. Jocelyn was lucky that no one ever questioned whether or not she was Olivia's mother. Jocelyn and Camille both favored their mother. Olivia—with her poker-straight brown hair, wide chestnut eyes, and straight nose—could pass as either one of their daughters.

"Raquel has a daddy," Olivia said. "He's a 'older."

"A soldier," Jocelyn corrected.

"Soldier," Olivia tried.

"That's right. Raquel's daddy is far away in Afghanistan."

"Aftercan?"

Jocelyn said the word a few more times, far better prepared to answer questions about war in a foreign country than about Olivia's father. But Olivia's attention had already waned, sleep finally claiming her. At that moment, Jocelyn felt the tightness in her throat ease as Olivia's eyelids drooped.

Skirting the edge of Fairmount Park, Jocelyn took Thirty-Third Street to Ridge Avenue. Three-story brick row houses with mansard roofs and dormer windows sat opposite the park, many of which were burned out or boarded up. Some had sagging porches and trash-lined sidewalks. The turrets and columns had long lost their aesthetic appeal. The larger homes gave way to two-story row houses with bay windows, most of which were painted in shades of brown and deep red. She passed Mount Vernon Cemetery and drove down

West Hunting Park Avenue, home to a slew of mammoth industrial buildings. Long abandoned, the shards of the broken windows were like fangs glinting at her as she passed. The streets narrowed as she drove down Germantown Avenue, but the houses and businesses looked no less desperate as she approached the Nicetown-Tioga section of the city. She was grateful that the rumble of cobblestones and old trolley tracks beneath her tires did not awaken Olivia. Foliage closed in from both sides of the street as Jocelyn drew closer to the neighborhood where the mother of her best friend, Inez, lived. Inez worked patrol in the Thirty-Fifth District. Her mother, Martina, provided day care for Olivia and Inez's four-year-old daughter, Raquel, while Jocelyn and Inez worked.

Jocelyn lived in the Roxborough section of the city, but she had to stop at Martina's house to pick up the treasured blanket that Olivia had left there the day before. They had only discovered it was missing last night. Olivia had thrown the tantrum to end all tantrums before finally falling asleep in Jocelyn's arms on a wave of hiccupping sobs. There were a few tense moments when Jocelyn almost broke down and called Martina to see if she could pick up the blanket, but she stood her ground. People forgot things, left them behind. Olivia would have to learn that sooner or later. A night without her blankie would not kill her—and it hadn't. Still, Jocelyn wasn't about to go another night without it. Raquel was spending the day with her paternal grandparents. With no children to watch, Martina had gone to Atlantic City for the day, but she had promised to leave Olivia's blankie in a plastic bag between her screen and front doors.

Chew Avenue was a busy street with wide single lanes of traffic in each direction and cars parallel-parked bumper-to-bumper on either side. As usual there wasn't a parking spot within a three-block radius. Jocelyn pulled over and double-parked with her hazard lights flashing. Cars zipped around her vehicle without so much as a beep.

In Philadelphia, double-parking is the norm. The blinkers were an added courtesy that most double-parkers didn't even bother to use.

Jocelyn glanced at the house. The screen door was cracked just a little, and there was a flash of a yellow plastic ShopRite bag peeking out. She peered back at Olivia and paused a long moment to see if she would wake up now that the car had stopped moving. But the snoring continued unabated. Jocelyn turned away from Olivia, catching her own smile in the rearview mirror. Just looking at Olivia made her grin. Most of the time, she didn't realize she was doing it. It amazed her that this tiny person could be such a powerhouse of joy.

Unless she doesn't have her blanket, Jocelyn thought wryly.

Jocelyn took a quick look up and down the street, gauging how long it would take her to sprint to Martina's door and back. It shouldn't take more than ten seconds. As a rule, she never left Olivia alone in the car—not even when she was paying for gas—but the door was only twenty feet away. It would be faster to run for it than to unfasten Olivia's seat belt and carry her to and fro.

Jocelyn slipped off her seat belt and got out, closing the door softly behind her. She sprinted up the steps and snatched the bag from between the doors. As she turned back to her car, she saw the figure, just a blur in her periphery. Then her Ford Explorer drove off down Chew Avenue with Olivia in the backseat.

Jocelyn leapt off the steps and ran into the street.

"Olivia!" she screamed.

She had never run so fast, and she was only vaguely aware of the other cars whizzing past, beeping and swerving to avoid her, expletives rolling out of the mouths of passing motorists. The Explorer made the first right onto North Twenty-First Street and Jocelyn followed, arms and legs pumping, feet slapping the pavement, her heartbeat thundering in her ears. She reached for her gun but quickly remembered she didn't have it. It was her day off.

"Dammit."

She was losing ground as the Explorer turned right onto Conlyn and out of her sight.

"Olivia!"

Every muscle in her body strained and screamed, her lungs burning. She turned the corner and almost wept with relief. The Explorer was stopped behind someone who had double-parked in the middle of the street. There wasn't enough room for it to pass. The other car's blinkers were on, the driver nowhere to be seen. For once, Philadelphia's narrow side streets were a blessing instead of a curse.

Breathing heavily, Jocelyn approached the Explorer from the driver's side and opened the door. She didn't look; instead she grabbed and grabbed until she had a handful of clothing. She pulled a skinny punk kid—maybe nineteen or twenty—out of the car by his collar.

His face was pimpled with a patchy five o'clock shadow. His white-blond hair was greasy, a shock of it falling across his coal-dark eyes as he glared at her. "Hey, what the fuck are you—"

The whole world went silent. Jocelyn knew the kid was speaking, but she couldn't hear anything. Her field of vision narrowed to his face. And when he met her eyes, for a brief, fleeting second, he looked afraid. Then Jocelyn hit him. She hit him again and again. He fought back, but his ineffectual punches glanced off her body, no match for her rage. By the time she was done, she had a few bruises and her right wrist throbbed, but she didn't remember the particulars. She only remembered hitting him until he lay at her feet, unmoving. Her vehicle had rolled forward, bumping the rear of the car that was double-parked. A few people had come out of their homes. They stood on the pavement and on porches, staring openmouthed.

Jocelyn's hearing returned slowly. Her labored breath was deafening. She left the kid on the ground and pulled open the back door of the Explorer. There sat Olivia in her car seat, face flushed with sleep. Her little round face was relaxed, her mouth open. A strand of brown hair stuck to one of her cheeks. She sighed softly in her sleep, one tiny hand clutching Lulu, the pink Beanie bear that accompanied them everywhere.

"Oh God," Jocelyn gasped. She put her Explorer in Park and then sat in the back, weeping uncontrollably. She dialed 911 on her cell phone.

"Nine-one-one. Where's your emergency?"

Sobbing.

"Miss? Where's your emergency?"

"Philadelphia. I want to report a carjacking."

TWO

October 4th

Anita Grant cranked the bathroom window open and blew smoke outside. Footsteps sounded in the hallway as she took another drag. She waited for the footsteps to continue down the hall, but they stopped near the bathroom. Even though she knew it was coming, the knock at the door startled her. Quickly, Anita ran her cigarette under the faucet. Her daughter Pia's voice came from outside the door. "Mom? What are you doing in there?"

Anita flushed her cigarette butt down the toilet and sprayed some of her mother's perfume. "I'm goin' to the bathroom, baby. What do you think?"

Her mother's footsteps followed behind Pia's. Anita always recognized the sound of her mama's footsteps—distinct from those of her own children. At ten and fourteen, Anita's children had heavy feet—they trudged and clomped; her mother's step was lighter.

"She's smoking," her mother told Pia. "Go get in there and do your homework."

Pia plodded off. Anita's mother rattled the doorknob. Anita opened the door and confronted her. Lila Grant seemed shorter, smaller than ever. The skin over her cheeks had hollowed out, making her face look sunken. Where they met at the hollow of her throat, her collarbones were two unnaturally large knobs, the skin shiny and taut around them. The cancer treatments were wasting her down to nothing.

"Mama," Anita said, her voice softening at the sight of her mother. "I'm thirty-four years old. If I want to smoke, I'll smoke."

Lila raised an eyebrow and sniffed the air, leaning slightly into the bathroom. "Long as it's just Newports." She took in Anita's clothes and makeup and folded her arms across her middle, her eyebrow a perfect steeple. "Where you goin'?"

Anita sighed and gathered the cosmetics she'd left on the counter. She swept them into her purse. "Out," she said.

Lila blocked the doorway. She stared at Anita hard, the look in her eyes popping the cork on Anita's long-held bottomless well of guilt. Lila glanced down the hall to where they could both hear Pia talking to her brother, Terrence. Their voices were whispers, barely audible over the sound of the television in the background. The smell of roasted chicken wafted down the hallway, mixing with the antiseptic scent of her mother's Cetaphil lotion.

"Nita," her mother whispered, the word something between a plea and a warning.

Anita looked at her feet, swallowed, and looked back at her mother, steeling her resolve. "It's not what you think, Mama."

They stared at each other for a long moment. Anita knew her mother didn't believe her. A thousand justifications flew through her head, but she said nothing. She pushed past her mother, kissed her babies good-bye, and hurried out into the waning daylight.

It was warm for October. She wished she hadn't worn her lace-printed leggings beneath her black miniskirt. Sweat gathered in the creases of her flesh—behind her knees and where her legs met her rear end. After shedding her thin leather jacket, she slung it over her arm and hurried down West Chelten Avenue. The heels of her black stiletto platforms clacked on the broken pavement.

The Dunkin' Donuts on Germantown Avenue was crowded as usual. Anita liked to meet prospective clients at places like this for exactly that reason. So many people came and went—no one noticed her or whom she was with. Usually she met her clients at a Starbucks in the heart of Center City, Philadelphia, but the clients she was meeting today had suggested something closer to where she lived in the Germantown section of the city.

She scanned the tables and saw LJ9124 immediately. *LJ9124* had been the first part of his e-mail address in the messages he had sent her. As promised, he was thin, black, and in his midforties with short, graying hair. He sat at a table with a younger, much larger, light-skinned black man. LJ9124's eyes darted around. The friend had a similarly wary, almost predatory look about him—like two men in a prison yard. Neither one of them had ordered coffee. A slow tingle started at the base of Anita's spine and snaked its way up to her neck. A dull ringing began in her ears. Her old self said, *Turn around and leave now.*

Then her mama's turbaned head flashed in her mind. She remembered the clumps of hair in the tub and on her mother's pillow. Since their apartment was so small, Anita and her mother shared the foldout bed in the living room so that both of Anita's children could have their own bedrooms. Anita was responsible for putting the foldout bed away each morning and had noticed her mother was losing more and more hair each week. Plus, Terrence needed new football equipment. Anita's day job as a receptionist kept the roof over their heads and some food on the table, but that was about it. Cancer meds and football equipment were extras they couldn't afford.

It couldn't hurt just to meet with LJ9124 and his friend. Maybe her instincts were wrong. She'd been off the street for over four years. The tingle could be wrong.

Anita made her way to the table, smiling insincerely—the tingle growing stronger and choking off her voice at first. *Relax*, she told herself. *It's just coffee. You don't have to go anywhere with them.*

LJ9124 stood and shook her hand briefly. His palm was warm and dry. "You Anita?" he asked.

He could have been someone's father—a factory worker, a bus driver, a regular guy—plain and unassuming. Why did his eyes give her the creeps? She studied him until she realized it was the deadness in his eyes that bothered her. They were flat and unemotional.

Anita took a seat, clutching her purse in her lap.

"I'm Larry," he said. "This is Angel. He don't talk."

Angel nodded at her, his dark eyes vacant. His enormous frame barely fit into the metal chair. For the first time, she noticed just how big he was. He seemed entirely made of fat, but she knew he could crush her like a bug if the impulse took him. His eyes drifted away from her, toward the front doors. Neither one of them was appraising her, she realized. They hadn't looked at her—checked her out. She wondered momentarily if they were cops.

"So," she said, forgoing the pleasantries she normally engaged in. "It would be you and Angel, then?"

Larry glanced around the crowded dining area—over one shoulder, then the other. *Definitely not a cop*, Anita thought. *Too jumpy.* He cleared his throat and looked at her. "Yeah."

"What are you interested in?" Anita asked, trying to remain calm and professional even though the tingle had reached her fingertips.

Larry's gaze left her again. He talked from the side of his mouth. "Uh, you know, me and Angel, we both do it. Straight. Nothing unusual."

Anita fidgeted with the strap of her bag. "How long?"

"Two hours."

"Can you host the gathering?"

His eyes darted back to her. "What?"

She gave him a tight smile. "Can you host? Do you have a place where we can go?"

"Oh. Yeah, yeah." He exchanged a look with Angel and met her eyes again. "How much?"

Nonplussed, Anita shrugged. Things were moving too fast. Usually there was a getting-to-know-each-other period—coffee and conversation. A chemistry check. This was too fast, too street. She racked her brain to come up with a way to get out of it. She wasn't doing this job.

"Fifteen hundred," she said.

For the first time, Larry's expression livened. His eyes widened; his lips twitched. "Fifteen hundred? For two hours of straight fucking?"

He looked at his partner, who nodded almost imperceptibly.

"Okay," Larry said, scratching the side of his nose. "But we only got three hundred in cash. We'll have to make a stop to get the rest."

Her entire body was abuzz. "I'm not—I'm not comfortable with that," she stammered. "Why don't we just meet again when you've got all the money?"

They stared at her, as if waiting for something. Then they exchanged another look. The flood of silent communication between them went on too long. Something wasn't right. She stood and smiled. "Well, it was nice meeting you gentlemen."

She left and didn't look back. Her breath came in huffs as she hurried down West Chelten Avenue, her heels clickety-clacking at machine-gun speed.

"Jesus," she mumbled. It hadn't gotten cold in the five minutes she'd been in the Dunkin' Donuts, but she pulled on her jacket anyway. She thought about the old days—all the times she'd been raped and beaten on Philadelphia's Kensington Stroll. Back when she was just a street hooker and a raging junkie. She thought about her babies and her sick mama.

She didn't even hear the car pull up.

By the time the large hands closed around her throat, it was too late to scream. She flailed her arms and lashed out with her purse, struggling silently as rough hands pushed her into the back of a car.

THREE

October 4th

No one on the street approached Jocelyn. They hung on their porches, watching the spectacle, mumbling among themselves, their words an indistinct rumble. The boy at Jocelyn's feet groaned and rolled onto his back. He slung a pale arm over his eyes. Blood streaked his forearm. She had definitely broken his nose.

Finally, a marked unit pulled up behind Jocelyn's Explorer. Officer Kyle Finch stepped out of the patrol car.

"Oh, Jesus Christ," Jocelyn muttered under her breath.

Furtively, she wiped her eyes and face, trying to compose herself.

Kyle Finch had been in the Thirty-Fifth District for six months, but it had been long enough for him to piss off just about everyone he worked with, especially Jocelyn. He had managed six years in the Northeast despite a series of small infractions. He'd been transferred to the Thirty-Fifth after accidentally shooting another patrol officer in his old district. He was a substandard cop, showing up late for urgent calls, spending an inordinate amount of time on simple tasks, and often leaving his fellow officers hanging. Many of the female patrol officers had crushes on him—he was handsome in a high school jock kind of way in spite of being over thirty—until he left them solo on a difficult call or dumped several hours' worth of paperwork on them while he flirted with witnesses.

Three months earlier, Jocelyn had been called out to a bar to investigate an armed robbery. After being attacked by a drunken patron outside the bar, she had called for backup. Finch hadn't answered the dispatcher, and Jocelyn had watched in horror as he cruised past the scene, leaving her to put down her attacker on her own and wait for a marked unit that was much farther away. In the time it had taken for the second unit to arrive, her assailant sliced her arm open with a broken beer bottle. It took ten stitches to close up the gash. A permanent scar was a constant reminder of the incident.

Without bothering to secure the scene, Finch sauntered up to the Ford Explorer and put his hands on his hips. He surveyed the scene as if he had all day, as if he were browsing in a goddamn department store. A smirk snaked its way across his chiseled face.

Behind him, another patrol car pulled up, lights blazing. Relief washed through Jocelyn as she saw Inez's compact frame emerge from the car, one hand on the butt of her gun. Inez approached them, the smooth brown skin of her face creased with worry lines. She shot Finch a look of disdain. "Your shift was over an hour ago, Finch. Get out of here."

Finch gave her a dirty look but didn't respond. He turned back to Jocelyn and gave a low whistle. "Well, well, well—Detective Rush—what do we have here?" He nudged the carjacker with his foot. "This looks like a case of police brutality."

Jocelyn stood up and straightened her clothes. Her right wrist throbbed like a heartbeat. "Fuck off, Friendly Fire. I'm not on duty."

Finch bristled at the nickname that had followed him to the Thirty-Fifth District. Inez muscled him out of the way and knelt next to the carjacker. She checked him over and secured his wrists with plastic ties. "EMTs are on their way," she said. "Finch, your shift is over."

His eyes snapped from Jocelyn to Inez, a flush creeping from his collar to his cheeks. "I'm the responding officer."

Inez stood and faced him. Even though she was shorter by more than a foot, her body seemed to fill up the space between them. She poked a finger at Finch's well-muscled chest. Jocelyn noticed he wasn't wearing his Kevlar vest.

"The hell you are," Inez said. "Get out of here. I got this."

Finch stared down at her. The tips of his ears flamed red, and his upper lip twitched just a little. Jocelyn could feel the indignation rolling off him. She didn't hear the unmarked car pull up or the footsteps of her unofficial partner, Kevin Sullivan, but then he was beside her, one hand gripping her elbow as he looked her over, assessing the damage. He was slightly out of breath. Midway through his inspection of Jocelyn, his eyes widened. "Olivia," he said. He pushed Jocelyn out of the way and poked his head inside the car.

"She's okay," Jocelyn said. "She slept through it."

Although the Northwest Detective Division didn't assign partners, she and Kevin almost always worked together. Kevin turned to Finch and motioned in the direction of the crowd gathered on the sidewalk. "Canvass," he said. "Get some statements, and I want cell phones confiscated too. I don't want footage of whatever happened here on the goddamn eleven o'clock news."

Finch rolled his eyes. "My shift is over."

Inez scoffed. "Of course it is, now that there's work to be done."

"Piss off, Graham." Finch pulled his cell phone out of his pocket, fingers sliding across the screen rapidly as he trudged off, apparently having lost interest in the entire incident.

"You guys got here fast," Jocelyn said.

"What happened?" Inez asked.

As Jocelyn recounted the events, she fought off a fresh wave of tears. She glanced back at Olivia, who stirred briefly. Jocelyn wanted to scoop her out of the car seat and squeeze her, smell her hair, and kiss her little face. Now that it was over and Olivia was safe, her mind raced through all the possibilities, all the things that could have happened to Olivia had she not caught up to the car. Her heart hammered so hard it felt as though her whole body was shaking.

"EMTs are here," Kevin said. "Why don't I drive you and Olivia to the hospital?"

Inez nodded. "Get them out of here before the press gets wind of this. We'll try to keep this quiet." She waved her hand toward the crowd. "They don't know you're a cop."

Kevin ushered Jocelyn toward the car. "Cell phones," he reminded Inez.

Jocelyn pulled the back door open once more. "I want to sit in the back with Olivia."

Kevin nodded. Inez signaled for the additional patrols that had responded to make way for them to leave. "I'll meet you at the hospital."

FOUR

October 4th

Anita woke to a rustling near her left ear. Her lips were dry and crusted together. Nausea spiraled up from her stomach. She opened her eyes, disoriented. Numbness had spread to her arms and legs, making her body feel cold and heavy. Blinking in the semidarkness, she wondered how long she had been here. The faded glow of a streetlight crept through a hole in the wall, barely cutting through the darkness. It had been dusk when Larry and Angel brought her here, and they had kept her for what felt like hours. How long had she been trapped here? It didn't matter. She was still alive. That was what mattered.

Squeezing her eyes closed again, she conjured images of her children's faces, thinking of all the silent promises she had made to them earlier while the men went at her. She had to get back to her babies. She had already failed them so many times in their short lives. If she lived through this, she would be better. A better mother, a better daughter. She'd make do with her receptionist job. She'd get two jobs. But she'd never put herself at the mercy of men like Larry and Angel ever again.

An involuntary shiver ran the length of her body at the thought of the other man, their friend. He had been waiting for them when they arrived. Larry and Angel called him Face although he wore a ski mask. She knew from his eyes that she was in deep, deep trouble.

Anita drew in a deep breath and almost choked. She'd forgotten about the smell—it was like sewage. Hot trash, a bathroom with a toilet that didn't flush, and cat piss. She'd spent some time cataloging the smells to keep herself from going into a full-blown panic attack. She was in some kind of house; she knew that much. Judging by the holes in the walls and floors and the smashed-out windows, it was condemned. Trash was strewn all over the floor. The three men had had to clear a space for her. There was no electricity. Face had used a crank-up camping light to illuminate the room.

Anita heard the rustling again and opened her eyes once more. She turned her head to the left and looked right into the beady eye of a giant rat. A hoarse scream tore from her throat. Her body tried to jerk away from it, and she felt the skin of her hands tear. Startled, the rat scurried off. Anita kept screaming. She couldn't stop. The movement woke the pain in her hands and feet, and it seared through her. She felt a warmth in her crotch and realized that she had wet herself. Her screams continued until she heard feet navigating through the trash.

Larry's face floated above her. "Jesus," he said. "Keep it down. Quiet now."

Anita's screams weakened to grunts. She craned her neck to look behind Larry, searching for Face—he was the worst. He had driven the nails in. Larry put a hand on her forehead and pushed her hair back, just once, gently. "Shh. Quiet now. He ain't here. He's gone."

She fell silent, her head dropping back onto the floor. Relief coursed through her.

Until she saw the pliers in Larry's hand.

Her screams returned with renewed vigor. She squirmed as much as she could without doing any more damage.

"Nonononono," she said.

Larry sighed and shook his head. He got down on his hands and knees, pliers in hand.

"Hold still," he said.

FIVE

October 4th

"Mommy, why are we at the hospital?"

"Because Mommy hurt her wrist, sweetheart."

At Einstein's bustling ER, they waited almost an hour, even with Kevin pressuring the staff. Jocelyn held her daughter on her lap as long as Olivia would let her. She kissed her head, her cheeks, her eyes, and her perfect little hands until Olivia wriggled off her lap. "Mommy, stop," she said.

Once they were ushered into a curtained partition, Jocelyn lay on the gurney. Kevin sat in a chair beside her and amused Olivia by blowing up a latex glove and holding it against the top of his head. He pretended to be a chicken, making "ba-gawk" sounds and flapping his free arm. He tried to peck Olivia with his nose, provoking endless giggles. Even Jocelyn had to laugh at Kevin's antics, in spite of her swollen, throbbing wrist and the suffocating anxiety that had set in since they'd arrived at the hospital. Her mind kept flashing to the moment she saw her Explorer pull away with Olivia in the backseat—a surreal moment that made her heart *tha-thump* unevenly just thinking about it.

Inez pulled the curtain aside. Her face was haggard. Wisps of black hair sprung from her ponytail. Olivia ran over and hugged her leg. Inez smoothed Olivia's hair back and bent to kiss her head. She looked at Kevin. "We got the guy in custody. He's waiting to be seen."

"Anything on him?" Kevin asked.

"His name is Henry Richards. He's twenty years old. Looks like a junkie. Been picked up for prostitution before."

"How is he?" Jocelyn asked.

Inez shrugged. "You definitely broke his nose, couple of his ribs. Maybe his jaw."

Jocelyn closed her eyes momentarily. "Oh my God," she moaned.

"He'll be fine," Inez said. "He had it coming. Oh, and we found blankie on Chew Avenue. It's in my car."

"Thank you."

Inez put her hands on her hips. "Kevin, would you take Olivia down the hall and get her a snack from the vending machines?"

Olivia jumped up and down. "A snack! Mommy, can I have Fritos?"

Normally, Jocelyn would try to steer her toward a healthier snack, but she didn't have the energy. "Sure, baby," she said, so grateful in that moment that Olivia was unharmed that she would have given her anything.

Kevin took Olivia's hand.

"Don't let her out of your sight," Jocelyn blurted.

Kevin rolled his eyes. "I'm not gonna lose her, Rush."

He scooped Olivia up into his arms and disappeared.

Inez made sure the curtain was completely closed and approached the bed. "You got ten minutes," she said. "Get it out now."

It didn't take long for the tears to come. With Olivia gone, it wasn't necessary to act calm. Jocelyn's shoulders quaked. A sob rose in her throat. Inez climbed onto the gurney with her and pulled

Jocelyn into a hug, her nightstick digging into Jocelyn's thigh. Jocelyn held on to her and let the tears overtake her.

"Oh my God, Inez. My baby. He took her. I wasn't even out of the car a few seconds. I can't believe I did that. He took her, and it was my fault."

"Jocelyn."

"No, Inez. What kind of mother leaves her three-year-old alone in a running car? I just—I can't believe I did that."

Inez squeezed her. "Olivia is okay."

Jocelyn shuddered. "But I almost got her killed today—or worse."

"But you went after her and got her back. She's fine."

Jocelyn wiped tears from her eyes and shook her head. "I fucked up. There's no way around that."

They were silent for a moment. Then Inez said, "I locked Raquel in the car over the summer by accident. I locked the keys in the car. It was that rental, remember?"

"The one you had after Ana totaled your Nissan?"

Ana was Inez's eighteen-year-old daughter. "Yeah," Inez said. "I only had one set of keys. I put Raquel in the car seat. I had put the keys down on the seat while I strapped her in, so the car wasn't even running. It was hot. She was stuck in the seat."

Jocelyn swallowed and pulled back to look into her friend's face. "What did you do?"

Inez smiled wryly. "I broke the window. Cost me a fortune too."

Jocelyn laughed. "I thought you said vandals did that."

Now Inez laughed. "You think I'm gonna go around telling people I locked my baby in a hot-ass car? Please. That's between me and the rental company. My point is we all screw up."

A commotion outside the curtain drew their attention. Inez extricated herself and peeked out. "It's the captain and—oh Christ—Phil's with him."

Jocelyn's throat constricted. The last thing she needed was to deal with Phil Delisi.

"Jesus Christ," Jocelyn said. "There are fifty ADAs in majors. He had to call Phil?"

Inez shrugged. "Who better than your ex-lover to help brush this under the carpet?"

Jocelyn shook her head. She stood up, wiped her eyes, smoothed her hair from her face, and straightened her clothes—the simple motions sent a white-hot streak of pain through her wrist. For the first time, she noticed the blood on the sleeves of her shirt. She shuddered.

"They're talking to Kevin," Inez reported.

"How do I look?" Jocelyn asked.

Inez didn't even look at her. "Like shit. What do you care? You guys broke up like a year ago, right?"

"Eighteen months."

Inez humphed as the curtain pulled apart. Phil stepped inside. Jocelyn hadn't seen him in months, but the sight of him still made her breath catch in her throat. He was, of course, impeccably dressed in a crisp charcoal suit with a yellow-and-black patterned tie. His thick brown hair was brushed away from his face. Without even trying, he gave off a vibe of importance and purpose. He was beautiful—strong and male. But he always stung her.

She glanced at Inez, but she was busy peeking around the curtain. Jocelyn braced herself for a steely reception. The last few times they'd spoken hadn't exactly been cordial.

"Jocelyn," Phil said as he neared, his brow knit with concern.

There was an awkward moment where he leaned in to kiss her cheek and she misread it, extending her uninjured hand instead. They settled on a stiff half hug. Phil cleared his throat as Jocelyn stepped back, putting some distance between them.

As much as she'd always been attracted to him, when he touched her she felt cold and closed off. Intimacy had been a big issue for them. Phil's overriding need to control everything about her life had chafed too.

He looked her up and down, assessing, and she was relieved to be out of the relationship. That look was a precursor to criticism. "Are you going to wear those shoes with that?" or "Aren't you going to iron your shirt?"

Now Phil simply asked, "You okay?"

She cradled her wrist and nodded. Inez moved aside to admit Captain Basil Ahearn, who was in charge of both Northwest Detective Division and the four districts it encompassed. Although Ahearn too wore a suit, he was considerably older and more rumpled than Phil was. Standing side by side, the contrast was almost comical. Phil was white, and he looked slick and neatly pressed. Ahearn was black, and, at the moment, he was a study in wayward wrinkles and smelled like cigarettes. Phil smelled as if he had just stepped out of the shower, a combination of soap and expensive cologne.

Captain Ahearn stepped toward Jocelyn and issued a heavy sigh. "Rush," he said. "I talked to Detective Sullivan and Officer Graham. I've consulted with Phil. I want you to take the next couple of days off. There will be an investigation, but since you were off duty and unarmed, there's no need for you to go on administrative leave. There are a couple of conditions, though. You'll have to enroll in anger management classes and go to therapy for eight weeks."

Jocelyn's cheeks burned. "Are you fucking kidding me?" she blurted. "Anger management? That piece of shit kidnapped my child!"

Phil exchanged a look with Ahearn. "He didn't know she was in the car," Phil said calmly. "You broke his jaw, his nose, and a few of his ribs. You used excessive force, given the situation. You'll be lucky if he doesn't try bringing a personal injury claim against you."

Jocelyn waggled a finger at Ahearn. "I was a private citizen whose child was kidnapped. I did what I had to do to get her back. I am not going to therapy."

Inez had come over to stand beside Jocelyn. She scratched her head, then put her hands on her hips. She regarded both men steadily and added, "This is bullshit."

Ahearn sighed again and raised an eyebrow at Inez. "I didn't ask for your input, Graham."

"Not that he's entitled to one, but Richards has asked for a restraining order against you, Jocelyn," Phil pointed out.

Jocelyn's anger was a hot knife slicing through her gut. If it was possible for her face to flush any deeper, it did. "I want a restraining order against *him*," she shot back. She turned back toward Ahearn. "If my child was missing right now, you'd all be singing a different tune and you know it. I did what I had to do. I do not need therapy or anger management."

Again, Ahearn and Phil exchanged glances. They were far too calm, which only pissed her off more. Clearly, they had discussed this and decided her fate before they even approached her. Ahearn's expression was blank, almost bored. "This is not up for discussion, Rush."

Jocelyn narrowed her eyes and took a step toward Phil, crowding him. He didn't back away. "This is coming from you, isn't it? Don't make this personal, Phil."

"This isn't personal," Phil said, but his blue eyes were filled with pity.

Jocelyn didn't know whose ass she wanted to kick more, Phil's or her own. He'd been hell-bent on the therapy idea ever since her parents had died two and a half years earlier. When he'd questioned her apparent lack of grief, she'd made the mistake of sharing an ugly family secret with him—one she had only ever shared with Inez and Kevin. He hadn't been able to let it go.

She held his gaze until he broke eye contact. He moved away from her, to the other side of Ahearn. It was a hollow victory.

"If that kid wants to make a stink out of this, it could be big trouble for you, Rush," said Ahearn. "If the press gets wind of this later, and it comes out that we did nothing to remedy your lack of control—"

"Lack of—" she spat, but Ahearn held up a hand to silence her.

"We have to cover our asses. If it ever came out that you were an off-duty cop, if someone leaked cell phone video to the press, half the city would be calling for your head on a platter, demanding to know why we didn't discipline you in some way."

"Yeah, the half that doesn't have kids," Inez muttered, drawing a glare from Ahearn.

Jocelyn crossed her arms in front of her, wincing as a stabbing pain pierced her arm. "This is a bunch of public relations horseshit," she said.

"He's right," Phil said.

She shot him a caustic look before speaking to Ahearn. "Fine. Anger management. No therapy, and I want a restraining order against that kid—if not for me, then for Olivia."

Ahearn glanced over at Phil, who shrugged. "It's your ass," Phil said.

Ahearn gave Jocelyn a long look. Finally, he turned to leave. "See you in a few days," he said.

SIX

October 4th

Two hours later, Jocelyn was still fuming, and still waiting to be taken for X-rays. Someone on the hospital staff had found crayons and a coloring book to keep Olivia occupied. They sat on the gurney together coloring while Kevin waited outside for Inez's daughter Ana to arrive. She had offered to take Olivia until Jocelyn was finished at the hospital. Although Jocelyn didn't want to let her daughter out of her sight for even a second, Inez had insisted.

"She'll be fine," Inez had said. "Ana will feed her and take her for ice cream. It'll be a hell of a lot better for her than sitting in here for six hours."

When Kevin came in to get Olivia, Jocelyn kissed her goodbye six times until she got annoyed and pushed Jocelyn away. Tears stung Jocelyn's eyes as Kevin walked out with her. "Make sure you get the car seat from my Explorer," she reminded him.

"Bye-bye, Mommy," Olivia called over Kevin's shoulder with a sunny smile. It was all a grand adventure to her.

Smiling tightly, Jocelyn waved. She didn't trust herself to speak again without bursting into tears.

Kevin returned five minutes later and tossed a folded piece of paper at her as he plopped into the chair beside her gurney. It landed in Jocelyn's lap. She picked it up, turning it in her hands. It was an origami crane. "What's this?" she said.

"It was on the front seat." He fished in his pocket for a tab of Nicorette gum. "Doesn't your sister do that shit? What is it? Origami?"

Jocelyn turned it in her hand. It was sloppily folded, not at all up to Camille's standards. "Yeah," she replied. "My uncle Simon taught us when we were little girls. I could never get the hang of it. Camille is way better than this, though, and Simon . . . Well, he's better than Camille."

"I heard he used to do it in court to distract the juries."

Jocelyn laughed. Simon, her mother's brother, had met Jocelyn's father in law school. He had introduced Bruce Rush to his little sister, and the two had quickly become engaged. Simon and her father later partnered up, opening what would become one of the best defense firms in the city. "Yeah, that was an old trick. He used to do the most elaborate origami there was while the prosecutor talked so the jury would be watching him and not hearing a damn thing the DA was saying. They don't let him do it anymore, though."

Jocelyn held it up. "I have no idea where this came from. Neither Simon nor Camille have been in my vehicle for weeks—maybe even months."

Kevin shrugged and opened his mouth to speak but was interrupted by an orderly who had come to take Jocelyn for X-rays. She tucked the crane into her pocket and let the man push her back and forth to radiology. Once she returned, Kevin pointed to the gurney and said, "Lie down. Rest."

Too exhausted to protest, Jocelyn followed his instructions. She closed her eyes and tried to quiet her mind. Her wrist ached and throbbed. No one had even offered her an ice pack, and she was too tired to make a fuss over it. Within moments, Kevin was snoring, chin on his chest. He'd always been able to sleep anywhere, under any circumstances. Jocelyn tried to follow suit, closing her eyes and trying to ignore the sounds outside her curtain.

Even for a Friday, Einstein Medical Center's emergency room was packed. Children wailed. Chairs scraped against linoleum. A young woman shouted, "I'm bleeding all over the place. Can I get some help over here?" Someone vomited. An incredulous male voice said, "Yo, look at this shit. Dude cut his motherfucking finger off." Nurses scrambled and shouted out instructions to other staff members, impervious to the suffering around them. A different male voice said, "My wife is having chest pains." Magic words in an ER. She heard a nurse say, "Come with me, please," as the couple was whisked out of triage and back to the treatment area.

Lucky for Jocelyn, the pain meds made her drowsy. Within a few minutes, all the voices and other noises blended together into a sonorous buzz, lulling her into a light sleep.

A half hour later, she woke to the sound of whimpering. She looked toward Kevin, who rubbed his eyes and pointed toward the other side of Jocelyn's bed. It was coming from the patient on the other side of the curtain.

Jocelyn heard a woman's voice, calm but firm. "Miss Grant, I have to call the police—"

"No, no. Don't. I'm fine," came another female voice, this one strained.

"You're not fine. Whoever did this to you—"

"Please, I don't want to talk about it."

"I have to call the police."

The other female's voice went up about three octaves. Her voice was squeaky and thick with tears. "Please, no."

Silence.

The nurse again. "All right, no police for now. Miss Grant, do I need to do a rape kit?"

Silence again. The nurse sighed. "I'll take that as a yes. You should know that I have a legal obligation to report this to the police."

"Please. Do you—do you at least have a more private room or something? Something besides these curtains?"

The nurse's voice was laden with sympathy. "I'm sorry, Miss Grant. We're completely full. We just had to put a guy with a severed leg in the hallway. This is the best I can do. If a private room opens up, or if I can switch you with someone else, I'll try."

"Thank you."

"I'll be right back."

Jocelyn and Kevin exchanged a look and raced into the hall after the nurse.

"Excuse me," Jocelyn said. "Were you just in with a patient named Grant?"

The woman nodded. Kevin stepped forward and flashed his credentials. "Detective Sullivan with Northwest Detectives. This is Detective Rush."

The woman arched a skeptical eyebrow at Jocelyn. "You're the carjacking."

"Yes," Jocelyn said. "But I'm also the police. You were going to call us. Well, we're here. You've got a sexual assault?"

The woman frowned. "You know your wrist is broken. The doctor will be in any minute to speak to you. You should really go back to curtain five."

Kevin stepped forward and smiled. Although he was in his fifties with thinning salt-and-pepper hair and a paunch, he could still soften up females. Jocelyn always thought it was the kindness in his hazel eyes. "Detective Rush is technically a patient, but I'm here in my official capacity. If you had called, I'd probably be the one coming over here to take an initial statement. If it's a sex crime, we have to call SVU, but we'd be happy to get the ball rolling and speak with Miss . . ."

The woman swallowed and glanced toward the nurses' station. "Grant," she said. "Anita Grant."

"Anita Grant?" Jocelyn said.

Kevin glanced at her. "You know her?"

"Anita and I go way back. She was a pro—I knew her when I worked in the Northeast, on patrol. She went through Dawn Court. She's been clean for years."

Project Dawn Court was a program for women who had multiple prostitution offenses. It offered refuge, mental health treatment, substance abuse counseling, and job training. It gave repeat offenders a chance to get their lives together and reenter society in a meaningful way rather than throwing them in jail.

Kevin turned back to the nurse. "What happened?"

The nurse shrugged. "I don't know. She won't tell us. She's got some pretty bad wounds. She's refused pain meds, though. Well, narcotics. We gave her Tylenol, but I don't think it's helping." She gave Kevin a tight smile. "My name's Kim, by the way. Come with me."

She led them to curtain four. "Miss Grant," Kim said as they entered. "These are Detectives Sullivan and Rush. They've come to talk to you."

Anita lay on the narrow hospital bed, her hands and feet bundled in gauze. She had put on weight since she'd left the street. Her brown face had rounded out, as had her figure. She looked healthy finally.

She met Jocelyn's eyes and quickly turned away. Still, Jocelyn saw the tears streaming down her cheeks.

"I got nothing to say," she murmured.

Blood seeped through the bandages on her hands in dime-shaped circles, front and back. The nurse probed gently at Anita's left hand. "This is bleeding through. We'll have to change it."

Anita winced as Kim pulled the gauze away from her hand to rewrap it. She turned Anita's hand over so that Jocelyn could see the damage. Blood leaked from a pen-size puncture hole that went straight through Anita's palm and out the other side. Jocelyn's stomach tumbled uneasily. She swallowed and turned back to Anita's face, willing the woman to meet her eyes.

Anita stared straight ahead, refusing to look at them.

Beside Jocelyn, Kevin cleared his throat. "What is that from?"

Kim shrugged. "Looks like a nail. I mean, it's small. Looks like it went clean through. It chipped the bone in the center of her hand, but other than that, she was lucky. Same for the feet."

"Someone crucified her?" Kevin said.

"Looks that way."

Jocelyn felt sick to her stomach. "Anita," she said. "What happened to you?"

Anita's frame trembled. She bit her lower lip. Jocelyn could see her holding it all back—the fear, the trauma. Her body shook with the unspoken knowledge of what had been done to her, but she did not speak.

Jocelyn turned to Kim. "Who brought her in?"

Kim shrugged again. "Don't know for sure. She says it was a friend, but whoever it was left her lying outside the ER."

"Anita," Jocelyn said softly. "I can help you. Whatever happened to you, I can help make it right, but you have to talk to me. Tell me who did this."

Anita shook her head and looked away. Another nurse pulled the curtain back. Beside her was a female doctor. "We need a moment with the patient, please," the nurse said. She pointed a finger at Jocelyn. "And you—you need to get back to curtain five. The doctor is looking for you."

"Anita," Jocelyn implored.

The woman wouldn't look at her.

"Just a minute," Jocelyn said. She retrieved a business card from Kevin and jotted the number to the Special Victims Unit as well as her own cell phone number on the back of it, sucking in a sharp breath at the pain in her wrist. "Kevin is going to make a report and send it over to Special Victims. The doctor will do a rape kit. There will be a file started with the SVU if you decide you want to press charges."

She put the business card into Anita's purse. "You call me when you're ready to talk, Anita."

SEVEN

October 5th

In her dream, Jocelyn stood at the door again, peering through the crack. There were four teenage boys. Were there four or five? She couldn't see all of them. Two of them held Camille down. All Jocelyn could see were her sister's white legs, pale and slender. They pushed them up into the air. "It will feel better that way," one of them said. They talked among themselves excitedly. There was a strange exhilaration in the room. They knew what they were doing was wrong, and they hurried about it. They could hardly contain themselves.

Jocelyn couldn't see Camille's face. Did any of them look at her face?

Then Jocelyn's dream-self was beside Camille, standing near her sister's head, her back to the atrocity. She held Camille's hand and wiped the fine beads of sweat from her brow, assuring her that it would be over quite soon. It would be over soon.

Jocelyn woke with a thrash, as if the wind had been knocked out of her. She tried calling out her sister's name, but all that came out was a strangled whimper. She sat up, clutching at her throat with her uninjured hand, willing air to move through her body again. Her T-shirt was soaked with sweat, locks of her hair plastered to her cheeks and the back of her neck.

For God's sake, it was only a dream. Breathe! a voice commanded. It sounded like her mother, but it couldn't be. Her mother was dead. Was it still a part of the dream? She cried out as the air filled her lungs once more. She gulped it as if she had just broken free from the depths of a deep, churning pool of water.

Tendrils of light from the hall night-light crept into her bedroom. A small leg was strewn across Jocelyn's middle. She gripped it and looked over at its owner. Olivia snored lightly; her tiny body fit into the space between the wall and Jocelyn, blankie clutched to her chest. Her little face was so peaceful. Jocelyn hadn't even heard her come in. Two weeks ago, she'd made the mistake of letting Olivia sleep with her while she battled bilateral ear infections. The ear infections had cleared up, but now Olivia moved stealthily each night from her toddler bed across the hall into Jocelyn's bed.

Looking at Olivia's face calmed her, soothed away the last vestiges of the nightmare. As her breathing returned to normal, she got out of bed and rifled through her dresser for another T-shirt. Goose bumps erupted all over her flesh as she changed her shirt, in spite of the warmth in the room. Back in bed, she pulled the comforter over her and laid her head on the pillow, staring at her daughter. She stroked the girl's brow gently and planted a kiss on her forehead.

Jocelyn knew she should scoop her up and return her to her own bed. But she didn't do it. After what they had just been through, Jocelyn couldn't imagine a better place for Olivia than cuddled up next to her, where Jocelyn could keep a watchful eye on her. She liked feeling Olivia's warmth right next to her, being able to kiss her little forehead or her tiny hands. She liked the sound of Olivia's breathing and the occasional soft sigh she made in her sleep. That sound was one of Jocelyn's favorite things in the world.

Jocelyn planted another kiss on Olivia's cheek and turned away from her, curling up on her side. She brought her hand up beneath her head and realized she was shaking. Her wrist, which was encased in an immobilizer, throbbed. She didn't want to think about the dream, but of course, there it was. It must have been seeing Anita Grant that brought it back. She hadn't had the dream for years.

Maybe I should have agreed to therapy, she thought with a heavy sigh.

She concentrated on the sound of Olivia's breathing and turned her thoughts to how she could help Anita Grant.

—

"Mommy, what kind of store is this?"

"A hardware store."

"Do they have toys?"

Jocelyn laughed as she tugged Olivia through the narrow aisles of Stanley's Hardware. It was the last small store of its kind in her neighborhood, run out of a large house with a long line of garages in the back. It had always amazed Jocelyn just how much crap the owners could cram into the tiny establishment. There was talk of tearing the old house down and putting up a new modern storefront, but so far it was just that—talk. Still, they seemed to have everything—except toys.

And nails.

"No toys, honey," Jocelyn said as she surveyed the last aisle in the store, searching for nails and finding none.

"What kind of stuff do they have?"

Jocelyn pulled Olivia toward the back of the store to what passed for a customer service counter. It was a wooden desk that took up half of the back of the store. Then again, the place was so small; a space heater would take up half the store.

"Tools and other materials that grown-ups use to fix stuff," Jocelyn explained.

They waited at the counter. Olivia looked up at Jocelyn, her tiny stuffed bear, Lulu, in her hands. She pinched Lulu's ears. "Are you going to fix the window in the back door?"

"No, honey. Not today."

"Are you going to fix the leak in the skylight?"

Jocelyn raised an eyebrow. "No."

Olivia's delicate little brow furrowed. She looked around at the tools, storage bins, painting supplies, and other home repair items. "Are you going to fix the hole in the carpet in the living room?"

Jocelyn burst into laughter. "No, I'm not. Since when do you catalog our home repairs, young lady?"

Olivia's face remained serious. "What's catalog?"

"It means to make a list of things. Honey, Mommy has to pick something up for a friend. Then maybe we can go get some lunch. We can go to any restaurant you want."

Olivia loved restaurants. Just the mention of eating at one was enough to distract her from her litany of questions. Her eyes widened and her lips curved in a huge smile. "Can we go to Cracker Barrel?"

"Sure," Jocelyn agreed as a man in a Stanley's polo shirt came to the counter. He was young with short brown hair and dark eyes. "Can I help you?" he said.

"I'm looking for nails."

"We have them in the back. What kind do you need?"

The kind you use to crucify someone.

"Big ones. I need to see the biggest nails you have," Jocelyn said.

The man looked down at the counter, barely suppressing a grin. He must have thought she was some kind of idiot. "Well, what are you using them for? You need roofing nails? Aluminum nails? Finishing nails?"

"Just regular nails."

"Common nails?" he said, sounding like a patient parent speaking to a child.

Jocelyn nodded. "Yeah, common nails."

"Okay. What are you using them for? 'Cause typically your nail should be three times as thick as whatever you're using it on. If you tell me what you're working on—"

Jocelyn smiled tightly, resisting the urge to tell him to just give her the goddamn nails. "I'm not using them. I'm not constructing anything. I—I need to match them up with something in my house."

"Do you need a screw nail or ring-threaded nail?"

Jocelyn stared at him blankly. "What does that mean?"

The man disappeared for a moment and returned with three small nails. Two of them had grooves snaking round the length of their shafts. The third was smooth. "That one," Jocelyn said, pointing to the last sample. The nurse had said that Anita's wounds were clean. A serrated or threaded nail would have done a lot more damage. The one the man handed her was only an inch long. "Do you have this in a larger size?"

The man dipped his chin and looked at her from beneath an arched brow. He cleared his throat. "Uh, this isn't like trying on clothes. If you just tell me what you're fixing—"

"I told you—I'm not fixing anything," Jocelyn said impatiently.

"My mommy's not a good fixer," Olivia put in, breaking some of the tension building between the adults.

The man laughed. "Is that right?" he said, leaning over the counter so he could look into Olivia's face. He lowered his voice conspiratorially. "Is she more of a breaker?"

Olivia smiled. She looked at Jocelyn, gauging her mother's reaction to the conversation. Jocelyn couldn't keep the smile from her face. Olivia turned back to the man, grinning. "Yeah, she's a breaker."

Jocelyn shook her head. An image of Henry Richards lying immobile and bloodied in the street flashed through her mind. *Sure*, she thought grimly. *I break faces.*

Pushing the image out of her mind, she turned her attention back to the man. "If you could just show me what you have—I'd only need one of each size."

He frowned and stared at her for a beat longer, as if debating whether or not he should try imparting some manly wisdom, before finally disappearing into the back of the store.

He returned with a pile of large nails. He left them on the counter for Jocelyn to sift through and moved on to another customer.

Jocelyn chose a few that looked three times the thickness of a human hand. She held each one up along the outside edge of her hand, placing the head of the nail flush with the surface of her palm.

Olivia stood on the balls of her feet to peer over the top of the counter. "Mommy, what are you doing?"

"Just trying to see how long these are, sweetie," Jocelyn said absently. She chose three candidates that would easily penetrate through her palm with an inch or more to spare.

"What are you going to do with those, Mommy?"

Probably not a whole hell of a lot. Sex crimes went right to Special Victims. It was their job to go to the hardware store and look for nails that were large enough to penetrate a human hand. It was their case. But that wouldn't stop Jocelyn from following closely to make sure Anita's attackers were brought to justice.

Jocelyn reached down and tousled Olivia's hair. "I'm going to help a friend, sweetheart. Now let's pay for these and we'll go get lunch."

EIGHT

October 6th

It was unseasonably warm for October, but still a couple of the homeless regulars had taken shelter in the vestibule of the Thirty-Fifth District. Jocelyn stepped over two prone figures and entered the building that housed Northwest Detectives.

The desk sergeant, a middle-aged man named McDowell, smiled at her. "Rush. Good to see you."

Jocelyn smiled back and gave him a mock salute. "I only took one day off, McDowell. But it's good to be back."

The other officer grinned. "It was a long day. Start anger management yet?"

"Had my first class this morning."

"How'd that go?" McDowell asked.

"I'm in class with five guys who routinely beat their wives and a woman who set her neighbor's car on fire over a parking spot. What do you think?"

McDowell scratched his head, both eyebrows rising. "Jeez, I think anger management is a good place to get pissed off."

Jocelyn laughed and made her way up the steps to the offices of Northwest Detectives, which was responsible for four police districts in the city. The upper floor of the building at Broad and

Champlost was like an old classroom with its hardwood floors and the faint smell of chalk. Desks were crammed together throughout, the walls lined with filing cabinets. A piss-smelling closet with a pilfered park bench in it served as an impromptu interview room.

Kevin sat behind a desk, his upper body nearly obscured by files and paperwork.

"Rush!" He stood, grinning widely, the skin at the corners of his hazel eyes crinkling. "You're back. How's Olivia?"

She looked around, smoothing her jacket with her left palm. "She's fine," she said. "She was thrilled that I got an extra day off."

"Hey, slugger," Chen, one of the other detectives, said as he passed. "How's the arm?"

Jocelyn held up her right arm and slid her jacket sleeve to her elbow, revealing the splint she had to wear for the next six weeks. "Good enough to kick your ass."

Chen laughed. "Good to see you, Rush. Glad you're okay."

A commotion behind her drew Jocelyn's attention. The closet door was ajar. A woman paced back and forth inside. She was in her early twenties, slender with long blonde hair in disarray. Her lavender wrap dress was torn, blood spattered down the front. She held an ice pack to the side of her head. When she turned, Jocelyn saw a black-and-blue mark by her eye. Her bottom lip was split and swollen.

"I already told you what happened," the woman said. "Can I go now?"

Jocelyn heard a male voice, calm but interested. "Ma'am, I just need you to stay here with me awhile longer. You need to be interviewed by Special Victims. Someone will come get you. We can talk about something else while you're waiting."

She recognized the voice immediately. Jocelyn turned back to Kevin, hooking a thumb back toward the closet.

"Is that Friendly Fire?"

"Yeah," Kevin said. "The Germantown Groper struck again today, only this time, the woman fought back."

The Germantown Groper had been accosting women in the Germantown section of the city for weeks. He approached them in broad daylight and touched their breasts and genitals. He never went further than that, usually fleeing as soon as the women protested. They had some grainy surveillance footage of him, but nothing more to go on. The composite sketch they had released produced no leads.

"No shit. Did we get him?"

"No, but she got into quite a fight with the guy. She knocked his hat off in the struggle, tried to pull out a clump of his hair. He hit her a few times and took off. She got the hair, though. We bagged it, but we're waiting for someone from SVU to show up and take her. She was a walk-in. She didn't want to go down there in a police car."

Jocelyn stepped toward the closet, and Kevin followed. "How long has she been in there?"

Kevin scratched his head. "Come to think of it," he said. "They've been in there a long time."

"Tell me about yourself," Finch went on.

"Are you serious?" the woman said, her voice rising. "Look at my face! I was attacked today. I don't want to talk to you. I want to go home—or to the hospital."

Finch again. "Ma'am, I'm sorry. I just thought you'd want some company while you waited. I didn't mean—"

There was a noisy sigh of exasperation. "Can't I just go? I mean, you can't just keep me here, right?"

Jocelyn swung the door open. Finch sat on the bench, slumped against the wall, arms spread across the top of the bench. If he was surprised to see her, he didn't show it.

"Ma'am," Jocelyn said, herding the woman out of the closet to where Kevin waited. "Detective Sullivan will escort you downstairs and arrange for some transportation. You need to be interviewed by Special Victims, and they will be sure that you're seen by a doctor."

Jocelyn turned to Kevin and fished her keys out of her pocket. She handed them to him. "Call Inez and have her come and take the witness down to SVU in my car."

Finch waited until Kevin and the woman were out of earshot before he stood and walked over to Jocelyn. He glared down at her, trying to use his height advantage—he was a foot taller—to intimidate her. She put her hands on her hips and thrust her chin up at him.

"What the fuck are you doing?" Finch asked.

"What the fuck are *you* doing?" Jocelyn challenged.

Finch motioned behind him, indicating the closet. "I was interviewing a victim."

Jocelyn laughed, the sound dry and hard. "That was not interviewing a victim. Where's your notepad? Where's your pen? Did you even take any notes?" She waved a dismissive hand in the air. "Forget it. She's SVU's problem anyway. How long were you in there with her? You trying to pull a Casanova on a woman who was just sexually assaulted? That's low, even for you."

Finch took a step closer to Jocelyn. His breath was on her face. It smelled like mints. *What the hell?* she thought. What kind of cop had minty breath? He went to poke her chest, but she slapped his hand away. "Don't touch me, Friendly Fire."

"Don't interrupt my interviews," he said.

Jocelyn crossed her arms and looked up at him defiantly. She sensed the crowd that had gathered at her back by the still silence that had overtaken the normally noisy unit.

"Rush," Kevin called. Jocelyn heard the rustle of bodies as he pushed his way to the front of the other officers. "Hey," Kevin said as he broke through and came up beside her. "Back up, kid," he said to Finch.

Finch snickered as his eyes slid up and down Kevin's frame. "Why, old man? You gonna do something about it?"

Kevin looked at Finch as if he was the stupidest person he had ever laid eyes on. "No, dumbass—she will, and you don't want to go toe-to-toe with her."

A ripple of laughter came from behind Jocelyn. Someone said, "Don't make her break her other wrist."

"Aren't you on shift?" Jocelyn asked. "You hiding in the closet so you don't have to do any work?"

She stepped into him, and Finch backed up. "Or were you just trying to get some ass? You know, there are these places that most men go to pick up women. They're called bars and clubs. Unless you like your ladies already roughed up."

The tips of his ears reddened. He swallowed hard, his Adam's apple bobbing in his throat. "Fuck you, Rush."

"Do your fucking job, you little prick. Get off on your own time."

Jocelyn turned away from him.

"Cunt," he said.

A collective gasp went up across the room.

"Hey, watch it, kid," Kevin said. "You're way out of line."

Jocelyn turned back and advanced on him, standing on the balls of her feet to get in his face. "You wanna go?" she said. Her anger felt like waves of heat rolling off her body. She pushed him. "You wanna hit me? Come on. Let's go."

Kevin stepped between them, a hand on Finch's chest, keeping him at bay. He looked at Jocelyn. "Rush, let it go. He's not worth it."

"Come on, you little bastard," Jocelyn said. "Hit me, and you'll see just how much of a cunt I really am."

Kevin shook his head and put his body directly in front of Jocelyn's. He looked at her sternly. "That's enough," he said. "Let's go."

When Jocelyn didn't move, Kevin took her arm and guided her away from the closet. "*Now*," he said.

The crowd dispersed. Finch headed for the steps, shooting Jocelyn a deadly glance before disappearing from sight. Jocelyn's good hand was clenched in a fist. The scar on her left forearm tingled. Heat rose from her collar and enveloped her face. Kevin gave her arm another tug, pulling her back to the present, keeping her from going after Finch. Jocelyn sat at the desk across from Kevin, eyes still on the space at the top of the steps where Finch had just been. Just once, she'd love to pound the shit out of him. Just once. But she was already in deep shit, and a punk like Finch was hardly worth her career. She had Olivia to think about now. She turned toward Kevin and sighed.

"Why do you do that?" Kevin asked.

"He's an asshole."

"That's old news, Rush. You just enrolled in anger management classes—you tryin' to get suspended too?"

Jocelyn shook her head. "Sorry, Kev—no, he just pisses me off."

Kevin shuffled some papers around on the desk. There didn't appear to be any system, although Jocelyn was certain that most of the paperwork would end up on her desk before the end of the night. "It's okay," he said. He smiled mischievously and leaned toward her. "I would have enjoyed seeing you put him in his place, though."

Jocelyn laughed. "If he's around long enough, that day will come. All right, forget about him. What do we have for tonight?"

Kevin leaned back in his chair and yelled back toward Detective Chen, who'd been fielding calls during the confrontation between Jocelyn and Finch. "What do you got?"

Chen rattled off the night's calls in a disinterested tone, as if he were reading items from a take-out menu. "I got a shooting at a playground with no injuries, two robberies—one armed—a lady found dead in her garage under mysterious circumstances and a suicide."

"A suicide?" Kevin said. "What kind?"

"Guy jumped off the Henry Avenue Bridge."

"How long ago?"

Chen looked at his notes. "About fifteen minutes."

Kevin looked back at Jocelyn, giving her his that-sounds-interesting look. "What do you think? We can start with something easy tonight. How's the suicide sound?"

"I don't know, Kev." Jocelyn immediately wondered what kind of family the guy had—if he had young children. How many lives had he ruined when he jumped off the bridge? She thought about the last suicide they'd covered six months ago. The guy had lived with his mother. He was her only son. Her husband was dead, and she didn't get out much. Jocelyn had told her the news standing in the woman's dusty, Bengay-smelling living room. She'd watched the woman's face crumple from polite disbelief to unbridled grief—the pain in the woman's eyes was so immediate and so palpable that by the time Jocelyn had left, she'd felt like going directly to the bar.

"No," Jocelyn told Kevin. "I can't do a suicide. Let's do the playground shooting. After that, I want to pay a visit to Anita Grant and see if I can get her to talk."

He looked disappointed but conceded, grabbing his jacket from the back of his chair.

"Rush," Chen called. "Call on three."

Jocelyn signaled Kevin to give her a minute and picked up the receiver on the desk in front of her. "Rush."

"It's me," Inez said.

"Did you get my keys? Can you take that woman down to SVU?"

"Yeah, sure," Inez said. Then she hesitated, clearing her throat. "I got your sister down here in CCTV. She hasn't been slated yet."

CCTV was a holding area downstairs monitored by closed-circuit television. Jocelyn slouched in her chair. She closed her eyes momentarily and took a deep breath. "What is she in for—drugs or prostitution?"

Inez hesitated again. "Prostitution."

Jocelyn clenched her hand around the receiver, white-knuckling and releasing. "Book her."

"What?"

"Book her."

"I'm gonna send her up to you."

"No, Inez. This is Camille's third arrest this year. *This year.* I appreciate the heads-up but no more favors. I'm done trying to help her. Just book her."

There was a long pause. Dead air. A rustling. Then Inez said, "Okay, fine."

Jocelyn hung up.

Kevin jangled his car keys. "You ready?"

Jocelyn nodded. They were at the top of the stairs when Chen called for her again. "You got a call on line two."

Kevin shot her an impatient look, one brow raised, his mouth turned down. "You sure are popular tonight."

"Give me a minute," Jocelyn said.

Kevin threw his arms in the air and called over Jocelyn's head, "Hey, Chen, give the playground shooting to someone else. We'll take the old woman in the garage."

Jocelyn snatched up the receiver. "Inez, I wasn't kidding. Charge her. I'm not going to change my mind."

"Detective Rush?" said an unfamiliar voice.

"Who is this?"

"I'm trying to reach Detective Jocelyn Rush," the woman said.

"You got her. What's this about?"

"Hi, Detective. I don't know if you remember me. We met in the ER two nights ago. I'm a nurse at Albert Einstein. My name is Kim Bottinger."

"I remember," Jocelyn said.

"Anita Grant asked me to call."

Jocelyn's pulse quickened, but she kept her tone cool. "I thought you were an ER nurse. Tell me she's not still waiting in the ER."

Kim laughed. "No, she's not. She was admitted the night you guys were here. I went upstairs to check on her a couple of times on my breaks to try to convince her to press charges. There was another detective here—a woman from Special Victims, but Anita wouldn't talk to her. I think she's ready to talk now, but she'll only talk to you."

"All right," Jocelyn said. "I'm on my way."

NINE

October 6th

Twenty minutes later, Jocelyn and Kevin stood outside Anita Grant's hospital room. Jocelyn had called SVU on their way to Einstein and spoken with Lieutenant Caleb Vaughn, who'd given her permission to take a statement from Anita. He'd promised to get back in touch with Jocelyn later in the evening. Kim Bottinger had met them in the ER and guided them upstairs.

"I told her you were coming," the nurse said. She glanced nervously at Kevin, giving him a tight smile. "I don't think she'll talk if you're there too," she said to him.

Kevin smiled back. "I understand," he said. "I can wait out here with you."

Instead of telling him she had to get back to the ER to finish her shift, she nodded. Her cheeks flushed.

Jocelyn suppressed a groan. Kevin was practically glowing. The nurse offering to wait with him was what passed for female attention in Kevin's world. He was twice divorced, and he logged double the hours Jocelyn did. There was no time for him to date or even flirt. Interviewing crime victims wasn't the best vehicle for meeting people either.

Jocelyn shook her head. "I'll leave the door cracked, Sullivan."

Kevin leaned against the wall and folded his arms across his chest, eyes never leaving the nurse. Jocelyn moved past Kim, and the nurse laid a hand on her forearm. "There's something else." She looked around, as if to make sure no one else was listening, and leaned in toward Jocelyn. "A few months ago there was another woman in the ER. She was definitely a hooker. She didn't say she was raped, but she had the same . . . wounds. We called the police, but she took off before they could talk to her. I don't know what happened to her."

"What are you saying?" Jocelyn asked, exchanging a look with Kevin.

"I'm saying this is the second one—that we've seen."

Jocelyn sighed. "Wait here. We'll talk later."

Anita's second-floor room was infinitely quieter than the shitty accommodations she'd been given in the ER. She lay on the bed, her feet propped on pillows. Her hands were still wrapped in gauze and rested, inert, in her lap. Jocelyn pulled a chair up beside the bed. Anita's eyes darted from Jocelyn to the door and back.

"Relax," Jocelyn said. "You asked for me, you got me. Just me."

Tension fell away from Anita's shoulders, and she let her head loll against the pillow. Jocelyn pulled out a notebook and pen, grimacing as she tried to write with her injured arm.

"What happened to you?" Anita asked.

"Carjacking. You?"

A faint smile crossed Anita's face. "You ain't changed at all, Rush."

Jocelyn smiled back. "Guess not. What about you, Anita? I thought you were clean."

"I am."

The two women stared at each other until Anita broke eye contact. She looked straight ahead. After a moment, her lower lip trembled. She crossed her arms and tried to hug herself, wincing at the pain in her hands. A small circle of blood leaked through the bandages on the top of her right hand. "I am clean. I don't do drugs no more. But I have an ad on Craigslist, okay?"

"Anita."

Anita glared at Jocelyn. "What? I'm a damn receptionist, Rush. I got two kids, and my mama's sick. I make twelve dollars an hour. It's not like I'm supporting a dope habit no more. It's just—it's easy money. I screen the clients, and I don't do it all the time. It's nothing like working the Stroll."

The Stroll was an area in Philadelphia where drugs and hookers were easily obtainable, but it was also one of the most violent and unsafe areas of the city—especially for prostitutes.

"I never had a problem until now," Anita continued. "Like I said, it's easier to screen my johns this way. Most of the time, I don't even have to do much. I meet them beforehand in a public place, and then we set up another time and place to meet for the . . . you know—"

"I know," Jocelyn said.

"So this guy answered the ad and said that him and his friend wanted to have a threesome."

"How did he answer the ad? Did he call you? Text?"

"He sent me an e-mail."

"I'm going to need that," Jocelyn said.

Anita bobbed her head in the direction of her bedside table. "I can forward it to you from my phone before you leave."

"What was this guy's name?" Jocelyn asked.

"Larry. Don't know his last name. His e-mail address started with LJ9124 so his last name might start with a *J*. Or the *J* could be for his middle name, I guess."

Jocelyn scribbled down some notes, pain streaking through her wrist. She hoped the bottle of ibuprofen she kept in her desk wasn't empty. She would need some when she got back to the Division.

"So, Larry and his friend want to have a threesome. What did you say?"

Anita shrugged. "It ain't nothing I haven't done before, so I said sure, let's meet for coffee, and we can talk about it then. Like I said, I screen them first. If they won't meet me for coffee, I don't do it. If we meet for coffee and I get a bad feeling, I don't do it. If I'm not what they expected, then they can walk away."

"Where did you meet?"

"The Dunkin' Donuts on Germantown Avenue. They were both there. Larry, and he said his friend's name was Angel."

"What did they look like?"

"They were both black. Larry was tall and kind of thin. I'd say about six foot. He was probably in his mid to late forties. His friend was younger, late twenties I'd say. He was shorter, probably about five-eight and fat. I am talking huge, like a damn house. He didn't say much. Larry said he didn't talk."

"Didn't talk or couldn't talk?"

Anita's eyes drifted up toward the ceiling as she considered the question. "Larry said, 'He don't talk.' But I think maybe he couldn't talk 'cause he didn't say a word the whole time. Like maybe there was something wrong with him that he couldn't talk."

"Did you agree on an arrangement?" Jocelyn asked.

Anita shook her head. "No. I had a bad feeling. I sat with them for a few minutes. I didn't like the way they looked at me. They seemed like the kind of guys who wouldn't respect the arrangement. I seen a lot of those guys on the Stroll. Been raped by a few of 'em. So I gave them a really high price, and they said they only had a few hundred dollars on them and wanted to 'make a stop' to get the rest. I told them they should call me when they had all of it, and I left."

Jocelyn looked up from her notepad. "Then what happened?"

Anita seemed to shrink in the bed. Her body curled into itself, as if she was trying to make herself smaller, more compact. Less of a target. She crossed her bandaged hands over her chest, making an *X* with her arms. "I was walking down Chelten Avenue, and they came up on me in their car. Angel got out and just pushed me into the car. I tried to get out, but Larry took off driving while Angel held me down in the back. I fought like hell. The really weird thing is that he didn't hit me. I thought for sure he'd hit me, as much as I was fighting, but he didn't. He just held me. He was so big."

There was a hitch in her voice, a sudden sharp intake of breath as she tried to hold down a sob.

"It's okay," Jocelyn said softly. "Take your time."

Anita didn't look at her, but she kept talking. "They took me to this house. I don't know where it was, though. I couldn't see where we were driving 'cause he had my face pressed into the backseat. It was abandoned. It was dark by then, but from what I could see, the whole row of houses looked condemned. It was disgusting—trash everywhere and rats. There was a big hole in one of the walls and the windows were smashed out. They dragged me inside, and there was another guy in there already. Larry and Angel called him Face. He had this room near the back of the house lit up with one of those crank-up camping lights. He had a mask on, but I could tell he was a white guy 'cause his neck and his arms were exposed."

"What kind of a mask?" Jocelyn interrupted.

"A ski mask. Black. I could see his eyes, though. They were blue. He talked real low, like a whisper. He told Larry and Angel to hold me down. They spread me out on the floor—" A sob erupted from Anita's throat. She had the look of a terrified animal, a rabbit that had just been caught by a larger beast, just felt the predator's teeth plunge into its tiny leg. Jocelyn reached over and squeezed Anita's forearm. Anita swallowed and took a moment to compose herself.

"They held me down, and Face hammered nails into my hands. He nailed me right to the floor. Big old nails. I was screaming—telling him no and begging them to let me go, but none of them listened. He kept on hammering. Then he sat in a folding chair down by my feet and he—"

She broke off and looked away, closing her eyes. Her voice was an uneasy whisper when she spoke next. "He told them to do it. He said—he said, 'It's your turn.'"

"Did he watch?" Jocelyn asked.

Anita nodded. "Yeah. He sat there and watched while they took turns. He was smiling the whole time. I could tell by his eyes. Then he jerked himself off. I thought that was it—that they were done, but then after all that, he got up and made the big one hold my legs. They bent my knees and put my feet flat so Face could hammer my feet into the floor. It was harder than my hands. He struggled a little with my feet, cursing and everything. I don't even know why he did it. They already got what they wanted. There wasn't no reason to nail my feet into the ground."

To quell the rising nausea in her stomach, Jocelyn stood and poured herself a drink of water from the small pitcher on Anita's tray table. She offered some to Anita, but the woman refused. She returned to her chair and picked up her notebook and pen once more. "What happened after that?"

Anita shrugged, the movement small and jerky. "I passed out. When I came to, Larry was the only one there. He took the nails out. Well, he started to, but by the time he got to my feet, I passed out again. I woke up on the sidewalk outside the emergency room."

Jocelyn pulled the small brown bag from Stanley's Hardware out of her jacket pocket. She shook the nails out and spread them on Anita's bedside table. At the sight of them, silent tears rolled down Anita's cheeks. "Were they like these?" Jocelyn asked.

Anita nodded. "Yeah," she said huskily. "They were just regular old nails. I remember they looked so big—like this one." She fingered a nail with a three-inch-long shaft.

"Regular hammer?"

"Yeah, like the kind you get at any hardware store."

"What can you tell me about Face?" Jocelyn asked, depositing the nails into the bag and stuffing them back into her jacket.

Anita shrugged and dabbed tears away with the back of her bandaged hands. "Nothing that will help. I only saw his eyes. He was a white guy with blue eyes."

"Short, tall, fat, thin?"

Anita swallowed. "Tall, probably about six feet. Thin. He was muscular. His arms were real muscular and his chest too. Like he works out."

"That's good. What was he wearing?"

"A black T-shirt and jeans. Black sneakers. He looked real neat, though, like put together, like he takes care of himself. He wasn't wrinkled or nothing."

"Any tattoos, moles, scars, markings of any kind?"

Anita shook her head. "Nothing that I could see. I only saw his arms and neck. He was all covered up. But he smelled—" She broke off and bit her lower lip.

"What is it?" Jocelyn prodded.

Anita blinked back another onslaught of tears. "This is going to sound weird, but he smelled good. Like soap or cologne or something. Clean."

"Okay," Jocelyn said. "That's good. How about the car? Can you remember anything?"

"It was gray. That's all I can remember. It was dark, and I was scared. I didn't get a good look at it."

"Two doors or four?"

"Four. Angel shoved me in the backseat."

"That's good, Anita. Is there anything else?"

Anita swallowed and took a deep breath. She motioned toward her purse, which sat atop her nightstand. "There's three hundred dollars in my bag. It wasn't there before. I only had about twenty dollars on me when I went to meet them."

Jocelyn stood and moved around the bed. "May I?" she asked, reaching for the bag.

Anita nodded. Jocelyn rifled through the bag until she found three crisp hundred-dollar bills, neatly folded in an inside pocket of the bag. "Is this the pocket where you found it?"

"Yeah. I didn't know what to do. I just put it back in there. You think you can get fingerprints?"

Jocelyn shook her head. "No, not from money. Too many people have handled it. Did you see one of them put it in?"

"No, but it wasn't there before. Who else would have put it there? They paid me. They nailed me to the floor, raped me, and then they paid me for it. You should take that money. Lord knows, I don't want it." A shiver shook Anita's frame.

Jocelyn folded the money up in a paper towel that she got from the bathroom. "Well, it's evidence now," she said. She put it in her jacket pocket, next to the nails, and sighed. She pulled her notebook back out. "I'm going to write down an e-mail address so you can forward me the messages from this guy. Is there anything else you can think of? Anything at all you can remember?"

Anita looked at her bandaged hands, staring at them for a long moment. Jocelyn noticed that the wound on the top of her other hand had started bleeding through. "No," Anita said. "That's all I can remember. I know it's not much."

Jocelyn closed her notebook and slipped it in her jacket pocket. "Hey," she said, drawing Anita's eyes to her own. "It's enough. Enough to start with."

TEN

October 6th

Outside Anita's room, Jocelyn briefed Kevin, although he had heard most of the conversation with Anita. "Where's the nurse?" Jocelyn asked.

"Bathroom," Kevin replied.

When Kim Bottinger emerged from the restroom down the hall, Jocelyn pulled her aside. "I need to know the name of the other woman—the prostitute."

Kim looked around, suddenly nervous. She jammed her hands into her scrubs' pockets. "There are HIPAA laws," she said. "I could lose my job. Get fired."

"Goddamn privacy laws," Kevin groused.

Jocelyn leaned into the woman, her brow furrowed in concern. "You called us, Kim. You've been checking in on Anita. I can see that this is eating at you. Now there are a group of sadistic rapists on the loose. I don't need the woman's records. Just a name. That's all."

Kim swallowed. She looked away for a moment. Her hands broke free of her uniform pockets. She stroked the inside of her palm with the fingers of her other hand—in the same place Anita had been crucified.

"No one has to know who gave us her name," Jocelyn added. "You give me a name, and we're done here."

Kevin caught the nurse's eye and smiled reassuringly. "You'll be helping a lot of women."

Kim looked back at Jocelyn, her face paler than it had been moments earlier. She glanced down the hall, but no one in or around the nearby nurses' station appeared to be listening. She lowered her voice anyway. "Alicia," she said. "Alicia Herrigan or Herman—something like that. She was tall, like five-nine, and she had a big tattoo on her throat. I don't remember what it was, but it was big."

Jocelyn laid a hand on Kim's forearm. "Thank you."

"How long ago was that?" Kevin asked.

"About six months ago."

Jocelyn pulled a business card from her jacket pocket and pressed it into Kim's hand. "Thank you. Call me if you think of anything else or if another victim comes in."

"What is this? Some kind of religious thing?" Kevin asked as they weaved their way through the parking lot, looking for the car. He popped a Nicorette tab. His lips smacked as he chewed.

"Keys," Jocelyn demanded.

Kevin tossed her the keys, and she unlocked the car. It had started to rain. A fine mist fell outside the car. Once inside, Jocelyn flipped on the windshield wipers. "I don't think there is any religious element here at all."

She didn't have to look at Kevin to know one eyebrow was raised skeptically. "They crucified her."

He took out another piece of gum, but Jocelyn snatched it out of his hand. "Will you just fucking smoke? You're killing me with all that lip smacking."

"This case has you cranky," he said as he glanced out the window, his chewing noticeably quieter. "I'd love to, believe me. Chicks don't like the smoke smell."

"Chicks who smoke do."

"Funny. It's not healthy. You used to smoke. Now you have Olivia, and you're all straight and narrow and shit. You're real fucking boring now, Rush."

Jocelyn thought about the anger management class she had taken that day and sighed. "Not that boring, Kev. Not that boring. Look, this was more about mutilation and humiliation. The guy watched, for fuck's sake. He hammered in the nails, and then he watched. He jerked off. It's sadistic."

"Well, let's turn it over to SVU."

Jocelyn pulled out her cell phone and called the SVU only to find out Lieutenant Vaughn was on the street. She had his cell phone number from their earlier conversation. She tried that three times, but it went to voice mail.

"They're pretty swamped down there," Kevin reminded her. "They got the Germantown Groper, the Center City rapist, and the Kaufman thing. Oh, and the usual stuff that doesn't make the news—like our friend Anita."

Jocelyn groaned. She leaned her elbow on the ledge of the window and rubbed her eyes. "I forgot about the Kaufman thing. God, I hope they find that girl."

Taylor Kaufman was a nine-year-old who had been abducted from her Northeast Philadelphia neighborhood in broad daylight two days earlier. In the weeks leading up to her kidnapping, there had been two prior abduction attempts by a man matching the description of Taylor's abductor.

Kevin's lip smacking grew in intensity. "Me too. Look, they aren't getting back to you today. Let's get back to the Division. We'll file our report and see what else comes in."

Jocelyn turned to him, holding his gaze intently. "I don't want to file a report."

Kevin stared back for a long moment and shook his head. "Rush, I know you and Anita go way back, but this isn't our case. You can't cherry-pick an SVU case. We don't handle sex crimes. We have enough calls without doing someone else's work."

"She said the car was gray," Jocelyn went on as if he hadn't spoken. "I thought I heard a GRM about a gray Bonneville on the way over here."

A GRM, or General Radio Memorandum, was Philadelphia's version of an APB. Jocelyn flipped on the police radio in the car and listened.

"It could be connected," she added.

Kevin sighed and scratched the thinning hair on the back of his head. "Rush. This. Is. Not. Our. Case."

Jocelyn swatted Kevin's arm, immediately regretting it as pain reverberated through her wrist. "Come on, Kev. We're already on the street. Let's just hit the Dunkin' Donuts on the way back to the Division and see if they've got surveillance. We'll save Vaughn the trip."

Kevin rolled his eyes. "Anything else you want to do for this guy?"

Jocelyn smiled and pulled out of Einstein's parking lot. "I want to find this Alicia Hardigan."

"I thought Kim said her name was Herrigan."

Jocelyn shook her head. "Yeah, she said Herrigan, but I think I know the girl she's talking about, and her name is Alicia Hardigan. She used to work the Stroll. She had a big butterfly tattoo on her throat."

Kevin shrugged. "Okay. But then we file the report and get on with our lives."

"Absolutely," Jocelyn agreed.

The manager of the Dunkin' Donuts showed them footage of Anita Grant meeting with two black men who matched the description Anita had given. They appeared to talk for less than five minutes before Anita stood and exited the restaurant. The two men stared at one another for a moment and left. The black-and-white footage was grainy, but Jocelyn and Kevin could use it to corroborate Anita's story. The manager promised to burn the footage onto a DVD for them by the end of the night. They returned to Northwest Detectives to prepare a report for SVU and download the e-mails Anita had forwarded to Jocelyn. Kevin went out to get cheesesteaks, and Jocelyn took the steps up to the detectives' offices.

She found her sister sitting next to her desk, wrists cuffed in front of her. Camille looked sunken and pale, with dark smudges beneath her eyes. The orange halter top she wore seemed too large for her. Her once pert breasts were flat. Her curves had given way to hard angles, bones straining against her skin. A short denim skirt barely concealed her legs, which made Jocelyn cringe. She was two pounds away from anorexic.

Camille's eyes lit up when she saw Jocelyn. She shifted in her seat like a dog on a chain as Jocelyn approached.

"What are you doing here?" Jocelyn said. "What is she doing here?" she asked more loudly, her question addressed to the handful of colleagues at their desks.

"Talk to Inez," someone called back.

"Jesus Christ," Jocelyn muttered. It had become common practice for the officers in the Division to bring Camille up to Jocelyn's desk so that she could decide whether or not to charge Camille whenever she got arrested. But Jocelyn had been clear with Inez that Camille was to get no special treatment this time.

"Joce, Joce, you got smokes?"

Jocelyn sat, facing Camille. "You know I don't smoke."

The handcuffs rattled. Camille deposited something onto the desk. It was then that Jocelyn noticed the twenty origami figures littering the desk. She unfolded one—it was an evidence voucher.

"Camille!"

Camille rocked back and forth in her chair, her eyes all lit up and hungry. "You were gone a really long time. I didn't have any smokes."

"This is important paperwork, Camille."

The rocking increased, causing the chair to creak a little. "I'm sorry. The folding—it calms me down. You know that."

Sighing, Jocelyn went to Kevin's desk and found his emergency pack of cigarettes in the middle drawer. She tossed the pack at Camille, who clutched it greedily, nearly crushing the pack in her hands. Sitting back down, Jocelyn used Kevin's lighter to light one for Camille. Technically, smoking wasn't allowed in the building, but the detectives routinely disregarded the rule when it came to witnesses and victims. And Camille.

The rocking slowed with her first inhale. Kevin had left a mostly empty can of Coke on his desk. Jocelyn grabbed it and set it in front of Camille to use as an ashtray. She smoked silently as Jocelyn unfolded each of her creations, smoothing out each page. The origami had become a nervous habit for Camille over the years. Concentrating on the intricate folds, creasing the seams over and over, always helped calm her when she was anxious. She'd always been good at it. Uncle Simon's star student. Jocelyn had never had the patience for it.

Jocelyn booted up her computer so she could log in to her e-mail account and print out the e-mails Anita had forwarded from her BlackBerry.

"Have you heard from Uncle Simon?" Camille asked.

"No," Jocelyn lied.

"Isn't he handling Mom and Dad's estate?"

"I'm sure he is."

"Do you think they cut me out?"

"Well, if they didn't, they should have."

Camille ignored the dig and moved on to something else. "How's Taffy?"

Jocelyn winced. "Her name is not Taffy. We've been over this."

Clink, clink went the cuffs. Camille lit a second cigarette from the first one.

"That's right. It's Olivia now. I don't know why you changed it."

"Because I don't want her to grow up to be a stripper," Jocelyn said flatly.

Camille humphed. "How's Olivia?"

"None of your business."

Camille quickly covered her wounded look with one of intense earnestness. "Can I see her? Just once?"

Jocelyn shook her head, eyes on her computer screen. "You just got picked up for prostitution. What do you think?"

Camille's shoulders sagged, rounding forward, making her look even more sunken. "She's my daughter," she said quietly.

Jocelyn tried to keep her voice down, the old anger bubbling up like bile in her throat. "She's *my* daughter," Jocelyn corrected.

Camille stared at her lap and deposited the second cigarette butt into the can. A tense moment passed. Jocelyn leaned toward her sister. "Do you know what Ramon said when I asked him to sign away his parental rights?"

Camille met Jocelyn's eyes, a small flicker of remorse in her gaze. "We weren't really together. I mean, I was going to break up with him."

Ignoring Camille's lie, Jocelyn continued. "He said, 'Take her. She can't earn me no money till she's at least four.'"

The memory still made Jocelyn sick to her stomach. Sometimes looking at Olivia now, it took her breath away to think of all the things Jocelyn had saved her from.

Clink, clink. Camille squirmed as if her chair were on fire. "But she was my baby," she pointed out weakly. "He wasn't the one taking care of her."

Jocelyn laughed, the sound a short dry bark. She pushed back in her chair. "You weren't taking care of her either. Unless you think raising a seven-day-old infant in a meth lab and putting her to sleep in the bathroom sink makes you mother of the year."

"It was only temporary—"

Jocelyn raised a hand. "I don't want to hear it. I don't care. She's mine now. My daughter. You come talk to me after you've been clean for a couple of years. Then maybe you can see your niece."

Camille slumped in her chair. Jocelyn could see her give up. Her eyes wandered around the room, the intense expression on her face gone flat. There wasn't much besides drugs that could hold Camille's attention for longer than five minutes. As Camille lit another cigarette, Jocelyn went back to printing out the e-mails Anita had sent her.

"One more and then you're going down to booking," Jocelyn said.

Camille looked stricken. "What?"

"You heard me."

Camille said nothing and took her time finishing the cigarette. When Jocelyn heard the sizzle of the lit butt being extinguished in the Coke can, she stood up and pulled Camille to her feet. "Let's go."

Camille held both hands out, palms up, the handcuffs knocking against her bony wrists. "Come on, Joce. Give me a break."

"No," Jocelyn said.

They passed Kevin on the stairs. He smiled at them and opened his mouth, Camille's name dying on his tongue when he caught

Jocelyn's icy glare. He clamped his mouth shut and gave them a wide berth. When Jocelyn returned to her desk, he stared at her until she snapped, "What?"

Kevin shook his head. "That's cold, Rush. Real cold."

ELEVEN

October 6th

Kevin tossed the three e-mails and Craigslist ad that Jocelyn had printed out onto the heap of paperwork already cluttering his desk. "This is useless," he said. He picked up the nub of his cheesesteak and popped it into his mouth. "The ad is for a companion—who sounds more like someone who cares for the damn elderly—and his response to it says nothing."

Jocelyn shrugged. "Well, it gives the time and location of the meet. I'll send it over to my friend in computer crimes and see if she can track down the owner of the Yahoo account. She owes me a favor."

Kevin scoffed. "I'll be in the nursing home before you get that back. Why bother? Just give it to SVU. You talk to the lieutenant over there? What's his name? Vaughn?"

Jocelyn nodded. "Yeah, Caleb Vaughn. He's still on the street and not answering his cell."

Kevin leaned back in his chair, eliciting a long squeal from its rickety frame. He stretched his arms over his head, lacing his fingers behind his head. Looking around, he said, "It sure is crowded in here. What the hell is going on?"

Jocelyn looked away from her computer screen, taking in her colleagues seated at their desks. It was very unusual to find them all in the office at one time. Answering calls kept most of them on the street throughout the shift. Normally, they'd be hard-pressed to find bodies to send out on investigations.

Chen walked by, nudging Kevin's chair and nearly sending him feet over head. "Slow night, Sullivan."

Kevin grabbed for the edge of his desk, steadying himself, the chair squealing again, this time even louder. "There are no slow nights in Philadelphia. Criminals must be on dinner break. Give it an hour and—"

"Look at this," Jocelyn interrupted. She tapped a finger against her computer screen. "A nine-one-one call came in last night at six o'clock. A witness saw a large light-skinned black male force a black woman into an older model gray Bonneville. Witness got the plate number. The car is registered to forty-nine-year-old Larry John Warner."

With a few clicks on her computer, Jocelyn brought up an old mug shot of Larry Warner, taken about five years earlier. His brown hair was shot through with gray. He looked like an emaciated Morgan Freeman. "Looks like the guy Anita described and the guy from the Dunkin' Donuts video."

"What's he been in for?" Kevin asked.

Jocelyn scrolled down all the arrests and convictions Warner had accumulated over the years. "Forgery . . . writing bad checks . . . receiving stolen property . . . identity theft. A couple of drug possession charges and a DUI."

Kevin's eyebrows drew together. "Anything violent?"

Jocelyn scrolled down further. "Aggravated assault . . . terroristic threats. Five years ago. He did eighteen months."

"Did he get picked up last night?"

Jocelyn clicked back to the first screen. "Inez responded to the call. Let's find out."

It took only a quick text to locate Inez. "She's downstairs in CCTV," Jocelyn said. "Let's go."

Kevin sighed. "Now just a minute there, Rush. I'm not running all over town for an SVU case. When's the last time we had a slow night? We should be enjoying this shit."

Jocelyn rolled her eyes. "You really want to be sitting on your ass when Ahearn makes his rounds?"

Kevin grimaced, his lips forming a thin line. "Good point."

"Let's just run with it till I get in touch with Vaughn."

Inez met them in the hallway. "Yeah, I talked to the witness. He was pretty shook up. We ran the tag, came up with Warner. He wasn't home. His mother was there. She let us do a plain view search of the house. There wasn't anything there. We put out a GRM on the vehicle. We got nothing. No one reported any black females missing, so there's no movement on it."

"The woman's at Einstein," Jocelyn said.

"She alive?"

"Yeah, but she wishes she wasn't," Kevin said.

Inez rattled off Warner's address. "You might take another ride past there to start. Maybe he's been home since then."

"Thanks, Inez," Jocelyn said. To Kevin, "Let's go."

Larry Warner lived in a run-down row house on North Sixteenth Street. Jocelyn rolled past the house once and parked three houses away. The gray Bonneville was parked across the street from Warner's house.

"It cannot be this easy," Kevin said as they got out of the car.

"Give it time," Jocelyn said as she locked the car. "I'm sure it will get harder."

Weeds sprung from the cracks in the pavement outside the house. Small piles of broken glass had collected in the creases of the porch steps. The house was an ugly red color—almost burgundy. The porch roof sagged, and one of the upstairs windows above it had been boarded up. The screen door let out a loud belch as Jocelyn opened it.

"Glad it didn't come off in your hand," Kevin remarked as Jocelyn rapped her knuckles against the door.

They waited a long moment. The rain had stopped. A cool October breeze drifted across the porch, bringing with it the sounds of children playing down the block. In the street, two men labored past, pushing a metal shopping cart with a disemboweled refrigerator atop it. Jocelyn knocked again, harder. After another moment, the door creaked open. Larry Warner stood before them in jeans and a worn black T-shirt. He looked them up and down. It was clear to Jocelyn by the way his eyes darted up and down the street that he knew they were cops. In neighborhoods like these, whether you'd done something to break the law or not, you didn't want to be seen talking to cops.

Larry remained calm. "Help you?" he said.

Jocelyn put a foot in the doorway and flashed her credentials. "I'm Detective Rush—this is Detective Sullivan. Can we come in?"

With the same feigned indifference, Larry shrugged and let them past. A musty smell greeted them. The floorboards in the living room bowed beneath their feet. A nubby green carpet covered the center of the room. There was a mismatched living room set that looked about as old as Jocelyn. The only thing modern was the fifty-two-inch flat-screen television that sat atop a rutted coffee table.

"Anyone else here?" Kevin asked, standing near the front door.

Larry nodded. "My mom's upstairs sleeping. My friend is here." Larry motioned down the hall to what looked like the kitchen. "Angel!" he shouted. "Police is here."

The man who emerged from the kitchen carrying a plate piled high with spaghetti was huge. His frame swallowed the kitchen doorway. Jocelyn estimated his age to be mid to late twenties. His jowly cheeks hung down over his neck. Rolls of fat strained against his red sweatshirt. He was exactly as Anita had described him. Kevin and Jocelyn exchanged a furtive look. Jocelyn could practically hear Kevin's thoughts.

It can't be this easy.

Angel nodded at them and sat on the couch, eating his dinner as if they weren't even there. "This is Angel," Larry said.

"Angel got a last name?" Kevin asked, flipping his notebook open.

"Donovan," Larry said. He sat on the love seat and began channel surfing with the remote control. "Angel don't talk," he added.

"Why's that?" Jocelyn asked.

"Got shot in the throat a few years back."

As if on cue, Angel stopped eating and pulled his collar down, revealing a large lump of mangled scar tissue at the center of his throat. Jocelyn caught Angel's eyes. They were brown and flat. There was nothing there. "How many years ago?" she asked.

Angel held up a hand and wiggled all his fingers. "Five," he mouthed.

"Mr. Warner, Mr. Donovan, we'd like you to come down to the Division to answer a few questions."

"About what?" Larry asked. His posture was wide-open, relaxed.

"About a woman being treated at Einstein for some pretty nasty wounds," Kevin said.

"Don't know nothin' about a woman in the hospital," Larry said. Angel nodded in agreement.

"You know a woman named Anita Grant?" Jocelyn asked.

"Nope."

"How about Nitaluv79?"

It was a split-second flicker in his eyes that gave him away. Jocelyn could tell he was trying to decide how much to tell them—how much trouble he was really in. He leaned forward. Angel finished up his dinner, setting his empty plate on the coffee table, and leaned back, watching with total disinterest.

"You said this about a woman?" Larry said finally.

"Why don't you come down to the Division, and we'll talk about it there," Jocelyn suggested.

Larry had been picked up enough times to know how the game worked. He didn't put up a fight. Instead, he stood and turned the television off. "Let me get my shoes," he said.

Kevin followed Larry upstairs as the man retrieved his shoes. Jocelyn looked at Angel. "You too, Mr. Donovan."

Wordlessly, Angel stood and walked over to her. He towered over her, the broad expanse of his chest blotting out the rest of the room. Jocelyn stood erect and looked up into his eyes. He stood close to her, but he wasn't trying to intimidate her, she realized. He was merely waiting for further instructions.

Larry returned to the living room with Kevin trailing behind him. Jocelyn glanced at Donovan again and pointed to the door. "Let's go."

TWELVE

October 6th

Back at the Division, Jocelyn and Kevin put the two men in separate interrogation rooms and headed upstairs to their desks. Jocelyn tried Vaughn on his cell phone again, but he didn't answer. As they started up the steps to the Detective Division, Jocelyn was struck by how preternaturally quiet the stairwell was—normally, the voices of detectives at their desks or on the phone could be heard trailing down the steps. A small sapling of dread sprouted in Jocelyn's stomach. What if the Division had been inundated with calls after she and Kevin left? What if there hadn't been enough detectives to respond to calls? Ahearn would have their asses if he knew they'd been out working an SVU case.

As if reading her mind, Kevin grumbled, "I sure hope they all fell asleep at their desks."

At the top of the steps, the tension mounting in Jocelyn's shoulders dissolved. Almost the entire shift was gathered around the tiny block of a television mounted on the wall in the corner of the room. It was hardly ever turned on, but tonight all eyes were riveted to the images moving across the screen.

Kevin and Jocelyn exchanged a curious glance, one tinged with relief. They sidled up to the rear of the pack. Jocelyn found herself next to Chen and nudged his ribs with her elbow. "What's going on?"

"Is that Kensington?" Kevin asked loudly.

The television showed an aerial shot of a few tightly packed city blocks, some of the residential streets no wider than an alleyway, lined with squat, flat-roofed houses. The words "Breaking News" scrolled across the bottom of the screen. Marked units flooded the narrow streets, lights blazing. From the sky, the images reminded Jocelyn of the old video game Pac-Man, the marked units moving steadily through the grid of city streets, searching for their prey.

"They found the Kaufman girl," Chen said, his tone disinterested.

Jocelyn felt her stomach constrict. For a split second, her breath caught in her throat. She coughed and tried to make her voice sound as normal as possible, but when she said, "Alive?" her voice cracked.

Chen didn't notice. "Yeah," he said. He rubbed a palm over his eyes, as if trying to wipe away some troublesome emotion. "Bound, beaten, and raped, but alive."

Jocelyn stifled the breathless "Thank God" that nearly escaped her mouth. Although Northwest didn't cover sex crimes, during her career Jocelyn had seen her share of crimes against children. Before Olivia, she'd been able to wall up the part of her that reacted emotionally—with hysterical rage at the criminals and aching sympathy for the victims—and do her job with the cool efficiency of a machine. But being a mother had put cracks in the wall, and, sometimes, her true feelings seeped through. It didn't prevent her from doing her job and doing it well; it just made it harder for her to sleep at night.

"They found her in this guy's basement. He escaped out the back, took off in a white Honda sedan. The Kenzos heard the police were pursuing a guy in a white sedan, and they pulled some dude out of his white car at Lehigh and Memphis and proceeded to beat the shit out of him," Chen related.

Kenzos was the nickname for people who lived in Philadelphia's Kensington neighborhood. One of the other detectives picked up the tale. "Yeah, so they realized they got the wrong guy, but in the meantime, the rapist crashes his car into a house on Cedar and takes off on foot."

"I hope the Kenzos find him first," someone else said, eliciting laughter from the rest of the unit.

"Nah," Kevin said. "I hope he pulls a weapon."

His comment was met with grim but approving nods. Jocelyn swallowed over the lump in her throat. She hated to admit it, but she agreed—everyone concerned would be better off if officers were forced to shoot and kill the child rapist while trying to apprehend him.

She glanced at her silent cell phone. "Guess I know where Vaughn is."

Kevin nodded. "SVU is ass-deep in this right now. What should we do with their suspects?"

"Hold 'em till SVU comes," one of the other detectives piped in.

Jocelyn kept her eyes on Kevin. She stared hard at him until he rolled his eyes. With a groan, he threw his arms in the air. "Fine," he huffed. "Let's go talk to them."

They tore themselves away from the television and sat side by side at Jocelyn's desk. She ran a quick background check on Angel Donovan. He was twenty-eight, a native of Philadelphia with a dozen arrests for drug violations. He had done a few years in his late teens. The rest of the charges had been dismissed before Donovan even got to trial.

"He's been clean for the last five years, unless you count the reckless driving ticket he got last year," Kevin said as he squinted at the computer screen.

Jocelyn leaned in toward the screen and scanned the report. "Five years, huh? Got shot in the throat five years ago. Suddenly stopped being a criminal? Unlikely."

Kevin shrugged. "Well, we know he hasn't ceased all criminal activity. He just hasn't been caught."

Jocelyn chewed her bottom lip briefly. "Five years ago, Warner had his first ever violent offense. I'm thinking we need to find out what went down five years ago and find out if Donovan was involved."

Jocelyn tried to pull up the file in the police computer, but there was nothing there. "That's weird," she said. "There's nothing here. A mug shot, the summary of charges, and that's it."

"No affidavit of probable cause? No reports?" Kevin wheeled his chair closer to hers and nudged her aside. His fingers worked quickly over the keyboard. He tried for ten minutes before a stream of expletives erupted from his mouth. "This makes no sense," he said. "This kind of shit doesn't just disappear."

Jocelyn leaned over and grabbed the phone. "The DA's office will have it. They've got everything."

Kevin's brow furrowed. "You calling Phil?"

"Not Phil. His paralegal, Lori. I always liked her better than him anyway. She still sends Olivia birthday and Christmas presents."

Lori couldn't find the file in the DA's computer system, but she promised to look in their boxed files to see if she could locate anything—although it would likely take a couple of weeks to track down.

"Something's not right," Kevin said when Jocelyn relayed the conversation. He popped another tab of Nicorette gum. "Well, I guess we might as well talk to these guys. We're gonna be here all night as it is."

Jocelyn grinned and headed toward the steps. "Good luck talking, Kev. You can question Donovan. I'm taking Warner."

She waited for him to remember that Donovan couldn't talk. She watched his blank expression turn to consternation. Then she took off down the steps, dodging the pen he threw at her. "You'll need that pen for Donovan," she called over her shoulder.

THIRTEEN

October 6th

In the interrogation room, Larry slumped in his chair, legs stretched out before him, his right foot moving ever so slightly back and forth. His arms were crossed in front of him. When Jocelyn entered, he remained still. Only his eyes flicked toward her, following her around the room. She pulled a chair toward him, its legs screeching over the tile floor. Sitting beside him, she turned her body to face his and rested one arm on the table.

He spoke little during her introduction and muttered a "yes" indicating he understood his rights once she had Mirandized him. "So," she began. "How long have you lived on North Sixteenth Street?"

His eyes lost some of their jitteriness. "About ten years. It's my mom's house."

"What's your mom do?"

"She used to work for a doctor, medical assistant or something. She's sick now."

"I'm sorry to hear that. Is it treatable?"

He shook his head. "Nah, not really. She has a little bit of dementia. But the real problem is her lungs and heart. She needs oxygen. Doctors said she has CHF. Something heart failure."

"Congestive heart failure?"

Larry nodded. "Yeah, that's it."

"I'm sorry to hear that, Larry. It can't be easy."

He shrugged.

"Larry, do you know why you're here?"

He swiped at the top of his nose with one hand. His eyes darted away from her. "Don't know," he said. "Guess it's about a woman."

"Yes, an escort. Her name is Anita Grant. But you knew that, didn't you?"

No response. The twitching movement of his right foot grew quicker.

"Is this the first time you've picked up an escort online?" Jocelyn asked.

Larry sat up slightly. The fingers of his right hand moved to the tattered collar of his T-shirt. "Online?"

"Yeah, over the Internet. Is this the first time you've used the Internet to find an escort?"

Larry licked his lips. His answer came slowly. "I don't go online a lot."

"Larry," Jocelyn said, leaning toward him. "We know you arranged to meet Anita Grant via e-mail. I've got copies of the e-mails. I know it was your computer because we've got your IP address."

Confusion crossed his face. "IP address?" he repeated.

This, of course, was a lie. Jocelyn hadn't gotten that far, but she was pretty sure that within a few days she—or someone in SVU—would have possession of his personal computer, and someone in computer crimes would be able to confirm that Larry Warner had sent the e-mail to Anita asking to meet with her.

"I have footage of you and Angel Donovan meeting with Anita Grant at the Dunkin' Donuts on Germantown Avenue at five forty-five, two nights ago. So you tell me—was this the first time you've looked for an escort online?"

"I wasn't looking for no escort," Larry began, but Jocelyn held up a hand to silence him.

"Larry, I've got an e-mail from you to Anita setting up the meet. I've got you on video in the Dunkin' Donuts. I know you answered Anita's ad and met with her to arrange a sexual encounter. Anita has been a prostitute for ten years."

Larry remained silent, looking anywhere but at Jocelyn. She let a moment pass. The only sound in the room was the frenzied tapping of his right foot on the linoleum. He licked his lips and looked toward the door.

Jocelyn tried another tack. "Did you know they call prostitution the oldest profession in the world? Hell, it's legal in Nevada. You—you're not that old, still got your looks. Got your mother to take care of. Everyone needs a little release. It's not a big deal, Larry. Maybe you went online, looked around. Maybe you wanted to find an arrangement that wouldn't get you into a big emotional mess."

He was nodding almost imperceptibly as she spoke.

"So," Jocelyn went on. "Was this the first time you used online services to find an escort?"

Larry sighed, tugged at his collar again. "Yes."

"Whose idea was it to find an escort?"

"What?"

"Was it your idea to hire an escort?"

He squeezed the bridge of his nose and squinted his eyes as if the light in the room had suddenly become too bright. "Uh, yeah."

Jocelyn knew he was lying but left it alone for the moment. "So you met with Anita. What did you discuss?"

"Discuss?"

"Yes, what did you talk about?"

"Uh, you know. Sex."

"What did you ask her to do?"

"She was—she would do it with me and Angel."

"She would have sexual intercourse with you and Mr. Donovan?"

He nodded.

"How much did she quote you?"

"Uh, fifteen hundred."

"Did you agree to pay the fifteen hundred?"

"Did we what?"

Jocelyn knew that lying suspects had a tendency to repeat the questions asked them to buy time, just as Larry had been doing since she walked in, but still, her patience was wearing thin. She didn't show it to him. With all the calm she could muster, she repeated the question.

"I don't remember," he said.

"Well, Ms. Grant says you didn't come to an agreement. She says you offered her only partial payment, and she left the Dunkin' Donuts. I've got an independent witness who says they saw Angel Donovan force Miss Grant into a gray Bonneville just fifteen minutes later."

Larry erupted into a coughing fit, his body folding in on itself.

"Let me get you some water," Jocelyn said.

She stepped out of the room and walked down the hall to the room where Kevin was interrogating Angel. She gave the door two knocks and walked back to the end of the hall, toward the watercooler. Five minutes later, Kevin emerged with several sheets of paper clutched in his hand.

"What do you have?" Jocelyn asked.

Kevin shook his head. "This not-talking business is a pain in the ass. And, oh yeah, this guy can't spell for shit."

He held up a sheet of paper. The letters looked like those of a first grader. *Dont no.*

Jocelyn raised an eyebrow. "What's he say about the other guy?"

"He says there wasn't another guy. Just him and Warner. He copped to just about everything else, though. He's not the brightest bulb on the tree."

"Three squares a day in prison. Can't see a guy that size being someone's bitch."

Kevin laughed drily. "You never know," he said. "He says Larry asked him to go get a girl. They went to the Dunkin' Donuts, met Anita. She wouldn't take the money they offered and left. They followed her, put her in the car. He claims he doesn't know the house they took her to—he was never there before."

"That's bullshit," Jocelyn said. "What's he say about crucifying her?"

Kevin shrugged. "Wasn't them. He says he and Warner took her to a house and had intercourse with her. He claims they dropped Anita back off at the Dunkin' Donuts, and he has no idea how she got crucified. That's it."

"So they're both denying the existence of the white guy. Did you ask him who Face is?"

Kevin nodded and held up a piece of paper in each hand. Makeshift letters spelled out *no gy at hose* on one sheet and on the other *dont no fase*. "He says he's never heard of anyone named Face before."

"Bullshit again." Jocelyn paced in the tiny hallway. "Jesus Christ. This sounds rehearsed to me."

"We're not getting lucky on this one. This guy will cop to forcing Anita into the car and even the rape—I asked him if Anita put up a fight and he said yes—but he won't give up the white guy. I don't get it."

"Whatever this guy has over them, it's big," Jocelyn said. "Let's see if we can crack them."

"All right," Kevin said.

"Hold on." Jocelyn took the stack of pages from Kevin's hands. She fished out a handful of them. A few that said simply *yes*, one that said *Put her in car*, and the one that said *no gy at hose*. She tore the *no* from the last page so that it just said *gy at hose*. She took the pages and a cup of water back to the interrogation room where Larry waited.

She put the pages on the table and set the water in front of him. He was hunched over the table. The tap-tap-tap of his right heel bobbing up and down filled up the room. He took a sip of the water, his eyes never leaving her.

Jocelyn sighed and took the seat next to him again. "Larry," she said. "Let's cut to the chase. I don't want to waste any more of your time. You're not an idiot." She flicked a finger off the stack of pages she'd brought in. "Clearly, you're the brains in this operation."

Larry's eyes rested on Angel's crudely drawn letters.

"We know you and Angel Donovan forced Anita Grant into your car. We know the two of you took her to a secondary location where one of your associates was waiting. Where did you take her?"

Larry stared at her silently. She could see him trying to work it out in his mind—how much to tell her, how much to leave out, what would make sense, and what wouldn't. He cleared his throat. "We didn't take her nowhere."

"But Angel put her in your car, correct?"

He tugged at his collar again. "Yeah. She was in the car, but we didn't go nowhere. We paid her. We paid for the sex."

Jocelyn sighed again. "Okay, Larry. Who paid? You? Angel Donovan? Or was it your associate?"

Larry's eyes darted from side to side. "My associate?"

"Yes, Larry. There was a third man involved. Who is he?"

Again, Larry licked his lips, his mouth making a smacking sound. "Wasn't nobody else."

"In the car, yes. When you got to the house, there was someone waiting. Who is he? I want a name, Larry."

Larry shook his head slowly, scratching his nose. "There wasn't nobody—"

Jocelyn held up her hand again, silencing him. "Larry, Miss Grant says there was a third man, and Angel Donovan has confirmed that. We know there was someone else with you that night. What's his name?"

She rifled through the pages from Angel's interview until she found the one that said *gy at hose* and pushed it across the table until it was under Larry's nose. "What happened, Larry?" Jocelyn asked. "I've heard from Anita Grant, and I've heard from Angel Donovan. Now I want to hear from you. This is your chance to tell me what happened in that house. If you talk to me now, I can help you. I don't think this was your idea, but I need to hear from you. Who's Face?"

Larry's eyes flitted from the page to her eyes. For a split second, he had the look of a deer in headlights. Recovering quickly, he cleared his throat and said, "Who?"

"Face. Who is he?"

"Don't know no Face."

"You don't know anyone named Face?"

"No."

Jocelyn leaned in toward him and lowered her voice. "Well, Angel Donovan does. Anita Grant most certainly does. Why are you lying for this guy, Larry? Tell me and I can help you."

He was silent. Jocelyn waited a beat before moving on. "Where did you take Anita Grant?"

Larry shrugged. "Don't remember."

"Is it in Kensington?"

"Don't know."

"You drove there, Larry. You must have some idea."

Again, he scratched his nose. "Don't remember."

"All right. Forget about the house. Between Anita Grant, the independent witness, and Angel Donovan, we've got you on kidnapping and rape. That's ten to twenty on each charge. You could be in prison till you're ninety. Think about that. You can go down or you can give me the name of the third man, and I'll see if I can get the charges reduced. I'm sure the DA will help you out if you're willing to do the right thing."

She saw the struggle in his eyes. The moment stretched out between them. "What's he got on you, Larry? Whatever it is, we can work something out. He drove the nails in, not you. Why go down for something he did? Give me a name, and I can work out a deal for you. I can help you."

His gaze danced around the room, catching her eyes fleetingly. His Adam's apple bobbed in his throat. The sound of his frame shifting against the chair seemed unusually loud.

"You're not stupid, Larry. Don't let this guy ruin your life. You have a sick mother to think about. Who's gonna take care of her if you get locked up?"

He lowered his head into his hands. His shoulders rounded. For a moment, Jocelyn thought he might capitulate.

"Who is he, Larry? Tell me his name."

He raised his head to look at her. His eyes had gone flat and vacant.

"I can't," he said.

FOURTEEN

October 6th

Jocelyn's breath caught in her throat. She swallowed, and, keeping her expression blank, said, "Why not, Larry?"

His fingers thrummed against the stack of pages Angel had written on. "Wasn't nobody else."

"Who are you lying for, Larry?"

"Nobody."

Jocelyn knew that continuing the interrogation was pointless. Warner and Donovan had worked this out ahead of time—what they would say if they were caught or questioned by the police. Their plan did not involve ratting out their associate. The staccato beats of Larry's fingers against the table grew faster and louder. Jocelyn watched him until he shifted in his chair and went back to bobbing his right heel. When the moment became painfully awkward, she leaned toward him and caught his gaze once more.

"I can't believe you're this fucking stupid, Larry."

She went at him for another half hour, but he wasn't budging. He was like a broken record. *Wasn't nobody else. Don't know no Face.* She and Kevin left both men in the CCTV holding area and went upstairs to regroup. Most of the other detectives had dispersed, sent out on calls. The television still played silently in the corner, flashing images of evening sitcoms with an occasional "Breaking News" alert.

Kevin plopped into his desk chair and loosened his tie. "I'm tired of talking to these two fuckers. Let's call SVU and have them picked up."

Chen breezed by, a stack of files in his arms, a pen hanging from the corner of his mouth. "Forget it, Sully. They got their hands full. The Kaufman suspect barricaded himself in someone's house. Hostages and all. They're in a standoff. Oh, and the Germantown Groper struck twice tonight."

Kevin rubbed his eyes with the palms of his hands. "Jesus H.," he said. "It'll take them forever to get here. Well, fuck it. Those two can sit in a holding cell for the next day for all I care."

Pacing, Jocelyn loosened the brace on her wrist and rubbed the skin lightly before tightening it again. Exhaustion made her legs ache. It was nearing the end of her shift, but she knew they'd be there well after their shift doing paperwork. She remembered she'd promised Olivia they would go get a Halloween costume in the morning.

"This isn't right," Jocelyn said. "Why are they protecting this guy?"

Kevin sighed. "Who cares? It isn't our problem anyway. Let's just charge 'em and leave 'em down there till SVU picks them up."

"With what?"

Kevin ran a hand over the thinning hair at his scalp. "Jesus Christ, Rush. With whatever we can. Rape, kidnapping, aggravated assault."

She stopped pacing and looked at Kevin. "We need the third guy."

"This is not our case. We're not going after the third guy. We're charging these fuckers, and we're going home."

Jocelyn stood before him and put her hands on her hips. She arched her brow until Kevin groaned loudly, leaning back in his chair and looking at the ceiling as if he wished aliens would abduct him right that very second. "What the hell, Rush?"

"When SVU takes over, I want to make sure we did our job."

Kevin shook his head and looked back at her. "We did our job. Look, we're not getting the third guy through these fuckers. Did you offer Warner a deal?"

Jocelyn nodded. She rifled through her desk for the bottle of ibuprofen she kept there. "He's not taking a deal."

"Neither is Donovan."

She found the bottle, opened it, and shook two pills out onto her desk. "Donovan is just the muscle. He does whatever Warner says because Warner is in charge. They practiced this. They planned this—how they would handle it and what they would say if they were ever questioned."

Kevin pulled a pack of Nicorette gum out of his jacket pocket and popped two tabs. "So we charge them. SVU can check out their known associates. They'll write up a warrant for the car, the phones, and Warner's computer. These guys must be calling this Face guy on the phone. SVU will track him that way. But this is not our problem anymore."

Jocelyn fished a warm bottle of Pepsi from beneath the paperwork on her desk and used it to swallow the ibuprofen, grimacing at the flat, saccharine taste. "I don't think SVU is going to find Face that way. Warner and Donovan had the foresight to get their stories straight. What makes you think a simple check of their phones is going to lead us right to the other guy?"

"So they try some other way. Who cares, Rush? Look, I know you and Anita know each other from when you were on patrol, but SVU handles all sex cases. That is not news to you. This is out of our hands."

Jocelyn reached up to rub her eyes with both hands, flinching as the coarse material of the splint scratched her cheek. She kept forgetting she had it on, despite the throbbing in her wrist. She dropped into her chair, leaned her head back against the headrest, and closed her eyes. Kevin was right, of course. Neither their boss nor the Special Victims Unit would take kindly to them pursuing a case that was not theirs, no matter how good their work was. There were plenty of other crimes in their own jurisdiction to handle.

She thought of Anita cowering in a hospital bed, blood-soaked bandages on her trembling hands. Jocelyn understood why Anita had returned to prostitution. The money was easy, and Anita was not wealthy by any standards. The prostitution had never been the worst of Anita's problems anyway. It was always the drugs—like it was for so many people. Like Camille. But unlike Jocelyn's sister, Anita had found it within herself to kick them and had been strong enough to stay off them the last several years. On the Stroll, Anita had been tough and resourceful. She was strong. Those were the qualities that had enabled her to clean herself up finally, to stop using drugs and make a life for herself and her children.

Jocelyn hated that anyone could reduce the vibrant, spirited woman she knew into a quivering mess. It burned her. Deep in her stomach, in her core. The things she wanted to do to the men who had hurt Anita tested the very limits of her humanity.

But she had to let go of the case.

She could always check up on Anita, but she had to do her job, and her job was not investigating sex crimes.

She sighed. "Okay, let's charge them."

Kevin turned to his computer. "Gladly."

FIFTEEN

October 7th

Jocelyn woke from the dream kicking, her mouth working to release the scream lodged in her throat. A glance at her alarm clock showed it was 3:24 a.m. Attempting to catch her breath, she extricated her legs from the tangled blanket and threw them over the side of her bed, sitting upright. She was relieved that Olivia had not yet crept into her bed. A thick bead of sweat slid down the side of her face. She swiped it away with the back of her wrist, scratching her cheek with the splint and making her wrist throb. She tried to slow her breathing.

It was the same dream from the other night. She had stood peering through the crack of her sister's bedroom door while those boys hurt Camille. Five altogether. One of them only watched. Then she ran, her parents' Main Line mansion turning into an endless maze of hallways. She ran and ran and ran, but she couldn't find her father or anyone who could help.

Is that how it had been? Had she been there? Had she really seen it? She couldn't remember—had never remembered, in fact. Only two weeks after the rape, at seventeen, she'd been in a car accident. She'd lost all memories from the week before the rape to the week after her accident, a month of her life completely gone. Her doctor had said it wasn't unheard of with major head injuries.

The last thing Jocelyn remembered was getting into her car after school sometime before all the bad things happened. She remembered waving good-bye to friends in the parking lot and driving to the exit. Then she was at home, in her bed. Her whole body ached. Her hair had been shaved where they did the craniotomy. Her mother kept vigil beside her bed.

"An accident," her mother had said. "You've been in an accident."

No one explained what had happened in the month she had lost. Her family scrupulously avoided the subject, no matter how incessantly she brought it up. *An accident,* was all her mother said.

The six months after that was a blur. Doctors, physical therapists, and schoolwork at home. Her family was wealthy enough that her father could afford to have almost all her medical treatment take place in their home. She rarely left the house, rarely had the time to think past walking and feeding herself again. All she knew was that her mother was weepy and tremulous, a tissue pressed against her mouth as if she was holding back a great wave of grief. Camille was moody and withdrawn. She wouldn't talk to any of them. She wouldn't look at any of them either. Jocelyn's father was exactly the same as he had always been—cold, distant, and mostly absent.

Jocelyn found out about Camille's rape by accident. She'd been unable to sleep most nights and spent them prowling the house, pacing mindlessly, willing the limp in her left leg to go away. One night, she headed for her father's study to look for a book that might interest her. When she reached the closed doors, she heard her mother's raised voice.

"We can't just do nothing, Bruce."

Her father's voice was considerably lower, and even with her ear pressed against the door, Jocelyn could only make out snippets of what he said.

". . . just boys. Do you understand how many lives would be ruined?"

"How can you even say that?" her mother had shouted. "Those boys gang-raped our daughter. Our daughter."

Something crashed behind the doors. Jocelyn jumped, her heart racing. Her father's voice sounded alarmed, almost afraid. "Elizabeth," he said.

"You bastard!" her mother railed. "You shit. You prick!"

Another crash.

"Elizabeth!" her father shouted, the sternness returning to his tone. Then he lowered his voice again. "I've already made this decision. We're talking about teenagers . . . no good will come of dragging this out . . . press coverage . . . out of control. I know what's best for this family. Let me handle this my way . . . not in court and not in the press. Those boys will be punished."

Her mother's voice was still loud but deadly calm. "What about Camille?"

Jocelyn heard what she thought was her father sighing. "I'll handle Camille," he said.

"And Jocelyn? She saw them."

Another sigh. "Jocelyn doesn't remember any of it. Not a thing—not after that accident. You know as well as I do that she will never recover those memories. Look at her, for God's sake. She can hardly even walk. We don't need to worry about her."

Her mother was silent for what felt like several minutes. Then the sound of glass shattering broke the silence. Jocelyn had never heard her mother sound so angry or so threatening. "I will not forget this," was the last thing she said.

Jocelyn kept replaying the conversation from that night in her mind. She could not let it go. She tried for a long time to talk to Camille about it, but Camille always shut her down. After many attempts, she refused to talk to Jocelyn at all. In spite of that, Jocelyn made every effort to undermine her father's plan to brush the whole thing under the carpet. She went first to the sheriff, then to the district attorney's office, where two ADAs listened to her with rapt attention and promised to thoroughly investigate the rape. They brought Camille in, along with their father, but Camille would not admit that any crime had taken place.

Jocelyn had then gone to a reporter at the *Times Herald* who was very interested in the story, but after a few weeks, he called to tell her there was no story. He too had spoken with Camille. There was no evidence whatsoever that a crime had been committed, and without Camille's testimony, without her confirming that the rape had, in fact, happened, there was nothing that they could do.

By the time Jocelyn left for college, several months after the accident, Camille had run away from home. Their parents tracked her down a few times on the streets of nearby Philadelphia. Camille was two years younger than Jocelyn. Since she was still a minor, their parents were able to take custody of her. By the time she was eighteen, she'd been in three different rehab facilities.

Elizabeth Rush's face had taken on a permanently shattered and bitter look. Gone was the loving, vivacious woman Jocelyn had known all her life. The woman who wrapped each one of their Christmas ornaments individually in bubble wrap to ensure that none of them broke, even the cheap ones. The woman who cradled other people's babies as if they were made of dandelion fluff. The woman who wrote motivational sayings and professions of love on napkins in her children's lunches. *You grow more wonderful all the time. Your brilliance will win the day.* Or just simply: *I love you with all my heart.*

Elizabeth Rush had become a dark, thorny husk of her former self. She was so angry, not even her oldest friends could stand to be around her. Only her brother continued to speak to her, and, as far as Jocelyn could remember, Elizabeth never spoke to her husband again unless it was absolutely necessary. She never even slept in the same bed as him again. She spent the years before her death trying futilely to track Camille down and keep her out of trouble. But Camille was too far gone.

"Mommy?"

Olivia's sleepy voice startled Jocelyn, making her body spasm a little and her heartbeat quicken momentarily. The hallway night-light illuminated Olivia's tiny form. The girl stood in Jocelyn's bedroom doorway in bare feet, her nightgown clinging to her with static, blankie clutched in her right hand. With her left hand, she rubbed her eyes one by one. Jocelyn reached a hand out to her daughter, and Olivia shuffled over. They lay down in bed, Olivia fitting her body perfectly against Jocelyn's with a contented sigh. Together, they fell into an easy, dreamless sleep.

SIXTEEN

October 7th

The rustling of bodies pulled Larry from the brink of sleep. His eyes popped open, and he turned his head to his right. On the cot beside him, Angel snored peacefully. The kid always slept well, no matter where they were. As big as he was, he didn't have to worry about other inmates making advances. Still, Larry didn't know how he slept with all the noise. Eighty men in one large room made for a lot of snoring, tossing and turning, groaning, farting, and even crying.

Larry sat up and looked up and down the cots lining Holmesburg Prison's retrofitted gymnasium. The prison, which sat like a medieval castle in the middle of one of Northeast Philadelphia's working-class neighborhoods, had been closed down in 1995. Then, in 2006, the city of Philadelphia had refurbished Holmesburg's gymnasium and reopened the prison to accommodate the overflow of prisoners from the larger Curran-Fromhold Correctional Facility. Larry had been in both before, and he preferred neither. He and Angel would likely be here while they awaited trial on the charges the lady cop had slapped them with.

"Bitch," he muttered.

As his eyes adjusted to the semidarkness, he found the source of the rustling about ten cots to his left. The bodies of two men rutting were just vague shapes. Soon Larry could hear the other sounds he'd come to associate with prison—the rhythmic creaking of a cot, skin slapping against skin, and guttural moans. He turned away, pulled the pillow from behind his head, and swatted Angel with it.

Angel woke at once, his heavy fist shooting out and landing on the edge of Larry's cot. Larry waited for him to wake more fully before he threw his legs over the side of the cot and sat on its edge. Angel did the same so that they were face-to-face. The kid's eyes were small, black marbles gleaming in the dimmed overhead lights on either side of the gym. Angel held up his left hand, palm facing away from Larry. *What?*

It was a shorthand the two had developed over the years. Angel didn't know real sign language, and neither one of them could be bothered with learning it, so they'd come up with their own language composed of gestures, mouthed words, and facial expressions.

"Why'd you snitch to the cops?" Larry whispered.

Angel rolled his eyes and wagged his index finger at Larry. *I didn't.*

"Yes, you did," Larry hissed.

Angel swiped a hand down his face and shook his head. *I didn't tell them about Face.*

Larry considered this. It wouldn't be the first time a cop had tried to trick him into confessing. The lady cop probably made the whole thing up.

"Did you tell them about the hooker?"

Angel shrugged. That was a yes.

Larry sighed. He rubbed his eyes with the heels of his hands. "That's why they got us on rape, you dumbass. You were supposed to stick to the story."

Angel raised both hands, palms up, and shrugged. *What for?*

Larry poked Angel's chest with his index finger. "So we don't go to prison, that's why!"

Angel waved a hand in dismissal. He pointed back and forth from him to Larry. Then he made the gesture for Face and a slitting motion across his thick throat. He ended the motion by flicking his wrist, as if he were trying to shake water off his hand. *We should cut Face loose.*

Larry scratched at his scalp. Face had been a thorn in their sides for years; it was true. The guy was a freak too, but their arrangement had been lucrative, especially after Dwayne's death.

"We still need him," Larry said.

Angel made a rolling motion with his fists, then hooked his thumbs together and fluttered his fingers, like a bird flying. *Let's roll on him and get out of here.*

Larry shook his head. "No. Not now. He's gotta do what he promised."

Angel shifted his bulk, and the cot squeaked like a mouse being crushed beneath his girth. He shook his head slowly from side to side. He rubbed his thumb over the index and middle fingers of his right hand. *We'll never get that money back.*

Larry met Angel's eyes. "Not just about the money—you know that."

Angel made the gesture for Face and flipped his middle finger. *Fuck him.*

"Not yet," Larry said.

Angel's normally flat expression pinched, the corners of his mouth dimpling. He pointed upward and tapped the top of his wrist with a finger. *I want to get out of here now.*

"We'll make bail," Larry assured him.

Angel's brow bunched up over the bridge of his nose. *How?* he mouthed.

"My mama will know what to do."

Angel rolled his eyes and then made a swirling motion with one finger near his temple. *She's crazy.* He made the rolling motion again. They'd have a better chance of getting out and staying out if they rolled on Face.

"I left her instructions."

Angel's shoulders quaked with silent laughter. It always freaked Larry out when he laughed. It was unnatural—him not making any kind of noise. Larry knew the bullet had severed Angel's vocal cords, but still, the sight of Angel laughing noiselessly made Larry's scalp itch. *She won't remember*, Angel mouthed.

It was quite possible that Hattie Warner wouldn't remember the instructions Larry had given her. She might not even realize he was gone, but she'd never let him down before, dementia or no dementia.

"Fifty bucks says she will," Larry said.

SEVENTEEN

October 7th

"Mommy, Mommy. Can I watch *Chicken Little* on the TV? Can I have chocolate milk in my cup? Can I eat soup for breakfast?"

At eight a.m. Jocelyn rose from bed bleary-eyed, mumbling "yes" to Olivia's litany of demands as she made her way to the bathroom. Olivia stood before her as she relieved herself, clutching her little pink bear, Lulu, and telling Jocelyn about her dreams.

"There was a big spider and he liked to eat pizza."

"Pizza?" Jocelyn exclaimed in a voice far more cheery than she actually felt.

Olivia smiled and nodded, swiping a brown lock of hair out of her tiny face. "Yeah," she said, rocking her whole body up onto her toes and back. "He liked to eat pizza, and he was a pizza spider!"

"Pizza spider? Wow!" Jocelyn responded as she flushed the toilet.

"And he drove an orange car," Olivia continued.

They brushed their teeth and hair and made their way downstairs, where Jocelyn flipped on the coffeemaker. As she waited for the pot to fill, she put *Chicken Little* on the TV, pausing momentarily to take in the latest breaking news on the Kaufman abductor. After a ten-hour standoff with Philly SWAT, he had put a bullet in his brain.

"There is a God," Jocelyn said.

"What, Mommy?"

Jocelyn tousled Olivia's hair and kissed the girl's forehead. "Nothing, baby. Watch *Chicken Little*. I'll fill up your sippy cup. How about an egg for breakfast?"

"Soup," Olivia declared.

Jocelyn sighed. The kid was on a soup craze. It was almost the only thing she would eat lately. The pediatrician said it was normal for toddlers to be picky eaters, but Olivia defied pickiness. She went through phases where there was only one food she would eat. Jocelyn had never worked as hard interrogating a suspect as she had trying to convince Olivia to vary her diet. She offered Olivia a wide variety of food, but it all went uneaten. Last month, her food of choice was macaroni and cheese. This month it was soup.

"You had soup for lunch and dinner yesterday. Let's have eggs for breakfast."

A pout. "Soup."

"Eggs," Jocelyn said firmly.

Olivia studied her for a long moment, assessing just how far she could push Jocelyn on the egg issue. "Okay," Olivia agreed finally. Then, "Can I color while I'm waiting for my egg?"

Jocelyn smiled. "Sure."

Olivia ran to the living room and began pulling out her crayons and paper. Jocelyn busied herself in the kitchen, making Olivia's egg and downing a cup of coffee. The doorbell rang. Olivia called out, "Mommy, Mommy! Someone's at the door."

Jocelyn set the egg on a Disney princess plate to cool and went to the front door. They didn't get many visitors. She peered through the peephole while Olivia tugged on the hem of her T-shirt. "Who is it, Mommy? Who is it?"

"It's Uncle Simon," she said, opening the door.

Olivia squealed with delight and promptly hid behind the couch. Simon Wilde stood on Jocelyn's porch. His suit was gray, his blue dress shirt open at the collar, revealing a few springy chest hairs. His black hair was nearly half gray—it had started going gray the day Jocelyn's parents died. Although he was thin and nearing seventy, his long rangy limbs and Al Pacino face still made him imposing. Except to three-year-old Olivia, whose giggles increased when she heard his voice. Jocelyn opened the door, and Simon slipped past her.

"Where did Miss Olivia go? I was sure she lived here," he said, scanning the room.

Olivia's head popped up from behind the couch. Never one to stand anticipation, she said, "I'm here! I'm here!"

Simon's face lit up. He chased her around the living room, finally catching her and scooping her into his long arms. He squeezed her and planted a loud kiss on her cheek before releasing her. Olivia made no move to escape. Instead, she tugged at his hand, urging him into the dining room to look at her toys.

Jocelyn positioned herself at the edge of the room, arms folded across her body. "What are you doing here?"

Simon gave her an impish smile—the one he'd been charming lady jurors with for almost forty years. When her father was alive, he and Simon had made a formidable team. Rush and Wilde was still one of the most feared and highly respected defense firms in Philadelphia. Jocelyn's dad had been the intimidator, Simon the charmer. Hard and soft, yin and yang. Jocelyn hated to admit it, but she'd always secretly liked Simon better than her father. She'd loved her father, but he'd been a hard man, and after the business with the rape, she had lost all respect for him.

"I'm here to see my lovely niece and grandniece," Simon said.

Jocelyn smiled wryly. "Please. I've never known a lawyer who didn't have an ulterior motive."

Simon laughed but didn't respond. Instead, he folded himself down onto the floor and took the Lalaloopsy doll Olivia handed him. They were new to the toy market, thin-bodied dolls with giant heads and button eyes—derivatives of Raggedy Ann and Andy but made entirely of plastic instead of cloth.

Jocelyn motioned toward the kitchen. "Well, if you're staying, you'll have to eat an egg."

Olivia looked at Simon with a serious frown, eyebrows drawn together, the skin at the bridge of her nose bunching. For a split second, she was the spitting image of Jocelyn's mother. Simon saw it too. Jocelyn could tell by the sudden, unguarded look of sadness on his face.

"Uncle Simon, do you like eggs?"

With a quick glance at Jocelyn, he said, "I love eggs. I eat two eggs every morning for breakfast."

Olivia beamed and jumped up and down. "Me too! Me too!"

An hour later, they'd eaten a half dozen eggs, played with every Lalaloopsy doll that Olivia owned, and moved on to crafts. Simon was knee-deep in Olivia's creations. They'd devised a system where he made an origami figure and she colored it. They were everywhere—flowers, cranes, swans, butterflies, and pinwheels.

Eventually, Olivia grew bored and went back to drawing. She drew a series of princesses with butterflies and lollipops before moving on to mermaids.

"She's very advanced for her age," Simon noted.

Jocelyn smiled. She sat on the couch, legs tucked beneath her, cradling her third mug of coffee in her hands. It was strange to be home with Olivia and not be the one on the floor with her. But when Simon was around, Olivia didn't even notice Jocelyn.

"So," Simon said. "Have you seen Camille?"

"Last night," Jocelyn said. "She got picked up for prost—for solicitation."

Simon shook his head and made a noise deep in his throat.

Without looking up from her drawing, Olivia asked, "Mommy, what's 'licitation?"

Simon looked alarmed. Without missing a beat, Jocelyn said, "Solicitation, honey. It means when you try to sell someone something."

"Like the man at the Super Fresh?"

"Sort of. Solicitation is more like when someone comes up to you or comes to your house and tries to sell you something."

"Like the ice-cream man?"

Jocelyn laughed. "Yeah, more like that."

Simon let out a long breath and raised an eyebrow at Jocelyn. "Impressive."

"She's in Riverside," Jocelyn said, referring to the Philadelphia prison system's correctional facility for women.

"Well, I need to speak with both of you about your parents' estate."

Jocelyn held up a hand. "I don't want to talk about it."

Simon looked around. As if for the first time, Jocelyn noticed the carpet peeling up in the corner of the living room, the subtle cracks in the ceiling, and the broken lock on the front window that she had wedged closed with a two-by-four. Things in ill repair. She barely registered them anymore.

"You could use the money," Simon said.

Jocelyn ignored him. Simon's lips pressed into a thin line. "There's something else. Your mother asked me to—"

"Uncle Simon, Uncle Simon! Look! Look at this!"

Olivia pulled on Simon's arm with all her might, drawing him closer. He leaned over her shoulder to see her newest drawing. "Wow," he exclaimed loudly. "Olivia, that is very beautiful."

Jocelyn leaned forward to look at the mermaid Olivia had drawn with pen and colored in with crayons. "Sweetie, that's incredible." She nudged Simon. "Look, she even drew shells where the breasts would be."

Simon laughed. Olivia shot Jocelyn a serious look. "It's a seashell bra, Mommy."

Jocelyn nodded. "You're right, honey, and you drew it so well."

"We have to put it on the fridge," Olivia said.

Simon's cell phone chirped, and he slid it out of his back pocket to look at the screen. He frowned as he scanned the text message and quickly responded to it. "I have to get back to the office," he said.

Olivia pushed the mermaid drawing in his face. "But first help me put it on the fridge."

Simon stood up with difficulty, his knees creaking. He'd always been so energetic, so vital. It was strange for Jocelyn to see evidence of his advanced age. He wouldn't be around forever. The thought made her heart heavy. She had so little family left. Still, she smiled as Olivia tugged him into the kitchen.

"Good luck finding room," Jocelyn called after them.

Her fridge was almost entirely covered with Olivia's artwork. Some days it was work finding the door handle. Jocelyn was unable to part with a single drawing. After a few hushed moments of rustling pages and magnets clattering to the floor, Olivia returned to the living room triumphant.

"Find room?" Jocelyn asked.

"Yep."

Simon came in behind her, a cream-colored page in his hand, his left eyebrow arched severely. "So you did get my letter," he said, handing it to her.

The letter was on heavy bond paper—Rush and Wilde letterhead. It had spent a month on Jocelyn's fridge being buried by Olivia's many drawings. Hidden but not forgotten. Simon slid his jacket on. "For God's sake, Jocelyn, you need to come to my office and meet with me. There are things we need to discuss." He glanced pointedly at Olivia, who was pressing buttons on the DVD player, trying to get *Chicken Little* to come back on for the second time that day. "Privately," Simon added.

Jocelyn stared blindly at the letter. She didn't need to read it again. She'd read it so many times, she could recite it word for word.

> *Dear Ms. Bishop:*

Simon had crossed out *Ms. Bishop* and handwritten *Jocelyn.*

> *I am writing at this time to notify you that your parents' assets have been liquidated after the sale of their home in Ardmore as well as their properties in New Jersey and the Poconos. The total value of their estate is $16,100,000.00. Your share of that is $8,050,000.00, which is presently in an estate account. Prior to making distribution to you and your sister, I must meet with you to discuss a codicil of your mother's will. Please contact me upon your receipt of this letter to arrange an appointment to discuss the same.*

Simon hugged and kissed Olivia good-bye. Jocelyn was still staring mindlessly at the letter when Simon bent to kiss her cheek. "Come to the office," he said. "It's important."

EIGHTEEN

October 8th

Jocelyn arrived at work the next afternoon with her ass dragging. Exhaustion tugged at every muscle in her body, making her limbs heavy and slow. Her eyes burned, and her broken wrist ached like something decrepit and arthritic. She hadn't gotten home the night before until four a.m. She and Kevin had been out on a late call. She'd slept just long enough to have the nightmare again before whisking Olivia back to Martina's house for the entire day so she could get to court by nine.

It was the part of her job most people didn't realize was necessary. Court appearances. She and Kevin were scheduled to testify in a trial that week for an armed robbery case they'd closed over two years ago. The trial had started that morning, and, despite the prosecutor's assurances that they would be put on for testimony the first day, they had waited all day in the hall of the Criminal Justice Center. The other witnesses' testimonies had gone longer than expected. Kevin had spent the entire day sleeping upright on the benches lining the hall, snoring lightly. Jocelyn had tried to follow suit, but she'd never been able to doze in public places.

By three thirty, it was time to go to work for the evening. Jocelyn was tired and cranky that she had wasted an entire day that could have been spent with Olivia. Guilt made her stomach burn. Basically, she wouldn't see Olivia for twenty-four hours; she hated days like that. She had already called Martina three times and asked her to put Olivia on the phone. She missed the kid like hell. Maybe later in the week she would take her somewhere special, like the Please Touch Museum.

Sighing, Jocelyn sifted through the paperwork on her desk. Kevin placed a cup of coffee in front of her. The scent immediately soothed her. He sat across from her at his own desk.

"You two look like shit," Chen said as he passed.

He dropped a stack of phone messages next to Jocelyn's coffee.

"No hard calls tonight," Kevin called to Chen. "I want easy calls, like suicides."

Jocelyn winced and looked up at Kevin. "What is it with you and suicides?"

Kevin shrugged. "What? No witnesses to track down. Very little evidence. No file to prepare for the DA. Come on—it's easy."

Jocelyn's brow creased. "The families, Kev. It sucks telling the families."

"You got issues, Sullivan," Chen said.

"Me? Please. You all work here too. We all got issues." Kevin waved a piece of paper in the air. Upon closer inspection, Jocelyn could see that it was an eight-and-a-half-by-eleven-inch sheet of cream-colored paper encased in a plastic sleeve. "Speaking of suicide, this ain't ours." He thrust the paper in Jocelyn's face. "This ain't ours, right?"

It was fancy letterhead—thick woven paper, the lettering at the top embossed in maroon ink, much like the letter she had received from Rush and Wilde. Pricey. At the top it said, "From the Desk of Michael Pearce." The name jolted her. She wondered immediately if it was the same Michael Pearce who had been involved in Camille's rape. Some of the names of Camille's rapists—like this one—were more common than others. She had seen a few Michael Pearces and some James Evanses during her career, but none of them were the same men who had raped Camille.

As a teenager, it had taken her some time to figure out who the five boys were, but it wasn't difficult to do. One by one, their fathers showed up at the Rush home, looking shamed, repentant, and scared shitless. Each one spent more than two hours behind the doors of her father's study. She knew them and their sons because four of the boys had been in her class. Only one of them was younger—in the class between Camille and Jocelyn. They were all popular, successful in academia and sports, headed for Ivy League colleges. One of them had already gained early admission into Harvard. They were all good-looking, neat, and put together. They were never without crisply pressed khaki slacks and polo shirts. They wouldn't look wrinkled if you ran them over with your car. Some of them had spiky hair, but even that was flawlessly tousled. They were chiseled and perfectly proportioned. Strong chins, straight teeth. Tan in the winter, bronze in the summer, with shiny silver watches that weighed three pounds and cost more than Jocelyn made in a week. They looked like they should be lifeguards. They were the type of boys who grew up to be doctors, lawyers, and accountants. They had perfect lives, perfect wives, and dirty secrets. Jocelyn hated them.

They had traveled in the same circles as Jocelyn and Camille, although Jocelyn never saw them after that summer—the summer after Camille's rape and Jocelyn's accident. The summer when their own perfect family fell completely apart. Jocelyn had finished her senior year at home, having already been accepted into Princeton.

She'd stopped checking on them years ago. One of them was dead, killed by a drunk driver. One of them was in prison for murder. She had no idea what had become of the other three. Unless this was the same Michael Pearce.

Kevin rustled the stationery inches from her nose, drawing her attention back to the letter. It was a typed note but had been signed in pen.

> *Dear Mom: Things were not as they appeared. I promise you that. Please take all my money and the house. Take everything. Find a good home for Nibbles. All my love, Michael.*

Jocelyn tried to swallow, but her throat felt like sandpaper.

"We didn't handle this call, right?" Kevin asked.

Jocelyn shook her head.

Chen had weaved his way back to their desks, and he leaned over Kevin's shoulder. "Oh, sorry," he said. "That's the guy who jumped off the Henry Avenue Bridge. Apparently, he was out on bail awaiting trial on child pornography charges. You're right—that's not yours. The mom is coming by to pick it up."

"His mom?" Jocelyn croaked.

"Yeah, she needs it for something."

Just then, Captain Ahearn stuck his head out of his office. "Sullivan, Rush. Get your asses in here," he bellowed.

Relieved to have an excuse to get away from the creamy suicide note, Jocelyn jumped up. Her chair skidded backward and nearly fell over.

"Slow your roll, Rush! I'm not in that much of a hurry to get my ass handed to me," Kevin said. He handed Michael Pearce's suicide note to Chen.

Jocelyn muttered a "piss off" and made her way toward Ahearn's office. Kevin followed close on her heels, his coffee breath on the nape of her neck. "We're fucked," he whispered. "This is about that SVU case. We shoulda let those assholes rot until SVU came."

Jocelyn rolled her eyes. "Shut up," she hissed as they crossed the threshold into Ahearn's office. They stood side by side in front of the captain's desk, like children in a principal's office. Ahearn sat behind the desk in just his dress shirt, his suit jacket slung over the back of his chair. His office was even warmer than the detectives' rooms and smelled like lemon. He studied his cell phone as he spoke to them.

"You guys handle a call for SVU the other night?" he said gruffly.

Beside Jocelyn, Kevin fidgeted, his feet shuffling back and forth. Jocelyn couldn't read Ahearn's tone. "Yeah," she said.

"Well, we didn't take it," Kevin clarified. "The vic would only talk to Rush. SVU approved the interview—"

Ahearn cut Kevin off with a wave of his hand. Annoyance pulled the corners of his mouth down. "Lieutenant Vaughn called me personally to thank me for our assistance with the case, especially in light of the Kaufman thing. It was all hands on deck with that shit-storm. Anyway, he said you guys did good work."

Jocelyn allowed herself a small sigh of relief. Kevin stilled beside her.

"Only thing he wanted to know is if you had anything else on." Ahearn paused and looked at a pad on the corner of his desk where he had jotted down some notes. "Alicia Herrigan."

"Hardigan," Jocelyn corrected, drawing a sharp glare from Ahearn.

"Vaughn wanted to make sure you filed everything with your report," he went on.

Kevin made a sound of exasperation. "Cap, we gave them what we had. It's not our job to follow up on leads."

Jocelyn elbowed Kevin sharply in the ribs, silencing him. "We'll double-check our notes," she said.

Ahearn stared at the two of them for a long moment with a look that said, *I don't know what's going on with you two, but knock it off.*

"Fine," Ahearn said. "But don't keep wasting your time on an SVU case. We're strapped as it is."

"No problem," Jocelyn said.

"Sullivan, Rush," Chen called as they stepped out of Ahearn's office. "I got a hospital case. Einstein."

"We'll take it," Kevin said.

NINETEEN

October 8th

"I spend more time here than I do in my own goddamn living room," Kevin grumbled as he and Jocelyn breezed through Einstein's ER doors. The automatic doors swished closed behind them. Kevin stopped in the vestibule and studied his reflection in the glass wall. He brushed the thinning hair on the top of his head back, dipped his chin for a better look, and then brushed it forward.

Jocelyn stood behind him, hands on her hips. "What are you doing?"

Kevin squinted at his ghostly reflection and rubbed the stubble on his chin. "How do I look?"

Jocelyn arched a brow. "You goin' to the prom or something?"

Kevin turned to her and smiled. He pointed to the second set of doors leading inside. "I want to look good in case Nurse Bottinger is on duty."

Jocelyn rolled her eyes and turned away. "Good lord."

Kevin caught up to her just inside the ER. "Come on," he said. "She's cute."

Jocelyn studied him momentarily. He had a flush that she hadn't seen in about four years—not since his ill-fated affair with a schoolteacher fifteen years his junior. They were hot and heavy for three months, and then the woman acted like Kevin never existed. It had crushed him.

Jocelyn sighed. At least Nurse Bottinger was more age appropriate. "You look good, Kev."

Again he stroked his chin. "Even with the stubble?"

"Yeah, makes you look rugged. Now can we go talk to this guy?"

She walked off without him, weaving her way through the various patients lingering in the hallway in chairs and on stretchers. One man sat hunched over in a wheelchair, vomit fanned out at his feet. Jocelyn stepped around it, cringing at the smell. They reached the curtained area of the ER, where Jocelyn and Anita had been the night of the carjacking. A male doctor with glasses and a dark buzz cut emerged from one curtained area. A splatter of blood arced across the front of his blue scrubs. He pulled his latex gloves off as he approached, bundling them together. "Oh good, you guys are here."

Jocelyn and Kevin showed him their credentials. He took a cursory look and deposited his balled-up gloves into the nearest trash receptacle. "You're here for the bar fight, right?" he asked, looking from Jocelyn to Kevin and back again.

"Yeah," Jocelyn said.

"All right, good. I need this guy out of my hospital. We're busy, and we need that room." The doctor turned, and Jocelyn and Kevin followed behind him.

"The lady he hit with the beer bottle is there," the doctor said, pointing to a curtained area on his left. "The bottle didn't break, so all she's got is some contusions."

Jocelyn poked her head around the curtain to have a look at the woman, who was snoring openmouthed, her arm propped on a pillow and hooked to an IV. She was in her midthirties with straw-blonde hair, tattooed wrists, acid-washed jeans that looked about three decades too old, and a black T-shirt that was at least two sizes too small. A large raised purple bruise made a path along her jawline, starting at her chin and spreading across her cheek to her ear.

"That's a nice one," Kevin said from behind Jocelyn. His breath stirred the hair near her ear. She smelled peppermint gum. Kevin's breath never smelled like anything besides coffee. Nurse Bottinger was really in for it.

"She had a pretty whopping headache. We gave her something for pain," the doctor explained. "You can wake her up, but I'm not sure how coherent she'll be. The bartender, on the other hand, is over here." The doctor pulled the curtain across from the woman, where a broad-shouldered older man sat on the side of his gurney. He was trying unsuccessfully to contort his body so that he could see the line of stitches running the length of his triceps.

"This guy intervened and actually did catch some broken glass. Twelve stitches. He's lucky it wasn't worse. He can give you the story. Down there," the doctor went on, pointing at a private room at the end of the row of curtained areas, "is the guy who started the whole thing."

Kevin frowned. "You gave him a private room?"

The doctor spun and stared at Kevin, impatience tugging at the corners of his thin mouth. "He needed a private room. He's quite belligerent, and his blood alcohol level is through the roof."

"Who brought him in?" Jocelyn asked.

The doctor shrugged. "I don't know, some officer. He's back there with the guy. Guy's name is Martin, Todd Martin. Anyway, the sooner you can get him out of here, the better."

He walked off, leaving them standing in the middle of the triage area. Jocelyn sighed. "You talk to the bartender. I'll check out the drunk."

Kevin gave her a mock salute and disappeared behind one of the curtains. Inside the private room, a large, barrel-chested man lay on the gurney, one of his meaty wrists bound to the guardrail with a set of handcuffs. He had long, stringy brown hair and a patchy beard. Jocelyn estimated Todd Martin to be in his midthirties. He wore a black Slipknot shirt and a pair of frayed jeans. She could smell the booze on him before she even walked through the door. A row of stitches kinked over his left eyebrow. His upper lip was split; dried blood caked in his facial hair. Beside the bed sat a tray table, a discarded suture kit and a pile of bloody gauze scattered haphazardly over its surface.

Martin's head swiveled in her direction as she entered. His eyes had all the glassy blankness of someone who'd been drinking like it was his job. "Get me the fuck out of here," he said, his voice rising in volume with each word. Jocelyn ignored him and scanned the room, muttering, "Fuck," under her breath when she saw Finch sitting in a chair in the corner of the room.

He looked up from the magazine he had been flipping through. "Christ," he breathed. The line of his chiseled brow wrinkled in consternation.

Jocelyn studied Martin for a moment. "I don't think this guy is in any shape to be questioned. Let's take him down to the Division and let him sleep it off." She motioned to Martin's wrist. "Those your cuffs, Finch?"

He nodded, and, with what looked like great effort, stood and walked to the bed to uncuff Martin from the bed.

Martin looked from Jocelyn to Finch, his eyes bulging out of his head. "Get me the fuck out of here!" he bellowed.

Jocelyn and Finch ignored him. "Sit up," Finch commanded.

"I said get me the fuck out of here, you fucking pig."

The blast of whiskey breath was hot on Jocelyn's face. Finch grimaced openly. "I said sit up!"

Martin reached over to the guardrail and rattled the cuffs, trying to pull them off. Jocelyn grabbed his legs and threw them over the side of the gurney. "Get up. Now," she said in her best no-nonsense voice. He stopped struggling with the cuffs and sat up. Silently, he stared at the two of them.

"Did you Mirandize him?" Jocelyn asked.

Finch slipped the handcuff key into the locking mechanism. "What do you think?"

"I ain't gettin' locked up," Martin said. "I ain't gettin' locked up." Once again, his voice rose in pitch and volume.

When Finch freed the cuffs from the guardrail and reached for Martin's other hand, the man shot upward, stumbling forward. He lashed out with one arm, knocking Finch backward, sending him flat on his ass. As he fell, Finch knocked the tray table over, and remnants of the used suture kit flew everywhere. Before her brain had even completely registered what was going on, Jocelyn's hand was reaching for her gun. She was too late. Martin lunged at her and crushed her against his chest before she could unsnap her holster. He wrapped a meaty forearm around her throat. She reached up and pulled down on it with both hands, prepared to struggle until she felt the cool blade of a knife against the flesh of her throat.

"Hold still," he breathed into her ear, the smell of alcohol burning her nostrils.

Where the fuck had he gotten a knife?

She had time for one word before the forearm clenched, leaving her only enough room to breathe, nothing more. "Finch."

Martin hollered again. She couldn't hear him because the adrenaline surging through her momentarily silenced the entire world. He kept squeezing her throat, then releasing slightly and pressing the blade against her skin. She strained her eyes, trying to see Finch in her periphery. He was getting up, slowly. His hand went to his holster, a little too slowly for her taste.

Martin looked at him, pressing the knife into her throat. "Don't do it, pig. I'll fucking slice her throat."

For a split second, she thought Finch would reach for his gun anyway. But he stopped and raised both hands in the air. "I'll fucking kill her," Martin said, alcohol-laced spittle flying.

All Jocelyn could think about was Olivia and the way she looked when she slept, the roundness of her cheeks and the way the fine blonde hair along her jawline shone by the light creeping in from the hallway. Jocelyn was going to die. She was going to get her throat sliced by a worthless drunk while Finch stood by uselessly, and all she could think about was Olivia. She'd made provisions of course, in her will, but as good a mother as Inez was, Jocelyn was the one who wanted to be there to watch Olivia grow up. This wasn't fair.

Her hands trembled as she pulled down again on Martin's arm. The rushing in her ears came back.

Then Kevin's voice, calm and slightly annoyed. "Finch, why does this motherfucker have a knife?"

Jocelyn looked front and center to Kevin, who stood in the doorway, his Glock trained on Martin's head. His eyes blazed with an intensity he rarely showed. He wouldn't look at her. He wouldn't take his eyes off the man with the knife, she knew. Not even for a second.

"Finch," he said again, his words slower, more pronounced. "Why does this motherfucker have a knife?"

It was the same tone he might use if he were asking Finch where his coffee was. From her left, Jocelyn heard Finch stammer, "I—I don't know. I—I—"

"Didn't you pat him down?"

A growl tore from Martin's throat. "Hey," he shouted at Kevin.

Jocelyn's breath sounded like Niagara Falls in her ears.

"Shut up," Kevin said quietly.

For a brief second, Martin loosened his hold, and Jocelyn sucked in a noisy breath. "What?" he said.

"I said shut up," Kevin replied. "I'm talking to this fucknut over here, who apparently forgot to pat you down."

"Hey—" Finch said, a hint of indignation in his voice.

"You shut up too," Kevin said. "This is a nice mess you've got us all into, isn't it?"

Now it was Finch's turn. "What?"

"Hey," Kevin said to Martin. "Look at this dumbass over here. He just fucked you."

Martin's grip loosened even more as he shifted to look again at Finch. For just a second, the blade left her skin. She squeezed her eyes shut against the tears of relief that stung her lids. Then he tightened his grip again, and the point of the knife needled her carotid.

"What?" Martin and Finch said in unison.

"He just fucked you," Kevin repeated.

"I'm the one with the knife, asshole."

"Exactly. You've got a knife that this dumb shit forgot to take from you when he arrested you—for what? Drunk and disorderly? Simple assault? You're holding it to the throat of a police officer. You know what that means? You're fucked, man. You put the smallest scratch on this broad, and the brass is gonna charge you with attempted murder—probably kidnapping too. Those are felonies. That's twenty to fifty years."

An audible scoff. "Kiss my ass, old man."

"I'll pass," Kevin said. "But don't worry, where you're going there will be plenty of men interested in your ass."

Jocelyn could feel Martin's hesitation even as he spit out a "Fuck you" in Kevin's direction.

"You like that?" Kevin asked. "Ass fucking?"

"Shut up!"

"I'm just sayin'. You'll get all the ass fucking you can dream about if you keep hanging on to this broad here. They'll even do you two or three at a time. They like that."

"I'm not going to prison," Martin hollered, his voice growing high-pitched.

Kevin laughed. "Yeah," he said. "You are."

The point of the knife threatened to puncture her skin this time. Only Kevin's voice stopped him. "Unless . . ."

Martin froze. Kevin let the moment stretch out, made the man come to him. "Unless what?"

"Unless you let her go right now. It's just the three of us in here. We keep it that way. You let her go—she gets to live. I don't have to shoot you, and this dumbass over in the corner doesn't get his ass handed to him by the brass for not patting you down. You walk with a drunk and disorderly—probation and a fine."

The man's grip had loosened considerably. Jocelyn sucked in great gulps of air.

"So what's it gonna be? You wanna drop the knife and let this broad go, or you wanna do hard time?"

Jocelyn waited. But he took too long to decide—just a beat too long. That was when Kevin finally met her eyes. It had the same effect as if he had yelled, "Now!"

The entire thing took only seconds. Jocelyn pulled down on his arm, her splint catching against his arm hair. She gripped the hand with the knife with both hands and held his entire arm out to the side, like an archway that she quickly slipped through, so that she was behind him. She kept hold of his wrist as she turned so they were both facing the same direction. Twisting his wrist sharply, she wrenched his hand up toward his opposite shoulder until the knife dropped from his grip. He cried out in pain, too stunned to react with his free hand. Kevin was at her side instantly, and together they took Martin down hard, Kevin's knee on the side of his neck. He pulled Martin's hands together behind his back and cuffed them with Finch's cuffs, which still dangled from one of his wrists. The sound of the cuff cinching closed was one of the best sounds Jocelyn had ever heard.

"Get the fuck off me," Martin yelled, squirming erratically.

Kevin glanced over at Finch, who remained stock-still. "Hey, limp dick."

Finch narrowed his eyes. "What did you call me?"

Kevin left Martin wriggling on the floor and retrieved the knife, handling it carefully as he deposited it onto the gurney. "Limp dick," Kevin said. "You know, a man who can't perform. Nice of you to jump in there."

Finch pointed a finger at Kevin, anger lining his reddened face. "Hey, you—"

He didn't finish. Jocelyn strode over to him and, in one fluid movement, sucker punched him in the jaw with her left hand. He wasn't expecting it. He flew backward for the second time that evening and hit the wall with a thud. Dazed, he slid to the ground. Jocelyn stood over him, chest heaving, her fist still clenched.

Finch rubbed his jaw and looked up at her, a look of pure hatred flashing in his eyes. "You're dea—"

"Shut. Up," Jocelyn said, her voice husky. They stared at each other a moment longer, neither one of them giving an inch. Finally, Jocelyn turned and walked out of the room.

TWENTY

October 8th

Jocelyn strode down the hallway to the doors she and Kevin had entered through. She kept her eyes straight ahead, not even stopping when the doctor in the blue scrubs called after her. Every muscle in her body was tensed up in an effort to keep from shaking. She went through the two sets of sliding glass doors and stopped outside. She moved down from the entrance and sat on a bench that smokers used. She leaned forward and put her head between her knees. She couldn't stop the trembling, but now with no audience, she let it run its course. She probably looked like she was having some kind of seizure by the time Kevin found her.

He sat beside her with a sigh. She didn't look at him but recognized the sound of him freeing a Nicorette tab from its wrapper and popping it into his mouth. He put a hand on her shoulder. "You okay?"

She lifted her head and glanced over at him. "No," she said. "I'm fucking pissed."

And she was. More than anything—more than she felt afraid or traumatized or lucky to be alive, she felt angry. It raged through her like it had been injected intravenously. For a moment, she felt as though she might split apart, explode into a thousand pieces. Her chest heaved with the effort it took to breathe around the anger. "That motherfucker. I could have been killed tonight, all because he can't do his fucking job—because he's fucking lazy and incompetent. I already have one scar because of him. Shit. I should have shot him."

"Hey, take a breath," Kevin said.

"I'm trying. It's not working."

He laughed. "And you thought you didn't need anger management."

Her hand shot out and punched him hard in the upper arm, splint and all.

"Oww," he said, rubbing his arm. He motioned to her wrist. "You're going to feel that in the morning."

"I don't really care."

She sat up straighter, focusing on drawing breath down deep into her diaphragm—like she had been taught in the one anger management class she'd attended thus far. She and Kevin watched people drive up and drop loved ones off. Some of them got out of their cars in a hurry, sprinting through the ER doors and emerging seconds later with a security guard wheeling an empty wheelchair. Others dropped their loved ones off and went to park, leaving the person to stand outside the door and wait for them to return. The red lights of ambulances flashed past now and then, headed around to the trauma bay. There were flurries of activity followed by dead silence, punctuated only by Kevin's incessant lip smacking.

"Hey, Rush," he said during one lull.

She turned her head to meet his eyes, realizing that her body had finally relaxed. The rage was fading. "Yeah," she breathed.

"Know how you punched Friendly Fire in the face back there?"

"Yeah."

"That was pretty badass."

Jocelyn laughed. It began as a chuckle and kept going. She laughed so long and loud that her sides hurt.

"It was," Kevin added.

She wiped tears from her eyes, her body still convulsing with laughter, shedding the rest of the tension from the confrontation in the hospital. "Well, it felt pretty damn good."

"I bet."

"He'll report me," Jocelyn said, her laughter subsiding.

"Fuck him," Kevin said, waving a hand in the air. "I'm reporting his ass too. What he did was worse. Plus, he's got a history. One of these days he'll get what's coming to him."

"Hey, Kev," Jocelyn said.

"Yeah?"

She smiled. "Don't ever call me a broad again."

It was his turn to laugh. "Deal." He clapped her on the knee. "Let me wrap this up, and then we'll get out of here."

Jocelyn was standing outside, waiting for Kevin, when a woman in a wheelchair caught her eye. She sat alone in the vestibule area of the ER entrance. It was the bandaged hands and feet that drew Jocelyn's gaze.

"Anita?" Jocelyn said as she approached. She crossed the threshold of the vestibule and the double sliding glass doors closed behind her automatically with a loud whoosh.

Anita looked up at her and then quickly looked back at her lap. She was dressed in street clothes that looked dirty and rumpled. A red cotton shirt and a pair of faded jeans. They didn't look at all like Anita's style. SVU would have taken the clothes she'd been wearing on arrival into evidence. These looked like donated clothes. Jocelyn would bet her week's salary that one of the nurses had supplied them. Anita hugged her purse to her stomach, her two bundled hands like large paws.

Jocelyn looked around. Anita sat off to the side, as if waiting for someone. Jocelyn watched the parking lot for a moment, but no headlights cut through the darkness.

"Anita," Jocelyn said again. "What's going on?"

There was a tremor in her chin. Jocelyn almost missed it. Anita swallowed hard and blinked back tears. "Got discharged," she murmured.

Again Jocelyn looked toward the parking lot. No one was coming.

"You want a ride home?" Jocelyn asked.

Finally, Anita met her eyes. Something like relief washed over her face, smoothing the lines out of her forehead. "Okay," she said.

Kevin met them in the parking lot twenty minutes later and helped Jocelyn maneuver Anita into the backseat of their vehicle. As Jocelyn folded the wheelchair and placed it into the trunk, one of Einstein's security guards called out from a nearby parking lot booth. "That's hospital property."

She flashed her badge. "It's police property now."

He flipped her off, and she yelled, "Fuck you very much," as she got into the car. Kevin drove, and, from the backseat, Anita chuckled softly. "You're something, Rush."

"You still live on West Chelten?" Jocelyn asked as they pulled out of Einstein's parking lot.

"Yeah, the Grove Apartments. I, uh, I live on the second floor."

"You got elevators?" Kevin asked.

"No," Anita replied.

Before Kevin could get through his eye roll, Jocelyn jabbed him sharply in the side with her elbow. He cleared his throat and smiled tightly at Anita in the rearview mirror. "That's okay. We'll get you up there."

They rode in silence for a few moments. Then Jocelyn asked, "Did someone from SVU come out to talk to you?"

"Oh, he was here," Anita said, clucking her tongue. "Name was Vaughn. But he was too pretty to talk to."

In spite of the tension that had been knotting Jocelyn's shoulder blades all night, she laughed. "Too pretty to talk to?"

She and Kevin exchanged a look. Kevin shrugged and kept his eyes on the road.

"Boy looked like a damn movie star," Anita continued. "I am not talking to him about—well, you know."

Vaughn had come out himself. Jocelyn felt a small wave of relief. Vaughn was a lieutenant. He didn't have to interview Anita. He could have sent one of his detectives to do it, but he had taken the time to go to the hospital himself, which meant that he was taking the case seriously—even if he was too pretty to talk to.

"I remembered something else," Anita said.

Jocelyn turned in her seat to look at the other woman. The backseat of the car seemed to swallow Anita. She looked so tiny. The white of her gauze bandages stood out in stark relief against the evening darkness.

"What is it?"

"The guy who drove the nails in," Anita paused to lick her lips, as if her mouth had gone dry just talking about the rape. "He had a big, thick silver watch. I think it was Michael Kors. It was expensive."

"What's Michael Kors?" Kevin asked.

"It's a brand of watch. Phil wears Michael Kors. I remember because I had to spend a half week's salary on the one he wanted for Christmas. He couldn't possibly settle for one of their less expensive ones," Jocelyn said.

Kevin let out a low whistle. "For a watch? That's bullshit."

"I know," Jocelyn said. Phil's expensive taste had been one of the things they'd disagreed on consistently. Sure, he made more than her, but even an ADA's salary wasn't enough to support the lifestyle that Phil aspired to. He saw nothing wrong with spending hundreds or thousands of dollars on needless things.

She had bought him the watch because he'd wanted it so badly, and she had wanted to please him. Even as he had exclaimed over it on Christmas Day and slipped it onto his wrist with a flush of delight on his face, all Jocelyn could think of was that he was wearing three months of electric bills on his wrist. He did not understand her frugality.

"But you came from money," he would say.

"Yes," she would respond, exasperated, "but I don't have any now."

Kevin's voice interrupted the memory. "How do you know it was Michael Kors?" he asked Anita.

"It had an MK on it. I know the brand because one of the men in my office wears it. This one was big and clunky."

"That's good, Anita," Jocelyn said. "Did you mention this to Vaughn?"

"No, I didn't remember till this morning."

"This is it," Jocelyn said to Kevin, motioning toward Anita's apartment building. Kevin pulled over. Together, he and Jocelyn carried Anita up to the second floor. The apartment was small and dated but neatly kept. It smelled like cinnamon and Lysol.

"Where's my babies?" Anita asked her mother as Jocelyn and Kevin half carried, half dragged Anita into the living room.

Arms crossed tightly across her thin chest, Lila responded, "Terrence is at football practice and Pia's at her little friend's house. They'll be home soon enough."

Kevin went back down for the wheelchair as Jocelyn helped Lila situate Anita on their pullout sofa bed. The woman was rail thin, her skull swathed in a turban. She barely acknowledged Jocelyn and Kevin, appraising her daughter with pursed lips and a wrinkled brow. Anita began to cry silently, sobs making her body hiccup. Wordlessly, Lila arranged a blanket over Anita's lap and shook her head, turning her back on her daughter. Jocelyn's throat felt suddenly tight. The tiny apartment seemed to close in on her, but she steeled herself against the unwanted emotion. She sat beside Anita and leaned in close.

"Pull it together, Anita. It's going to be okay. I already got two of those fuckers behind bars." Jocelyn glanced over her shoulder. Lila had disappeared down the hall. "I don't give a rat's ass what your mama thinks. This wasn't your fault."

Anita smiled and wiped her tears gingerly with the backs of her gauze-bandaged hands. When she met Jocelyn's eyes, the sadness in her gaze set Jocelyn back on her heels. Anita had been through a lot in her short, tortured life, but this had damaged her in a place her former life had never been able to touch. Her lips pressed into a thin line and lifted ever so slightly at the corners—a cross between a smile and a grimace.

"There's always more, Rush," she said. "You put those men away, but there will always be more."

TWENTY-ONE

October 20th

"Rush, what are you doing?"

Kevin's voice startled her. The chair she sat in creaked loudly as she jumped. Her splinted hand flew to her chest. "What the hell, Kev?" she said. "Don't sneak up on me."

Across the room, a knot of other detectives chuckled. "You're concentratin' awful hard there, Rush. Whadda you got on that computer? Porn?" one of them called.

She flipped them off and shifted her chair over as Kevin dragged his own chair around the desks and insinuated himself next to her. He plopped three thick files onto her desk, dislodging a stack of papers and sending them scattering to the floor. "We got reports to write, Rush."

"Goddammit, Kev," Jocelyn said, reaching down to the floor to retrieve them. She was already halfway under her desk when she realized that from across the room it would look like her head was in Kevin's lap. She raised one hand in the air, middle finger extended once again, at the barrage of oral sex jokes that floated over toward the two of them.

"You're no fun anymore, Rush," one of the other detectives called.

She sat back in her chair, face flushed, wisps of her brown hair escaping from her ponytail. Kevin was leaning over her desk, squinting at her computer screen. "Are you working on that SVU case again?"

She pushed him aside and clicked out of the screen she had been in. It had been almost two weeks since they had taken Anita home from the hospital. Jocelyn had left several messages for Lieutenant Caleb Vaughn, but he hadn't called her back. She'd wanted to talk to him about the watch Anita had remembered and whether or not he had tracked down Alicia Hardigan.

The lines at the corners of Kevin's eyes crinkled. He rubbed a hand over his thinning salt-and-pepper hair as he regarded her. "Rush," he said, lowering his voice. "What are you doing?"

"Vaughn hasn't called me back." She pulled one of the files he'd plopped on her desk toward her but didn't open it.

Kevin fingered the packet of Nicorette gum sticking out of his jacket pocket. She realized suddenly that for the first time in weeks, Kevin didn't smell like smoke. It was slightly disconcerting. "So what? Who gives a shit? In case you didn't notice, we've got our own cases to worry about."

Jocelyn looked away momentarily. A muscle in her jaw twitched. She looked back at Kevin, right into his hazel eyes, and whispered two words. "Rasheedah Jones."

He paled immediately. He leaned back in his chair, away from her, away from the mention of the single case of his career that had truly gotten under his skin.

"That's not fair," Kevin said. "Why are you bringing that up?"

"Anita," said Jocelyn, holding him with her gaze, "is my Rasheedah Jones."

Rasheedah Jones had been a seventy-eight-year-old woman who was beaten in a subway stairwell by five teenage boys for no apparent reason. She'd had less than ten dollars on her, and they hadn't even taken it. One of the things they'd used to beat her—besides their fists and feet—was her own cane.

Kevin had gone around for weeks after that night muttering, "Her own cane" at random times. They'd closed in pretty quickly on the teenagers. The criminal youth of Philadelphia weren't the brightest, and Kevin and Jocelyn managed to track down pretty good surveillance footage of the boys before and after the beating, including a video showing one of them carrying Jones's cane off with him as a souvenir.

Then Rasheedah Jones died from her injuries, and the case was turned over to homicide.

But Kevin couldn't let it go.

Kevin was a pro. He had fifteen more years on the force than Jocelyn did. In fact, he could retire soon if he really wanted to, but he was a bachelor in his midfifties. He ate TV dinners and spent most of his off time at the nursing home visiting his mother. His sister and her family lived in Maryland, and he didn't see them much. Every year for Olivia's birthday he dropped hundreds of dollars on ridiculously extravagant gifts. He had no idea how to function outside work.

And that was okay because Kevin could do his job, and it didn't get to him. But Rasheedah Jones had kept him up nights. He couldn't let it go, wouldn't let it go. He harassed the homicide squad, inserting himself into the investigation where he didn't belong until he got himself formally reprimanded.

"Anita didn't die," Kevin growled. "She'll survive this."

Jocelyn stared hard at him until he had the good sense to look at his feet. "Who had your back, Kev?"

A moment of silence passed. Then another. Kevin rubbed his hands over his eyes and sighed heavily. "I guess I can always take early retirement if the shit hits the fan," he said. "What did you have in mind?"

"I want to find Alicia Hardigan."

TWENTY-TWO

October 22nd

Hattie Warner rocked back and forth in her recliner, watching dust motes float and drift in the afternoon sunlight that streamed through her living room window. She listened to the furnace go *knock, knock, knock*. Still, she felt cold. She tugged the corners of the nubby blue-and-white afghan wrapped around her shoulders, pulling them to the center of her chest. She watched the big TV, but there was nothing on. The remote was nowhere to be found.

Knock, knock, knock.

Her fingers worked at some buttons beside her chair, but they didn't turn the TV on. The oxygen tank roared to life, though. Now where did she put her nasal—

Knock, knock, knock.

Damn furnace. "Larry!" she called. The boy never listened. Up in his room, blasting music, cutting school.

Knock, knock.

Then the furnace spoke. "Mrs. Warner," it said.

Hattie froze in her chair. *Knock, knock.* "Mrs. Warner."

She stood and went to the furnace. When she opened it, there was a man there. She looked behind him and saw her porch. "Mrs. Warner?" the man said, leaning down to peer into her face. He was tall and white, and he looked like he should be on TV. He wore a black suit like a preacher.

"He's in his room," she told him. "I said, 'You better go to school now,' but that boy never listened to me. How's he gonna raise his own boy with no education and no job?"

The man smiled. He handed her his wallet. There was no money in it. "Mrs. Warner, my name is Lieutenant Caleb Vaughn. I'm with the Philadelphia Special Victims Unit."

She stared at his wallet. Then back at him. He had thick, silky hair and a five o'clock shadow. Was it five o'clock? She had to make supper. "From where?" she asked.

Gingerly, he took his wallet back from her outstretched palm. "The police," he said. "I'm with the Philadelphia Police Department. The Special Victims Unit."

"You on TV?"

Vaughn chuckled. "No. Not the show. I'm with the police department. Can I come in?"

Hattie shrugged. "Guess so. I don't have no rent, though. I'll get paid on Friday. You can come then."

Vaughn followed her to the living room. He looked around, the lines of his face turned downward into a grimace. "I'm not here for your rent, Mrs. Warner. I'm here about your son, Larry."

She sat in her chair and slid her fingers into the cracks between the arms and the seat cushion, feeling around until the man reached down and handed her the nasal cannula hooked to her oxygen tank. "Thank you," she said.

Vaughn perched on the pockmarked coffee table, at eye level with her. He smiled again, and she couldn't remember what TV show she had seen him on. "You have kind eyes," she said. "Are you a doctor? I sure wish Larry would have been a doctor."

"No, Mrs. Warner, I'm with the police."

"Them police was just here taking all kinds of stuff—computers and phones," she said.

The man nodded. "Those were my investigators. They were executing a warrant—taking those things into evidence. Mrs. Warner, I'm here about Larry."

"He in trouble?"

"Yes, ma'am."

"I told him to leave those checks alone. Forgery's against the law." She shook her head. "There's no telling him."

"I'm not here about checks. Your son's in a lot of trouble. He's been charged with kidnapping and rape."

Hattie's hands flew to her chest. She sucked in a breath that didn't reach all of her lungs. "Rape?"

"Yes, ma'am. Larry's in jail. He's there with his friend, Angel Donovan. Do you know him?"

She stared behind him, her eyes drawn to the dancing dust motes. Why wouldn't the damn TV come on? The man repeated his question, bobbing his head to catch her eye.

Her mind lit on one word. "Jail? Larry got locked up?"

"Yes," the man said.

"He told me—" Hattie began, but she couldn't find the rest of the words. "I was supposed to do something."

She looked around, but nothing sparked her memory. Larry had said, "Mama, if I ever get locked up, you need to—"

"What did he say?" she asked. She looked at her feet.

"Mrs. Warner, I'm here because there was another man involved with the crimes that Larry's been charged with. A white man. Do you know the names of any of Larry's friends who are white?"

"Larry don't have no white friends," she replied. Her feet. Her feet. Something about her feet. But all she saw were her threadbare pink slippers, now a dirty rose from age and overuse. What had Larry said?

"Larry doesn't associate with any white males that you know of?"

Hattie shook her head. "No. Larry run with Angel and Dwayne, although I don't know why Dwayne gives him the time of day after the way Larry ignored him the whole time he was growing up. His own son. He don't want nothing to do with that baby."

Vaughn's brow furrowed. "Dwayne is your grandson?"

Hattie stared at her slippers, crossing and uncrossing her ankles. Something about her damn feet. "Who?" she said.

"Dwayne."

"Don't know no Dwayne."

It was under her feet! She clapped her hands together and smiled broadly at Vaughn. "What's your name?" she asked.

The man sighed. He ran a hand through his thick brown hair. "Lieutenant Caleb Vaughn."

She stood up, and he stood with her. "Mr. Vaughn," she said. "Can you move my chair?"

She pointed to the other side of the room. "Over there by the window."

Another sigh, heavier this time. *Damn movers.* She hoped he didn't expect a tip after acting so put out about doing his job. "Sure," Vaughn said. "Sure I can."

He dragged her recliner to the window, thanked her for her time, and left. Hattie knelt in the empty space where her chair had been and pulled the green carpet, peeling it away from the wall.

"Larry's in trouble," she mumbled.

It took her three tries to dislodge the false floorboard. She reached into the dark hole and rooted around until her hand closed over a large Ziploc bag. Once she had freed it, she dumped its contents onto the floor. Seven or eight thick stacks of hundred-dollar bills tumbled to the floor. There was a business card, small and white. Bail bondsman. On the back were the handwritten words: *Larry said call this guy.*

She turned it back over. Larry had told her to call his friend about the money. He'd get Larry out and bring him home. She studied the number for several seconds before shoving all the money back into the bag.

Now, where was the damn phone?

TWENTY-THREE

October 27th

Jocelyn hadn't been to the Kensington Stroll in years—not since she was on patrol. But it hadn't changed much. If anything, it had grown dirtier and grimier. The El spanned the length of Kensington Avenue like a giant blue thousand-legger whose body cast a dark metal shadow over its inhabitants. The buildings that still stood were mostly brick and grouped tightly together. The houses on the side streets were in such ill repair that the whole neighborhood looked haphazardly thrown together, as if someone had tossed them all onto the concrete and smushed them together to make room for something better—something better that never got built. Many of the buildings were various shades of red, painted as if someone had started putting on a fresh coat and never finished. Some row houses had been torn down, giving the blocks a gap-toothed look. Used needles gathered in the cracks and crevices.

Abandoned warehouses stood defaced, covered in graffiti with the windows smashed out. The signs on the businesses lining Kensington Avenue looked like something someone had hand-painted in his basement. Most shops had either the accordion-style garage door security closures or wrought-iron bars lining their windows. The upper floors of most all the buildings had boarded-up windows.

The closest thing to grass you could find were the weeds springing from the broken pavement. Abandoned, trash-strewn lots occasionally broke up the pushed-together buildings. It had the look and feel of desperation, of life trying to climb out of the bowels of the concrete only to be violated and crushed over and over again.

"Watch where you step," Jocelyn cautioned as she and Kevin stepped out of their car.

As Jocelyn had predicted, Alicia Hardigan was a lifer. She had arrests for prostitution going back ten years—from her eighteenth birthday. She'd been in and out of prison for minor drug violations, and her list of former addresses could fill a phone book. Jocelyn and Kevin had waited a week for another night that was slow enough for them to do some investigating and track Hardigan down without their absence being noticed or reported to Ahearn.

They decided to hit the Stroll, flashing Hardigan's last mug shot, trying to find someone who knew her. The prostitutes they talked to weren't in the habit of trusting—or talking to—police. No matter how many times Jocelyn assured the women that Hardigan was not in trouble, she was turned away with a stony expression and an "I don't know her." She knew at least half of them were lying.

Kevin met her on the corner of Kensington and Allegheny Avenues after an hour. "I got nothing," he said. "But I did see a couple of people humping next to that house back there."

Jocelyn shook her head. "That doesn't help us."

Kevin motioned behind her. "How about this one?"

Jocelyn turned to see Delores Halsey striding toward her, a wry smile on her leathery face. "Jocelyn Rush," she said. "I heard you were out here."

Delores was in her fifties, but she looked like she was in her sixties. Her hair was bleached blonde, straggly and brittle. Her skin was wrinkled and sagging, bronzed from too much sun and worn thin from exposure and life on the street. Her denim miniskirt and high-heeled shoes seemed completely inappropriate for her age—not to mention the cool weather. At least she had a jacket—denim like her skirt. She had liberally applied some blue eye shadow and rouge that her skin seemed to reject—it sat atop her face, occasionally loosening in chunks and sloughing off.

Jocelyn smiled back. "Delores, how are you?"

Delores shrugged. "Same," she said. "You know how it goes. Who's your friend?" She eyed Kevin up and down until he shifted his feet and folded his arms across his chest.

"This is Detective Sullivan," Jocelyn said.

Delores appraised him a moment longer, apparently deciding he wasn't worth her attention, before turning back to Jocelyn.

"I hear you're asking about Alicia."

"What do you know?" Jocelyn asked.

Delores smiled a mostly toothless smile. "Enough to get me a free lunch."

Twenty minutes later, they were ensconced in a booth at the Tiffany Diner, Kevin looking disgusted and Delores drawing shocked looks from the other patrons. She ordered two entrees. Jocelyn had coffee and Kevin had water. Delores ate like it was her last meal, and it occurred to Jocelyn that, working on the Stroll, it might just be.

"So what do you know about Alicia Hardigan?" Jocelyn asked.

Between bites, Delores asked, "Is she in trouble?"

"No," Kevin said. "Someone else is—someone we think might have hurt her."

Delores looked at Jocelyn, who nodded her confirmation.

"Well," Delores said, signaling their waitress for more soda. "She's been on the Stroll for years. I seen her about two months ago, and she was all fucked up."

"Fucked up how?" Kevin asked.

"Bitch could hardly walk she was in such a stupor. Her nose kept bleeding, and she was so out of it she didn't even know it.

Couldn't get no johns because she'd be covered in blood. Some of 'em don't even care if you wet yourself, but ain't none of 'em touching you with blood all down your front."

"Is she still working?" Jocelyn asked.

Delores shook her head. "No, she OD'd last month. Heard they took her to Episcopal. She was in a coma for two days. Her brother came and got her. He put her in rehab somewhere up on the Main Line."

"No shit," Kevin said. "Nice of her brother to show up after she OD's."

Delores wagged a finger at him. "Her brother been trying to help her for years. She don't want no help. I'll bet you she's miserable in rehab. She won't last. The street is her home. She ain't never changing. She sure as shit ain't going straight. She'll be back."

"She got any other family?" Kevin asked.

Delores shook her head, finishing off her cheeseburger. "No, just a brother. They came up in foster care—separated. The brother found her a few years ago. Been trying to get her straight ever since."

"Do you know the brother's name?" Jocelyn asked.

"No."

"How about the rehab facility?"

"Booster or Brewster something. Something with a *B*. But give it two weeks, she'll be back on the Stroll."

"Do you remember her getting messed up earlier this year?" Jocelyn asked.

The skin between Delores's eyebrows knotted up. "Messed up?"

Jocelyn leaned forward, elbows resting on the table. "She get in trouble?"

Delores thought about it for a moment. "Not that I remember, but she did disappear for awhile. Around April. She was gone a couple of months. She was a lot fatter when she got back."

"You notice anything different about her? Besides her getting fat?" Kevin asked.

Delores froze, her fork and knife poised above her plate. She looked at Jocelyn, her gaze flinty. "What's going on?"

Jocelyn lowered her voice. "We think there might be two or three men picking up prostitutes, crucifying and raping them."

"Crucifying them?"

"Yeah."

"Like nailing their hands?"

"And feet."

Delores's expression went flat. Her hands quivered momentarily. "Jesus," she said. "You think they got Alicia?"

"Yeah, we need to talk to her."

Delores leaned back in her seat, pressing her thin shoulder blades into the booth behind her. She put her utensils down and picked up a napkin, tearing little pieces from it and balling them up between her thumb and middle finger. She didn't speak for several moments. Jocelyn's coffee had grown cold.

"You lookin' for them?" Delores asked.

"We got two of them," Kevin put in.

"We're looking for the last one," Jocelyn said. "These are going unreported. So if you hear anything, call me."

Jocelyn handed Delores a business card with her cell phone number scrawled on the back. Delores stuffed the card into the pocket of her impossibly small miniskirt and stared at her half-eaten meal. She put her napkin down and picked at her French fries. "I'll ask around," she said finally.

"I'd appreciate it," Jocelyn said. "Call if you find out anything."

TWENTY-FOUR

October 27th

The Main Line was a collection of wealthy suburban towns in the neighboring counties of Philadelphia. It was where many of Philadelphia's rich people lived small-town lives—safe and secure in their opulent and pristinely manicured mansions and only minutes from the bustling city in all its glory and squalor. With a ten- or twenty-minute drive or train ride, Main Line residents could gain access to everything the city had to offer: a Broadway show, illicit drugs, a museum, or a violent assault. Jocelyn had grown up in one of those towns in a mansion not far from where Alicia Hardigan now resided temporarily for her latest stint in rehab.

Evening had descended gently, almost imperceptibly. The golden glow of the lit windows gave Brewster House a welcoming feel. It was housed in a mansion surrounded by rolling crisply cut lawns as far as the eye could see. Jocelyn expected to see golfers milling about. It looked more like a country club than a rehab facility. There was a small parking lot in front of the house marked for visitors. Jocelyn and Kevin climbed the expansive marble steps and entered a set of double doors that led to a large reception area decorated in bland taupe and tan tones. The desk was empty. To their right was another set of locked double doors. A sign drew their attention to the black intercom box on the wall for after-hours use.

It took twenty minutes of finagling, which included a call to the administrator, who was at home, before they were allowed to see Alicia Hardigan. An aide led them to a small community area—two couches and a recliner grouped around a thirty-six-inch flat-screen television. Tabloid shows flashed across the screen. Alicia used the remote to turn the volume down as Jocelyn and Kevin entered the room. She eyed them warily from the corner of one of the couches. She was curled into a ball, her feet tucked beneath her. Even in baggy jeans and a sweatshirt, she looked emaciated. Her blonde hair was cropped very short, the top of it stiff and spiked with gel. The skin was taut and shiny over her face, making her look more like a starved preadolescent boy than a twenty-eight-year-old woman. A large multicolored butterfly wrapped its wings around her throat, the bottom of its wings disappearing beneath the collar of her sweatshirt. She raised a hand to her lips, picking at the skin, and Jocelyn noticed her gloves. They were thin and black, and the fingers had been cut off.

"You the cops?" she asked.

"I'm Detective Rush. This is Detective Sullivan," Jocelyn said, flashing her credentials briefly.

Jocelyn perched on the edge of the recliner, catty-corner from Alicia. Kevin remained standing.

"You guys from Philly?"

She stared at Kevin, the skin picking increasing in tempo and fury. Jocelyn nodded at Kevin, and he sat on the other couch, as far from Alicia as he could get. He stared at the television, looking bored.

Alicia seemed to relax a little, her body unfurling slightly.

"Yes," Jocelyn answered. "We're with Northwest Detectives."

"I ain't done nothin' lately. I'm not on probation—"

Jocelyn held up a hand to silence the woman and smiled. "We're not here for anything you did."

Alicia's brown eyes darted from Jocelyn to Kevin and back. Slowly, her legs unfolded from beneath her.

"We're here about something that happened to you—about six months ago."

It was remarkable how quickly Alicia shut down again, her feet disappearing beneath her like the feet of the wicked witch disappearing under Dorothy's house in *The Wizard of Oz.* Her eyes turned glassy, and she crossed her arms over her chest, hugging herself.

"I don't know what you're talking about," she said quietly.

Jocelyn waited a long minute. Alicia's haunted gaze flicked toward Kevin, but he had leaned back in his seat and closed his eyes, hands clasped over his belly as if he were dozing.

"I just need to ask you a few questions about what happened, Alicia," Jocelyn said gently. "That's all."

"I don't know nothing. Nothing happened."

"A few questions and we're gone from your life."

Alicia scoffed, but her eyes brimmed with tears and her body shook. "Sure. Cops always say that shit. 'Let me help you, Alicia. We're on your side, Alicia.' Next thing I know, I'm locked up."

Jocelyn shifted closer to Alicia. "Well, I'm not here to offer help or make any promises. I just need some information. That's all."

Alicia stared past Jocelyn, her teeth working her lower lip until it was raw. "I don't know nothing," she repeated.

Jocelyn moved to sit beside Alicia. "May I see your hands?"

Alicia turned toward Jocelyn, eyes wide, horror turning her face gray. "What? I—"

Jocelyn looked at her lap for a moment. When she spoke, her tone was calm and gentle, almost a whisper. "Alicia, I don't want to make you relive it. I certainly don't want to cause you any stress, not while you're in rehab, but they did it again—a couple weeks ago—to a woman I've known for several years. A woman a lot like you. Someone who was trying to clean up her life and make things better for herself. I want to get these guys, but I need a little help. Anything you could tell me might help me put them away."

Alicia had been looking at Jocelyn as she spoke, but now she looked back at the television. The silence stretched on so long that Jocelyn pulled out her business card to hand to the other woman. Finally, Alicia spoke. "I ain't going to clean up. My brother—I don't know how he turned out so good—he thinks I can clean up, get my life together. Get back on track. That's what he always says. I keep doing this—" She waved an arm around the room, indicating the rehab facility. "Not because I'm gonna get better. I do it for him. 'Cause he always looks so sad and disappointed all the time. When I come to a place like this, he gets all happy. I wanted to die. I meant to die the last time I OD'd. But I can't even do that right."

"You must be doing something right," Jocelyn offered, wanting to keep Alicia talking. "Your brother obviously loves you very much."

Alicia shrugged. "He deserves better than me," she said matter-of-factly. "He's all good-looking and successful, and he's got this junkie hooker for a little sister. I should have died. At least if I was dead I wouldn't have to keep thinking about what they did to me."

A shudder worked its way through Alicia's body. She fingered the cuff of the glove on her left hand, eyes darting toward Kevin, who still pretended to be asleep. Finally, Alicia shifted toward Jocelyn and peeled the glove back. She put her hand in Jocelyn's lap and squeezed her eyes shut. Two gnarled lumps of flesh, about the size of a nickel, marred either side of her hand. The one on the top of her hand was much worse than the one on her palm. Jocelyn touched them gently, her throat constricting. For a moment, she couldn't catch her breath. With infinite care, she pulled the glove back down over the scars and relinquished Alicia's hand.

Alicia opened her eyes, cradling her left hand as if it were a dead thing. "The right hand is the same. I wear the gloves because I can't stand looking at them," she choked. "I got tracks that look worse than that." She pulled up the sleeve of her sweatshirt to reveal the crook of her arm, a decimated, pockmarked piece of flesh that looked like it might fall off. "But the scars on my hands—they remind me. When I think about it, all I want to do is score."

Alicia's body rocked back and forth. Jocelyn let her talk, keeping perfectly still, not wanting to break the spell. "I ain't no saint," Alicia continued. "I been doin' shit since I was sixteen. Hooking since I was eighteen. I had a foster dad who would give me a twenty for a blow job. It was dope money. It was so easy. Of course, it got a lot harder on the Stroll. Most of it I don't remember—it's all a blur. I never got raped, but I did a lot of shit I didn't really want to do. There was a cop who used to leave me alone if I gave it to him for free. I got stiffed a lot in the beginning, till I learned how to handle the tricks. I seen some bad shit too—a lot of bad shit happens to other girls, but that night—"

She stopped abruptly and swallowed, her throat working, making the butterfly ripple, its wings undulating.

"Can you tell me what happened?" Jocelyn prompted.

"It was a walking date. An older black guy came up to me, corner of Kensington and Monmouth. He said he wanted to do it while his friend watched. We went into an alley. He gave me the money. His friend came from the other direction. He was huge and lighter skinned than the old guy. He didn't talk. He kept pointing to the end of the alley. The older guy acted like he didn't want to go with the big guy. Then he said his car was around the corner, that we should do it in his car. I said no. Then they changed real quick. The big one lifted me up under his arm like I didn't weigh nothing. I kicked and screamed, but it didn't do no good. They stuffed me in the car."

"What kind of a car? Do you remember?"

Alicia shook her head. "I just remember it was gray."

"Gray," Jocelyn said. "Okay, that's good. So they put you in the car. Then what?"

"Well, the big one held me down in the backseat while the other one drove. He kept my face pressed into the seat so I couldn't see where we went. When they took me out of the car, they threw a jacket over my head. All I could see was pavement. The big one carried me into the house—"

"How long do you think you were in the car?"

Alicia shrugged. "I don't know. Maybe ten minutes. It was hard to tell. I thought they were going to kill me. I wish they had."

"So they took you into a house?"

"Yeah, but it was abandoned. It smelled like fire and piss. They dumped me on the floor in the front room. The windows were boarded up. They had a light—one of those lights like people take camping. There was trash everywhere—a lot of roaches. The big one held me while the other one went into the back of the house. When he came back, there was a white guy with him. He had on a ski mask, but I could see his neck and his hands were white. He looked at me for a long time."

"What was he wearing?"

"Jeans and a long-sleeved black shirt. He was solid. I mean, muscular like he worked out. He just looked at me for a while. Then he said, 'Hold her down.'"

Alicia closed her eyes again. Her upper teeth scraped against her lower lip, drawing blood. "I sure could use a smoke."

Jocelyn glanced around the room. "Can you smoke in here?"

Alicia laughed loudly. "Hell, no. Only in the smoke room. Besides, I'm on suicide watch. I'm not allowed to play with fire."

Jocelyn looked at Kevin, whose head slumped downward to the right. "How about Nicorette gum?"

Alicia perked up. "You got some?"

Jocelyn shook her head. "Not me." She made a show of tiptoeing over to Kevin and stealthily extracting the Nicorette from his right jacket pocket. Alicia chuckled a little as Jocelyn handed her a tab. She chewed slowly. "Thanks," she said.

Jocelyn waited patiently for Alicia to begin again. "The two black guys, they held me down on the ground. I fought like hell, but they were too strong. The white guy disappeared, but once the other two had me pinned down, he came back. They had my arms out like this—" She spread her arms wide. "When the third guy came back, he had a hammer and nails. He nailed my hands into the floor. I cried and cried, but they ignored me. Then they left me alone with him."

"Did he nail your feet?"

"My feet? No. He pulled down my jeans and tried to fuck me, but he couldn't. He was limp."

"Did he say anything?"

"No, just a lot of grunting. Then when he couldn't do it, he called the other two back in. He said, 'Your turn.' The other two—they didn't have no problems. The white guy, I saw him. He stood in the corner while they raped me, and he was hard as a rock. He jerked off while I got raped."

Rage caused Alicia's voice to go up a few octaves.

"Then what happened?" Jocelyn asked.

"I passed out. When I came to, only the skinny older one was there. He was sitting in a corner, in a folding chair just watching me. I started crying when I saw him. He didn't say nothing—well, he said, 'Hold still,' and he pulled the nails out with pliers. He pulled me up and put the jacket over my head. It smelled like cigarettes and fried food, but it was better than the smell in that house. I couldn't feel my arms. He put my jeans on backwards and took me out to a car. He dropped me off a couple of blocks from Einstein."

"How long were you in the house?"

Alicia made a face of disgust. "Long enough for a cockroach to crawl in my goddamn ear. I think I was there overnight. It was Wednesday when I picked up the walking date and Thursday when I got to the hospital. They patched me up, got the roach outta my ear. Then they said they were calling the cops—even though I never told them what happened."

"Why did you run, Alicia?"

Alicia humphed. "No offense, but I don't trust no cops. You think anyone would believe me—or care? I got spooked. I just wanted to go somewhere I could forget. But I can't. I can't forget it."

Jocelyn spread out ten mug shots on the coffee table. Alicia picked out Warner and Donovan without hesitation. "One last thing," Jocelyn asked. "Is there anything else you can remember about the white guy? Anything at all? It doesn't matter how small or stupid it might seem. It could be important."

Alicia chewed her gum thoughtfully. "Well, he had blue eyes. He was muscular like I said."

"How tall was he?"

"Probably five-ten and he was real clean."

"Clean?"

Alicia nodded. "Yeah, his clothes were neat and clean, and he smelled clean—like soap."

"Any particular kind?"

"I don't know. I'm just saying he smelled clean like he just got out of the shower."

Jocelyn pulled out a business card and scrawled her cell phone number on the back of it. She handed it to Alicia. "If you think of anything else, call me."

"Was I any help?"

Jocelyn stood and walked over to Kevin. She kicked his foot, and he made a show of waking up, stretching, and yawning.

"Yeah," Jocelyn said. "You were a big help."

Alicia studied the card. "You're a nice lady," she said. "For a cop."

TWENTY-FIVE

October 27th

"Nice work in there," Kevin said as they got into the car. "You owe me some Nicorette."

Jocelyn laughed, but Kevin feigned seriousness. "I'm not kidding. That shit is expensive."

"How about a Dunkin' Donuts coffee?"

He clapped his hands together. "Now you're talking. So did Hardigan ID Warner and Donovan?"

"Sure did," Jocelyn confirmed.

"Well, that was easy," Kevin said. He reached forward and toggled the radio dial until he found the oldies station. "So here's what I don't get. Neither Warner nor Donovan bothered to hide their identities. They didn't wear masks or disguises. I mean if you're going to kidnap and rape a woman, wouldn't you try to be a little stealthy about it?"

"They didn't think it would come to that," Jocelyn said.

"They didn't think they'd get caught? They drop their vics off at the fucking hospital."

"No," Jocelyn said. "They didn't think any of their victims would report it—or press charges if it came to that. Alicia ran. Anita didn't talk at first."

She glanced at Kevin just in time to see his face tighten as the realization dawned on him. "Because they're doing it to hookers."

"Right."

"Why not just kill them? Why leave them alive?"

Jocelyn shrugged. "A murder charge carries a heavy sentence. Heavier than rape. Plus they can always say they paid for it and have the charges thrown out—like you said, they're targeting hookers."

"So there could be a lot more victims out there."

"Could be."

"But wait, what about the white guy? Why does he wear a mask?"

"Because whoever he is, he's got a lot more to lose than Warner and Donovan."

The nearest Dunkin' Donuts was on West Lancaster Avenue. Jocelyn wanted to go through the drive-through, but Kevin insisted on going inside to see the donut selection. Jocelyn thought of Olivia and how she loved Munchkins, especially the chocolate ones. She had even learned to identify the Dunkin' Donuts sign, so that whenever they drove past one, she went nuts. Sometimes Jocelyn had to consciously avoid the place while they were driving around. The thought of Olivia brought a smile to her face, which quickly faded at the sound of a man's raised voice inside the store.

A familiar tall, sandy-haired man about Jocelyn's age stood by the counter yelling and gesticulating wildly at an iced drink on the counter. The woman behind the counter stared at him with a wilting look. "This is coffee," the man said. "Coffee! I asked for tea. Tea. This tastes like shit. It's disgusting. I stood right here and ordered tea and you gave me coffee. Coffee that tastes like shit, no less. What is wrong with you? I'm the only one in here, I ordered one thing, and you can't get it right?"

"Excuse me, sir," Kevin said, but the man kept going as if Kevin hadn't spoken.

"Are you deaf or are you just that fucking stupid?"

Kevin stepped between the man and the counter. "Hey, man," he said. "Relax. I'm sure this nice lady will be happy to get you some tea."

The woman took the offending coffee and disappeared. The irate man turned to Kevin, disdain curling his upper lip. "Mind your own fucking business."

"All right," Jocelyn said, stepping toward the man. "That's enough. Sir, step outside please."

The man turned toward her, disdain morphing into shock, the angry lines of his face slackening as he registered her authoritative tone. Then his belligerence returned. "Who the—"

Jocelyn cut him off. "Who the fuck am I? I'm the fucking police, and you're the fucking douche bag who's going to step outside. Now."

In a single fluid movement, she flashed her credentials in his face and took his elbow, guiding him outside to the parking lot. She gave him a little push as they stepped outside, and he stumbled down the three steps, barely maintaining his balance. For a moment, he seemed dazed. "Rush?" he said as he studied her face beneath the faded glow of the parking lot lights.

"Detective Rush, yes. Now, unless you want to be charged with harassment and terroristic threats, you'll get into your vehicle and move on, and I would strongly suggest you not patronizing this business ever again."

He smoothed the lapels of his suit jacket and turned to face her. He peered into her face. Then he stuck out a hand, palm upturned. "Let me see your badge again."

"Sir—"

"James," he said haughtily. "James Evans."

Jocelyn froze. Ice seemed to flow through her veins, spreading rapidly throughout her body. She swallowed. Her hand went to her holster.

"What?" she croaked.

She wouldn't recognize them of course—not by sight. She had no memory of that time period. It had been years since she'd studied their photos in her high school yearbook, and by now they would look differently. It had been eighteen years. They would have grown and changed, and, like James Evans, they might not be easily recognizable.

"James Evans," he repeated. "I went to high school with a couple of Rush girls. Which one are you?"

Quickly regaining her composure, Jocelyn pushed him along toward the only other car in the parking lot, a Porsche. "I'm the one who is telling you to leave. Right now."

He ignored her. "A police officer, huh? That doesn't surprise me. You put my family through hell."

A sound like thunder rushed in her ears. Her vision narrowed to the area directly in front of her, and Evans filled up her entire field of vision. She unsnapped her holster. "Excuse me?" she said incredulously, her voice raising an octave.

He narrowed his eyes as he studied her. Then, "Your sister, though—what's her name? Karen? Cameron? We had a great time together, her and I. Kinky stuff, though."

Then the barrel of her Glock was pressing into the skin under his chin. Jocelyn crowded him, pinning him against the Porsche, the length of her body pressed against his, her hand steady.

"What the fuck?" Evans cried, throwing his hands up in the air.

"I don't think you want to go there with me, you piece of shit."

"Are you crazy?" he asked, eyes frantically darting around, searching for rescue.

Jocelyn dug the barrel of the gun into his skin, making an imprint of the barrel in the soft underbelly of his chin. "I don't know, am I? Keep talking and we'll find out."

She heard Kevin's voice from behind her and his feet jogging toward her. "Rush! Jesus Christ."

He pulled her away from Evans, pushing the barrel of her gun toward the ground. Evans opened his mouth to speak, but Kevin said, "Do yourself a favor, and get the fuck out of here like we told you in the first place."

Evans's hands trembled as he pulled his keys from his jacket pocket. He clicked the key fob to unlock the car and got in. With a pale, frightened glance at Jocelyn, he tore out of the parking lot, tires squealing.

Kevin shook his head. "Put that away," he said. "Get in the goddamn car."

Jocelyn stared after Evans's car, gun at her side as the thundering in her head receded. Kevin stood by the car. She was barely aware of the cherry-red hue that had risen to his cheeks. A vein throbbed on the side of his forehead. Finally, he slapped the roof. "Jesus Christ, Rush. Right now. Get in the fucking car!"

Silently, Jocelyn got in and pulled away. Although his breathing sounded slightly labored, Kevin didn't speak for almost five full minutes. That's how Jocelyn knew he was really angry with her. She chanced a look at him. His face was still flushed from collar to roots. Once they crossed the Green Lane Bridge back into Philadelphia, Kevin spoke. "What's with you lately, Rush? You're totally out of control. I should be reporting you right now. You're already on thin ice. We're not even supposed to be out here. This isn't even our goddamn case."

"I know," Jocelyn said tightly.

"What if that guy files a complaint against you?"

"He won't."

"You don't know that."

"Yeah, I do. He was one of the guys who raped Camille when we were teenagers."

Kevin lost some of his bluster. He looked away from her and let a few seconds pass. "Oh," he said, followed by a short pause. "Still, Rush. You can't go pulling your gun on civilians—scummy or not. Are you trying to lose your job or what?"

"You know I'm not. I have a child now."

"Then what is your problem?"

Jocelyn swallowed, trying to think of a reply that would pacify him. Finally, she said, "I don't know."

Kevin shook his head and sighed, his breath a loud huff. "That guy is a piece of shit, no doubt, but reaming out the clerk at Dunkin' Donuts is not a crime. You can't go waving your gun around at every entitled prick you see—even if you know about the skeletons in their closets. You're not a rookie, for fuck's sake. You're better than this."

"I know," Jocelyn said.

"Get your shit together, Rush. I don't want to have to report you. Ever." He reached a hand toward the empty cup holder in the center console. "Son of a bitch."

Jocelyn glanced at him. "What is it?"

"After all that, I still didn't get my coffee."

TWENTY-SIX

October 30th

The next three nights, they caught two shootings, two stabbings, and a robbery. Two of those nights, Jocelyn didn't pick Olivia up from Martina's house until three a.m. Olivia slept through the transfer, and having had a good night's sleep, woke promptly at seven each morning. By the fourth night, Jocelyn felt like the walking dead. Kevin was off, and she thanked the great, unknowable Universe that it was a slow night. The next day was Halloween, and she wanted to be awake and alert enough to have a good day with Olivia. Even though she was still too young to really understand trick-or-treating, she loved to dress up. Jocelyn had planned to take her to a few trusted neighbors' houses. She couldn't wait to see Olivia all decked out in the Disney princess costume she had chosen.

She put her head down on her desk and tried to doze, drifting fitfully in and out of sleep. Fragments of a disturbing dream involving Olivia dressed as a princess and being kidnapped afflicted her, waking her with a start every few minutes.

Chen appeared at her side. He set a Styrofoam cup of coffee next to her head. "Sometimes the sleep just isn't worth it," he said.

Jocelyn lifted her head and stared at him, bleary-eyed, until he smiled and said, "Nightmares. I get 'em too."

Smoothing the hair away from her face with her good hand, she rubbed her eyes before curling a hand around the coffee cup. Inhaling its scent, she lifted the plastic lid to see if Chen had put cream and sugar in it. He had. She sipped it gingerly and nodded her thanks. She tried to catch up on the large stack of paperwork ever present on her desk, but her mind kept going back to Anita Grant and Alicia Hardigan. She had left four messages for Caleb Vaughn. He had called her back once, but she had been on the street and missed his call.

Jocelyn looked around at the mostly empty desks. She fished her car keys from the mess on her desk and grabbed the coffee cup. "Chen, call me on my cell if all hell breaks loose."

Chen waved without taking his eyes off his computer screen.

She drove to Second and Westmoreland where the SVU had its offices. It was a five-story unmarked brick building nestled among dilapidated row houses. They sagged, cracks like spider veins in their exterior walls. On the other side, running parallel to Westmoreland, was new construction. Sparkling new apartment buildings and high-rise complexes rose out of the dirt and decay looking so clean and new; it hurt Jocelyn's eyes just to look at them. She wondered how long it would be before they too were pulled down into the muck.

All over the city there were efforts to revitalize crime-ridden neighborhoods and beautify them. In some neighborhoods, revitalization took, and the houses were bought up by doctors, lawyers, and college professors who wanted the quintessential urban experience without actually getting shot when they left the house. Crime went down in those neighborhoods, at least for a time. The houses were rehabbed by their new owners and small businesses flourished. It became trendy to go there and even trendier to live there. In other neighborhoods, crime was too much a way of life, too deeply ingrained, to ever lift the stain.

Mercifully, SVU had a parking lot. The city had been working for years to have their facility moved and integrated with the Department of Human Services Abuse Investigations Division, the Philadelphia Children's Alliance, and prosecutors from the district attorney's office. The city wanted all these agencies in one central location, which made sense to Jocelyn. Unfortunately for them, no neighborhood in the city wanted the Sex Crimes Division in their midst. Drug dealers, murderers, and prostitutes were A-OK but not sex crimes victims and investigators. Jocelyn thought she had read that they'd finally closed the deal on a new location, but it had taken years and it would be years before SVU actually moved into their shiny new facility.

At the front desk, she flashed her credentials and said she was there to see Caleb Vaughn about a case.

"He's on the street," the disinterested desk sergeant said without even looking at Jocelyn. The woman continued working on her crossword puzzle.

"I didn't know they let psychics work the front desk," Jocelyn said. "Must save you a lot of phone calls."

The woman looked up at her, one eyebrow raised, the corner of her mouth dimpled in a scathing smirk. "Excuse me?"

Jocelyn matched the raised eyebrow and pointed to the phone on her desk. "How about you call up there and find out if Vaughn is here or not."

Jocelyn expected resistance, but instead the woman picked up the phone and dialed. She kept her eyes on Jocelyn as she spoke into the receiver. "Is Vaughn there? Yeah. Someone down here to see him. Yeah. Northwest. Okay."

She hung up. "He'll be right down," she said, resuming her crossword puzzle.

"Right down" turned out to be a half hour. Jocelyn was ten seconds from storming past the reception desk when a tall man with thick, wavy brown hair appeared. He looked to be in his forties. Small lines appeared at the corners of his brown eyes as he surveyed the room. His gaze settled on Jocelyn, and in that split second, she felt a jolt, like a spark of electricity. She heard Anita's voice in the back of her mind: *too pretty to talk to.* Jocelyn swallowed. Vaughn walked over to her and extended a hand. "Caleb Vaughn."

Jocelyn, who had been ready to read him the riot act five seconds earlier, took his hand and stared at him blankly. Up close, she could see laugh lines around his mouth as well. His eyes were dark, flinty, and kind at the same time. He didn't look like a cop. He looked like a high school English teacher—a really hot one. He reminded her of the kind of man who actually got better looking as he aged. A bit of George Clooney mixed with Patrick Dempsey's hair. Yet, he was unkempt—his tie was loosened, the first two buttons of his wrinkled white dress shirt undone. There was a small tear in his shirt to the left of his tie.

"Divorced," she blurted.

Caleb's hand was still in hers. He didn't let go but gave her a quizzical look and laughed warmly. "No," he said. "Never married but single. You?"

Jocelyn wished she could hide the blush that rose to her cheeks. She hadn't meant to say it out loud. She cleared her throat. "Same." Glancing down at their locked hands, she was glad he didn't comment on her splint. She didn't feel like answering questions about it.

They realized at the same time that the handshake had gone on entirely too long. Caleb released her hand. From the corner of her eye, she saw the desk sergeant shake her head. Caleb kept smiling at her. "Now that I know your marital status, how about your name?"

She fumbled in her pocket and produced her credentials. "Rush. Jocelyn Rush. I'm with Northwest Detectives. I worked on the Grant case. I've left you about six messages."

He ran a hand through his hair, tousling it further as he gazed down at her police ID. "Yeah, the Grant case. I called you about that. Sorry about the phone tag. I've been on the street."

"So I've heard."

He handed her credentials back to her. "What can I do for you?"

The words *come home with me* flew through her mind. Luckily, they didn't come out of her mouth. "I spoke with Alicia Hardigan. She had some interesting information. I wanted to touch base with you because I think we might just be scratching the surface on this one."

"You found Hardigan, huh? Okay," he said. "You like coffee?"

"What? Yeah, I—"

"Wait here," he said and left her standing there openmouthed. The desk sergeant looked up over her crossword and shook her head again. Blushing for the second time in five minutes, Jocelyn turned away from the woman. This time, she didn't have to wait long for him.

Again, he smiled at her warmly, his dark eyes glinting. Over one arm he carried a suit jacket. In his hand, two slim files. "You can drive," he said as he ushered her out of the building.

The diner he directed her to was only five minutes away. It was small, cozy, and mostly empty. One of those neighborhood places run out of a converted corner row house that only the locals dared enter. One waitress sat behind the register engrossed in a paperback novel while another worked the only two tables with customers. Caleb chose a booth in the corner, out of earshot of the other diners. When the waitress came over, he ordered two coffees and two pieces of key lime pie.

"You've got to try their key lime pie," he said. "It's unbelievable and also one of the only edible things on their menu. Oh, you're not allergic, are you?"

She shook her head and stared at him, dumbfounded. He wasn't acting like a cop. She'd inserted herself into his investigation, and he wasn't giving her one ounce of shit. Instead, he was buying her pie. He was too pretty to talk to and he was buying her pie. She tried to tamp down the uncharacteristic thrill spiraling up from her center and focus on the reason she had come—the investigation. "No, I'm not allergic."

He winked at her. "Good. You'll love it. I promise."

Caleb's cell phone rang. He looked at it and shot her an apologetic glance. "I have to take this," he said. "It's my son."

"Your son?"

He held up one finger, signaling for a minute, and answered. The call lasted about thirty seconds and seemed to have to do with a lost set of keys. Caleb ended the call and flashed her a grin. "I was twenty-two," he explained. "We broke up before he was three. She married someone else and moved to North Carolina when he was eleven. Brian stayed with me. He just started at Temple University. You have kids?"

Still taking him in, Jocelyn said. "Yeah. Olivia. She's three."

"You and her dad . . ."

Jocelyn waved a hand dismissively. "She was my sister's—my niece—but my sister couldn't care for her, so I adopted her."

The waitress brought their coffee. "Pie will be up in a minute," she said.

Jocelyn couldn't help but notice they prepared their coffee exactly the same way—two level spoons of sugar and three creams.

"So, we found six prepaid cell phones in Larry Warner's home, all of which had been used to call only two other prepaid cell phones in the last seven months. None of the numbers can be traced to a person. We ran all the numbers in both his and Donovan's real cell phones, but none of their contacts fit the description of the third man."

"What about the computer? Did you get his computer?"

The corner of his mouth dimpled. He shook his head. "We got it, but it was completely useless. I mean we can connect him to Grant via the e-mails, but that's all we got. Doesn't help us with the remaining suspect. So, tell me about Alicia Hardigan." He sipped his coffee with a hissing sound and a grimace. Jocelyn stirred her own coffee idly while she recapped her interview with Hardigan and told him about the Michael Kors watch Anita had remembered.

When she finished, he slid the two manila files he'd brought with him across the table to Jocelyn. "You're right. What you said earlier—we are just scratching the surface. That one," he said as she opened the one on the top, "was the first one. Happened about four years ago. Her name was Raeann Church. She'd been working in Atlantic City for about three years. She was approached by a black male in his late forties in a blue, late-model Ford for sex. They agreed on the services and the price. He drove about three blocks and picked up another black male, big guy. Never said a word. The big guy crowded her, kept her from getting out of the car. They drove for hours, she said, until she didn't recognize where she was. They ended up here, of course."

"Let me guess," Jocelyn said as she thumbed through the file. "They took her to an abandoned house. There was a white male there wearing a ski mask. He nailed her to the floor, tried to have intercourse with her, and couldn't get it up. He told the other two to have sex with her while he watched. The next day, the driver pulled the nails out and dumped her off at the hospital."

There was a police report, a few interview logs, a victim statement, and photos of Raeann Church. She was white and thin—too thin—the way Camille had looked when Jocelyn had last seen her. She had a large nose that had obviously been broken a few times and small sunken eyes. She might have been attractive if the street hadn't turned her into a ghostly pale stick figure. She had greasy brown hair and sallow skin. There were photos of her hands, but only the left one bore the mark of a nail.

"Close," Caleb said. "They took her to a motel in the Northeast—"

"Do you have security footage?"

Caleb sipped his coffee again and frowned. "Not the kind of motel that has security cameras, if you know what I mean. The white guy was there. He tried to have intercourse with her but couldn't—so yeah, he told the other two to do it. Then the white guy gets the idea to nail her to the floor. Raeann doesn't know where the tools came from, but they left her with the skinny one for a while and came back with a hammer and nails. They got one nail through her left hand. She screamed her head off, and the owner of the motel threw them out. The driver dropped her off a few blocks from Frankford Torresdale Hospital."

"Sounds like their first time," Jocelyn said.

The waitress returned with two pieces of key lime pie. Jocelyn took a bite. It melted in her mouth. Before she had taken her second bite, Caleb was halfway through his. She moaned softly. "This is incredible," she said and meant it. She knew she'd be craving it later, long after she'd gone back to her own Division.

"I know," Caleb agreed. "It's bizarre, isn't it? This little diner no one even knows about and they've got the best key lime pie you ever had."

Jocelyn laughed and tapped an index finger on Caleb's notes. "This doesn't say anything about the white guy wearing a ski mask."

"Because he wasn't."

Pages flew across the table as Jocelyn searched frantically for composite sketches. "Where are the composites?"

Caleb grimaced. "Do you know how much it costs to use a sketch artist? Back then we were only allowed to bring them in on serial offenders and crimes against kids."

Jocelyn's fork clanged against her plate as she dropped it. "Are you fucking kidding me?" she said, but she knew exactly what Caleb was talking about. Like anything else, police departments were run on money, and their budgets only went so far. There had been plenty of cases in her career that she would have loved to bring in forensic help, but she couldn't because of budget constraints. Real police work was about as far from the television shows depicting CSI as you could possibly imagine.

"Raeann was a known prostitute. A high-risk victim. She agreed to have sex with one of these guys—things went south. In her statement, she said she didn't put up much of a fight until they brought out the hammer and nails. She was hoping if she went along with things, she'd live another day. And they paid her. If I spent thousands of the Division's money on composites in a case like this, I'd get fired."

Jocelyn groaned. "I know, I know. I've heard it all before. Forget it. Is this woman alive at least? Can we talk to her?"

He didn't even balk at her use of the word *we*. "Yeah, last I heard she was still alive. She was based out of Atlantic City, though, so it could take a while to find her."

"Okay, how about the second victim?"

"Well, that scenario was a lot closer to the one you described. Happened about six months after they got Raeann. The victim's name was Honey Mae."

"Really?"

Caleb laughed. "Yeah, really. I don't know what some people are thinking—do they want their kids to grow up to be hookers?"

Jocelyn thought of the argument she'd had with Camille over Olivia's original name—Taffy. "My thoughts exactly."

"Anyway, Honey Mae was working here in Philly. The two black guys drove up, tried to negotiate something. She wasn't going for it. They left and came back later, stuffed her in the car, took her to a crack house, and you know the rest."

"White guy can't get it up; he nails her to the floor—"

"He nails her to the floor right away this time. Now he's got the idea in his head, and he likes it, so yeah, he nails both her hands and has the other guys have intercourse with her while he jerks off in the corner."

Jocelyn flipped open Honey's file. She glanced over the reports and Caleb's notes. "The white guy wore nylons over his head?"

"Yeah. So I guess he got wise and decided it was best to try to disguise himself."

The description of the third unknown subject was the same from both women. The guy was young, probably in his late twenties, early thirties, well built, and muscular. Like Anita, they described him as clean. Raeann Church had said his eyes were blue, his hair brown and close-cropped. Caleb had handwritten, *Clean-cut. Looked like a frat boy. (Military?)*

The descriptions of the black males matched that of Larry Warner and Angel Donovan exactly. The car used to abduct Honey Mae was different from the one used to transport Raeann Church. Perhaps they'd borrowed the vehicles or rented one for the occasion.

"Where's Honey now?"

"Dead," Caleb said. "One of the other girls stabbed her last year in a dispute over some drugs. She bled out on the street."

"Shit," Jocelyn said. "What about the motel owner from the first case?"

Caleb shook his head. "More useless than a corpse. I got two things out of him—he doesn't talk to cops and he doesn't speak English. Now, it's been four years, no way he'll remember these guys."

"Well, at least we've got them in custody," Jocelyn said. "You read my notes on the interrogations. They won't roll on the third guy. I can't figure it out."

Caleb shrugged. "Well, either the third guy has something on them or there's something in it for them."

"That's what I'm thinking."

"If we really want to find the third guy, we should take a closer look at these guys. Anita Grant was a prostitute?"

Goose bumps rose along her arms at his use of the word *we*. "More of an escort. These assholes were upping their game, moving from street prostitutes to online escorts."

Caleb's brow crinkled, the lines at the corners of his eyes deepening. "She wouldn't talk to me or my female detective. At all. You know that she'll only speak with you."

Jocelyn nodded, scraping up the last bits of pie. "I know. Anita and I go back a-ways."

"Well, my problem is that this case is not very high priority. You know how it is. I mean if it were a college student or a housewife, I might be able to throw more manpower behind getting the third guy, but a prostitute—two guys already in custody . . ." He drifted off as she stared at him.

"I hear you," she said. "But I think it would be a mistake not to pursue the third guy. We need him—before he decides to do this to a housewife or college student."

He smiled. A megawatt, movie star kind of smile. She suddenly and inexplicably wanted to kiss him. "I'm guessing you want to help."

"You think?"

He laughed.

"My captain will never go for it. I'm sure you've got many competent investigators in the SVU to help out with this," she conceded.

"Yes, but the victim won't speak to any one of them. Let me pull some strings. Bring you on as a special consultant or some bullshit like that. Then I'll see if I can find Raeann. She's the only person who saw his face."

Jocelyn smiled. "Ahearn will flip his lid. Let's do it."

TWENTY-SEVEN

October 30th

He insisted on buying her a piece of pie to go. She drove him back to SVU headquarters. She parked the car and turned off the ignition before she realized what she was doing. She didn't want to start the car again with Caleb in it and draw attention to it. They sat side by side for a long, awkward moment. Jocelyn could hear his breath. Or was it hers?

Later, she was hard-pressed to remember how it started. Had they looked at each other first? Had their eyes met meaningfully like in the movies or had they just gone for it, instinct drawing their bodies together, without the need for locked gazes or words?

What she remembered clearly was him touching her knee—familiarly, as if they'd known one another for years instead of an hour. She turned into him, and their mouths crashed into each other. His lips were soft, the kiss hard and frantic. He tasted like key lime pie. Then they were reaching, grasping, and sliding their hands over the top of each other's clothes like two blind people searching for something. She maneuvered over the center console, her lips barely leaving his, and straddled him. He slid her jacket down over her shoulders. The right sleeve caught briefly on her splint before falling to the passenger's side floor, a soft sigh. She tugged at the knot of his tie and he pulled it off, breaking contact for a few seconds. His mouth closed back over hers with renewed urgency. She leaned into him, pulling him by his shoulders—closer. She wanted him closer. A tingling heat broke open between her legs. She pressed herself down into him and felt his hardness through both their pants.

Caleb pulled her collar apart and teased her collarbones with his tongue. His hand snaked its way under her shirt, beneath the underwire of her bra. When it closed over her breast, she moaned softly. Never in her life had she wanted a man the way she wanted Caleb in that moment.

I want you inside me.

Her eyes flew open. Had she said it aloud? She couldn't seem to control her thoughts or words around him. If she'd said it out loud, he hadn't noticed. His head was bent to her chest. He'd liberated one of her breasts. She watched as he took her nipple in his mouth—the tingling heat between her legs a raging inferno. His hands were warm as they moved downward, palming her ass.

"Jesus," she said, and this time it did come out. He made some muffled noise against her breast in response.

She closed her eyes and ran her hands through his thick brown locks. She tried to slow her breathing, think about something besides his mouth and hands on her and his hardness pressing into her inner thigh. She wanted to tear her clothes off and fuck him right in the car, in the parking lot, while she was on duty.

"Jesus," she said again. "We have to stop. Stop."

She went limp in his hands. Slowly, with lingering hesitation, he released her breast, brought his hands back to neutral territory. She pulled away from him and looked into his flushed face. He grinned at her. Tufts of his hair shot out in every direction. It made her want to kiss him again. He pulled the lapels of her shirt together and leaned his mouth toward hers, hovering a half inch away, testing the tension between their mouths, the motion of his head matching hers. She tried to put some distance between them, but he kept close.

"We can't," she said into his face.

He kissed her chin, nipped at her bottom lip. She smiled and put both hands on his shoulders, pushing him firmly against the seat.

"Really," she said.

He lifted his hands in surrender and closed his eyes, a lazy grin on his face.

Jocelyn straightened her bra and shirt and fished her jacket from the floor. As she pulled it back on, Caleb opened his eyes, seriousness overtaking his expression. "I'm sorry," he said. "I don't normally act this way."

I never act this way. She disentangled herself, settling back into the driver's seat. "Me either," she said. "That was . . ."

"Fantastic?"

She smiled again. "I was going to say weird."

"I'll take weird as a compliment if I can see you again."

Her hesitation was automatic. She didn't even think about it. It was ingrained. Between the post-Phil baggage and Olivia coming before all else, her knee-jerk response to any advance by a man was to blow him off.

"Don't say anything," Caleb said. "I know where to find you."

Jocelyn immediately felt badly. "I—" she began.

He reached over and squeezed her knee. "I'll find Raeann Church. When I do, I'll call you. I'll get you on this case with the Anita Grant connection. You'll have dinner with me, if you want to. You choose the time and the place."

"Okay," she said, feeling dumbstruck.

"If you want to," he said again.

She felt like a starstruck teenager. "I do."

A business card appeared in his hand. He pressed it into hers. "My cell phone number is on there," he said. "You probably already have it, but just in case. I'll be in touch."

She watched him saunter away, his stride long and relaxed. She found herself smiling as he stopped to check his reflection in the tinted window of a nearby truck. He spent a few seconds smoothing his hair back down.

She drove back to Northwest Detectives in a daze, acutely aware of the moist, hot wanting still coursing through her core. It was a completely foreign sensation. Her entire response to Caleb was foreign. From the moment she'd seen him to them making out like teenagers in the car. *This must be what real attraction feels like.* Certainly, she'd found men attractive before. She'd always thought Phil was attractive, and yet their sex life had always been problematic. She had occasionally enjoyed sex with Phil, but most of the time she'd found herself enduring it. Phil had suggested to her—and she had often wondered—if she had some kind of hormonal imbalance that kept her from getting turned on or enjoying sex.

"Frigidity is a real medical condition," Phil used to tell her in that way he had of saying things matter-of-factly that just happened to make her feel like shit.

She'd never brought it up to her ob-gyn. Then Olivia came along, she and Phil broke up, and Jocelyn's sex drive—or lack thereof—was the least of her concerns. When she was fifteen, she had had a boyfriend for about six months. They had done it like the world was about to end. Jocelyn remembered feeling a vague sense of titillation at doing something her parents would most certainly disapprove of coupled with curiosity at what the other girls at school had already been doing for two or three years. But mostly she had felt uncomfortable. She kept waiting for the sex to feel better, but it never did. Even the making out and heavy petting was lacking for her. The first time the boy pushed his fingers inside her, rooting around like a kid rifling through a bag of Halloween candy, she'd wondered what it was about sex that people liked anyway. After she dropped out of Princeton and joined the police academy, she'd slept with a couple of men. One-night stands that barely registered and were more a result of alcohol consumption than any desire for sex on her part.

But Caleb—she'd wanted him, wanted to touch him, kiss him, fuck him. His touch made her dizzy with desire and his mouth . . .

"Oh my God," she groaned aloud. "What the hell is wrong with me?"

She tried to act normal as she returned to Northwest Detectives. She ran into Inez on her way up the steps.

"There you are," Inez said. "What happened to you?"

Jocelyn looked down at her clothes, smoothing her jacket. "What?"

Inez eyed her skeptically, one hand on her outthrust hip. "You're all flushed. You never get flushed. You never do anything worth getting flushed over."

Jocelyn raised an eyebrow. "That's not fair—or accurate."

Inez shrugged noncommittally, the hand still on her hip. "I'm just sayin'. Where you been?"

Jocelyn trudged past Inez, continuing up the steps. "SVU," she said over her shoulder.

Inez followed her up to her desk. "Well, you're gonna love this," Inez said as Jocelyn plopped into her chair and thumbed through her messages.

"What is it?"

"Those guys you hauled in a couple weeks ago—Warner and Donovan? They're back on the street."

The message slips fluttered from Jocelyn's fingers onto the floor. Her mouth hung open as she stared at Inez, waiting for the other woman to say it was a joke.

"I saw them an hour ago," Inez went on. "I got a call across the street from Warner's house. Came out and there he was standing on his porch with his friend, watching with the rest of the neighborhood rubberneckers."

"What the fuck?" Jocelyn said.

"I thought you should know," Inez said. "I gotta run. But we'll talk about SVU later."

With a wink and a grim smile, she was gone.

The last vestiges of the warm, tingly feelings Jocelyn had had from her encounter with Caleb slipped away. She leaned across the paperwork on her desk and booted up her computer. It only took a moment to pull up the dockets on Warner's and Donovan's cases. They had made bail two days earlier. The rape charge had been dismissed, although several lesser charges still stood. Their next preliminary hearing was in a month.

Jocelyn scanned the dockets for the name of the ADA assigned to their file. "Son of a bitch," she breathed, a squall of cold enveloping her as her gaze landed on the name.

Philip Delisi.

TWENTY-EIGHT

October 31st

The bus shelter at Ninth and Market, which was just a rectangular, three-walled, plexiglass-and-steel cove, was crowded at three forty in the afternoon. Three different buses stopped there in ten- to twenty-minute intervals. People stood beneath the shelter, trying to keep from touching one another in the tiny space. They studied their phones or tablets or listened to iPods to avoid any chance of interaction with their fellow passengers. There were three secretaries in skirts and nylons with running sneakers on their feet and purses damn near as big as steamer trunks. Larry had already dipped his chin as he and Angel passed to see if any of them carried anything of value in their giant purses, but he didn't find anything of interest.

The smokers stood outside the shelter, some of them behind it where Larry and Angel leaned against the scarred plexiglass. On one pane someone had grafittied RRAZR U REAL in black spray paint. Someone else had spread a wad of pink gum over the double *R* in RRAZR. Angel tapped his wrist and hooked a thumb over his shoulder. *If he doesn't show soon, we're out of here.*

Larry nodded. A young white blonde woman—wearing the tightest damn business dress Larry had ever seen—walked under the shelter. She was directly on the other side of the plexiglass. Her wine-colored dress hugged every curve on her body. Her breasts bobbed up and down as she moved, making them look as if they were fighting to get free of the V-neck. Her thick legs were covered in nude-colored nylons, and on her feet she wore UGGs with fur rims. She leaned back into the shelter, her ass pressing against the glass. Larry gave a low whistle.

"Damn," he said.

Angel looked down, where the outline of the cleft of her ass was just visible beneath the skintight dress. He smiled and cupped his genitals. The woman talked loudly on her cell phone, completely oblivious to their stares. "I told him, 'You are not going there with her.' She is trying to get in his pants, and damn if I'm going to let her." Her litany of complaints about the woman who was apparently tempting her boyfriend went on unabated. She went silent when Face crossed the front of the bus shelter. He didn't acknowledge her or the fifty-year-old secretary beside her, who was much more subtle in her ogling.

Larry glanced at Angel, who was rolling his eyes. *Women.* They couldn't get enough of the guy—until he was nailing their hands into the floor. Larry snickered at the thought. Face sauntered up beside him so they were back-to-back. He pulled out a cell phone and pressed it to his ear. He spoke quietly, and Larry replied as though he were talking to Angel. Anyone spotting them would think Face was on his phone and that Larry and Angel were talking among themselves. No one passing by would connect them.

"I see you dumb shits made bail," Face said.

Angel held up a middle finger behind Face's back.

"You need to make this go away," Larry said. "Making bail on reduced charges ain't good enough."

Face laughed. Larry could feel the quaking of Face's shoulders as he backed up a step closer to them. "If fat-ass here had just stuck to the story, you would've been fine. It's not my problem he's got shit for brains."

Larry tried to keep his cool. The muscles in his shoulder blades began to knot. Angel made a slitting motion across his throat. Larry swallowed. "If you want us to do another job for you, you will pull some strings and make this go away."

Silence. Face was rarely at a loss for words. Larry knew they had him by the balls. Almost the only thing the dude cared about was nailing girls into the floor. It was like an addiction. The more he did it, the more he wanted to do it. But he wouldn't do it without them. They were his muscle, he always said. That was bullshit, of course. Face was no slouch. He was buffed out and didn't need help subduing a woman. He'd also claimed he needed them to get the girls—also bullshit. Women were creaming in their pants over this fucker. No, Face needed them because he liked to watch. He was one sick fuck, but he kept them in it—money, drugs, whatever they needed. He had connections. That was why they'd hooked up with him in the first place.

"Okay," Face finally conceded. "I'll see what I can do."

"And there's one more thing," Larry added.

Face chuckled softly. "You're a demanding fucker, aren't you?"

"Only when motherfuckers like you don't do what they promised."

Angel nudged Larry with his elbow as a young college-aged couple came around to the back of the packed bus shelter to wait. They stood on the other side of Face. They talked quietly enough, but they were too close for the three men to carry on their cell phone ruse. A tense moment passed. Angel sauntered away. Larry turned and bumped Face hard with his shoulder. The cell phone flew out of Face's hand, clattering to the ground. The back of it snapped off and the battery fell out.

"Oh, man," Larry said, his voice oozing fake sincerity. "I'm sorry. I didn't see you there. I apologize, man."

He and Face knelt at the same time to retrieve the pieces of the phone. The young couple fell silent and watched them warily as if they might start swinging at one another. Face glared at Larry as they stood. A muscle in his chiseled jaw twitched. "It's okay," he said with a forced smile. He held out his palm for Larry to return the battery.

Larry dropped the piece into his hand, stepping closer, his back to the young couple now. He held Face's gaze and whispered one word before walking off in the direction Angel had gone.

"Fox."

TWENTY-NINE

October 31st

Overnight, the uncharacteristically warm weather had given way to autumn, complete with gusty winds. A cold blast of air batted Jocelyn as she stepped out of her Explorer. She held her cell phone pinned between her cheek and shoulder as she opened the back door to get Olivia from her car seat.

Inez's voice was unusually loud in Jocelyn's ear. "*Phil* is the ADA on the Warner and Donovan case?"

"Can you believe that shit?"

"Mommy!" Olivia gasped as Jocelyn unfastened the seat belt.

Jocelyn grimaced. "Sorry, baby," she said. "That was a bad word."

"Actually, I can," Inez replied. "Assholes stick together. I swear they have some kind of secret club."

Jocelyn snorted. "Yeah, initiation consists of fu—screwing over some unsuspecting woman—figuratively or literally."

"Did you call him?"

Jocelyn lifted Olivia out of her seat and carried her across the Wawa minimarket parking lot. "No. I know him. He won't take my call right away, and then he'll wait two days to call me back. I don't need him thinking I'm calling for personal reasons. His paralegal said he'll be in court tomorrow around one. I'll just surprise him there."

"I'd love to be there for that," Inez said, chuckling lightly.

"Are you coming over for trick-or-treating?"

"Yeah, Raquel and I will meet you at your house in a half hour."

"Mommy, can I have a milkshake?" Olivia asked as Jocelyn set Olivia on the ground and ended her call with Inez.

She brushed Olivia's hair with her hand and steered her through the Wawa doors. "Sure."

"Wawa has strawberry milkshakes," Olivia said, fingers worrying Lulu's ears. "I want strawberry."

"Okay, but don't let me forget the bread."

The Wawa was crowded as usual. It was the only Wawa in their neighborhood, and the only minimarket worth its salt. For years it had been across the street with a parking lot so small, it defied explanation. Someone very intelligent had come up with the idea of moving it to a much more spacious lot, the site of a long-defunct car dealership. The result was better parking and a larger Wawa but even more customers.

Jocelyn guided Olivia over to the frozen drink machine and let her pull the frozen strawberry cup out of the freezer. Jocelyn peeled back the lid.

"Look, Mommy. It's the same color as Lulu!" Olivia said, rocking up onto the balls of her feet and pointing to the pink concoction inside the cup.

"It sure is," Jocelyn agreed. She put the cup into the blending machine and pushed the Blend button. As the cup ascended into the machine, she chose a lid and threaded a straw through it. The machine made a grinding, whirring sound. Jocelyn smiled at Olivia and arched a brow. "Does that mean Lulu is a strawberry bear?"

Olivia grinned. "She's not a strawberry bear, Mommy. She's just a bear."

"I don't know. I think I should taste her and see."

Olivia giggled convulsively as Jocelyn bent and pretended to bite Lulu's leg. Her giggles rose to high-pitched squeals. Jocelyn looked around to see if they had drawn stares from the other customers.

That's when she saw him.

He stood across the aisle, at the coffee kiosk. His face was still swollen and bruised. When he smiled at her, she could see the metal bracing in his mouth holding his jaw in place.

Henry Richards.

What the hell was he doing in her neighborhood? In her Wawa?

She didn't notice how hard her heart was thundering until she felt Olivia's little hand tugging hers. "Mommy, Mommy, it's done. Can I put the lid on?"

Instinctively, Jocelyn scooped Olivia up without taking her eyes from Henry. He took a step toward them.

"Don't," Jocelyn said. The edge in her voice froze him. He looked momentarily confused.

Once again, Jocelyn wished she had her gun. She'd have to start carrying an off-duty weapon.

People passed between them, oblivious.

"You're in violation of a restraining order," Jocelyn said.

Henry laughed, his gnarled smile framing his wire-gritted teeth. "Like I give a shit."

Jocelyn glanced around. Surely, he wouldn't try anything in a crowded minimarket.

"Mommy—"

"Just a minute, honey."

Jocelyn panned the store again, hoping to see a uniformed officer. The Wawa was directly across from the Fifth District. Didn't any of them need coffee or snacks?

She swallowed hard over the lump in her throat. She reached for the milkshake and handed it to Olivia. Then she reached for the lid. Olivia took it from her and fit it onto the top of the cup.

"What do you want?" she asked Richards.

Henry reached inside his jacket. Jocelyn's voice turned sharp and loud like the report of a gun. "Don't," she said again, this time drawing the attention of several people around them. She turned her body so that as little of Olivia was exposed to him as possible. Again, Henry froze, nervousness slackening the sneer on his face. He looked around at the faces now gaping at him.

Jocelyn lowered her voice and narrowed her eyes. Even though she didn't want to be near him, she stepped closer. "Unless you want me to break your face again, you'll take your hand out of your pocket and get out of here."

Slowly, he removed his hand. He put both hands up, trying to smile again. The seam where Jocelyn had split his lip cracked. A small bead of blood formed.

Olivia grew heavy in Jocelyn's arms. She shifted her hold, jostling Olivia. The strawberry milkshake toppled to the floor, landing with a splat. A Wawa clerk who'd been watching the exchange between Jocelyn and Henry rushed over. Olivia wailed, fat teardrops rolling down her face. "I'm sorry, Mommy!"

"It's okay, honey," Jocelyn soothed. "We'll clean it up and get another one."

The clerk smiled at Olivia. "Don't worry, sweetie. That's what we have mops for. Why don't you get yourself another one? No charge."

Jocelyn mumbled a thank-you to the woman, trying to force a smile. When she looked back at Henry, he was gone.

The clerk already had the milkshake machine a-whir as another worker came out to clean up the milkshake. Jocelyn's gaze swiveled around the minimarket, but she didn't see Henry. The clerk gave her a napkin, and she dabbed Olivia's cheeks.

"I'm sorry about this," Jocelyn told the clerk. "I'll pay for both."

The woman smiled, her eyes warm and sympathetic. "Oh, sweetie, don't you worry about it." She held out a crudely folded origami crane. "Is this yours?"

"Yes," Jocelyn said. It wasn't hers, of course. But it was meant for her. Her hand trembled as she took it.

THIRTY

October 31st

At home, Inez got the girls ensconced in the living room with a pile of Lalaloopsies on the floor and the Disney Channel on television. They had dumped their Halloween costumes on the coffee table and were helping one another get dressed up. Jocelyn raced down the basement steps and flipped the light on in the laundry room. The crane Kevin had found on the day of her carjacking was still there, nestled among spare change and gum wrappers in the little plastic basket she kept next to her washer.

Back upstairs, she and Inez lined them up on the kitchen counter and compared them. They were nearly identical. Inez unfolded them and smoothed the pages out on Jocelyn's kitchen counter. "Oh, shit," she said.

"What?" Jocelyn said, looking over her shoulder. "Oh my God."

Side by side, the message was obvious, written in ballpoint pen. One of them read, "Back off," and the other read, "Bitch."

Inez turned toward Jocelyn. "Where'd you get the first one?"

"It was in my car after the carjacking. Kevin found it on the front seat. He thought it was Simon's, but Simon hasn't been in my vehicle for months."

"So it was definitely Richards. Which means the carjacking wasn't random, and since he keeps showing up in places you frequent, that means he's been stalking you."

"I don't know him, though. I never saw him before that day," Jocelyn pointed out. "What does he want me to back off from? What does he think I'm doing to him? And besides that, what was his plan? He took the car. Why leave a crane on the front seat of a car that I no longer have?"

Inez fished two wineglasses out of Jocelyn's cabinet and filled them with a cabernet-merlot from the fridge. "Numbnuts like Richards rarely do anything that makes sense. He's a junkie, Joce. Maybe he has you confused with a detective in some other district who did bust him. Maybe he's got a court date coming up and thinks you're going to testify against him. Maybe someone you did bust made him do it. Maybe he was going to drive the car around for a while and leave it somewhere. Or maybe he was just supposed to drop the crane in the window, but he saw the opportunity to steal the car and took it. Eventually the car would have been recovered. You sure you never arrested the kid?"

Jocelyn took a sip of wine. It was bitter on her tongue. "Okay, so I don't remember every arrest I ever made, but I'm pretty positive I've never picked up that kid before. Even so, what would he want me to back off from—testifying against him in court? When we had him for the carjacking, he didn't have any hearings pending. This doesn't make any sense."

"Junkies don't do things that make sense," Inez repeated. "Who are you scheduled to testify against? Maybe Richards is doing someone else's dirty work."

Jocelyn sighed and tried to think through all the cases she had pending. There was nothing particularly incendiary. No suspect she could think of who would go to such lengths to prevent her from appearing in court. She shrugged. "I really can't think of anyone."

"Well, we'll check out all of Richards's associates, see what pops." Inez peeked around the corner into the living room. When they heard the knock on the door, both women jumped. Jocelyn's wine sloshed around in her glass, spilling on her wrist. "That's gotta be Kev," Inez said.

Jocelyn looked through her peephole before she opened the door. Kevin smiled grimly at her and stepped inside.

"Uncle Kevin," Olivia cried, jumping up from the floor and dashing into his arms. He scooped her up and held her on his hip.

The corners of Kevin's eyes crinkled when he smiled at Olivia. Briefly, Jocelyn wondered why he had never had children. He probably would have been a good dad. But he made a pretty fun uncle.

"How are you girls?" he asked, winking at Raquel. "Look at you beautiful princesses! Where did Olivia and Raquel go?"

"I'm Rapunzel," Raquel said, twirling in her purple dress.

"Did you get me a treat?" Olivia asked pointedly.

"Olivia," Jocelyn chided.

She gave Jocelyn a blank what-did-I-do look as Kevin fished inside his jacket pocket and pulled out a pack of Skittles. Olivia squealed, wrapping her arms tightly around his neck. She clasped the bag as he placed her back on the floor and straightened the tiara that threatened to tumble off her head. "You have to share," he called after her. But she was already seated among the pile of Lalaloopsies next to Raquel, trying to open the Skittles. Jocelyn didn't even bother to police Olivia's candy consumption. It was Halloween, after all. Instead, the three of them went into the kitchen and spoke in hushed tones.

"I pulled the surveillance from the Wawa," Kevin said. "We've got him on tape violating the restraining order. I'm going to have him picked up. We'll see what he has to say for himself. Take me through it again."

Jocelyn recapped the encounter with Richards and showed Kevin the message in the cranes. He studied the words as if he were trying to read something in a foreign language. Finally, he said, "It never occurred to me to open it at the hospital that night."

"You thought it was from Simon. Why would you open it?" Jocelyn said.

He shrugged and rubbed a hand over his scalp. "You never met this guy before?"

Jocelyn shook her head. She felt very tired suddenly and wished she hadn't had the wine. Inez sidled up to her and let Jocelyn lean into her side. Jocelyn wanted to lay her head on her friend's shoulder but resisted the urge.

"I'll come up with a list of Richards's known associates and see if you recognize any of them. When we pick him up, we'll see what he has to say about these—and what he wants you to back off from." Kevin folded them carefully and put them in his pocket. He shot a glance at Inez. "You staying over here tonight?"

Inez slid an arm around Jocelyn's shoulder. "Yeah. We're going trick-or-treating and then coming back here. The girls love it when we have a slumber party."

Kevin nodded. Jocelyn walked him out to the porch after he said good-bye to the girls and exclaimed some more over their costumes. "Thanks, Kev," she said.

"We'll get to the bottom of it, Rush." He started down the steps and paused on the landing. He looked back up at her, squinting against the glare of her porch light. "In the meantime, you and Inez better take your guns with you trick-or-treating."

THIRTY-ONE

November 1st

Jocelyn paced the eighth floor of the Criminal Justice Center, pausing every so often to look at the people bustling about the streets below. The city looked so peaceful from her vantage point. From where she stood, it was almost hard to believe what a cesspool of violence and depravity it really was down there. Almost. She paced to stay alert. She hadn't slept well after she and Inez found the notes inside the sloppy cranes. Trick-or-treating had been uneventful, but it was hard for her to enjoy it with the specter of Henry Richards and whatever misguided issues he had with her looming large in her mind.

From the bay of elevators at the end of the hall, Phil emerged. He pulled a trial box behind him. He wore a gray suit, the pant legs creased perfectly, with a pink shirt and matching pink-and-gray-striped tie. Jocelyn used to think only Phil could make pink sexy. He was about ten feet away when he noticed her. He smiled. "Jocelyn."

He stopped a few feet away from her this time, keeping distance between them.

"How are you?" Jocelyn asked after an awkward beat.

"I'm well."

Well. Not "I'm good," as most people Jocelyn knew would say, but a more proper, "I'm well."

"Good," she said. She jammed her hands into her jacket pockets.

Phil shifted his trial box, rolling it back and forth on its wheels. He glanced behind her and motioned down the hall. "I'm due in court."

Jocelyn pulled her phone out of her pocket to check the time. "Not for another half hour," she noted. "This won't take long."

Phil sighed, a wry half smile on his face. He gave her the once-over before meeting her eyes again. "Okay, *Detective*," he said. "What can I do for you?"

"Anita Grant. She was raped and mutilated a few weeks ago. We arrested Larry Warner and Angel Donovan. Not only are they out on bail right now but some of their charges have been reduced."

Phil rolled his eyes, and Jocelyn resisted the urge to punch him in the face. She crossed her arms in front of her and studied him with a frown.

"You're not going to get the rape charge," Phil said without preamble.

Jocelyn felt her face flush and hoped it didn't show. "They nailed her into the floor and had sex with her against her will."

Phil shook his head and looked down at her as if he were looking at her over a pair of glasses. "Your unknown subject nailed her to the floor. Donovan and Warner paid her for sex."

Jocelyn made a noise in her throat. She couldn't keep the edge from her voice. "Oh, you think she was okay with being crucified?"

"Joce, I'm not saying any of it is okay. I'm just telling you, you've got a known prostitute who admits to soliciting on Craigslist who met with Warner and Donovan with the intention of having sex for money."

Jocelyn arched an eyebrow. "That's bullshit. They raped her. They didn't make any kind of deal. She left the Dunkin' Donuts.

They followed her and forced her into the car. I have a credible witness."

"And I can give you the kidnapping charge, but I'm pleading them down on the rape charge. It's a done deal."

Jocelyn glared at him. She stepped toward Phil and pointed at him. "If this was a white college student or a soccer mom, you'd be all over this. You'd never even consider pleading down."

Phil's tone was one of infinite patience. "But this wasn't a college student or a soccer mom. It was Anita Grant. A high-risk victim. A college student or a soccer mom wouldn't be meeting these guys to talk about how much it would cost to fuck them."

"Phil—"

"I could just as easily charge Ms. Grant with soliciting."

Jocelyn clenched her jaw, but the words slipped out anyway. Confrontational. *You're always so confrontational*, he used to say, *and crass*. "Don't be a prick."

Phil sighed. "Look, either way they're going to do time. Why do you care about this?"

Her mouth hung open. "What?"

Immediately, Phil's face softened. He held up his hands and gave her his best conciliatory expression—the one he used in court that made female jurors swoon. "I didn't mean it like that—I didn't mean that the case doesn't matter. A woman was raped, and I'm sorry for that, but, Jocelyn, you and I both know how this works. You know as well as I do that we get dozens of these cases every month. Why is this one under your skin?"

Jocelyn shook her head and paced before him, eyes on the cream-colored tile floor. Phil's eyes followed her as though she were a metronome. "I don't know," she said.

"Is it because you knew Anita?"

Jocelyn shrugged. "I know a lot of girls."

He stepped closer to her, stopping her in her tracks, and lowered his voice. He used what Jocelyn always thought of as his faux sympathy tone. “Is this about Camille?”

Jocelyn froze, her cheeks stinging with heat. “Don’t you dare bring my personal life into this. That’s off-limits, especially to you.”

Phil stepped back. He had folded his arms across his chest, and now they inched upward, making him look taller and larger. The impenetrable fortress. His mouth twisted, as though he had eaten something sour. “Oh, is it? Like everything else, huh?” he said, giving her a pointed look.

Jocelyn thrust her chin up at him. “Fuck you.”

Phil rolled his eyes, dismissing her. It was familiar territory. “It is personal,” he insisted.

“When I was on patrol, I saw thousands of rape cases. This is no more personal than any other.”

Phil shook his head. “Please. This woman was basically gang-raped just like your sister.”

“Camille was fifteen, and she wasn’t a prostitute.”

“But she was gang-raped and your parents did nothing about it. You don’t think your whole career is about finding *this* case?”

“You have no idea what my career is about, and clearly you have no idea what this case is about or you wouldn’t be trying to make it about me.”

She stopped pacing and looked at him. Tension knotted the muscles of her shoulders. “They crucified her, Phil. They held her down and put nails through her hands and feet. That’s sadistic. This unknown subject—I have a bad feeling. He may just be getting started. If he escalates—”

“You think he will?”

“Yeah, I do. He’s doing prostitutes now because they’re easy victims that no one cares about. Some of these didn’t even get reported. But one day it could be someone society does care about.”

"You think he's going to continue to do this without his muscle? Warner and Donovan will be going away soon."

"They're out there now, Phil. Thanks to you. And if you think for one minute that they're not going to do this again while they're out on bail, then you're pretty fucking naive."

"Really, Jocelyn." There was the patronizing tone. "Do you think they're that dumb?"

She held his gaze until he looked away from her, fidgeting with the handle of his trial box again. "Not dumb," she said. "Vicious."

THIRTY-TWO

November 2nd

The next night Jocelyn and Kevin were called out to a stabbing and a suspicious death, which they suspected was due to alcohol poisoning. Toxicology would take weeks. By nine o'clock, they sat at their desks, sifting through paperwork, which mostly meant Kevin moving all their paperwork from his desk to hers.

"Hey, Chen," Jocelyn called as Chen fought with one of the filing cabinet drawers. "Anyone pick up my friend Henry Richards yet?"

"You'll be the first to know," Chen replied. "You didn't recognize any of his criminal colleagues?"

She shook her head. "No. Not even one."

Chen walked back past her desk and dropped a manila envelope into her lap. "Someone from the DA's office dropped that off for you."

Kevin wheeled his chair over toward hers. His lips smacked as he chewed a wad of Nicorette. "What is it?" he asked.

Jocelyn slid a finger beneath the flap and opened it. "It's the affidavit of probable cause in Larry Warner's assault case. Phil's paralegal has delivered again."

"No shit. What's it say?"

Jocelyn skimmed it quickly, flipping pages. Kevin leaned back in his chair, his eyes on her. The chair squeaked loudly. She let out a puff of air as she finished. She handed it to him, but Kevin shook his head. "I forgot my reading glasses, Rush. I'm in the over-forty club, remember? Just give me the gist."

"Officer Vincent Fox responded to a domestic on the fifty-two hundred block of Hawthorne," Jocelyn began.

"That's in the Northeast."

"Yeah. Fox arrives to find a man and a woman in a struggle over a handgun. Dwayne Knowle and Shasta Deeb—"

Kevin laughed. "Wait, wait. The woman's name is Shasta? Like the soda?"

Jocelyn rolled her eyes. "Let's not speak ill of the dead, Kev."

Kevin threw his arms into the air. "She dies? We didn't even get to that part yet! You're ruining the suspense for me here, Rush."

She picked up an empty paper clip holder and threw it at him. His body shook with laughter as he dodged it. It clattered to the floor behind him, drawing a disinterested glance from Chen. "Okay, okay. Keep going. Dwayne and Shasta are locked in battle over a gun."

"Fox calls for backup. He tries to separate them, Dwayne gets hold of the gun and shoots Shasta, at which point Fox puts one in Dwayne. Dwayne later dies of his injuries."

"What's this got to do with Larry Warner?" Kevin asked.

Jocelyn held up a finger. "Wait for it. In the next room they find another man who evidently had been shot in the throat by either Dwayne or Shasta before Fox arrived. Guess who?"

Kevin whistled under his breath. "Angel Donovan."

"Correct. Backup arrives. Then Larry Warner crashes the scene—acting erratically, yelling, cursing, and generally causing a big shit-storm. He tries to get in the house, Fox restrains him, and Warner assaults him."

"Did Warner live there?"

Jocelyn shook her head. "House belonged to a known drug dealer. Dwayne and Shasta were just staying there. It doesn't say why Angel was there or what his relationship to them was."

"Were there drugs in the house?"

"Yup."

"Well, that's why he was there. So Warner shows up for Angel, and when he sees cops swarming the place, he goes ape shit."

Jocelyn sighed and tossed the affidavit on top of the monster pile of paperwork already on her desk. "This doesn't really help."

"Someone should talk to—what's his name?" Kevin leaned over and squinted at the affidavit. "Officer Fox. He might know a lot more than what's in that report—might even know who Warner and Donovan were hanging out with back then."

Jocelyn glanced at the clock hanging above Chen's head. "Why don't we see who they're hanging out with now?"

Kevin's face creased with confusion, then slackened in disbelief. "No," he said. "No way, Rush."

Jocelyn stood and stretched her arms over her head. "I'll drive."

Kevin wiped a palm over his eyes and groaned loudly. "Rush, come on."

Jocelyn put a hand on his shoulder and leaned down so that her mouth was only inches from his ear. "Her own cane," she whispered. "Her own cane."

The shudder that worked its way through Kevin's body was barely perceptible. Jocelyn might not have even noticed it except that her hand was still resting on his shoulder. Without looking at her, he stood, his knees cracking. He fished a pair of keys from his pocket and threw them to her. "You fight dirty, Rush. Real dirty."

—

They sat outside Larry Warner's house for an hour before he and Angel Donovan emerged. The two men got into Larry's car and pulled away. Jocelyn drove, staying three or four cars behind them. They weaved their way through the streets of North Philadelphia languidly, as if they didn't really have a destination. They stopped for steak sandwiches at a small corner place—like most in Philadelphia, it was run out of a converted row house. The smell of fried food drifted across the street to where Jocelyn and Kevin were parked. They watched the two men eat in silence, and then followed them several more blocks to where the boundaries between North and Northeast Philadelphia blurred. The two men parked in front of a row of dilapidated homes, the last two of which were burned out. They went inside, Warner stumbling on the trash-strewn porch. A black male in jeans and a black button-down shirt let them in.

"Who is that?" Jocelyn asked. "Run the address."

Kevin called Northwest Detectives and asked Chen to run a check on the address. When he got off the phone, he rattled off a name that wasn't familiar to her. "Local drug dealer," Kevin added. "Small-time stuff."

Jocelyn sighed. "Well, that's definitely not our guy."

They waited another hour in the darkness. Jocelyn had to nudge Kevin several times to keep him awake. Finally, she said, "There's a corner store two blocks back. Go see if they've got coffee."

Grumbling and rubbing his eyes, Kevin got out of the car. Jocelyn watched him in the rearview mirror until he was just a gnat-size form in the gathering darkness. A few minutes later, Larry and Angel emerged from the house. Instead of going back to their car, they approached her vehicle. Slowly, heads down. Larry came to her window, and she rolled it partway down. She kept her eye on Angel, who stood at the front of the car, one large hand on the hood. His eyes darted up and down the street as Larry spoke with Jocelyn.

"Mr. Warner," she said.

Larry rested one forearm on the roof and leaned down into her window. "What're you doing here, Detective?"

His breath smelled like whiskey and cheap light beer. She eyed him. "What do you think I'm doing here?"

Larry turned his head and spit on the ground. Jocelyn kept her hands on the steering wheel, although the car was not running. She was aware of Angel's large form moving around the car, toward the passenger's side door. The line of streetlights behind Larry cast a pallid glow over the street. The bumping sounds of a bass stereo coming from a house down the street seemed to pulse in the air, nearly obscuring the more ambient sounds of people talking as they walked down the street or congregated on porches. Cars whizzed past far faster than the speed limit allowed. There was no good reason to drive slowly in a neighborhood like this. People didn't come for the scenery. A cool, light breeze filtered in past Larry and licked the back of her neck.

"You got nothin' else on me," Larry said.

"I told you, Mr. Warner. I'm not interested in you."

She had to keep her body from jumping when she heard Angel try the door. Kevin had locked it when he got out. He always did. Her heart thundered in her chest, but she kept her gaze on Larry. Calm, unflinching.

Larry motioned around them. "This ain't exactly a safe place for a little girl like you."

She didn't have to fake her laughter. It sent Larry's head rearing back just a little. She heard the ineffectual snap of Angel trying the door handle again. Where the fuck was Kevin? Not that she couldn't handle these fuckers, she reminded herself, only half believing it.

"I'm not a little girl, Mr. Warner."

He made a scoffing sound. "Oh, what? You gonna whip out your gun?"

Jocelyn ran her fingers over the top of the steering wheel before wrapping them tightly around it. She had a sudden flash of Anita Grant in her foldout sofa bed, weeping because her mother wouldn't look at her. Alicia Hardigan's gnarled hands. This time she didn't feel nauseous. She felt angry and sick to death of men like Larry and Angel, who took what they wanted and left nothing in their wakes but ruined lives. Who hurt women for the sake of hurting women and for no other reason. Whose existence on this earth accomplished absolutely nothing but to inflict pain and suffering on others. It was a disgrace and an abomination that men like them should even be allowed to exist in the same world where goodness and innocence existed. Anita was right, she could put Larry and Angel away—she could even lock up their sadistic associate, the third man—but there would always be more.

And she wanted to kill every single one of them.

The world started to recede—the noises, her peripheral vision. Adrenaline was a dull roar, growing louder as it coursed through her. Rage—like the kind she had felt the day she'd pulled Henry Richards out of her car and punched his face in—quickened her heartbeat. And yet she felt calm and focused. She lifted her right hand in front of her and studied her splint. Slowly, she undid the Velcro and discarded the splint on the passenger's side seat. She straightened her wrist, her fingers pointed upward toward the car roof like a spear. She used her left hand to caress it, as though it were a sleek, deadly weapon. As if it were a serrated knife she could drive into Larry's heart, or a shiny Glock 19 with a magazine full of exploding rounds. She considered all the ways she would like to torture these two men while she studied her hand. From her peripheral, she saw Larry shift his weight. She turned toward him and smiled, a wicked, nasty grin. She stared hard into his beady eyes, imagining what it would feel like to torture him the way he had tortured Anita and Alicia. She stared until he looked away. When he looked back at her, she spoke, her voice low and even so that he had to lean in to hear her.

"What makes you think I need a gun?"

Jocelyn felt a thrill of satisfaction when she saw the flicker of doubt in Larry's eyes. He backed away from the car and bobbed his head toward Donovan. She sensed Angel moving away from the passenger's side. Relief flooded her chest, slowing her heartbeat.

As the ambient sound returned to her ears, she heard hurried footsteps. Then Kevin's voice. "What the fuck is this?"

Angel was already walking away. Larry stood in the center of the street, looking at Kevin across the roof of the car. When Jocelyn saw Kevin's tie dangling at the passenger's side window, she unlocked the door.

"What the fuck are you doing, Warner?" Kevin asked. "You got a name for us or what?"

Larry didn't say anything. Jocelyn watched his back as he retreated across the street. Mumbling expletives under his breath, Kevin got into the car and handed her a small Styrofoam cup. The smell of coffee filled the car.

"I'm warning you now, it tastes like shit," he said as he settled his own cup into the cup holder. He lifted his rear off the passenger's side seat and fished her splint out from beneath him. He stared at it, his brow wrinkled, until she snatched it away from him and fastened it back onto her wrist. "Chen called," Kevin said. "We gotta get back."

Jocelyn started the car and pulled into traffic, heading back to Northwest Detectives, leaving Larry and Angel behind. The coffee was thick and bitter. It burned Jocelyn's tongue.

"What the hell was that about?" Kevin asked.

Jocelyn kept her eyes on the road. "Nothing."

THIRTY-THREE

November 3rd

Inez pulled her cruiser into the Sunoco parking lot at Germantown Avenue and Washington Lane, next to another police unit. Window to window, she could see Officer Melody Brock's blonde ponytail as the other woman bent over some paperwork. She looked up at Inez and smiled. "Hey, Graham. What's going on?"

"Nothing," Inez said. She motioned over her shoulder toward Germantown Avenue. "See anyone who looks like a groper?"

Brock laughed. "Coupla dudes that looked like bona fide perverts but no groper. Unless you count the homeless guy playing with his own junk all the way down the street."

Inez laughed. "That's Skinny Joe. Only thing he puts a hurtin' on are his own balls."

They both chuckled. "The Groper did hit here twice in the last week," Brock said.

Inez scratched her forehead. "Maybe the third time's a charm."

The two women sat in companionable silence for a few minutes. Absently, Inez listened to the squawking radio, hearing the words but registering only static.

"When's Mark coming home?" Brock asked.

Inez shrugged. She reached inside her collar and fingered her thin gold wedding band, which she kept on a chain around her neck while on duty. "Don't know. They keep extending his deployment. We're hoping for a Christmas miracle, though. Maybe he can get a furlough."

"This his second tour?"

"Sure is," Inez said. She looked away from Brock, swallowing hard over the lump in her throat. She didn't like to think about it too much—to dwell on it—her husband a world away in a hostile foreign country, not even readily accessible by phone or e-mail. The physical and emotional distance between them, which grew just a little bit wider each day. Or the fact that at any moment of any day, men in stately dress blues could show up wherever she happened to be and completely shatter her world. And Raquel. She couldn't bear to think of having to tell their four-year-old that Daddy wasn't coming home.

Brock reached through the windows and poked Inez's shoulder. "Sorry, Graham. Shouldn't have brought it up."

Inez cleared her throat and managed a weak smile. "It's okay. Bringing it up doesn't change it."

"Hey, look at that," Brock said, pointing to the corner diagonal from where they were parked. Inez shifted in her seat to crane her neck. "What?"

Brock tapped Inez's side mirror and Inez looked. Across from them, exiting a pawnshop, was Kyle Finch.

"Think he pawned his cruiser?" Brock snickered.

"Wouldn't surprise me."

Brock sighed. "It's a damn shame."

"What's that?"

"That such a prick got those good looks."

"I know. It's a total waste."

"All the girls have a thing for him," Brock added. "Well, the ones who don't know any better." She studied him a beat longer. He looked around and slipped his hands inside his coat pocket. He pulled out a cell phone and punched some numbers, his gaze intent on the screen. "I guess if he didn't speak, he'd be doable."

Inez snorted.

"Janelle seems to think he doesn't like women," Brock went on.

"No shit. You think he's gay?"

Brock shrugged. "That would explain all the macho overcompensating. Gay or not, he's a fucking tool. Did you know he's got money? He doesn't even need to work."

Inez's lips twisted in disgust. "Are you kidding me?"

Brock shook her head, ponytail swaying. "No. Janelle told me. They went on a few dates before she realized his dick didn't work. Apparently, his dad is loaded, and his mom died when he was a teenager and left him a shitload of money."

"Let me guess, he joined the police force to help people."

Both women laughed. Inez checked her phone. Her shift had just started. Seven more hours to go. She sighed.

A guy passed Finch on the pavement, walking hurriedly. Although his back was to them and his maroon hoodie was pulled over his head, he had the skinny, hunched-shoulder look of a kid. His posture was stooped as though he were ducking under something. He stopped abruptly as Finch called out to him. From where they sat, Inez couldn't hear what Finch had said, but the kid stopped. One of Finch's hands rested on the butt of his gun. He grabbed the kid's shoulder and turned him into the wall of the pawnshop. The kid put his arms up as Finch kicked his feet apart and started patting him down.

"What's he got?" Inez said.

Then the kid turned so they could see his face. Brock said, "Isn't that—"

"Henry Richards," Inez filled in, already half out of her squad car. She ran—hand on the butt of her pistol. "Finch," she yelled. "Cuff him."

She was halfway across Germantown Avenue. Finch and Richards looked up at her at the same time. Finch stared at her dumbly, but Richards paled, and in one swift movement he spun on his heel and elbowed Finch hard across the jaw. Finch stumbled backward, reaching for his face and swearing. "Shit, Graham, what do you think I was about to do?"

He stuck a foot out, tripping Richards, but the kid was quick. He saved himself a concrete face-plant by bracing against the pavement with both hands. Then, like a runner in the starting position of a race, he took off in a dead sprint. Luckily, Brock had pulled out onto Germantown Avenue. She slid the cruiser in between two parked cars, angling it onto the pavement to block Richards. But he was already over the top of her hood, his sneakers making staccato *pow-pow* sounds as he ran across.

"Goddammit, Finch," Inez grumbled as she moved past him. She slid over Brock's hood on her rear end and hit the pavement running.

"Richards!" she hollered as he bolted ahead of her. He raced down Germantown Avenue, his maroon hoodie flapping at his sides. He pushed two elderly pedestrians out of his way. They grabbed on to each other, teetering, before they found their balance again and stood frozen in place as Inez ran past them. A group of teenage boys sitting and smoking on the steps of a walled-in cemetery hooted and laughed as Richards darted past them with Inez hot on his trail.

Richards glanced over his shoulder at her and increased his speed. Inez was gaining on him. She looked to her left and saw that Brock was cutting in and out of traffic, trying to head him off. She finally got in front of him, pulling up on the pavement again. The car shuddered when she braked abruptly, the frame still traveling forty miles per hour but the wheels stopped. Brock emerged at a sprint.

Richards froze for a split second, being pursued from the front and back. He glanced at the street on his left, clogged with traffic. To his right was an empty lot overgrown with thick oak trees and knee-high weeds. The trees had lost most of their leaves, but the gnarled branches seemed to reach inward toward the center of the open space as if they were trying to reach one another across a small chasm. A tall chain-link fence stretched across the front of the lot, where its weedy floor met the sidewalk. Before Inez could even open her mouth, the kid was climbing the fence like damn Spider-Man. He dropped to the ground on the other side as if he weighed nothing and headed straight for the trees.

"Shit," Inez huffed.

Brock was talking into the radio on her shoulder as Inez flew up and over the fence after Richards, the metal making a light tinkling sound. She used her momentum to carry her up and over, but still, climbing the fence with her Kevlar vest on was like trying to maneuver with a bunch of cast-iron frying pans strapped to her torso. She dropped to the other side with a much less graceful thud and, unlike Richards, landed on her ass, grunting irritably.

She scrambled back up and sprinted in the direction he'd gone. Over the sound of her own rapid breath, she tried to listen to the crash of his body through the dry brush ahead. She saw flashes of his hoodie as she ran after him, but by the time she emerged from the trees onto a lot of burned-out container trucks, she had lost him. She checked each blackened shell, but there was no sign of him.

She kept moving, hopping a much smaller fence into someone's backyard. The sound of snarling registered only a split second before someone tackled her to the ground full force. For a moment, the wind was knocked out of her. Her body flailed, struggling against the man on top of her until she realized it was Finch.

"Graham, get up. You have to run," he breathed into her ear. Dazed, she sucked in a noisy breath. She tried to concentrate on his words, but she could barely hear him over the frenzied growling of the large pit bull tearing into Finch's pant legs. The dog seemed to be everywhere at once, barking, snarling, nipping, pawing, and spraying foul-smelling saliva all over them. For a second, she wondered if she had stumbled into a yard filled with pit bulls, but a quick glance from the cover of Finch's body confirmed that it was only one. Inez heard fabric tear, followed by Finch grunting. She tried to take a deep breath, but her lungs seized up. Fear and adrenaline warred within her, making her limbs stiff and her brain foggy.

"Graham, get up!" Finch rolled off her, onto his rear, keeping his legs between him and the dog, kicking at the dog's head, his boots moving like pistons. As he pulled his nightstick from his belt, Inez stumbled to her feet. The dog tried to leap over Finch, straight at her. Instinctively, she threw her arms up. Finch swung his nightstick, making solid contact with the dog's head, eliciting a strangled yelp.

Momentarily stunned, the dog listed to its left and bit the air. As it moved back toward Finch, Inez unsnapped her holster. She froze when she saw a shape move in her periphery. Then she heard an unfamiliar male voice. "Champ, down!"

The man was tall and thin, clothed in a Phillies shirt and gray sweatpants. She noticed he was barefoot as he sprinted toward them and quickly took hold of the dog's collar. "Shit, man. I'm sorry. Champ, down!"

The man yanked the dog away from them, dragging it toward the back door of the house. Champ wasn't inclined to listen to his owner. White foam dripped from his bared teeth as he pulled away from his owner, still intent on attacking. Finch stood and backed away from man and dog. Inez could still hear the dog barking, even after it had been stuffed inside the house. The owner returned to them, his hands out in a gesture of apology. "I'm so sorry. He don't normally act like that, but you guys are in our yard. He knows to protect the house, you know?"

Inez was still trying to catch her breath. "We shouldn't have been in your yard," she conceded.

"We were in pursuit of someone," Finch put in.

"Did he bite you?" the man asked.

Finch reached down and pulled his pant legs up. There were several scrapes, a few deep puncture wounds beginning to ooze blood, and a lot of saliva. His pants were shredded.

The dog owner looked like he might cry. "Oh man, that's bad. I'm really sorry. I—"

Finch managed a smile. "It's okay. A couple of stitches and I'll be fine. Right now we're looking for someone." He glanced at Inez and she nodded. Heart still thundering in her chest, she stood by while Finch questioned the man, but he hadn't seen Richards. Hoofing it past the side of the house, they emerged onto Baynton Street.

Inez paused to straighten her uniform and smooth her hair back. All she could smell was dog saliva.

Finch glanced at her. "You okay?"

She pointed at her chest. "Me? Yeah, I'm fine. You're the one who got bit. You need to go to the hospital, Finch."

He waved her off. "I'll be fine." Looking up and down the street, his ears glowed red. "Where the fuck did Richards go?"

"I don't know," Inez replied. "We lost him."

He reached both hands to the top of his head, clenching tufts of his hair in his fists and tugging. "Fuck!"

"Hey," Inez said.

"I fucking lost him," Finch dropped his hands to his sides. A muscle in his jaw ticked as he met her eyes.

"Finch," she said. "Don't worry about that right now. I'm serious, you need to go to the hospital and get those bites looked at—at least get them cleaned out."

He nodded but walked off, peeking into alleyways as he went. Inez trotted after him, clamping a hand onto his shoulder. "Hey," she said, stopping him in his tracks. She looked him in the eye and swallowed. "Thanks for that, back there. I mean it."

The beep of a horn startled them both. They turned to see Brock pulling down the street and ran up to the car. "You got him?" Inez asked.

Brock shook her head, grimacing. "No."

Inez pressed the heels of her palms against her eye sockets. Finch walked away from the car, pulling at his hair again. Almost in unison, they said, "Son of a bitch."

THIRTY-FOUR

November 4th

"So, Finch got bested by a twenty-year-old male prostitute?" Jocelyn asked Inez. She held Olivia's hand as the girl wobbled in a pair of high heels across the Please Touch Museum's play shoe store.

"Mommy, Mommy, look at these," Raquel cried, pulling out a pair of boots from the myriad of cubbies lining the small room. They were fluorescent green and rubber. Jocelyn's eyes hurt just looking at them. Inez even squinted as she helped slide them onto her daughter's tiny feet. Raquel clomped after Olivia, who had abandoned the heels in favor of a pair of big red clown shoes. High-pitched giggles erupted from the two girls as they chased each other around the mock store.

Inez sighed. Her smooth brown forehead wrinkled. "Yeah, a lousy elbow and the kid got away from him. But he saved me from a pit bull. I guess he's not a total fu—" She glanced around her. Two other children had wandered in, mothers trailing behind them. They too began trying on shoes, the mothers oohing and ahhing over each pair, talking to their children in that overly loud, fake Mommy voice that Jocelyn had noticed most mothers used on their young children—like they were deaf or mildly retarded.

Inez lowered her voice so as not to be overheard by the moms with the faux Mommy voices. "He's not as much of a fuckup as I thought. I mean, I would have been screwed if he wasn't there. That dog was vicious and mad as hell."

Jocelyn folded her arms across her chest. She blew out a breath. "I appreciate him taking a dog bite for you, but he's a pansy. You know how many times I've been elbowed trying to arrest someone? Or kicked or choked or spit on? One time, when I was on patrol, I had to arrest a guy who had shit himself and thought it was a good idea to try finger-painting a bus stop with it."

Inez snickered. One of the faux Mommies shot Jocelyn a look that was somewhere between worry and horror.

"I probably spooked the kid when I ran up. I didn't think Finch was going to lose him, but it all happened pretty fast. I mean I don't think Finch expected Richards to resist."

"But you should always be on your guard in case any suspect you're arresting resists," Jocelyn argued. "I mean, what you're saying is he can take on a pit bull, but he can't take down a twenty-year-old kid?"

Inez walked up behind Raquel and pointed at the fluorescent green boots. "Put those back if you're finished."

Raquel scurried over to the wall and stuffed the boots into a cubbyhole, one of the soles left dangling. She rooted through a few other cubbies until she found a pair of blue sequined platforms. She ran over to Olivia, who was clomping around in a pair of black man shoes. When she saw the platforms, she immediately discarded the boxy man shoes, but Raquel was already teetering on them.

"Can I try?" Olivia asked.

"Let Olivia try," Inez instructed after Raquel ignored Olivia for several seconds. Inez turned to Jocelyn. "All right, so he could have handled the arrest better, but Finch did go after him. That damn kid disappeared like a puff of smoke."

Jocelyn shook her head. "Friendly Fire is incompetent."

She wondered if Finch had tried as hard as he could to catch and keep Richards in custody. If maybe his incompetence was just a little bit intentional. With the way things had been between them, especially in the last few weeks, he might jump on the opportunity to screw her in some small way—half-assing it and letting Richards get away with a puny elbow. Any other officer would have handled Richards. Now she had to live with the fact that the guy was still out there and after her for reasons she couldn't even imagine. As it was, the guy had twice gotten close enough to Jocelyn's daughter to pose a threat.

"Your face is turning red, Rush," Inez pointed out. "You need to relax."

There was the anger again, like a wild animal caught in a sack, flailing every which way, trying to burst loose. Jocelyn closed her eyes and took a deep breath. In through her nose and out through her mouth. Maybe those anger management classes were good for something after all.

She opened her eyes and looked at her friend. "I'm glad he saved you from the pit bull, but thanks to him, Richards is still out there. Taking on one pit bull doesn't make up for his general laziness. Shit. I should have shot that son of a bitch that night at Einstein when I had the chance."

A sudden still silence drew their attention to their left where the other two mothers stood staring at them. One woman was frozen bent halfway over with a shoe dangling from her hand, her son's outstretched foot arcing up toward her.

The silence stretched on. One of the women swallowed and licked her dry lips. She opened her mouth to speak, but Inez held up a hand. "If you knew this guy, you'd feel the same way," she said matter-of-factly.

The half-stooped woman flushed, and the other mother paled. They hurried their children out of the room like it was on fire, bumping against each other to get out the doorway at once. Jocelyn laughed so hard, her sides hurt.

"Mommy, what's so funny?" Olivia asked. Jocelyn looked down to see her daughter standing before her in the blue sequined platforms, her hands on her tiny hips.

Jocelyn reached out and stroked her hair. "Nothing, baby. Nothing."

"So," Inez said as Olivia flitted off to try on a pair of lace-up work boots in the corner of the room. "Are we going to talk about SVU or what?"

Jocelyn felt the heat return to her face once again, but this time it wasn't anger. Not even close. She could still feel Caleb's mouth on her as if she'd just come from making out with him in her car. "Let's just say that there is a certain lieutenant there who left a very, very good impression."

Inez wiggled her eyebrows suggestively and grinned, a wicked tilt to her mouth. "Scandalous good or lunch date good? Don't tell me. I can tell by your face. It was scandalous good."

"A little bit," Jocelyn acknowledged.

Inez swatted her in the arm and whooped. She grabbed Raquel's arm and twirled her around. Olivia clomped over to where they were in a pair of fireman's boots. "Mommy," she said, "what's sandluss?"

Jesus. These kids had sonic hearing. Inez hid a giggle behind her hand and continued to twirl Raquel around in the sequined platforms. Jocelyn knelt in front of Olivia. "It means something very bad."

Olivia quirked a brow. "But how can something be sandluss and still good?"

Jocelyn sighed. "I'll explain it to you when you get older. Right now, Mommy has to leave. I have some errands to run, and then I have to go to work."

Olivia's face seemed to droop, her mouth turning down in a crescent frown. "Awwww, but I want you to stay."

Jocelyn felt a little stab in her heart. "I know. I want to stay too, but we're all out of soup, and I have to work. But you're going to see the rest of the museum with Inez and Raquel, and then Inez will take you back to her house. Martina is going to watch you girls tonight while Mommy and Inez work. I'll come get you later. I put blankie and Lulu in your bag. It's in Inez's car."

Olivia's eyebrows drew together. She looked at Inez. "Can we eat ice cream?"

"Of course," Inez said.

"No," Jocelyn said at the same time.

Jocelyn glared at her friend. Inez folded her arms across her chest. She gave Olivia a quick wink and then pretended to stare Jocelyn down. "We eat ice cream at my house," she proclaimed. "House rules."

Jocelyn raised an eyebrow in mock skepticism. By now, both girls were watching the women, giggling silently. "House rules, huh?"

Inez stepped toward her, into her personal space, challenging her. "That's right."

Jocelyn tried not to laugh. She gave Inez her best cop stare. They let the stare-down go on for several seconds as both girls watched intently, trying not to make a sound. Then in her most serious tone, Jocelyn said, "But what about the ice-cream monster?"

"I arrested him last week," Inez responded matter-of-factly, as if she were talking about a real suspect.

"Mommy, you arrested the ice-cream monster?" Raquel said excitedly.

Jocelyn shook her head and widened both eyes. She glanced sideways at the kids. "He got out on bail this morning."

She could see the corners of Inez's mouth twitching as she tried not to laugh. Olivia tugged on Jocelyn's hand. "What's he do, Mommy? What's the ice-cream monster do?"

Abruptly, Jocelyn turned and dropped into a squat in front of Olivia and Raquel, her voice a roar. "He tickles little girls who eat ice cream!" she hollered.

Both girls squealed as she grabbed them and tickled their bellies and under their arms. Raquel escaped easily. Jocelyn scooped Olivia up and kissed her all over her face. When Olivia's laughter subsided, Jocelyn set her back down. "Okay, love. You can eat ice cream at Inez's house."

Olivia's eyes grew wide. "But what about the ice-cream monster?"

Inez put a hand on top of Olivia's head. "Guess I'll have to arrest him again."

Jocelyn laughed. As she made her way into the hallway and toward the stairs to the first-floor exit, she heard Raquel and Olivia's little voices: "Can we watch? Can we watch you arrest him?"

THIRTY-FIVE

November 4th

The house was entirely too silent. Jocelyn dumped her grocery bags on the coffee table, a half dozen cans of chicken noodle soup spilling out, and locked the front door behind her—both locks. She turned back and surveyed the room. A sheaf of Olivia's drawings had fallen from the coffee table onto the floor—rainbows, butterflies, hearts, and stars. Bright, happy things. Olivia's drawings were exquisite and yet heartbreaking in their delightful innocence, knowing what Jocelyn knew about the world. A tangle of Lalaloopsies and discarded dress-up clothes were piled high on the love seat. A pink tiara peeked out from beneath one of the cushions. Only the couch sat unsullied by evidence of the resident three-year-old.

Jocelyn walked over and stretched out on it, moaning in pleasure at the realization that she could lie down and do absolutely nothing for the next hour completely undisturbed. Her visit to the grocery store had gone more quickly than anticipated, which left her with some time to herself—a completely foreign concept post-Olivia.

After about fifteen minutes, Jocelyn began to miss Olivia. That's how it always happened. Once, the year before, Jocelyn had caught the flu. Her entire body ached, and she could barely get out of bed. Desperate for rest, she had called Inez and asked her to take Olivia for one night, but after only a half hour alone, Jocelyn wished Olivia were still there.

Of course, she missed the sleep. What little she used to get. She checked her phone. She still had a half hour before she had to leave for work. Closing her eyes, she focused on her breathing, concentrating on the rise and fall of her chest. She was just drifting off, floating free in the nowhere place between waking and sleeping, when a noise snapped her awake. She sat up quickly and listened. There was a rattle at her front door—like someone trying to get in. Her heart hammered in her chest. She picked up her gun and went to the door. She peered through the peephole, but all she could see was the back of a man wearing a brown jacket. There was something very familiar about him, but she couldn't place it.

Quietly, she turned the locks and flung the door open, the barrel of her gun pressed against the glass of her screen door. The man whipped around, the smile dying on his face as he stared down the barrel of her gun. She realized at that moment that she had been expecting Henry Richards. Instead, Caleb Vaughn stood on her doorstep.

THIRTY-SIX

November 4th

Face burning, Jocelyn holstered her weapon and pushed the door—it didn't budge.

"It's locked," Caleb said, pointing to the door handle. "Your doorbell is broken. I was going to knock on the door."

She twisted the lock and opened it, smiling apologetically. "I'm sorry," she said. "I thought you were . . . someone else."

He smiled as he slipped past her. "I wouldn't want to be that guy."

Jocelyn closed and locked the door behind him. "What is that?" she asked, pointing to a plastic container he held in one hand with what looked suspiciously like key lime pie.

Caleb's smile widened. He arched an eyebrow suggestively. "I think you know what it is."

She moved closer to him, trying to think of something witty to say in response, but her mind was completely blank. All she could think about was his mouth. He still had the pie in his hand when their mouths met. Jocelyn rocked up on the balls of her feet to pull his mouth down to hers. With one arm, he pulled her in, tight against his body. He smelled like coffee and aftershave. He tasted like Altoids.

The plastic container dug into her lower back. She pulled it from his hand and tossed it on the coffee table. Stumbling over a pair of Olivia's dress-up shoes, they fell onto the couch. There wasn't room enough for them to lay side by side, not with his large, rangy frame. They shifted so she lay atop him. His hands moved up and down the length of her body. He tugged at her waist, separating his mouth from hers. "Your gun," he said. "We should take our guns off."

Breathless, she raised her face to look at him. "Yeah," she agreed. They disentangled and stood up. He pulled off his jacket and removed his shoulder holster. She took her belt off and dropped it onto the table beside his. They turned back to each other, regarding one another for a long moment before bursting into laughter.

Caleb smoothed her hair back from her face. "What *is* this?"

Grinning, Jocelyn shrugged. She caught his hand and held it. "I don't know," she said. "I'm never like this. I mean, with men. I mean, I don't usually—"

Caleb silenced her with a quick kiss. "It's okay. I know what you mean. I haven't had this reaction to a woman in over twenty years."

Jocelyn smiled. "I'll take that as a compliment."

He squeezed her hand, and they sat next to each other on her couch. "It is," he assured her. "But I think we should slow down."

"Yes, we should," she agreed, even though every inch of her body was afire and tingling with his proximity.

"How about if I take you on a date?" he suggested.

"I have next Thursday off," Jocelyn said. She already felt guilty. She treasured her time off because she got to spend it with Olivia. But surely one Thursday wouldn't be so bad. Inez was always after her to spend more time with adults.

"Socially," Inez always said. "Not at work."

Caleb grinned from ear to ear. "Thursday it is. I'll pick you up at eight."

Jocelyn glanced at the clock on her cable box. Hesitation rooted her to her seat even though she knew she would probably be late. All she wanted to do was drape herself all over Caleb and let things take their natural course. She kept her face averted from his so he couldn't see the hot flush creeping up her neck to her cheeks. She pushed images of the two of them naked out of her head and cleared her throat. "That will be great," she said. "So, uh, I've got to leave for work soon."

"That's actually why I came here," Caleb said, inching away from her, putting some space between them on the couch. As much as she wanted to touch him, she was grateful for the small distance between them—it made it easier for her to turn her thoughts to work. Caleb went on. "I talked to Captain Ahearn about bringing you on to the Warner–Donovan case given your connection to Anita."

Jocelyn raised an eyebrow. "That must have gone over like a lead balloon."

Caleb laughed. "Yeah, that's about right. But I could use your help if you're up to it. I found Raeann Church. She's living here in Philly in a halfway house."

Jocelyn sat up straighter, a cool little frisson of excitement shooting down her spine, dissipating some of the heat in the room. "Really? I'd like to be there when you interview her."

Caleb nodded. He checked his phone. "I'll meet you at Northwest in two hours."

"Great," Jocelyn said. "I just have to put these groceries away and then I'm on my way."

Caleb laughed and motioned to the coffee table. "Like soup much?"

Jocelyn smiled. "Not me, my daughter. I can't get her to eat anything else. I'm starting to get concerned about her health at this point."

She shuffled the cans back into the bag and took it into the kitchen. Caleb followed, glancing around at her house. She never had houseguests besides Inez, Kevin, and Simon. As she followed Caleb's gaze, she realized just how messy the place was. "I'm sorry about the mess," she stammered, "I—"

Caleb grinned and waved a hand in dismissal. "You should see my place. Do you have a piece of paper and a pen?"

She gave him a puzzled look but went over to Olivia's craft bin and fished out a piece of construction paper and a crayon. "Will a red crayon do?"

"Sure," he said, taking it from her. He plopped down at her dining room table and began drawing a chart of some kind—three columns of boxes with five boxes in each column.

Jocelyn stood over his shoulder. "What are you doing?"

Without looking up, he said, "What does your daughter like?"

"What?"

"Olivia, right? What kind of toys does she like?"

"Lalaloopsies—they're dolls, but what are you drawing?"

She trailed off as he drew a crude stick figure below the chart. He gave it curly hair and a dress. Jocelyn laughed.

Caleb met her eyes, his grin somewhat bashful. "Okay, so I didn't go to art school for good reason, but bear with me. Pretend this is a Lalaloopsy. Later you can print out a picture of a Lalaloopsy or something and glue it to the chart."

Jocelyn folded her arms over her chest. "Chart?"

"Yeah, it's like an incentive system. So, you see all these boxes? Every time she eats something besides soup, she gets a sticker. Once she fills up all the boxes, she gets a prize. Something she really likes, like a Lalaloopsy."

Jocelyn studied the chart. "That is actually a great idea."

"She's three, right?"

Jocelyn nodded.

"So don't make the chart too big. If she has to wait too long for her prize, she'll get bored with it and not be motivated to earn stickers."

Jocelyn pointed to his stick figure Lalaloopsy. "This could get costly."

Caleb laughed. "My son—by the time he was seventeen, he had every LEGO set and PlayStation game known to man. But he graduated high school at the top of his class, and I never had any major behavioral issues with him. Oh, and he had proper nutrition."

Caleb winked. Jocelyn hoped he didn't notice her sway on her now wobbly legs. That wink almost brought her to her knees. He stood up and handed her the chart before going back into the living room to strap his gun on. "Just try it," he called over his shoulder.

She studied it a moment longer and left it on the table. "I will," she said, strapping on her own gun.

She ushered him onto the porch. As Jocelyn locked her front door, their conversation moved back to interviewing Raeann Church. The smell of coffee and chocolate reached her before Phil's voice.

"Oh, I didn't—"

She looked over to find Phil paused in his climb up her front steps. He had a take-out cup holder with two Starbucks coffees in it and a small brown bag—containing a brownie no doubt. As always, he was dressed impeccably in a charcoal suit, his hair slicked back neatly.

"Phil?" Jocelyn said. "What are you doing here?"

He didn't take his eyes off Caleb, who stared back with a bland smile. Phil's face flushed red. He didn't do awkward very well. "I came to—" He cleared his throat. "I didn't realize you were seeing someone."

Jocelyn regarded him silently, not giving an inch. Phil cleared his throat again. He motioned toward her with the cup holder. When he spoke, there was a bit of petulance in his tone. "I thought

I might smooth things over after the other day. I felt badly about how things went."

Jocelyn raised a brow and placed one hand on her hip. "You mean you feel badly about putting a couple of rapists back on the street after I arrested them—after I got a confession from one of them?"

Phil looked nonplussed. "No, I meant—"

"Don't make more out of things than are really there, Phil. I'm a detective. You're an ADA. We disagree about a case. End of story. You can go now."

She should have known he would react badly. No one dismissed Phil Delisi. Red-faced, he turned toward Caleb. The cup holder trembled in his hand.

"You don't know what you're getting into," Phil said. "If you were smart, you'd walk away."

Caleb's smile hardened into a firm, angry line. "And if you were smart, so would you."

Phil looked from Caleb to Jocelyn and back. Then, "She's frigid," he blurted.

"Phil," Jocelyn said, stepping toward him, pushing him back down the steps. "That's enough. Leave. Now."

But Phil would not be deterred. Although he let her shuffle him along toward his car, he called over his shoulder at Caleb. "She's cold. You'll see. What kind of woman doesn't go to her own parents' funeral?"

She gave him a final push and he stumbled, dropping the coffee cups into the street. They splattered, coffee flying up onto Phil's pant legs. He didn't look back at Jocelyn. He kicked the empty cups as he made his way back to his car. Jocelyn waited for him to drive away before she picked up the cups and cup holder and deposited them into her recycling bin.

Caleb waited on the porch. She swallowed hard over the lump in her throat. She wished her face wasn't burning. "I'm sorry," she said. "He's—"

"An asshole?" Caleb supplied. "Yeah, I got that."

Jocelyn smiled but shook her head. "What he said, I—"

Caleb reached out and tipped her chin so he could look into her eyes. "Don't sweat it," he said. "My ex has nothing good to say about me either. It's just the nature of the beast."

She sighed. She opened her mouth to try once more to explain, but she had no idea what to say. Caleb didn't wait for an explanation. He cupped her cheeks in his palms, the skin of his hands dry and soothing against her face. She nearly swayed looking up into his eyes. She couldn't remember the last time she'd wanted to kiss a man the way she wanted to kiss Caleb—not even Phil. She wanted to devour him. He leaned down and kissed her, slowly and deeply. Afterward, he continued to hold her face in his hands and gazed down into her eyes. "Seriously," he said. "Forget about that guy. I would prefer you think about me instead."

THIRTY-SEVEN

November 4th

An hour later, Jocelyn was sandwiched between Inez and Kevin as the three of them stood in Basil Ahearn's office. Friendly Fire was there too, on the other side of Kevin. He kept a good foot and a half between himself and the rest of them. His face was a mask of disinterest, but Jocelyn noticed the tips of his ears reddening. Ahearn sat at his desk, his cell phone in his hand, looking alternately at the phone and back at them. He pointed his phone at Finch. "You," he said. "Consider yourself officially reprimanded. You're to go for training on how to pat down suspects—and arrest them."

Jocelyn and Kevin glanced over at Friendly Fire, but he remained impassive. Jocelyn thought she was the only one who could hear Kevin's snicker, but Ahearn never missed much. He shot Kevin an icy glare, silencing him, and looked back at Finch. He motioned Finch over to his desk with his phone and handed him a piece of paper. "This is your official reprimand. The next time you see Henry Richards, you put his face into the concrete. You know he's wanted for violating the restraining order Detective Rush's daughter has against him and for generally harassing one of my people. Do not let him get away. And after you detain him, pat him down, Finch. Properly."

Jocelyn looked over at Finch again. He stared straight ahead, his expression blank, but she could see a muscle ticking in his jaw. "Now get out of my sight," Ahearn added.

Wordlessly, Finch left. She listened to his footsteps, into the common area and down the steps. Then a loud clatter, like something metal being thrown or kicked, followed by a voice she didn't recognize. "Jesus Christ, Friendly Fire. Watch it."

Ahearn sighed. He pointed his phone at Inez, who had cleared her throat loudly. "What?"

"Sir," Inez said. "Friendly—Finch took on a pit bull for me."

Ahearn's brows drew together; then he rolled his eyes. "That's admirable, Graham, but I don't care. Now look, all of you, I'm not running a goddamn preschool here. Get your shit together and work it out. I don't want the four of you in my office again for dumb shit. And keep your hands to your goddamned self," he said pointedly, looking right at Jocelyn. "You got that?"

"Yes, sir," the three of them said in unison. Jocelyn wanted to point out that Finch not patting down Todd Martin wasn't dumb shit—especially since it had nearly gotten her killed. Kevin must have sensed that she was about to speak because he elbowed her. "Let it go," he said between gritted teeth.

"And, Rush," Ahearn continued. "You don't like it here at Northwest or what?"

Jocelyn met his eyes. "Sir?"

"Lieutenant Vaughn was here earlier and asked if I could *loan* you to him for an SVU case." He said the word *loan* as if it were something extremely distasteful. Like Vaughn had asked him to clean the SVU toilets for a month—with his own toothbrush.

"Anita Grant will only speak to me," Jocelyn said.

Ahearn waved his phone back and forth in the air. "I heard it all from Vaughn. I don't give a rat's ass who's talking to who. I need bodies in here, and if you're not going to be one of them, put in for a damn transfer."

"That's not necessary, sir," Jocelyn said.

Ahearn looked at her with one bushy brow arched high over his right eye. He let a moment slip by as he regarded her, skepticism in every line of his face. Finally, he said, "Just wrap this up fast, Rush. And you," he added, pointing at Kevin. "You stay here. I need you on Northwest calls, not following Rush all over the damn place on this SVU case."

Kevin nodded. "Yes, sir."

Ahearn flicked his wrist, making a shooing motion toward the door. "Now get out. Go do your jobs."

They filed out and headed back to the Detectives' room. "Got yourself assigned to that SVU case, did you?" Kevin grumbled in her ear as they returned to their desks.

"It's only temporary," Jocelyn said. "I'm just helping out."

"Well," Inez interrupted, "if I see Richards tonight, I'll—whoa!"

She pulled up short and gripped Jocelyn's arm as Jocelyn's and Kevin's desks came into view. Caleb perched casually on the edge of Jocelyn's desk, his head bent to his cell phone.

"Who the hell is this?" Kevin asked.

Jocelyn swallowed. Caleb hadn't seen them yet. She paused a moment to take in his thick, tousled brown hair and the line of his jaw. She'd just seen him of course. Just kissed him on her front porch, but still, the sight of him made her limbs feel slack and boneless.

"That's Mr. Scandalous," Inez whispered.

Kevin turned to her, his eyebrows drawn together in confusion. Jocelyn gave Inez a shove and looked at Kevin. "That's Vaughn," Jocelyn explained.

"*That's* Vaughn? He looks like he should be teaching high school English or some shit."

Jocelyn laughed. "That's exactly what I thought when I met him."

Inez snorted. "Yeah, I bet that's all you—" A sharp elbow jab stopped Inez from finishing her thought. At that moment, Caleb looked up and smiled. And Jocelyn's whole body felt like a sigh.

"Good lord," Kevin muttered as he stalked off to greet Vaughn.

Jocelyn and Inez followed him. There was a round of introductions followed by some awkward small talk during which Inez did nothing but grin like a Cheshire cat. Then Kevin interrogated Caleb on everything from his résumé to his dating history. Jocelyn pulled Caleb away, dragging him by his wrist.

"We have a witness to interview," she said.

Caleb met her eyes, an amused smile on his face. "But I'm talking to your friends," he said.

"Yeah," Jocelyn said. "I noticed. That'll be quite enough of that."

Caleb laughed the whole way down the steps.

THIRTY-EIGHT

November 4th

Raeann Church was living in a halfway house in Northeast Philadelphia. She'd been locked up for petty drug charges and released from jail to the house on Orthodox Street. Once Caleb assured the coordinator that Raeann wasn't in any trouble, the woman backed off. She let them use her dingy office to conduct the interview. The desk was metal. The room smelled like must and cigarettes. Its once eggshell walls were now yellow, punctuated by brown water stains.

Raeann looked normal enough—her waist-length brown hair was clean and neatly brushed. She was curved at the hip with thick thighs, unlike most of the emaciated junkies Jocelyn had encountered. Only her flickering gaze and fidgety hands gave her away. She was a meatier, less attractive version of Camille.

She recognized Caleb instantly. "It's you," she said.

Caleb sat in a chair next to her. Jocelyn pulled the chair out from behind the desk and placed it across from Raeann, the three of them forming a loose semicircle. Caleb smiled at the woman. "Raeann," he said. "How are you?"

She rubbed her palms together and squeezed her clasped hands between her legs. "I'm okay. I'm in here, you know?"

Caleb nodded. "Yeah, I know. You still smoke reds?" From his jacket pocket he pulled an unopened pack of Marlboros.

Raeann's face lit up. "Thanks, man."

"So, Raeann. I'm here with my colleague, Detective Rush, because we think the guys who attacked you four years ago are still at it. You're the only person to see all their faces. We'd like to ask you some questions."

She turned the cigarette box around and around in her hands. "I told you everything I know already."

Caleb smiled, and Jocelyn could see he had the same effect on Raeann because her face flushed instantly. "It will only take a minute, Raeann."

She looked at the floor, her body pitching back and forth in the chair. "Okay."

"I know it was a long time ago," Jocelyn broke in. She took out a stack of photos and spread them along the edge of the desk. "But can you tell me if any of these men were involved in the attack on you four years ago?"

Raeann stood and bent to the photos. She chewed the cuticle of her left index finger as she studied them. "This one," she said, pointing to the photo of Larry Warner. "He was the nice one." She laughed nervously. "Well, not nice. But not mean. He wasn't as rough as the other one. He took the nail out."

She turned her right palm toward Jocelyn. In its center was a small, silvered lump. Anita's and Alicia's wounds had been far worse.

"And this one," Raeann said, fingering the photo of Angel Donovan. "He didn't talk."

"What about the third guy? Can you tell me about him?"

"Well, he was white. He seemed kind of young, his late twenties maybe? He could have been in his thirties, I guess. He was real clean, like he took good care of himself. He had brown hair, and he kept it real short. He was tan and real muscular. Blue eyes. At first I didn't understand why he wanted a prostitute. He could have gotten any woman."

"Most women draw the line at crucifixion, no matter how good-looking the guy," Jocelyn said.

More nervous laughter. "He looked like—he looked like a frat-boy type. Like a yuppie or something. You know, like one of these rich white people who drive their Benzes into the ghetto to buy drugs. He smelled good. He was arrogant too." Raeann frowned, thinking.

Jocelyn leaned forward, elbows on her knees. "Like a cop?"

Jocelyn caught the look Caleb gave her. She hadn't voiced this suspicion before—not to Caleb or even Kevin. She'd been kicking it around in her head for days—ever since she saw Caleb's notes. He had written "military" in his notes, but somehow that didn't fit. For one thing, Warner and Donovan didn't seem to have many associates with military experience. They had both had plenty of run-ins with cops, though, and there was no shortage of dirty cops in the city.

Raeann nodded vigorously. "Yeah," she said. "He could have been. Something like that. A cop or a lawyer or something. He was take-charge. He seemed, you know, like he had a lot of school maybe. He used words I didn't understand."

"Raeann, would you be willing to sit down with a sketch artist to come up with a picture of the guy?"

"Sure," she said. "Why not?"

Outside, Caleb said, "We'll never get permission for the sketch artist."

Jocelyn grimaced. "Just wait," she said. "Sooner or later they're going to do this to someone the brass can't ignore. If we can't convince them now, they'll give us the sketch artist then. We'll request it now, and let them turn it down. We can revisit the issue later."

When they reached her Explorer, she leaned her rear against the driver's side door. Caleb stood in front of her. He placed a hand near her roof and leaned into her. She could smell his aftershave. God she wanted to do things to him. Dirty, dirty things.

His cell phone buzzed, and he reached into his jacket pocket to silence it.

"We're on the job," she reminded him.

He smiled. "I know. That's why we're out here and not in the car."

Dizziness overcame her as she thought about the last time they were in her vehicle together. His cell phone buzzed again. He silenced it once more and looked back at her, his expression less playful. "So," he said, "you think our unknown suspect is a cop."

Jocelyn shrugged, forcing herself to focus on the case instead of Caleb. "Makes sense. From the way the victims described him—the way he looked, the way he acted. That would explain why he's gone to such great lengths to keep his identity a secret."

"Raeann thought he might be a lawyer."

"I suppose it's possible, but I think it's more likely a cop. Warner and Donovan have had enough contact with the law to have crossed paths with a dirty cop."

"So this guy has something on them," Caleb suggested.

"Probably. Maybe he caught them doing something and instead of arresting them, he used the crime as leverage."

"For what?"

"To get them to do what he wants. Who knows what else they're into together—drugs, running numbers. There's no shortage of laws to break."

Caleb's phone buzzed a third time. Finally, he looked at the screen. His brow drew downward. He scraped his teeth over his bottom lip. "Shit," he said. "We got a break in this child pornography case we've been working on. Immigration and Customs Enforcement brought us in on their task force. I've gotta go. But first, where do we go from here? There are a lot of cops in this city. It will take too long to investigate every one."

Jocelyn laughed. "Well, it's not me or you, so that's two down."

Caleb grinned. "You're funny."

"I know where we can start," she said. "The cop who was on the scene five years ago when Donovan got shot in the throat and Warner got nailed for his first violent offense." She quickly recapped what she'd found in the file Phil's paralegal had unearthed for her. "I'll check him out tonight."

"Great," Caleb said. "Keep me posted. And"—he leaned even closer to her, his lips inches from hers—"can I still see you Thursday?"

"Yes," she said, her voice coming out more breathy than she would have liked. When his mouth closed over hers, she tried not to kiss him like she was trying to suck the air out of his body. His hands on her hips set her whole body afire. She finally understood that old expression about taking a cold shower.

She was glad to be leaning against her Explorer when he released her because her legs had gone all rubbery.

"Talk to you later," he said. Then he strode off toward his own car, phone pressed to his ear.

Jocelyn sighed. *Back to work.*

THIRTY-NINE

November 4th

Vince Fox was retired and owned a sports bar in the Northeast. Jocelyn pulled into its large parking lot just before happy hour. She parked next to a shiny new Hummer that had to be his, judging by the "SexyFox" vanity plate. The car looked like it cost more than her house did. Not bad for a retired cop. She slipped inside through two sets of double doors. It was cool and dark inside. The bar spanned the entire length of the building and gleamed in the daylight that managed to creep through the tinted windows. The tables and chairs were shiny chrome. The place was immaculate, and everything in it looked brand-new. The walls were lined with sports memorabilia from the city's pro sports teams, each wall featuring a different sport. The biggest wall was reserved for the city's football team, the Eagles, which was no surprise since Eagles' fans were a veritable cult. There were at least four flat-screen televisions on each wall, all in varying sizes. Between the televisions and the memorabilia, the content of the walls in Fox's were worth more than Jocelyn's house as well.

Vince Fox was doing pretty well for himself. Jocelyn didn't know many single, retired cops who could afford to open a place like this.

"Help you?" asked a man standing behind the bar. In one hand he held a remote, in the other an open bottle of Corona. He was in his fifties with greased-back black hair graying at the temples. His face was puffy and ruddy. He sported a short-sleeved button-down shirt that revealed a set of muscular arms. Resting in the center of his open collar were two thick gold chains and a bushy gathering of chest hairs. His eyes were dishwater gray and bulged from his head. He frowned at her without using any of his facial muscles.

Jocelyn pulled out her credentials and handed them to him. "Vince Fox?"

He nodded, studying her police ID. "I didn't realize they let the girls take the detective exam." He made a show of looking her up and down. "Does it still have an oral component?"

She sighed. "I've got fifteen years on the force, so if you're coming at me with inappropriate sexual innuendo, you'll have to do better than that. You wanna try again, or should we just talk about why I'm here?"

He sneered. "You some kind of dyke?"

In her flattest tone, Jocelyn said, "Why? You got some well-used dyke comment stored up just for little old me?" She feigned feminine eye batting and snatched her credentials out of his hand before hardening her expression. "Let's stipulate the fact that you're a dumb, misogynist pig, and that I don't like you. I've got questions and I don't have all day, so are you done?"

His mouth hung open, the remote dangling from his hand. He recovered quickly and took a long swig of Corona. "What's your problem?"

"What's *your* problem?" she shot back. She sighed again. "Let's just skip the witty banter and move on." She slid Larry Warner's mug shot across the bar. "You remember this guy?"

Fox picked up the photo. Jocelyn saw instant recognition in his face, yet he remained silent for almost a full minute, staring at the picture.

Finally, Vince looked up. The mug shot seemed to sober him even more than her response to his detective comment. Still, he set it aside and looked back at the flat-screen hanging behind the bar. He flipped channels, finally settling on Channel Ten news.

"Drink?"

Jocelyn shook her head and put her hands on her hips. "I'm on duty."

He didn't look at her but raised his eyebrows. With a smirk, he asked again, "Drink?"

"No."

"You dykes are no fun," he said. He laughed heartily and poured her a shot of whiskey anyway.

Jocelyn took a seat on the bar stool. "Funny, I say the same thing about misogynist pigs."

Fox's laughter petered out, but a slight grin remained on his face, widening when Jocelyn picked up the shot and tasted it.

"Larry Warner," he said. "What's he in for?"

Jocelyn filled Fox in. He gave a low whistle. "Jeez, sounds like Larry's got himself into a world of trouble."

"The night you arrested him five years ago was his first violent offense. What happened?"

Fox blinked and scratched his chin. "I, uh, got a call for a disturbance house over on Somerset near Front Street. I been over there before a couple times. Dwayne lived there with his girlfriend, Shasta. He was runnin' girls outta there, including his woman. I guess she didn't like him sampling the product. She got in Dwayne's face, he slapped her around, and she took his gun. Least that's what Dwayne told me when I got there. Shots were fired. Neighbors called the police. When I went in, Dwayne had the gun and Shasta and Dwayne's friend had both been shot. I told him to put the gun down, he didn't. So I shot him."

"You killed him."

Fox nodded. "Warner shows up after the fact. He was a maniac. He just went after the first person he saw, and that was me."

Jocelyn raised a brow. "He just attacked you?"

Fox turned away from her, talking over his shoulder. "Dwayne was Warner's son."

A cold shock jarred her. "And you killed him?"

Fox looked back at her and smiled. "Yup."

"Warner never mentioned a son."

"Warner didn't raise him—never took any responsibility for him—wasn't interested in Dwayne until he was an adult and started making money running prostitutes and dealing drugs. Warner sure as hell wasn't paying no support."

Jocelyn traced the rim of her shot glass with an index finger. "How'd you come by that information?"

Fox stared at her for a beat, and she knew he was hiding something. He took a long sip of his beer, keeping his eyes squarely on her. "Well," he said, "when you work the same area for a lot of years, you come by a lot of information."

She nodded. "What about Donovan? Were he and Warner into a lot of shit together?"

Fox shook his head. "No. Donovan ran with Dwayne. Him and Dwayne came up together."

So Warner hadn't gone off the deep end because of what happened to Donovan. It was his son's death that had likely set him off. His association with Donovan must have begun after he got out of prison for attacking Fox.

"Dwayne and Donovan ever run with any white guys?"

Fox humphed. "They sold drugs to a lot of white junkies, but no, none of the guys they ran with were white."

"How about Larry?"

Fox thought for a moment, staring blankly at the television. Finally, he turned back to her. "No, not that I remember."

"So what happened to you? You take early retirement?"

Fox smiled. "Got shot."

"On duty?" Jocelyn asked, wondering why she hadn't heard about it. A cop getting shot in Philadelphia rarely went unnoticed by the press or by other officers.

Fox's eyebrows arched suggestively. He licked his lips. "Accidental discharge."

"Oh." He wasn't the first cop to shoot himself in the foot while on duty. She made a show of checking her phone. "Well, I've got to get back to work, but thanks for the drink."

Fox nodded at her and turned back to the television. "Come by when you're off duty, and I'll make you a real drink."

She didn't respond, instead making a beeline for the door. Once safely in her car, she shuddered. She hated men like Fox. After the way their conversation started, did he honestly think she'd be interested in having a "real" drink with him? Of course he did. Her mother would have called him smarmy, although Jocelyn could think of quite a few other words for him. Sleazy. Disgusting. Creepy. Asshole.

She pulled her phone out of her pocket and checked the text message that had arrived while she was in the bar. It was from Caleb.

I'd rather be with you. In your car.

She laughed. *Same here*, she texted in return.

Did you talk to Fox?

Her fingers flew across the screen. *Yeah. He's not our guy. He had no information other than he shot Warner's son five years ago. I think he's hiding something, but I'm not sure it's related to this case.*

We'll keep working the leads, he replied. *See you Thursday. Can't wait.*

FORTY

November 7th

The e-mail came in just before fifth period ended. The students in Jennifer Maisry's fifth-period art class were engrossed in their latest assignment. Besides the susurrus sounds of rustling paper and snipping scissors, the room was silent. She wished all her classes were so easy.

Her BlackBerry buzzed atop her desk, signaling she had a new e-mail. A little wave of excitement went through her as she realized it was a response to her Craigslist ad. She'd taken the ad down for a month but recently decided to repost it. She read the e-mail. The guy's name was Larry, but he was careful not to say anything that could later be construed as damning. That was always the first test—discretion. The ones who'd picked up escorts online before were always careful about the language they used so they didn't incriminate themselves or Jennifer. The newbies were the ones she steered clear of.

Larry was a black male in his forties looking for a ménage à trois with a friend, also a black male.

"Mrs. Maisry?" the student's voice made her jump. It was one of the blonde girls. They all looked the same to Jennifer. This one stood at Jennifer's desk, staring at her expectantly. She couldn't remember the girl's name. Audra? Audrey?

"Yes?"

"Can I go to the bathroom?"

Jennifer smiled sweetly. "Of course. Don't forget to take the hall pass."

As she watched the girl leave the room, her BlackBerry buzzed in her hand. It was a call from her husband.

"Babe," he said. "What are you doing?"

Jennifer sighed. "What do you think I'm doing? I'm at work."

A noise of exasperation. "Still?"

"Still? Michael, I work the same hours every week."

"It seems like you're always there."

She almost said, "How would you know? You're never home," but she bit back her response. She kept her voice calm. "I'm here the same amount of time during the same hours every week."

"Well, whatever. I'm doing happy hour with Sal, so I'll be late, okay?"

Even though he couldn't see her, she arched an eyebrow. "Sal, huh?"

He coughed. "Uh, yeah. So don't make dinner, okay?"

"Fine," she said and hung up.

Although Sal was a real person—Michael's sales manager at their Conshohocken dealership—Jennifer thought of Sal as a code word for "I'm going to be fucking my eighteen-year-old blonde greeter while you're home alone, so don't wait up."

Jennifer had caught them once—a year earlier, when the girl wasn't even legal. She'd gone to surprise Michael at the dealership with Chinese takeout—General Tso's chicken was his favorite—and she'd seen the two of them through the crack in his office door.

Michael in the chair, his pants around his ankles, knees spread wide. The girl's head bobbed up and down furiously, Mike's hand tangled in her ponytail, controlling her movements. His head was tipped back, eyes closed. He groaned. Jennifer stood by the crack in the door, her whole body trembling till the girl finished. She listened to Mike's satisfied grunts of "Oh yeah" as she ran back through the empty showroom. She sat in her car, gripping the steering wheel till her hands ached. A few minutes later, the blonde girl emerged, looking impossibly young and pert—and happy. Jennifer resisted the urge to run her over as she drove out of the parking lot.

She didn't leave her husband. Their marriage had been a sham well before that. Jennifer had long suspected that Mike was having an affair. Although the proof of it was shocking, and even though she cried every time Mike stayed late for a month after that, she didn't confront him and she didn't leave.

They had an arrangement of sorts. Don't ask, don't tell. Successful dealership owner. Gorgeous schoolteacher. Beautiful, expensive home. To the outside world they were the perfect couple. A success story. But it was a facade, and after ten years Jennifer didn't mind keeping it up as long as she got to stay in her beautiful home, drive a hundred-thousand-dollar car, and buy anything she wanted. She liked nice things and didn't want to give them up just because of some stupid teenage slut.

She didn't even need the job at the school. Mike would be happier if she stayed home redecorating their house and going to the spa every day—as long as she cooked dinner every night. But she'd tried that. Teaching gave her something to do, and although the kids occasionally got on her nerves, they looked up to her. Most of the boys had crushes on her. She loved the way it felt to walk across the room and feel all those eyes on her. Sometimes she wore low-cut shirts just for the openmouthed stares she got. Her principal would have reprimanded her if he wasn't so busy staring at her tits. Her sister called her a narcissist, but Jennifer chalked it up to being incredibly lonely. Although Mike could be controlling and jealous, he hadn't really looked at her in years.

"Mrs. Maisry?"

Jennifer looked up from her BlackBerry. It was the girl again.

"Yes?"

"Here's the hall pass."

What did she want, a medal?

"Thank you." Jennifer smiled, taking it back.

She turned her attention back to her BlackBerry, reading the e-mail from Larry. She'd only done a threesome once before, but she found it incredibly erotic—two men touching her, kissing her, fucking her at the same time—two men wanting her at the same time. She felt a flush of anticipation envelop her as she typed in a reply.

Can you meet me today at 3 p.m. at the Starbucks at Germantown and Evergreen?

The reply came as she was leaving school for the day. *See you there*, it said.

She typed back, *Ask me if I've ever tried the pumpkin latte.*

She drove back to the Chestnut Hill area of Philadelphia and parked in the parking lot on East Highland near Germantown Avenue. She walked down Germantown Avenue, pausing to check herself over in the window of the Chestnut Hill Bootery. At thirty-two, her body was still tight and toned. She hit the gym three times a week. Her skin was smooth and tanned. The sun glinted against the blonde highlights she'd gotten in her long brown hair. She looked good.

She strode toward Starbucks, wondering if Larry had a place to go. She'd run into that problem before. She refused to bring them home, even though Mike would never find out. When she first started, she'd made the mistake of bringing one of them home. He'd shown up unannounced three times after that. "You have the sweetest ass," he'd said by way of explanation, as if he couldn't stay away from her. Luckily, Mike wasn't home. She'd done what he asked and charged him double what she had the first time. After the third time, she never saw him again, but his unannounced visits had freaked her out sufficiently. She stopped bringing them home.

Them. That's how she thought of the men who paid her for sex. Not as johns or dates. Just them. She didn't really consider herself a hooker. She liked to meet men who wanted to fuck her. Why shouldn't she charge them for it? She didn't want to have an affair. She didn't want complications. She didn't want the rigor or the tedium of something long-term. What she really wanted was a few hours now and then to satisfy her need to be desired, wanted, and touched. That's all her trysts with "them" ever were. It wasn't a real threat to her marriage—not as much as the teenage blonde was. Plus there was the titillation of doing something taboo, something so far out of her element. There was no beating the adrenaline high.

She waited in the Starbucks, sipping an iced tea until a tall, thin black man in his midforties dropped a few coins near her table. As she knelt to help him pick up his change, he smiled at her and said, "Have you tried the pumpkin latte?"

She smiled back. "Yes," she said. "It's very good."

FORTY-ONE

November 7th

Caleb's fingers trailed up Jocelyn's thigh, creeping under the hem of the black dress Inez had lent her for their date. His mouth was on hers before they even made it through her front door. As soon as she closed it behind them, he pressed her against it, and she wrapped her arms around his neck, focusing entirely on the kiss.

He'd taken her to dinner at Valley Green, a semifancy, expensive restaurant along the trail that bordered the Wissahickon Creek—what the locals referred to as "the crick." It was twenty-three miles and meandered its way through Philadelphia. Although Jocelyn had taken Olivia to the Wissahickon Creek to feed the ducks, and responded to calls of women being pulled off the trail and raped, she'd never been inside the restaurant that sat along its banks.

She'd had the lamb, Caleb the duck. The food was delicious. She was heady after two glasses of wine and two hours of great conversation. She had no idea how the adult dating thing worked, but she knew as she and Caleb walked hand in hand back to his car that she wanted him to touch her. So she invited him back to her house. They moved away from the door and fell onto the couch in a jumble of limbs. Caleb pulled a Lalaloopsy doll out from under Jocelyn's back, and they both laughed.

He tossed the doll aside and bent his mouth to her neck. Jocelyn's skin felt hot. As Caleb's fingers brushed across her pelvic area, she quivered. She felt the same desire she'd felt in the car the night she'd met him, but when his hand slipped inside her panties, her body tensed. It was almost imperceptible, the shift inside her. Phil had never noticed it. But she did. It was her body shutting down. She knew in that instant that no matter how much she wanted Caleb or how expertly he touched her, she would not fully enjoy the sex.

Caleb's head shot up from where it had been buried in her neck. "What's wrong?" he said.

Jocelyn froze. "What? Nothing, nothing." She forced a smile. Caleb shifted, putting some distance between their bodies. His brow furrowed. The crinkly lines next to his eyes deepened. "I'm going too fast," he said. "I'm sorry."

Jocelyn shook her head. She touched his cheek, trying to draw him back to her. "No," she said. "It's not that. It's not you. I just . . ." She trailed off, thinking about what Phil had said about her being frigid.

"It's okay," Caleb said. He moved his face closer to hers, catching her mouth in a soft, slow kiss. His hands rested on her hips. She could feel his hardness against her thigh. He lifted his head again and smiled at her. "Tell you what," he said. "We are not having sex tonight."

Flustered, Jocelyn shook her head. "It's okay," she said. "I want to be with you."

"Well, I'm glad to hear you say that, but I think we should slow this down. Enjoy it a little. So here are the rules."

"Rules?" Jocelyn arched a skeptical eyebrow.

"Rules, yes. No sex and no removing clothes."

Jocelyn laughed. "No taking our clothes off? How will that work exactly?"

He gave her a playful grin. "You'll see."

His mouth moved downward from the hollow of her throat, over her clothes and down her body. He stroked her bare arms and moved his hands along the contours of her body, slowly, lightly. She closed her eyes, focusing on his touch and her shallow breathing until pleasure woke again at her center. She was seriously considering breaking both of Caleb's rules when their cell phones rang.

They had dropped them on her coffee table. Hers was set to vibrate as well as ring. It danced on the table when she didn't answer right away. She didn't want to check it, but she had to in case it was Martina calling about Olivia. She and Caleb disentangled and picked up their respective phones.

"Work," they said in unison.

As Jocelyn answered, Caleb stood up and moved away from her to answer his own.

"Rush," Kevin said without preamble. "Can you get a babysitter? You're gonna need to come in."

Jocelyn watched Caleb arguing quietly into his own phone. His erection still strained against the front of his pants. She smiled. "This better be goddamned good," she said to Kevin.

Kevin made a noise deep in his throat. "Oh, you'll want to be here for this one. How soon can you get to Einstein?"

She felt a tickle at the back of her neck. Her skin felt cold. "Is it Warner and Donovan?"

"Yeah, and your unknown subject—this time they did a schoolteacher from Chestnut Hill. It's already on the news. Ahearn is down here, and word is they're calling Special Vics now. How soon can you get here?"

"Give me thirty."

FORTY-TWO

November 7th

Jocelyn changed out of her dress, and they drove separate vehicles to the hospital. She had the local a.m. news radio station, KYW, on during the drive. The droll, tinny voice filled up her car, sounding as though it were coming through some kind of filter. "A Philadelphia schoolteacher was brutally attacked in the Chestnut Hill section of the city this afternoon. She was abducted from Germantown Avenue by two men, who assaulted and crucified her. The police investigation is ongoing."

The schoolteacher turned out to be Jennifer Maisry, who was thin with delicate features and the kind of tan one only got from a combination of summers down the shore and winters in a tanning salon. Her long brown hair, although mussed, was expertly cut and shiny enough to earn her an endorsement from any number of high-class hair products. She sat on the edge of the hospital bed, her well-toned legs dangling above the floor, her feet wrapped in gauze. Just above the collar of her hospital gown, Jocelyn spied a gold chain plastered to her sternum with sweat. From across the room, she could tell the chain itself was worth more than she made in a month, and peeking from the bundles of gauze were two sets of perfectly manicured toenails. From what Jocelyn could see of her fingernails, they too were manicured.

The nurse checking her IV said, "Sweetie, don't get up. You have to keep those feet elevated."

Jennifer vomited all over the floor.

"Oh, sweet Jesus," the nurse said. She reached across the bed and pressed Jennifer's Call button. Within moments, another nurse pushed Jocelyn, Kevin, and Caleb out of the doorway and set about changing Jennifer's hospital gown. She shot the trio of detectives an acerbic look. "Come back in a few minutes," she said.

Jocelyn pulled the door to the room shut, noting that a white schoolteacher, Maisry, rated her own private room with solid walls and doors while Anita Grant had to bear her humiliation behind a semiprivate curtain for anyone to hear.

"She's wealthy," Jocelyn said. "Why is she teaching school?"

Kevin scratched his head and flipped open his notebook. "She teaches art at some swanky private school in Plymouth Meeting. Her husband owns a bunch of car dealerships. They have a mansion in Chestnut Hill. She got bored doing yoga and redecorating their house, so she dusted off her teaching degree. She has a minor in art history."

Jocelyn rolled her eyes. "So, what happened?"

Kevin flipped another page in his notebook. "She was shopping on Germantown Avenue, stopped at the Starbucks for a latte. She was walking back to her car, which she says is parked on West Highland Avenue next to Valley Green Bank, when she was grabbed and forced into a gray Bonneville. She was taken to an abandoned building—she's not sure where it was—by two black males. They held her down while a white male in a ski mask nailed her hands and feet into the floor."

Kevin frowned. "I think you know the rest of the story."

Caleb said, "Did she ID Warner and Donovan?"

"Yeah, we showed her a bunch of mug shots. She picked them right out."

Jocelyn arched a brow and folded her arms across her middle. "So, these guys are out on bail for kidnapping charges, and they abduct a wealthy stranger in one of the more affluent areas of Philadelphia? In broad daylight?"

Kevin shrugged. "You were the one who said they'd escalate."

"Yeah, but this is fast. I would have expected them to lay low for a while, not to go out and pick the most high-profile victim they could find. This doesn't fit."

Caleb tipped his chin in Kevin's direction. "No chance that Maisry is an escort?"

Kevin shook his head. "I asked her that right away. She was pretty offended. She says no way. I don't know why she would be—she's happily married to a rich guy. Teaches kids."

Jocelyn cracked the door to Jennifer's room and looked in. She was still sitting on the side of the bed. Blood trickled out from under the gauze and dripped down the big toe of her left foot. She vomited again, this time into a basin one of the nurses held in front of her.

"You never know," Jocelyn said, thinking of Camille. "People do strange things."

Before Kevin or Caleb could respond, their attention was drawn down the hall near the entrance to the treatment area, where a male was yelling. As the doors swung open, Jocelyn heard the words, ". . . my wife, goddammit."

Caleb grimaced. "Three guesses who that is."

A tall, pudgy man with thick, greasy black hair and a neatly trimmed beard strode toward them. He wore a long brown coat and, beneath that, a blue polo shirt that read "Maisry Lexus" over his left chest area. The top button was open, revealing thick rolls of fat where his neck should be and an unruly thatch of chest hair, punctuated by a chunky gold chain. He wore gray slacks and black dress shoes. A Bluetooth device was affixed to his right ear.

"You the cops?" he said, speaking directly to Caleb.

Caleb drew up to his full height and said, "I'm Lieutenant Vaughn. This is Detective Sullivan and Detective Rush."

Maisry gave Jocelyn a sideways glance and, looking back at Caleb, hooked a thumb behind him. "You need to talk to your boys back there. They weren't gonna let me through."

Jocelyn suppressed a groan.

Your boys.

Maisry was rich, well dressed, and well groomed, but he need only open his mouth to let the world know the elegance was purely external. Minimal education, major attitude. A lot of bluster and very little trace of manners.

"Where's my wife? They said she was in an accident. She okay?"

Caleb and Jocelyn exchanged a glance. He obviously hadn't heard or seen the news, or, if he had, he hadn't made the connection.

"It wasn't an accident, Mr. Maisry," Jocelyn said.

"Where is she? Did they tow the car? I gotta take pictures for the insurance company."

"Mr. Maisry," Caleb said. "Your wife—"

But Maisry was already pushing Caleb aside, heading for the door to Jennifer's room. Jocelyn put her body between him and door. For the first time, he looked at her. His face pinched into a look of annoyance.

"Mr. Maisry, I'm very sorry to tell you this. Your wife was not in an accident today. She was attacked. Two men abducted her. She was taken to an unknown location where a third man crucified her before the other two men sexually assaulted her."

He froze and stepped back. His face was ashen. "What?"

Jocelyn didn't repeat herself. She knew he had heard her because he looked like he might throw up on her shoes. She gave him a few seconds to collect himself. Then he said, "They crucified her?"

Jocelyn held his gaze evenly. "Yes. They nailed her hands and feet to the floor. I'm sorry, Mr. Maisry."

A shudder worked its way down from Maisry's shoulders to his feet. For a moment, he looked like he might faint. His fat throat worked, but no words came out. Kevin took his elbow and steered him toward a chair.

Maisry stared up at them. "How—how does this happen?"

Jocelyn put a hand on his shoulder. "Your wife has already identified two of the suspects. We've got the whole city looking for them. We're working on identifying the third suspect, but it will be extremely difficult since he was wearing a mask."

Jocelyn wasn't sure if Maisry was listening to her or hearing anything she said. His gaze was blank and pleading. He looked at each of them, as if willing one of them to say it wasn't true. He finally opened his mouth to speak, but a howl issued from behind the door to Jennifer's room. The sound was like a skewer to Jocelyn's gut. She made a conscious effort not to wince.

Maisry jumped up and pushed past them. "My wife!"

He burst through the door. Jennifer lay in the bed, tears streaming down her pale cheeks. One of the nurses was changing the dressing on her left foot. When Jennifer saw her husband, she turned away. He went to her anyway, gathering her awkwardly in his arms and talking softly into her ear. Jocelyn couldn't make out his words, but, after a minute, Jennifer nodded into his chest. Her shoulders shook, and he stroked the skin between her shoulder blades.

Feeling like a voyeur, Jocelyn pulled the door closed. They waited a half hour before Maisry emerged. Some of the color had returned to his face. "I'm going to go get her some of her own clothes," he said. "She says it will make her feel better if I do."

Jocelyn nodded.

"Oh, wait, the car." He turned back toward Jennifer. "Babe, where's your car? I'll have someone pick it up."

"It's in the parking lot behind the Starbucks on East Highland," she said.

Jocelyn looked at Kevin, but he didn't show any sign of having caught the discrepancy.

After Maisry left, Jocelyn slipped into Jennifer's room and introduced herself. "Mrs. Maisry, I know you're exhausted, but I just have a few more questions for you."

Jennifer nodded weakly without meeting Jocelyn's eyes.

"What did you buy today?" Jocelyn asked.

Jennifer's eyes darted toward her. "What?"

"You told Detective Sullivan that you were out shopping. What did you buy?"

Jennifer swallowed, her delicate throat quivering. "I—uh—I didn't get that far. I had coffee at Starbucks, and then I was abducted."

Jocelyn nodded along. "You were forced into the car while walking down West Highland Avenue?"

Jennifer hesitated a second. "Yeah. I was walking back to my car."

"Your car?"

"Yeah."

"The one your husband is going to have someone pick up in the parking lot behind the Starbucks on East Highland, which is in the opposite direction?"

Caught in the lie, Jennifer's already pale face turned an unhealthy shade of gray. Her eyes widened. She opened her mouth to speak, but Jocelyn went on. "You had coffee and then you went immediately back to your car? Without shopping as you had planned."

Jennifer stammered. "I—I—"

"How long have you been an escort, Mrs. Maisry?"

Jennifer's mouth clamped shut. Fresh tears filled her eyes. Her bottom lip trembled, but she didn't speak. Jocelyn moved closer to the bed, making her tone as nonthreatening as possible. "The last four women they did this to were prostitutes. Today you lied to the police about what you were doing and where you parked your car. The only reason that I can see for you lying about such trivial matters is that there's something you don't want your husband or anyone else to know. Either you're having an affair or you're an escort."

Jennifer stared at Jocelyn in horror, her entire body shaking.

"Here's what I think happened," Jocelyn continued. "You have an ad on Craigslist. Warner answered it. You met them for coffee at Starbucks. You closed the deal. Their car was parked on West Highland Avenue. You left your car in the East Highland parking lot behind the Starbucks and followed them on foot to their car. The rest happened exactly as you said."

Jennifer closed her eyes. A long moment passed. The sounds of the bustling ER outside the door became impossibly loud. Then Jennifer whispered, "Don't tell my husband."

Jocelyn sighed. "I won't tell him, but it will probably come out at some point. Especially if we catch these guys. That's going to be their defense—that they paid you."

Jennifer's eyes popped open, tears flowing freely. "They crucified me!"

Jocelyn gave her a grim frown. "I know. But they paid you for sex, and they will use that to their advantage. I'm not saying it's right. It is a horrible, horrible thing, especially after what they did to you. I'm just telling you that you might want to tell your husband so he's prepared for it."

Jennifer shook her head. She brought her gauze-bundled hands to her face. A dot of blood leaked through one of them. "Oh my God, this is such a nightmare."

A moment passed between them in silence. Jennifer brought her hands down and touched her fingers to the gold chain around her neck. Jocelyn could see the blood seeping through the bandage on the top of her right hand.

She met Jocelyn's eyes, her own pleading and moist. "You probably want to know why I was doing it—I'm rich. I have a beautiful home. I don't need to work. I certainly don't need to—"

Jocelyn held up a hand to silence her. "Mrs. Maisry, that's not important to me. I don't need to know why you became a prostitute." Jennifer bristled at the word, but Jocelyn went on. "My job is to find the man who put the nails into your hands and feet and arrest him so he cannot do this to anyone else. That's what I care about. That's what I am going to do."

FORTY-THREE

November 7th

Back at Northwest Detectives, Jocelyn, Kevin, Caleb, Finch, and Phil gathered in a loose semicircle around Jocelyn's desk. Patrol officers dodged in and out of the unit to deliver paperwork or discuss cases with the detectives on duty. Some of them lingered to listen to the informal powwow. Jocelyn hid her grin in a cup of coffee as Inez slid in behind Finch and made an obscene gesture behind his back.

"What do we have?" Kevin asked.

"We have mug shots out on Donovan and Warner. We have to find the third suspect, but we don't have much. We have one witness who saw his face four years ago," Jocelyn said.

Caleb nodded. "She's at a halfway house on Orthodox. I sent a couple of units to pick her up, but she was out. We'll pick her up as soon as she gets back. We put out a GRM in case she doesn't come back. We got authorizations for composite sketches."

"So as soon as we pick her up, we can get a sketch," Kevin said.

Inez nodded. "Okay, but what if you can't find this chick? Can you get Donovan and Warner to roll on this other guy?"

Jocelyn shook her head. "They won't. I already tried when I had them in for Anita Grant. Whatever this guy has on them, it's big."

Kevin looked at Phil. "Can't we hit 'em heavy with charges?"

Phil had a hangdog look. Dark circles smudged beneath his eyes. He refused to take his jacket off and scrupulously avoided Caleb's gaze. "They paid Jennifer Maisry for sex. She had sex with them. All we can hit them with is solicitation. She went with them willingly. At least with Grant they forced her into the car. We had the kidnapping charge. Here, besides the solicitation, there's not much I can do."

"They held her down," Kevin said.

Phil shrugged. "They didn't drive the nails in."

Kevin's face twisted in disgust. Jocelyn put a palm on his forearm to quell the outburst she knew was coming.

Phil held up a hand. "I can charge them with everything we've got on the books—I'm just telling you a lot of it won't hold up. Most of the charges won't make it to trial."

"Because you'll cut them a deal?" Jocelyn asked bitterly.

Phil's brow drew low over his eyes. He glared at her and opened his mouth to respond, but Caleb spoke.

"We'll need to hold a press conference," he said. His cell phone buzzed. He looked at it and frowned. "The press is already in a frenzy as it is," he added as he punched keys on the phone.

"How do they know so many details already?" Kevin said.

"Hospital staff," Inez piped in.

"Well, we need to decide how much more to give them," Phil said.

"Meaning you don't want it getting out that Jennifer Maisry was a prostitute," Jocelyn said flatly.

Phil sighed loudly. Before he could respond, Kevin asked, "Did anyone tell the husband?"

They all shook their heads. "That's not our problem," Caleb said. He went to put his phone back in his pocket, but it buzzed again. He held it in his hand and looked at each one of them. "But for our purposes, it may be best to simply omit that fact for now. The press is already going nuts over this. You add the prostitution angle, and it's even more salacious. They'll only be focused on that. Right now, we need to use them to find Warner and Donovan and our unknown suspect. We need them working for us—focusing on the crime and not the scandal."

Caleb looked at his phone again and fired off another text. "No names," Phil said. "At least for now. The Maisrys have asked that we not release Jennifer's name just yet."

"What about Anita Grant?" Kevin asked. "You gonna mention her?"

"Not by name," Jocelyn said quickly. "I want her privacy protected as well."

"I don't think we should mention her at all," Phil said.

Jocelyn glared at him. "Why? So your office doesn't look bad?"

"No," Phil said. "Because there's no sense in putting this city in a panic when these men are targeting a very specific demographic. If they think there is only one victim, the press will be less likely to cause said panic."

"They're going to find out one way or another," Jocelyn said pointedly. "They're reporters. Their job is to find shit out."

"A little panic is not the worst thing that could happen here," Caleb said. "We should warn people that they are dangerous. That might get them caught faster. However, I would not bring Anita up at this point. If they find out, then we address it, but let's not volunteer anything. I want them to have as little information as possible so we don't have to worry about them second-guessing everything we do."

There were nods of agreement. When no one spoke, Phil cleared his throat. He looked at Caleb, who was texting furiously. "You'll take point?"

Caleb met Phil's eyes, his face impassive. He held his phone up, the screen on display but too far away for Jocelyn to make out the series of text messages. "I can't. We're really close to cracking this child pornography ring. I've got to get back to the task force." He gestured toward Jocelyn. "Rush can do it. She knows the case inside and out. Plus, I'd like the public to see a female face on this one."

Phil raised a brow. "You want Rush on this?"

He said her name as though Caleb had suggested that Big Bird give the press conference. Both Caleb and Jocelyn opened their mouths to speak, but Kevin beat them to it. He stepped toward Phil, his neck thrust forward, index finger extended like he was going to poke Phil's chest. "What's your problem, Delisi?"

Phil raised both hands. "Hey, hey," he said. "Relax, Sullivan. There's no problem. Jesus." He looked around the semicircle before lowering his voice. "What? Are you fucking her too?"

For a split second, every last bit of oxygen seemed like it had been sucked out of the room. No one breathed, let alone moved. Jocelyn's face felt scorched. She looked at Caleb. He stared at Phil with unbridled anger in his eyes. She hadn't seen him look anything but affable. Well, affable and hot. This was new and surprisingly intimidating. Something brushed Jocelyn's side. She looked down to see Inez clenching and unclenching her right fist. She was like a racer raring to go, waiting for the starting shot.

Kevin, who had looked stricken for a fleeting moment, took the high road, defusing the situation. He turned back to Jocelyn, addressing her but hooking a thumb back toward Phil. "Is this guy for real?" he asked incredulously.

Jocelyn took his cue. She sighed impatiently and stepped in front of Kevin. She looked Phil right in the eye. "No one is fucking anyone. We're all here for one reason—to catch these assholes. So let's just do that. And, yes, I will be taking point on the press conference whether that suits you or not."

She looked around at the rest of her colleagues. "Let's set up downstairs."

She strode toward the stairs, Inez and Kevin close behind her. "And that, ladies and gentlemen, is how it's done," Kevin said. Inez's quiet laughter trailed them down the steps.

FORTY-FOUR

November 7th

Jocelyn stood before the bank of cameras and near-blinding lights. A cluster of microphones had been set up atop one of the tables in the lobby area. She stood behind it, her mouth dry. She licked her lips, but it didn't help. In spite of the cold November air flowing in through the open window behind her, a bead of sweat slid down her temple. The crush of bodies and lights had caused the temperature in the room to rise. They had opened as many windows as they could, but it made little difference. The only sound in the room was the rustling of bodies. Oh, and the sound of her swallowing. She wished Caleb had been able to stay. In spite of her bravado with Phil, the last thing she felt like doing was giving a press conference.

Kevin sidled up to her. "You about ready to get started?"

"Yeah," she said, the word scraping raw across her throat. "Let's go."

The room quieted. With the cameras on, their steady whirring sounded like a nest of angry hornets.

"Jocelyn Rush, Northwest Detectives," she announced. Clearing her throat, she looked around the room. "I know why you're all here. This is an ongoing investigation, so we're not at liberty to disclose details. The victim has asked that we not identify her by name. What I can tell you is that a thirty-two-year-old resident of the Chestnut Hill section of the city was assaulted by three men in the late afternoon today. Two of the suspects we believe to be Larry Warner and Angel Donovan, whose mug shots you've been given by Detective Sullivan. The third suspect is a white male, approximately five foot eleven, two hundred pounds, brown hair, and blue eyes. We are working on getting a composite. We believe that all three of these men are extremely dangerous. If you see them, do not attempt to detain them yourself. Call nine-one-one right away."

Phil, who had been standing behind her to her right, stepped forward and leaned into the bank of microphones. "That's all we have. We'll take a few questions, but then we need to get to work on this."

"Is it true the victim was a schoolteacher?" someone called from the back. Deciding that this was a question that interested all of them, the other reporters fell silent, staring at Jocelyn expectantly.

"Yes, the victim is a teacher," she confirmed.

"What school?" someone else asked.

"I can't tell you that," Jocelyn said.

Quickly trying to keep control of the situation, she pointed to a reporter from Channel Ten whose hand was raised. "Is it true that she was crucified?"

Jocelyn glanced at Kevin and Phil briefly. "The suspects took her to an unknown location—we suspect it was an abandoned house in the Northeast section of the city—where they nailed her hands and feet to the floor and sexually assaulted her."

Some of the reporters tapped away on their phones or iPads. Few looked sobered, but that didn't surprise Jocelyn at all. They were well acquainted with the myriad of violent crimes that Philadelphia had to offer.

"What information do you have on the third suspect?" someone shouted from the back.

"Just what we've told you," Jocelyn said. "As I said, we are working on getting a composite sketch. At this time, we have very little information. As soon as we know more, you'll know more."

A reporter from Channel Six who had obviously done his homework raised his hand but didn't wait for her to nod before speaking. "Is it true that Warner and Donovan are out on bail for a similar crime?"

Jocelyn cleared her throat. Another bead of sweat rolled down the side of her face. She brushed it away and met the stares of the roomful of reporters. "Yes," she said. "A month ago, they committed the same crime against a different woman—a receptionist."

"Why are we just hearing about this now?" A woman from Fox News asked, disdain dripping from every word.

Because that woman was poor and black, Jocelyn nearly blurted out. She caught herself and stared the woman down hard. For a moment, she thought the woman was angry that they'd set Warner and Donovan loose on the unsuspecting women of Philadelphia, but then she realized it was more likely about them not getting a potential story. The media thrived on scandal, just as Caleb had said. The idea that law enforcement officials had had two predators in custody and allowed them to go free to prey on a rich white woman from an affluent section of the city was just the kind of scandal they dreamed of when ratings were down.

Jocelyn sighed. "That arrest is public record," she said flatly. "Warner and Donovan were in custody, and we were actually pursuing the third suspect when they made bail."

In other words, blame the DA's office and the judge who set their bail.

A low grumble went through the room. She swore she could feel Phil's glare boring a hole in the side of her face. Before they could shout any more questions, Jocelyn held up a hand. "That's all for now," she said. "You guys have the mug shots and the number we're asking the public to call for tips." The room erupted in a cacophony of questions, but she stepped away from the podium and kept going.

FORTY-FIVE

November 8th

They met on the Stroll this time, which Larry had protested against. It was very public and out of their routine. Larry almost hadn't come, but now his and Angel's mug shots were all over the news. He had to talk to Face to find out what they should do. He really wanted to beat the shit out of the guy, mess up that pretty face that had earned him the nickname. He told Face the Chestnut Hill woman was a bad idea, but Face had insisted. He had specifically picked the ad. Larry thought they should cool it so soon after Anita Grant.

He waited inside the stairwell of an entrance to the El. He was getting ready to leave when Face strolled in. "Walk with me," he said.

"Fuck you. I could get spotted by the police out there."

Face sighed impatiently. He looked too clean for this neighborhood—black shirt and jacket, blue jeans, and black boots. He was trying to blend in, but there was something too fresh, too neat about him.

"There's a dive bar two blocks from here where no one will care who you are. Let's go."

Reluctantly, Larry followed. As promised, the bar was indeed a dive. There were five men inside—old-timers with gray hair or no hair at all. Hunched over their beers, eyes glassy, and faces puffy with drink. They spoke to each other in gravelly voices, discussing the latest loss of the Philadelphia Eagles. Three of them were black, two white. They gave Larry and Face a cursory glance and turned their eyes back to the 76ers game playing on the only television in the tiny room. Larry's living room was bigger than this place.

Face ordered two beers, which the bartender delivered without a word. Face waited for the man to meander back to the other end of the bar before he spoke. "Where's Angel?"

"Where do you think? He's hiding."

"Where are you guys staying?"

Larry shook his head. "Fuck if I'm telling you. We are really screwed this time, and that lady cop—she's got a real hard-on for you."

Face's eyes darted to Larry. "What lady cop?"

Larry rolled his eyes. "She's with Northwest. You know her. She was on TV last night. She's real pretty. Brown hair. Rush, I think her name is—she wants you real bad, and unless you do what you promised, I'm going to give the lady what she wants."

Face sighed again, feigning nonchalance. "She'll take you down too. Don't doubt that, my friend."

"I ain't your friend," Larry said. "Now, you promised me something, and I expect you to deliver."

Face turned toward him. "You know what I've never understood, Larry? That thing I promised to do for you—why don't you do it yourself?"

Larry lowered his voice to a hiss. "'Cause I'm not going down for killing a cop—even a dirty one. You said you could make it look like an accident—"

"A *retired* cop," Face corrected. "You won't go down for killing a retired cop, but you'll go down on rape, aggravated assault, conspiracy—"

Larry cut him off. "You already know I'll plead down and be out in a couple of years. Murdering a cop—any cop—is life—or death if y'all get to me first. Now I told you, we are takin' a lot of heat. What are you going to do about it?"

Face shrugged. "Nothing I can do, Larry. You're right. We're in hot water."

Larry's voice was a snarl. "No, motherfucker, me and Angel is in hot water. Unless we give you up. That last bitch—I told you she was a mistake."

Face scoffed. "She was a whore, just like all the others. Sure, she smelled nice, dressed better. She wasn't a junkie, but she was a whore just the same."

"She's rich," Larry said. "Why else would they be making such a big deal of this on the news? A rich white bitch. I told you it was a mistake."

Face smiled at Larry in a smug way that made Larry very uncomfortable. "Then why'd you do it, Larry? Why'd you pick her up and bring her to me? Why'd you fuck her, Larry?" He waited a pregnant moment, but Larry had no explanation. Face lowered his voice. "You liked that rich white whore, just like you liked that black bitch and that skinny, tattooed freak we did before her. You like it, Larry. I didn't make you do this shit. This was a good deal for you. You get sex on my dime and you get what you wanted."

"But you didn't do it," Larry pointed out.

Face's features tightened. "I tried."

"But he ain't dead, and I don't got my money back. You kill him, get me that money, and I'll go down for the white chick. I won't turn you in, but you gotta do it."

Face looked away. A long moment stretched out between them. Finally, he said, "One more job."

Agitated, Larry stood up. "Fuck you," he said. His bar stool tipped over as he headed for the door. Six pairs of eyes turned toward him. The silence in the bar was palpable.

"Sit down," Face snapped.

Larry stood at the door for a long time, weighing his options. Finally, he returned to the bar. He righted the stool with a mumbled apology to the bartender.

Face bought two more beers even though Larry's first one sat untouched. He waited a full five minutes before speaking again. "One more," he said. "Then I kill that motherfucker. As promised."

Larry slumped and finally took a sip of beer. It tasted bitter. Face pulled out a cell phone—his personal phone, not one of the throwaway prepaid phones he normally used to contact Larry. He slid his fingers across the screen, pulling up a photo. He handed the phone to Larry.

The woman hadn't known that Face was taking her picture. It was three-fourths profile in waning daylight from several feet away. She looked very familiar.

"She's on the Stroll," Face said.

Larry shook his head and handed the phone back. "She's a junkie. What do you want with her? She probably got more diseases than I got hair on my balls. I thought we weren't doing no street whores no more."

Face put an index finger over the woman's face. "She's more than that. I want her."

Larry rolled his eyes. "When?"

"Give me a few days. There's something I gotta take care of. Pick up a prepaid and text me the number. I still have minutes on the last phone. I'll pick out a place and call you when everything is ready."

"Last job," Larry reminded Face. "You do what I asked, or I turn your sorry ass in."

FORTY-SIX

November 9th

It had been two days since the press conference and what the press had dubbed the "Schoolteacher Attackers" were still on the loose. Jocelyn sat at her desk with her cell phone pressed between her ear and shoulder, sifting through her messages while she listened to Olivia recount all the things she had eaten at Martina's that evening.

"And grapes and a cup of water and a fish stick, Mommy," she said proudly.

"No soup?"

"No soup," Olivia confirmed. "Can I have stickers?"

Jocelyn smiled. "Yes, you definitely get stickers for grapes and fish sticks. I'll give them to you in the morning, okay?"

"Then I'll get my dolly?"

"Well, we'll see. You have to get all the way to the top of the chart first, remember? Remember how we talked about how you get the doll once you fill all the boxes with stickers?"

There was a pause. Jocelyn could hear *Mickey Mouse Clubhouse* playing in the background and Raquel singing. "Did I fill it up yet?" Olivia asked.

Jocelyn laughed. The chart was great, and she wanted to kiss Caleb for suggesting it. Well, she wanted to do a lot more than kiss him, but it was still a slightly difficult concept for Olivia to grasp. Caleb assured her that once they filled up the first chart and she got her reward, Olivia would get it. Until then, Jocelyn had to keep going over the logistics of the chart repeatedly.

"I don't think so, honey," she said. "We'll check it in the morning, okay?"

Jocelyn heard Raquel in the background, "Olivia, Olivia, let's play Mommy and baby."

Then Olivia's voice, the chart already forgotten. "Bye, Mommy, love you!"

"Love you too, sweetheart," Jocelyn replied, but Olivia had already hung up. No sooner had Jocelyn tossed her cell onto her desk, than it rang. She recognized Caleb's number immediately. It hadn't taken her long to memorize it. She had considered saving him as a contact, but she didn't want to jinx things.

"Hey," she answered, trying to sound professional and not giddy. She was at work, after all. "You got something on Warner and Donovan?"

There was a hesitation. She heard people talking in the background and then in what sounded like a strained voice, "No, not that."

Jocelyn frowned. "Any word on Raeann?"

"No. I—this isn't about that case," Caleb said.

Jocelyn hunched over her desk. She glanced around, but only Chen and two other detectives were there, and all three were engrossed in their own phone conversations. "What's going on?" she asked, lowering her voice.

Caleb cleared his throat. "You know that child pornography case I've been working on?"

She suppressed a groan. She had no idea where this was headed, but nothing that started with those words could be good. Her hands suddenly felt clammy. "Yeah," she said.

"I've got a suspect here. He, uh, he wants to talk to you. In fact, he will only talk to you."

"He asked for me by name?" she said, nonplussed.

"Yes. Think you can come down here?"

"Uh, sure," she said. "Caleb, what's this guy's name?"

"Whitman," he replied. "Zachary Whitman."

She recognized his name, of course. After the run-in with James Evans, she'd looked up the list of her sister's rapists to see what had become of them. She didn't recognize Whitman's face. He bore a passing resemblance to the rail-thin, longhaired boy in her yearbook. He was fatter and his brown hair was cut short, parted in the middle and brushed back into a feathered look. He wore wire-rimmed glasses, a well-kept goatee. *Very professorial*, Jocelyn thought, which was appropriate. He was now a criminology professor at the University of Pennsylvania. He had made a life of studying crime and its patterns. The irony was not lost on her.

Whitman sat alone in the interrogation room, wearing a sport jacket over a pink collared shirt. He leaned his elbows on the table, hands folded in front of him. He looked pretty serene for a man facing a slew of child pornography charges.

As Jocelyn studied him through the tiny square in the door, Caleb hovered beside her. "What've you got on him?" she asked.

"A cache of pornographic photos on his computer. It was old stuff. The photos he had have been circulating for several years. We can get these fuckers off the street, but the photos are out there. The digital age, you know? Anyway, they were all of girls—probably ten to twelve years old. Some naked, some in various sex acts. We got a couple of other guys last month, same photos. They appear to be from the same source. We're trying to track it down, but it looks like it might be overseas. ICE—Immigration and Customs Enforcement—is working on that end of things. So for now, we'll just charge the sickos and take away their computers."

Jocelyn glared through the small window, although Whitman couldn't see her. Her stomach felt weightless and hollow. She clenched and unclenched her jaw, grinding her teeth.

Caleb studied her. "You know him?"

Jocelyn nodded. "When we were teenagers, he helped gang-rape my sister."

Without waiting for Caleb's reaction, she pushed through the door.

Whitman smiled when he saw her, like she was an old friend. "Jocelyn Rush."

She kept her face impassive. "Detective Rush," she corrected.

His eyebrows rose. "Ah, yes. Detective. My apologies." Another amiable smile.

Jocelyn remained standing, arms crossed in front of her. "What do you want, Whitman?"

"Dr. Whitman."

"You're in police custody for child pornography. I'll call you whatever I want. Now, shithead. What do you want?"

Whitman sighed and looked at the table. Jocelyn noticed the dark smudges under his eyes, the sallow look beneath the glasses and facial hair.

"I'm gay, Detective."

"So, you like to jerk off to pictures of little boys instead of little girls. That still makes you a piece of shit. Why should I give a rat's ass?"

A tiny, grim smile remained on his face. He let a moment pass. Then, "In high school I got teased a lot. The other boys—they were always thinking up new ways to torture and humiliate me. They called me faggot. Before that night—"

Jocelyn stepped forward and laid a palm on the table. "Before the rape."

Whitman hung his head and averted his eyes. "Before the rape, I was an object of ridicule, a punching bag, a receptacle for all their hatred and fear."

Jocelyn exhaled noisily. "If you expect me to feel sorry for you, you're talking to the wrong person."

He met her eyes. "I was the lookout," he blurted. "I didn't even participate, but I was there. I saw—"

She had a sudden flash of Whitman's eye peering at her through a crack in the door to her sister's bedroom. *The door opened and a hand reached for her.* The image was like an uppercut to her solar plexus. She spun on her heel and turned away from the table where Whitman sat, barely suppressing the gasp that escaped her lips. This wasn't the same as the nightmares. This felt like a real memory. She paced before him. She didn't want to remain stationary and give him time to study her too closely. Her heart thumped hard in her chest. She swallowed. "You watched."

He nodded. "Yes. I watched," he said, his voice small and mournful. "After that, they treated me with respect. They treated me like one of them. When your dad came around asking questions, I ratted them all out without hesitation. They thought Camille had told, they never even suspected—"

"Is there a point to this?" Jocelyn asked impatiently, finally coming to rest before him, her composure intact.

He held her gaze, drawing each word out. "I'm sorry."

Jocelyn chuckled. "You're sorry? It's a little fucking late, Whitman. If you were that sorry, you would have confessed before the statute of limitations was up, you prick. We're finished here."

She turned to leave. He said, "I watched that night and I didn't stop it, but I have never engaged in the exchange of child pornography. Look at what they've got on me, Detective Rush. Little girls, all little girls. I'm gay and I like men, not boys. I think you know who is doing this to me, and I'd like you to ask them to back off."

She turned slowly, trying to keep her face blank. "What did you say?"

The cordial smile remained on his face. "I'm asking you to back off."

She advanced on him, coming to the table, and poked a finger at her own chest. "Me?"

He said nothing. He merely held her gaze, unwavering. "You can't change a person's sexuality," he said quietly. "Think about it. Are you gay or straight, Detective?"

Jocelyn shook her head. "Are you fucking kidding me? None of your fucking business."

"So, you're straight then."

Jocelyn remained silent, glaring at him from across the table.

"If you knew that it was illegal—harmful, even—to be with men in a sexual way, could you force yourself to become attracted to women? You might be able to put on a good show, have some superficial relationships, but your attraction to men would never go away. You can't change your sexuality."

Jocelyn said, "Again, I ask, do you have a fucking point?"

"I like men, not children. I've always been attracted to men. I'm not a pedophile."

Jocelyn rolled her eyes. "The evidence would suggest otherwise."

He raised a skeptical brow. "You and I both know that evidence was planted—"

She put a hand on her hip. "You think I *planted* child pornography in your home? You really are a sick fuck."

"How do you explain it, then?"

"Explain what?"

"There were five of us. One dead. One in prison. Of the three that remained, all of us were charged with child pornography in the last year—the worst possible thing to be accused of—even if we're exonerated, we'll carry a stigma for the rest of our lives. It didn't start until your father died. Our deal was with him—we paid and he didn't prosecute. He's dead, and the statute has run. Now the rest of us are accused of these awful crimes. Do you really think that's a coincidence?"

Jocelyn shrugged noncommittally. "You're all rapists. *That's* not a coincidence. I don't think it's a stretch that you're all perverts too."

"What about the crane? I talked to Michael. A few months before he was arrested—before he killed himself—he found one in his home. It was on top of his computer monitor. There was no sign of a break-in. Nothing was disturbed, but a crane was left for him. Just like me. And James—he was arrested last week. He found a crane on top of his home computer just a few weeks ago."

Cold crept up Jocelyn's limbs. "Did you leave the crane in my car?"

Whitman smiled. "Henry did. I couldn't get the hang of folding them, but he picked it right up. It wasn't as good as the one I got, but I think he made his point."

"Henry Richards? You sent him?"

"I asked him to give you the cranes. He had followed you for a few days, figured out where you went on a routine basis so he could wait for you. He was just supposed to leave it for you. I didn't ask him to steal your car. But I guess you took care of that."

"My daughter was in the backseat."

"I'm sorry about that. I doubt he would have hurt her. Henry can be impulsive, but he's not violent."

She wanted to scream at him. She wanted to lunge across the table and rip his throat out, but the cop in her had taken over. Calm, cool, trying to get to the truth.

"Are you lovers?"

Whitman's eyes dropped to his lap. "Henry is a prostitute. Yes, we are lovers but only because I pay him. I had hoped it would develop into more—I offered to pay for rehab, for him to go to college if he wanted to, but he always turns me down. I try to help him out when I can."

"You're in love with him."

Whitman nodded, the skin on his face tightening into a grimace, as if it physically hurt him to admit it. "I just wanted to send you a message. Ask you to back off."

"You couldn't call me on the phone?"

Whitman looked at her again, one eyebrow raised. "You couldn't call *me* on the phone before you decided to ruin my life? Even if I am exonerated, these charges will ruin my reputation. My job is as good as gone, tenure or no tenure."

"You really think I did this to you?"

"Then who else? When I talked to James, he told me about your . . . encounter."

Jocelyn winced.

Whitman went on. "Who else would do this to us?"

She knew the answer to that, but she'd never admit it to Whitman.

"What do you want from me?" she asked.

"Your help."

Jocelyn rolled her eyes. "You've got to be kidding me."

He kept his gaze on her. "I'm a lot of things, but a pedophile is not one of them. I think this is happening because of you, and I think you're the only person who can stop it."

Jocelyn stared at the man—her sense of fairness warring with her baser need for revenge. She swallowed. "What goes around comes around, shithead," she said and strode toward the door.

"I can help you."

Jocelyn turned back, hand on the doorknob. She couldn't suppress her incredulous laughter. "This ought to be rich," she muttered to herself before addressing him. "Help me? Really? With what?"

Whitman folded his hands on the table. "With the case you're working on. The rape. I saw you on the news."

"You rapists belong to some kind of support group or something? What are you telling me? You know the guys I'm looking for?"

Whitman shook his head. "No. I don't. You said you have very little information on the unknown suspect."

"So?"

"You had the other guys in custody before—they didn't give you anything?"

Jocelyn rolled her eyes again. "If you think I'm going to discuss the details of an open investigation with you, you're fucking crazy."

Whitman nodded, conceding her point. "Okay," he said. "But it's a crucifixion, right?" She stared at him as though he had completely lost his mind. He forged ahead. "A few years after the rape, your father defended that kid from Society Hill. He was seventeen, I think—old enough to be tried as an adult. He was accused of killing his mother and crucifying her. Turned out two men did it. Her husband had left her for a younger woman. She kept the son. She had a generous amount for child support but not enough to support her habit—she was a drug addict. She started prostituting herself for drugs. The son, he saw most of it. He even got into it with a couple of her dealers. Then one day, one of her trysts went a little too far."

"What does this have to do with anything?"

"The men—they crucified her and the son saw it. Of course, no one believed him when he said it was two black men. They thought he was making it up—typical rich white racist. Your dad's investigators found the men—got one to turn on the other. They said that the son watched them and didn't try to stop them. They said the kid was aroused."

He paused, staring at her face, waiting for some sort of reaction, but she gave him none.

"It's about the fantasy," he continued patiently. She imagined this was the same tone he used to give lectures. "The son developed some sort of paraphilia—his sexual arousal is triggered by something atypical, something others would consider extreme. In this case, I believe it is the mutilation and humiliation that gratifies him sexually. He is attempting to re-create the fantasy. Tell me, does the third subject in your case participate in the crime? Sexually? Or does he only participate in the crucifixion?"

Jocelyn tried not to show her shock at how close Whitman had come. She didn't answer his question. Taking a page from the book of just about every suspect she'd ever interrogated, she asked her own question instead. "You think this is the only crucifixion case to come down the pike? Happens more than you think."

"But this is so similar—a wealthy woman, two black men. The third man, the white man, he doesn't participate, does he?"

Jocelyn stared at him, silently hoping her face didn't betray her.

"As I said, it's about the fantasy," he went on when he realized she was not going to answer his question. "These women are surrogates for his mother. He's replaying the scenario over and over again for sexual gratification. None of his victims were prostitutes?"

Jocelyn sighed. "I'm not doing this Hannibal Lecter shit with you. Either you give me a name or I'm out of here."

"I don't know his name. It wasn't released. Your dad fought hard for that."

Jocelyn grasped the doorknob again. "Then we have nothing to talk about. I should not have even wasted this much time on you."

She opened the door to the interrogation room. For the first time, his eyes widened and moistened with desperation. He stretched his upper body, leaning toward her. "Detective, please," he called. "Please."

She turned her back on him and walked out of the room.

FORTY-SEVEN

November 9th

Raeann Church walked up and down Orthodox Street, pulling her hoodie over her head and shrugging it off again. It was dark, although the street was well lit, and a few other people made their way along the sidewalk. Her feet were freezing. The sneakers she'd gotten from the donated clothes at the halfway house were tight on her feet. She didn't have any socks. And she was starving.

She didn't want to go back. She'd spent a few days on the street, thinking that anything could be better than the house on Orthodox. She hated that place. It smelled like mildew, and the paint peeled off the walls in every room. She'd been in rent-by-the-hour motels that were cleaner and better smelling. The food there wasn't much better. But after three nights in the cold, it was looking nicer and nicer. Of course, she'd really have it coming to her, having gone AWOL for three days. But she could take her punishment in a warm place with a full belly.

As she neared the corner of Orthodox and Tacony, the smell of hot food drifted out of Angelina's Pizzeria. Pizza. Cheesesteaks. French Fries, maybe. What she wouldn't do for a big, extra-cheesy piece of pizza. Her mouth watered. She stopped before she reached the door. She couldn't bear to look in there and see what she couldn't have.

She dug inside the pockets of her hoodie and pulled out seventy-eight cents and three bus tokens. Not enough for pizza. Not enough for a soda. At least she still had a few smokes left from the cops that had come to see her last week. She pulled out the crushed pack of reds. There were two left. No lighter. She turned back and walked toward the Melrose Pub. A few guys stood outside smoking. Two of them looked like they were in their twenties. Their skin was thick and deeply bronzed, arms covered in faded-color tattoos. *Roofers*, she thought. *Or landscapers*. The third guy was older with a large paunch and a trucker hat pulled low over his brow. He eyed her as she walked up to them. She didn't like what she saw, so she ignored him and approached the younger men. "Can I get a light?" she asked.

Wordlessly, they each offered their lighters. She took the one closest to her and lit her cigarette. "Thanks."

"No problem," the guy said. He gave her a slight smile and turned back to his friend. They began discussing the Philadelphia Eagles in earnest. Raeann drifted away from them and leaned against the side of the building. She was wondering if she could get one of them to buy her a pizza when the shadow of the third, older man fell across her feet.

"Hey, girl," he said. Girl. Of course. He was already making her smaller, reducing her, letting her know that he would talk to her—he'd probably even fuck her—but he'd treat her as if she were less than.

Raeann ignored him, turning her head and looking down the street as if she were waiting for someone. He stepped closer, his body blotting out the glow of the streetlight. He stunk like beer. Too much beer. "I ain't seen you around here before," he said.

She met his eyes, thrust her chin up at him defiantly. "'Cause I ain't been around here and I ain't staying."

He laughed softly and stepped closer to her. "Relax, girl," he said, his voice smooth and low. The roofers were too engrossed in their conversation to overhear him. Raeann shot a glance at them. Soon they'd be finished with their cigarettes and they would go back inside. She had to get away from this creep before they left her alone with him.

"You workin'?" the man asked, his beer breath hot on her face.

She blew smoke back into his face. "Not right now," she said pointedly. She shifted away, sliding against the concrete wall, her hoodie catching on the uneven paint job.

He caught her arm, wrapping his fingers around her biceps. She pulled away. "What the fuck?" she said loudly.

The roofers, who were partway through the bar door, stopped and looked back at them. "Everything okay?" one of them called.

The creep pulled back and put both hands up, as if in surrender. A small smile played on his lips, sending a chill straight up Raeann's spine. "Everything's fine," he said. "Just fine."

While the creep was focused on the roofers, she turned on her heel and strode away from the bar, trying to keep a brisk pace without actually running. When she reached the corner, she looked back toward the Melrose, but all three men were gone.

She sighed. Her stomach growled loudly. So much for pizza.

"Hey," a man's voice called. She looked toward the street. A black Lexus had pulled over, the passenger's side window rolled down. Cautiously, she approached.

"You okay?" the man asked.

Raeann leaned down and peered inside the car. It was too dark to see his face well, but she could make out a smile and the glint of his eyes. She glanced over her shoulder. The sidewalk was still empty. "Yeah," she said. "I just—I was just having a smoke is all."

The man motioned over his shoulder, toward the Melrose. "Those guys bothering you?"

Raeann swallowed. What could she say? The older guy made her skin crawl and touched her arm? That wasn't really bothersome in most people's books. She shook her head. "No. Just bumming a lighter."

Again, her stomach growled. She was glad it was relatively dark and he couldn't see her face flush. "You hungry?" he said.

"No, no, I just—"

"It's okay," he said. "Look, I just pulled over because I saw you hauling ass away from that bar. You looked spooked. If you're hungry, I can drop you off at the pizza place down the street."

She shifted uncomfortably. "Thanks, but I don't got no money."

A ten-dollar bill appeared from the darkness. He held it out to her, across the passenger's side seat. The heavy, silver watch on his wrist gleamed in the light cast by the streetlights overhead. She could just make out the MK on it. Expensive. Like his car.

Her insides twisted. Here it was. In her world, nothing was free. Nothing was without a price. There was no kindness. A rich man in a fancy car didn't stop a woman like her on the street to come to her aid. There was really only one reason a man like him would stop for a woman like her. She wondered what he was going to ask her to do, and if she would do it for ten dollars. It wouldn't be the first time, but she was trying to clean up.

Sensing her hesitation, he placed the bill on the seat next to him. "It's okay," he said. "I don't want anything. I'm just trying to be nice."

She smiled weakly and thrust her hands into her hoodie pockets. "Nobody's nice."

"I'm sorry you feel that way."

There was a long moment of silence. Raeann listened to the sounds of cars driving up and down Orthodox.

"Okay," he said. "I'll get going. Take care of yourself."

He shifted the car into Drive. Raeann's heart leapt into her throat. She was so damn hungry. So what if he did want something from her? It couldn't be anything worse than the things she'd done for ten dollars in the past. She clapped her hands onto the passenger's side windowsill. "Wait," she croaked. "Okay, okay. I really am hungry. Angelina's is right back there."

He flipped the locks up. "Hop in."

She slid into the seat and pulled the door closed. "Thank you so much," she said as he pulled away. Immediately, she felt warmth beneath her. Heated seats. Maybe she wouldn't have to go back to the halfway house tonight. "I really appreciate this," she added.

"No problem," he replied. He looked over at her and smiled. As they passed under a streetlight she could see his face plainly. Her breath froze in her body. She tried to move air in and out of her lungs, but her body wouldn't cooperate. Her mouth was so dry it felt as if it were full of cotton. In her lap, her hands trembled violently.

Before his fist made contact with her face, she had time for two words. "It's you."

FORTY-EIGHT

November 9th

Simon answered on the third ring.

"I just talked to Zachary Whitman," Jocelyn said without preamble.

Hesitation. So he recognized the name. She kicked her foot lightly against the wall outside the bank of SVU's interrogation rooms. She glanced up and down the hall. It was blessedly empty except for Caleb, who stood several feet away, signing off on a report for one of his detectives. She had confirmed James Evans's arrest with him as soon as she'd emerged from talking with Whitman. Thankfully, he didn't ask her for details about the "encounter" Whitman had mentioned.

"How long have you known about the rape?" Jocelyn asked.

Simon sighed. She pictured his brow wrinkling, the vertical line appearing over the bridge of his nose. "Your mother came to me a few years after it happened. You had already left Princeton to join the academy. Jocelyn, please come to my office. We need to talk about this."

"Zachary Whitman is being charged with multiple counts of child pornography. James Evans has been charged as well, and

Michael Pearce was arrested and charged for exactly the same things right before he killed himself. Do you know anything about that?"

A long silence. Then, "Are you asking me as my niece or as a cop?"

Jocelyn's heart raced, her stomach dropping to her feet. She closed her eyes for a moment, trying to stay focused. "Well, that answers my question," she murmured.

"Jocelyn, if you come see me we can talk about"—he hesitated—"things."

He was arguably the best defense attorney in the city. He wasn't going to say anything to incriminate himself, even to her.

"We'll talk about that later. First, I need something from you. My father defended a juvenile about seventeen years ago. He was accused of crucifying and strangling his mother. They lived in Society Hill. He was exonerated. It turned out two drug dealers did it. Ring a bell?"

"No, but that was a long time ago, your father's case. We've had a lot of cases over the years. I'd have to look through our files, if they even go back that far."

"I need the name of the kid."

"Jocelyn, unless you have a warrant or a court order—"

She snorted. "Really? You want to talk to me about the law? You? After I just got done talking to Zachary Whitman? His prostitute lover carjacked me and accosted me in the Wawa. Olivia was in danger twice because a crane appeared at his house a few months ago."

Silence.

"You get me the name. Then we'll talk about 'things.'"

She hung up.

Caleb watched her. He approached her slowly, as if he was afraid she might lash out. He wasn't far off. She wanted to put her fist through a wall. She concentrated on keeping her hands still and on her breathing, like she had learned in anger management.

"So this guy is saying you planted evidence of child pornography on his computer to get revenge on him for raping your sister?"

Jocelyn rubbed her temples with her fingers in a futile attempt to stave off the headache she felt coming on. "He's saying someone planted evidence and, yes, he thinks it's because of the rape since the other living, nonincarcerated rapists also went down on child porn charges."

Caleb regarded her steadily. "You think your uncle did it?"

Jocelyn dropped her hands to her sides and shrugged. "If Whitman is telling the truth—he's innocent and someone planted evidence—then it would have to be Simon. My sister is a junkie. She can't think past her next score, let alone hatch an elaborate plot to frame these guys for child porn. That only leaves Simon. He certainly has the resources to do it. He wouldn't do it himself, obviously. He'd hire someone—probably someone he defended. I'm sure he's defended his share of burglars."

Caleb grimaced. "If Whitman is innocent—"

Jocelyn held up a hand to silence him. Her head pounded. "I know, I know. I'm not going to protect Simon, if that's what you're worried about. If he framed those men, he needs to be held accountable—even if they deserve to go to prison. My parents gave them a pass nineteen years ago. Nothing will change that."

Caleb touched her cheek briefly—a furtive movement, dropping his hand before any passing detectives could see. She looked into his eyes.

"I can see why you didn't go to their funeral," he said softly.

Her throat felt hot and thick. She didn't speak.

Finally, Caleb said, "You really think this old case has to do with the Maisry and Grant cases?"

"I have no idea, but at this point we've got nothing more to go on."

"But even if you get a name we'd have to connect it to the case."

Again, she shrugged. "Then we will. Look, we've got less than nothing on this guy. Raeann Church, the only person besides Donovan and Warner to see his face, is missing. We haven't picked up Warner and Donovan, but even when we do, they are not rolling on this guy. I will see what I can dig up. Anything I find, I'll turn over to you."

Caleb tried a smile, but it turned into a grimace. He motioned toward the interrogation room, where Whitman still sat. "I'm sorry," he said. "I had no idea. I didn't—"

She shook her head and smiled sadly. "It's okay. How could you have known? It's not something I tell many people. It's not something that usually comes up."

Caleb laughed nervously. "I guess not."

He glanced up and down the hall before leaning into her, one hand against the wall above her head. She lifted her face to his, concentrating on his laugh lines and his wide mouth. His lips hovered near hers. "I'd really like to see you again," he said. "In a way that is completely unrelated to these cases."

"Me too," she said. "Me too."

FORTY-NINE

November 12th

Camille tucked the man's money into her bra and stared at the floor. She winced as a cramp worked its way through her lower abdomen. Her feet dangled over the edge of the bed. She swung them back and forth over top of a carpet that was about two hundred different shades of brown, breathing through her mouth as the cramp eased. The carpet looked like it had been an entirely different color at some point, maybe when the motel first opened. Orange maybe. She tried not to wonder what the wet spot near the door was from.

She lit a cigarette and listened to the sounds of the man leaving. The rustle of his shirt, the shushing sound of pants being pulled up. Buckle. Zipper. Feet sliding into shoes. A heavy jacket shrugged over shoulders. Then, the exquisite sound of the door closing.

"Ahhh," she sighed. Alone at last.

Camille pulled her purse out from under the bed where she'd stuffed it and pulled out her pipe, which was wrapped in an old tank top. The meth was at the bottom of the bag. Her lighter had just flicked to life, the tiny flame licking the bottom of her pipe, when the door to the room swung open. She jumped up and turned to see a short Asian man in the doorway. He wore black slacks and a white button-down shirt. A thick shock of black hair fell across his forehead. "You," he said, waving his hand at her. "You go. Time up. You go."

Camille groaned and looked at the bedside clock. She had at least fifteen more minutes. "Come on, man," she complained. "We paid for the whole hour. I don't feel good. Give me a break."

The man shook his head. "Hour over," he insisted. He waited in the doorway, staring at her expectantly. She sighed and wrapped her pipe back up, dropping it into her bag. "Fine," she huffed as she walked past him. "But you owe me fifteen minutes."

The November air stung her face. She pulled her coat tighter around her and fumbled with the zipper. By the time she reached Kensington Avenue, a fine sheen of sweat had broken out over her forehead. Her entire body felt hot and weak, like she hadn't eaten in days. She'd eaten just a few hours ago, though, and soon that threatened to come back up. Squatting down in front of a pawnshop, she rested her face in her hands and waited for it to pass. She peeled her coat off, relishing the frigid air until she got the chills and pulled it back on.

When she felt steadier, she stood and lit a cigarette. She leaned her head back against the pawnshop window. Another cramp seized her abdomen. She hugged herself with one arm and clenched her jaw, waiting for it to stop. They'd been coming for a couple of days now. It wasn't her period—those cramps didn't feel quite this bad and were not usually accompanied by such drastic bouts of hot and cold. She had something. She was hoping it was just a virus, and she'd feel better in a few days. Camille didn't feel like dealing with any doctors. They were so judgmental. Who needed that? She'd promised herself she'd call Uncle Simon if it got much worse.

Camille checked her funds. She had enough money for the night. Probably enough meth to make it till the morning, but she was cold as hell and she felt like shit. She wanted a warm place, somewhere she could lay down for a while. The place she usually stayed was out of the question, at least for tonight. Her friend's pimp had taken up residence there while Camille was in jail. The last thing she needed to deal with right now was that asshole. She worked for herself, and, judging by her friend's scars, he wasn't the type to take no for an answer.

If she earned a little more, she might be able to rent a room just for herself. Or she could try to find some dates who would take her to a motel. They were usually good for an hour or two if she was lucky. Of course, she wasn't going back to the shithole she'd just been kicked out of fifteen minutes early.

She smoked two more cigarettes, praying the cramps and sweats would hold off for a while. She made a quick ten bucks with a teenage boy in a nearby alley. Then an old guy in a sedan. He didn't last long, and she was back out in the cold. She waited out another cramp and walked up and down the avenue with achy feet. Then a gray four-door with two men in it pulled up. The older one was driving. Beside him was a mountain of flab.

"You workin'?" the driver asked.

She smiled. "Maybe. You got somewhere to go?"

He shrugged. His friend looked straight ahead, seemingly disinterested. "Sure," the man said. He looked behind her, then back to her face. "It would be both of us."

"Sure," Camille said.

"How much?"

"Fifty."

He nodded. "Get in."

She got in the back and they pulled away. The inside of the car was worn and smelled like fried food. A spring in the seat beneath her poked her thigh. They drove down the Stroll a few blocks and then he turned onto a cross street.

"Mind if I smoke?" Camille asked.

"Nah," the driver said. "Just open the window."

She put it down a few inches and lit up. She sucked the smoke into her lungs and blew it out through the cracked window, watching the blocks whip past. They were getting pretty far away from her usual working area. Camille tapped the driver's headrest. "Hey," she said. "Where the hell are we going?"

"It's not far," he said, but the next block he drove down was dotted with condemned houses. They stopped in front of a large three-story that seemed to list to the left. It was red brick and crumbling. The second-story windows had long since lost their glass. Their frames stretched open to the elements. A tree branch poked out of one of them. The first-floor windows were boarded up, as was the front door. The porch bowed in a V shape.

"I thought you had somewhere to go," Camille said.

She'd done it in crack houses in worse shape than this one, but this place didn't look like it could keep out the cold, and that was the whole point. She wanted an hour or so of warmth and maybe the comfort of a bed. She shook her head and threw her cigarette butt out the window slit. "Look," she said. "I'm not doin' it in the cold, so let's just do it in the car."

She pulled her jeans down. "Who's going first?"

They looked at each other, and it was only when the big one got out of the car without uttering a word that she realized something was wrong. Despite having spent more than fifteen years on the street, Camille's instincts weren't the greatest. All those years of drug addiction, homelessness, arrests, getting stiffed by johns and rolled on by other girls had not served her well in terms of sensing dangerous situations. Other girls had the natural street savvy that Camille had been after her entire life. As always, the realization came too late for her to do much about the impending danger.

When the big one opened the back door and reached in for her, she bolted out the other door, hitching her jeans up as she ran. A car door slammed, and she heard the sound of feet slapping pavement behind her. It had to be the older one; she couldn't imagine the fat one running that fast. She didn't look back. Before she could get a good lead on the guy, a cramp seized her, starting out as a band across her pelvis and wrapping around to her back beneath her rib cage. Her knees hit the pavement hard, her breath coming in gasps. She swayed from side to side, trying to will the pain away. Fever enveloped her entire body. The sweats came on in a matter of seconds.

Get up. She had to get up.

An arm looped around her waist and picked her up. An involuntary scream escaped her. It felt as if someone were slicing through her insides and him jostling her didn't help. She flailed, kicking but finding only air. Swinging her bag behind her, she tried to make contact with something. He clasped her back to his chest and carried her back toward the house. The fat one met them halfway and lifted her out of the older one's arms like she was a grocery bag. In spite of several kicks to his fleshy stomach, he slung her over his shoulder as if she weighed nothing.

The cramping began to ease. Fat drops of sweat poured from her face onto his T-shirt. She pounded on his back and tried to elbow the back of his head. "You fuckers!" she shrieked. He carried her around to the back of the house. As they passed through the back door, she grabbed on to the door frame and held on as tightly as she could. Splinters dug into her fingers, but that pain registered as little more than an annoyance.

The older one walked up behind them and peeled her fingers one by one. "You son of a bitch," she snarled. She got a wild punch in on him before the fat one carried her into the bowels of the house. Her cries echoed off the crumbling barren walls. They came to a room that was lit by some kind of large flashlight. It cast strange, misshapen shadows on the walls. The place smelled like piss.

"This one's wild," the older one said.

The sound of laughter stilled her momentarily. She looked around for its source. A figure emerged from the shadows on her left clothed in all black from head to toe—even a ski mask. For a moment, he looked like just a pair of disembodied eyes and a floating mouth. He smiled beneath the mask, revealing perfectly straight white teeth. "She won't be when we're finished with her," he said.

That was when she saw the hammer dangling from his right hand.

FIFTY

November 12th

Kelly Drive was a four-mile stretch that snaked its way alongside the Schuylkill River between Jocelyn's neighborhood and the heart of the city. It was two lanes in either direction with no shoulders and absolutely no room for error. Every time Jocelyn drove it, she felt as though she were playing chicken with the cars coming in the opposite direction. Aside from that, it was a beautiful ride. "The Drive," as locals referred to it, was sandwiched between a lush, hilly, forested area and the riverbank, which was lined with manicured grass and dotted with statues and sculptures. The hilly side of the Drive skirted around some of the less savory neighborhoods in the city.

In true Philadelphia fashion, jogging along the open space next to the river you were relatively safe—at least in broad daylight—but if you went a quarter mile up one of those hills, you would find yourself on dangerous ground. The Drive terminated at the rear of the Philadelphia Museum of Art, which sat next to Philadelphia's famous boathouse row. When the drive wasn't clogged with Regatta traffic, joggers and cyclists frequented the path beside the river year-round. In the summers, people went fishing or had picnics along the riverbank. About six or seven times a year, someone drove his or her car into the water. Slightly less frequently, bodies had to be fished out of the river, like the one the Philadelphia Police Department's Marine Unit had fished out of the Schuylkill before Jocelyn and Kevin pulled up.

She found a space in one of the parking areas the city had cut along the riverbank, behind a large cluster of police cars, most of which sat haphazardly in the grass along the bank.

"How many police officers does it take to pull someone out of the river?" Kevin said. "Jesus, did they leave anybody to patrol the rest of the city?"

Jocelyn counted the vehicles. There were twelve and twice as many officers gathered alongside the riverbank. "Guess we'll find out," she said.

"You know," Kevin said. "Last time I checked, we weren't homicide."

Jocelyn shot him an acerbic look, her left eyebrow arched. "Caleb said it was important."

Kevin put a hand to his chest and batted his eyelashes. In a faux breathy voice, he said, "Oh, Caleb."

Jocelyn flipped him off as she climbed out of the car, hoping he wouldn't notice the blush that rose to her face.

"He's not homicide either," Kevin called from across the top of the car.

Jocelyn had a bad feeling about this. A very bad feeling. She and Kevin had been out looking for a place to score some dinner after an armed robbery call when Caleb called her and told her she needed to get down to the Drive right away. She didn't know if it was related to the child pornography case involving her sister's rapists or the "Schoolteacher Attackers." Either way, it would be unpleasant. The wind whipped around them fiercely, nearly causing her to stumble and making the balmy forty-degree day feel more like twenty degrees. The three news helicopters circling overhead didn't help. She and Kevin walked shoulder to shoulder toward the cluster of police personnel, keeping their heads down.

Some of the Marine Unit guys were erecting a pop-up tent at the very edge of the bank so the news helicopters wouldn't be able to get a high-definition shot of whoever they had pulled out of the water before the police could even identify them. It was a three- to four-foot drop-off from the wall at the edge of the bank to the water. A small boat bobbed along the bank, a diver swimming alongside it, hanging on to the outermost edge of the vessel. A larger police boat idled about thirty feet from the shore.

Jocelyn and Kevin shouldered their way to the edge, beneath the tent, where Caleb stood, a yellow transfer flat at his feet, the body inside limp and motionless. He turned toward them as they approached. "Sullivan," Caleb said, nodding at Kevin. He met Jocelyn's eyes and smiled. She resisted the urge to touch him in greeting. She felt a small tick of anxiety when she noticed that his smile didn't reach his eyes.

"What's going on?" she said.

He motioned to the body at their feet. "I think we found Raeann Church."

It was like a sharp punch to her gut. For a moment, she couldn't quite breathe. Then her words came out on a heavy exhale. "Son of a bitch."

"Are you kidding me?" Kevin said.

Jocelyn dropped to her knees beside the mummified body and watched as one of the Marine Unit guys carefully pulled the flat away from the head of the body. The woman's face was bloated and pale like the belly of a fish. The skin beneath her left eye was marred by a large purple bruise. Her brown hair was frayed and even stringier than when Jocelyn had met her. "No," Jocelyn said.

The medical examiner knelt on the other side, hands gloved. He pushed her hair away from her neck and adjusted her chin so that Jocelyn could see the finger-size bruises mottling her throat.

"Strangled," Kevin said.

Jocelyn nodded and took his hand as he helped her stand. She met Caleb's eyes. His face contorted as if he were in pain. "That's definitely her."

"Yeah," Jocelyn agreed, her voice throaty.

The sound of digitized music drew her gaze toward Kevin. He slipped his cell phone out of his pocket and glanced at it.

"That's new. Is that the theme to *The A-Team*?" she asked.

He smiled at her briefly in response and touched the screen with his index finger to answer. He turned and walked a few steps away as he talked. The conversation lasted less than a minute, and when he turned back to her, his face was the color of ash. His forehead creased. He stared at her until a shiver ran down her spine.

"What? What is it?"

He tried to speak and failed. He cleared his throat and tried again. "That was Kim—Nurse Bottinger. It's Camille." He looked down at the body, and when he looked back up at her, Jocelyn swore she saw a sheen of tears filming his eyes.

Panic rose inside her chest, making it feel tight. She had been freezing since she stepped out of the car, but now her whole body felt white-hot. Sweat broke out along her forehead. Had her sister finally overdosed?

"What happened to Camille, Kevin?" she asked, her voice far calmer than she felt. Caleb stepped toward her, not touching her but close enough that she could have leaned into him. She wanted to lean into him and close her eyes. Disappear into his warmth. Whatever it was, she didn't want to hear it. She didn't want to know it. She didn't want it to be.

"She's at Einstein," Kevin said. "They got her—Warner, Donovan, and the third guy. They got her."

FIFTY-ONE

November 12th

Caleb stayed at the scene, promising to follow up with Camille personally once he had wrapped things up there. Kevin hadn't stopped babbling since they got back into the car. As Nurse Bottinger guided them through Einstein's ER once more, he kept talking, although only part of what he said penetrated the haze that had fallen over Jocelyn's mind.

"This doesn't make sense," Kevin said. "They're going backwards. They started with girls on the street and moved on to online ads. Camille is a street hooker. No offense, Rush, but she's no Jennifer Maisry. Why would they go back to picking up street girls?"

Jocelyn ignored him. Kim stopped in front of a curtain. "She's in there."

The silence made Jocelyn cold from the tip of her nose to her fingertips. Grant and Maisry had both cried—howled and whimpered like wounded animals. Camille was silent. Kevin paced in front of the curtain. Jocelyn pulled it back slightly and stepped through, her heart thumping loudly in her chest. Her sister lay on the hospital bed, her bandaged feet elevated on pillows and her hands, similarly bandaged, also resting on pillows at her sides. An IV dripped clear fluid into her right arm. She wore a hospital gown stained with droplets of blood. Her eyes were closed, her breathing even. For a split second, she looked just like their mother. But as Jocelyn got closer, there was no mistaking her gaunt, jaundiced look. The scars left by needles in the crooks of her arms and the sharp lines of her collarbones jutting through the thin gown.

Jocelyn stepped toward the bed and placed a hand on Camille's forearm. It was white-hot.

Kim stepped in behind Jocelyn to check the IV. "It was really tough finding a vein on her," she remarked. "She has a kidney infection. That's why she has a fever. She's probably had it for a while now—she's almost septic. That's not from the assault obviously, but we're giving her IV antibiotics and fluids. She's very dehydrated. We gave her morphine for the pain. The shape she's in, I don't know how lucid she'll be. We already took the rape kit."

Kim left. Jocelyn kept her hand on Camille's arm, trying to stem the tide of tears threatening to overcome her. It wasn't working. As the first sob worked its way up her windpipe, Jocelyn wiped away a few tears.

"Oh, Camille," she cried softly.

With a moan, Camille awoke, turning her head from side to side. She opened her eyes and saw Jocelyn. She blinked several times before smiling weakly.

"Camille," Jocelyn said, her voice cracking.

Camille shifted, wincing in pain. "Are you crying?"

Jocelyn nodded. She wiped her nose with the back of her hand. She pulled a chair over and sat in it.

"You never cry. Even when we were kids you hardly ever cried," Camille said. Her voice was slow and thick, as though it took great effort to speak. Then abruptly, she drew a sharp breath and closed her eyes, face reddening considerably.

"Camille?"

"Just pain," Camille gasped. "It'll pass."

A few minutes later it did, the tension in Camille's face softening, her color returning to its normal shade. Jocelyn thought she had fallen asleep, but then she spoke, her voice weak and wavering. "They told you what happened? What those men did to me?"

Jocelyn swallowed, biting back more tears. "Yes," she said. "Camille, I'm so sorry."

"No . . . don't be," Camille said. She didn't speak for several seconds. Jocelyn expected her to start snoring. Then she said, "I'm sorry too."

Jocelyn bit her lip. "What are you sorry for?"

Without opening her eyes, Camille waved one of her bandaged hands. "I'm sorry that . . . that this is how I turned out."

"Camille."

She was silent again. A single tear slid from one of her eyelids and trailed down her cheek. Her speech was beginning to slur. Jocelyn didn't think she would be alert much longer. She had to lean in close to hear Camille's next words. "I want to be done with this," she murmured. "Done with this life . . . the drugs . . . the men. All of it."

Jocelyn smoothed her hair away from her forehead. "You can be, Camille. I'll help you."

Camille shook her head from side to side very slowly, stopping midturn as though she had drifted off. But then she said, "No, you . . . won't. You're always so . . . so angry . . . with me."

Jocelyn smiled through her tears, realizing that in that moment, for the first time in nineteen years she was not angry with Camille. She was tired of being angry. Where had it gotten her? Where had her anger gotten Camille? Who was she really angry with? Camille for folding when their father brushed the rape under the carpet? For her becoming addicted to drugs? Was she angry with herself because she couldn't remember what she had seen and therefore couldn't help Camille? They had been teenagers—kids still. How could they have been expected to take on a world of adults who were prepared to act as though the heinous crime had never happened at all? It was their parents she was really angry with, and they were gone. Her rage lived on, but it had never done either one of them any good.

"I want to be done with that," Jocelyn said.

She stroked Camille's hair until her sister started to snore lightly. Jocelyn pulled her chair up closer to the bed and sat by Camille's side. After several minutes, Camille jerked awake, her face red and contorted in pain, her body folding in on itself. Her breath was labored. Jocelyn stood and squeezed her bicep. "You okay?"

Camille nodded. "Cramps."

As the pain eased, so did the tension in her body. She relaxed against the pillow, her face paling once more. "Sit," she said to Jocelyn. "Sit down and tell me something good."

"Okay," Jocelyn replied, easing back into her chair. She thought for a moment. Then, "Your half of our inheritance is eight million dollars."

Camille's eyes widened. For just a moment, she looked awake, lucid. "What?" she croaked.

"Yeah." Jocelyn smiled. "And if you spend it on drugs, I'll fucking kill you."

Camille met her eyes. Her shoulders shook. At first Jocelyn thought she was crying. She reached out to her sister. "I'm sorry," she said. "That was a joke. I mean, I don't want you to spend it on drugs, but I was trying to—"

Laughter spilled out of Camille's prone form. Her smile looked pained, but it was there. "I know," Camille spluttered. "I know you were joking. It's okay." Once the laughter subsided, she looked back at Jocelyn. Again, she fought to keep her eyes open.

"You don't have to stay awake," Jocelyn said. "I'll stay here. I'll sit with you as long as I can."

Camille nodded. As she drifted back to her morphine-induced slumber, she mumbled, "We'll be okay now. It's . . . it's . . . over. Everything will be . . . okay."

An hour later, Jocelyn found Kevin lingering at the nurses' station. He looked at her the way he looked at child victims. She held a hand up in his direction. "Don't do the pity thing."

He inched his way over to her, his phone held in his outstretched hand. "I called Inez," he said. "She's on a call, but she said she would text you when she's done."

Jocelyn pulled her phone out of her pocket. There were three missed calls from Caleb, one from Inez, and two texts from Inez. She pulled up the text messages from Inez from five minutes earlier.

Kevin told me what's going on. Call me.

I have to go home for an hour. Meet me there.

Jocelyn put the phone back in her pocket and looked at Kevin. "Caleb should interview her. Will you stay with her till he gets here?"

Kevin nodded. "Of course."

"I'll meet you back at the Division in an hour or two."

"Sure," Kevin said as she walked away. "Rush," he called after her. She turned back toward him. "I'm sorry," he said.

FIFTY-TWO

November 12th

"The girls are asleep in Raquel's room," Martina said as Jocelyn entered the house.

The older woman motioned to the video monitor on top of her television. The two-inch-by-two-inch screen showed the girls curled up next to one another. Olivia snored openmouthed, Lulu tucked tightly against her chest, blankie covering her legs.

"I thought you were on until midnight," Martina said. She stood, pulling a green-and-white afghan over her shoulders. She was a few inches shorter than Jocelyn, but she peered up into Jocelyn's eyes, the wrinkles in her caramel face deepening. "What's going on?"

Jocelyn managed a weary smile. "Nothing. Just work stuff. I need to talk to Inez. Is she here?"

Martina motioned over her shoulder. "She's out back."

Jocelyn raised a brow. "Out back?"

Martina nodded solemnly. Jocelyn made her way through the darkened dining room, which Martina had long ago converted into a playroom for the girls. Jocelyn dodged a hippity-hop ball and a miniature stroller on her way to the kitchen. The back door was closed, but Jocelyn could see through the sheer curtain affixed to the block of windows in the door that the backyard light was on.

The door creaked slightly as she opened it. There on the other side of the screen door, standing in the circle of light cast by the outdoor bulb was Inez, wearing nothing but her bra and underwear—plain white cotton, both of them. She called them her utilities or her "utes." She only wore them to work. She saved the fancy stuff for her husband. In spite of everything weighing on her mind, Jocelyn laughed.

She stepped out into the yard. "What are you doing?"

"Watch where you walk," Inez said.

Her uniform lay in a pile behind her. To her left were her boots and vest. Her gun rested at her feet. She picked up a spray bottle of cleanser from the outdoor patio table and started spraying her boots. Whatever it was had bleach in it. The smell stung Jocelyn's eyes.

"I got a domestic," Inez explained. "Over on North Third. You should have seen this place. There were so many fleas, I think they were signing a petition for squatter's rights in the back room. They were goddamn everywhere. I could feel them jumping up into my pants. I left that place in a flea cloud."

Jocelyn smiled grimly. "Let me guess. The caller didn't press charges."

Inez snickered. "Of course she didn't press charges."

After spraying her boots liberally, she moved on to her vest. She motioned to her uniform. "That's the third one this year. I can't believe the way these people live." She hopped from foot to foot to keep warm. There were goose bumps over every inch of her flesh. She glanced at Jocelyn. "We gonna talk about this or not?"

Jocelyn folded her arms and looked at the ground. "Raeann Church is dead. She was the only one who saw this guy."

Inez froze, her hand still wrapped around the neck of the spray bottle. "That's not what I meant," she said. "Are we going to talk about Camille?"

Jocelyn's lower lip trembled. "They got her, Inez. They crucified her. They hurt her."

Tears leaked from her tired eyes. She flopped down on the back steps and wiped her cheeks with the sleeve of her jacket. She thought of Camille laying in the hospital bed, violated, mutilated, and broken—for the second time in her short life. Jocelyn had been powerless to stop it both times. Perhaps if she had been strong enough to see justice served for her sister the first time, Camille would not be in that bed now. Perhaps if things had turned out differently, Camille would never have turned to the streets. She opened her mouth to try to share her thoughts with Inez, but she couldn't bring herself to do it. She didn't want to talk about it. Not yet. What she really wanted was a few moments of silence—a few moments without demands. A few moments hidden from the world so she could grieve; Inez gave her that, letting her weep quietly on the steps while she bagged up her uniform and finished spraying her boots and vest.

She tugged the hose over to Jocelyn and handed it to her. "You gotta hose me down. Really get my feet."

Jocelyn looked up at her friend. "Are you crazy? It's freezing out here."

Inez put a hand on one hip and pointed at the back door. "I can freeze my ass off for five minutes, but I cannot bring fleas into the house where my baby sleeps. So hose me down."

Inez hugged herself as Jocelyn aimed the nozzle at her. "Listen," Inez said as Jocelyn's finger pressed against the nozzle. Jocelyn paused and met Inez's eyes.

"Yeah?"

"Camille's got a lot of problems, a lot of flaws. She's made a lot of mistakes. But you know what she is? She's a survivor." She paused a moment to let that sink in. "She's a survivor," Inez repeated. "She will survive this."

Jocelyn swallowed. It was true. She had never looked at it that way, but Camille survived everything and just kept going. She said a little prayer that Inez was right—that Camille would survive and that maybe, just maybe, she would turn a corner in her sad, tortured life.

"But the next woman these guys pick up may not survive," Jocelyn said. "Our only witness is dead. Even if we get Warner and Donovan, they'll never give the guy up. It's awfully fucking convenient that immediately after we got authorization for a composite sketch, Raeann Church turns up dead. Inez, I think this guy is one of us, and whoever it is—he's close to us. How else would they know we were looking for her?"

Inez sighed. She crossed her hands in front of her and rubbed her upper arms vigorously while walking in place. "Joce, they sent a GRM out. The whole police force knew we were looking for her. If it is a cop, it could be anyone. If you think it's someone close, I don't think we're looking for a cop."

Jocelyn's brow furrowed. "What do you mean?"

Inez motioned toward the hose. "Get my feet, would you? I can't stand out here all night."

Jocelyn squeezed the nozzle, shooting cold water at her friend's feet.

"Whoo," Inez hooted, hopping up and down. "What I mean is," she continued, her teeth beginning to chatter, "there was someone else there the night of the press conference, someone who's been close to this case all along."

Jocelyn sprayed upward toward Inez's waist and over her upper body. She gave her friend a puzzled look as Inez bent to get her hair wet. Inez flipped her hair back up and rolled her eyes at Jocelyn. "Jesus H.," she said, exasperated. "You are so fucking thick. Phil!"

Jocelyn's fingers went limp against the nozzle, the stream of water dying in her hand. Her mouth hung open. Inez walked behind her and banged on the back door. A minute later, Martina's hand poked through a crack in the door, a thick, blue terrycloth robe in it. Inez took it and wrapped it tightly around her glistening body.

"Phil?" Jocelyn said dumbly.

Inez stepped toward her and took the hose, stowing it back on its hook, her hands trembling with cold. "You're looking for a good-looking white male with blue eyes, brown hair. Someone who takes care of himself. Didn't you tell me that Raeann Church said he could be a lawyer?"

Swallowing over the growing lump in her throat, Jocelyn nodded.

"He reduced the charges on Warner and Donovan, which allowed them to make bail." Inez lowered her voice in a faux male imitation that sounded nothing like Phil. "He's the one who keeps saying, 'They didn't drive the nails in.' He was there when you and Caleb told everyone about Raeann Church and the sketch. And Joce, I hate to break it to you, but this shit is personal. They went after Camille. What are the odds?"

Jocelyn practically fell back onto the steps, staring at the water pooling around Inez's feet. She tried to imagine Phil—the man she had dated for so many years, the man who had touched her so many times and so intimately—driving nails into a woman's hands and feet.

"No," she said automatically. She hadn't meant to say it out loud. The word just came out.

Inez squatted in front of her, peering into her face. "Joce, think about it. You've been at each other's throats over this. Who would make this more personal than Phil? They got Camille." She placed extra emphasis on Camille's name, as if Jocelyn didn't already grasp what had happened to her sister.

"How many hookers are in this city? These guys weren't even targeting street hookers before this. Anita Grant? Jennifer Maisry? They're high class. They're escorts. Why go from women like them to Camille—no offense," Inez said, echoing Kevin's earlier sentiments. "It's too much of a coincidence."

Jocelyn chewed her lower lip, her mind trying to work through it.

This is going to sound weird, but he smelled good. Like soap or cologne or something. Clean.

He had a big, thick silver watch. I think it was Michael Kors. It was expensive.

He could have gotten any woman.

He was take-charge. He seemed, you know, like he had a lot of school maybe. He used words I didn't understand.

She hung her head and laid her face in her hands. "Oh, good God," she groaned.

Could it be? Could Phil—straight-laced, power-suit, Lexus-driving, cutthroat Assistant District Attorney Phil—be a serial rapist? A man who got off on hurting women? He was a prick and a major pain in the ass. He was insensitive, petulant, and—as evidenced by the scene with Caleb on her porch—mean. But a sadist? A criminal? In cahoots with the same types he put in prison on a daily basis? He would have to be living a double life.

"Jocelyn?" Inez said.

She met Inez's eyes. "Phil's mom," she said. "She lives in Delaware."

Inez's mouth twisted. "What?"

Jocelyn stood. "Phil's mother is still alive. Zachary Whitman said the third guy was playing out a fantasy about his mother. That's why he thinks it was that kid from Society Hill who was exonerated back in—"

"Stop," Inez said, curling a hand around Jocelyn's biceps. She shook her lightly. "Listen to yourself. You're not looking at the evidence—at what's right in front of you. Are you really going to base your investigation on something you got from a dude who's being charged with child porn—"

"I think Simon set him up," Jocelyn put in quickly. "He's a criminologist."

Inez shook her head, droplets of water flying. In the half-light of the backyard, her lips began to look blue. "He's a piece of shit. He was the lookout the day your teenage sister was gang-raped. Are you really going to go on something he told you?"

Jocelyn winced. When she didn't speak, Inez shook her again. "Jocelyn."

She pulled her arm away. "I don't—I can't—" she stammered.

"Look, I know it's a lot to take in," Inez said, her demeanor softening. "I'm just saying you should take a closer look at Phil. Maybe I'm wrong. Maybe I'm crazy—"

"No," Jocelyn said. "You're right. I mean what else do we have to go on? And I shouldn't be basing my investigation on anything Whitman says—I mean I shouldn't rely on it."

I need evidence.

Her cell phone rang. As she pulled it out, Inez opened the back door and ushered her inside. The warmth of the house was overwhelming—a hot blast causing an almost immediate sheen of sweat on her face. She pressed the phone to her ear as Inez put on coffee. "Rush," she answered.

There was silence. "Hello?" She pulled the phone away from her ear to check the number, but she didn't recognize it. "Hello?"

Then the soft sound of a familiar voice. "Rush?"

"Anita?"

"Yeah, I uh—"

"Are you okay? Did you remember something about the attack?"

"I'm fine. No, I didn't. I need your help. It's Pia. She's at Northwest. Apparently, her and her friends were in a store on Germantown Avenue when it was robbed. She talked to someone there, but I can't pick her up. I was wondering if you could bring her home. I don't know who else to call. My mama's in the hospital, and Terrence is on the road with his football team."

"Anita, I'm not a taxi service," Jocelyn said. There was a heavy exhale on the other end of the line, and immediately Jocelyn felt guilty. She rubbed her eyes with her free hand and sighed. "I'm sorry. I'm having a bad night. I've got a lot going on and—"

"I know," Anita said quickly. "I know. You know I don't like asking for help. I never would. I'd come down there and get her myself for sure, but I'm—well, you know. I'm not getting around so great right now. Please, Rush. It's getting late. I need her home with me. She's ten years old. She's my little girl."

Her little girl. Jocelyn felt a small pull inside, like a strained muscle. A heartstring, maybe. What if it was Olivia? What if Jocelyn were the one battered and injured, unable to get to her daughter to get her home safely? What if she swallowed her pride and reached out to someone for help for Olivia's sake and that person turned her away? She was a single mom, just like Anita. She was lucky to have Inez, Martina, and Kevin, small support system though they were. Anita had no one.

"Okay," Jocelyn said. "Sit tight. I'll ride over to the Division and get her."

FIFTY-THREE

November 12th

Luckily, when Pia Grant and her friends went into the minimart on Germantown Avenue to get soda and candy, she had been in the back of the store trying to decide between regular and Diet Coke—already at ten years old—when two armed robbers entered from the front of the store in a pretty rapid blitz attack. Pia had the good sense to hide behind a display of chips and had miraculously emerged unscathed. Her friends were not so fortunate. Their phones, iPods, iPads, and the little bit of cash they had on them was stolen. All three of them were thoroughly terrorized, and yet, Jocelyn couldn't help but think they'd been lucky.

The other girls had been picked up hours ago. Pia sat in a chair next to Chen's desk, playing idly with her iPod, one earbud in her ear and the other dangling over her lap. She was completely silent on the ride home, despite Jocelyn's efforts to engage her in conversation. At the apartment, she unlocked the door with a key she pulled from her coat pocket. She gave Jocelyn a backward glance and left the door ajar after scurrying through it.

Jocelyn closed it behind her, following Pia into the living room where Anita sat in a recliner. She had puffy brown slippers shaped like dogs on her feet, a square of gauze showing along one of her ankles. Thin white bandages looped around each of her hands, just covering the holes left by the nails.

Pia jumped into her lap, jarring the chair. Its springs let out a loud groan. Anita squeezed her daughter and stroked the back of her head. She tried to gather Pia in more closely, but the girl was almost as tall as Anita and her long, gangly legs sprawled over the arm of the chair. Jocelyn realized that she was going to hate it when Olivia got too big to hold in her lap any longer.

"It's okay now," Anita whispered. "You did good. It's over now."

After a few minutes, Anita sent Pia to her room with orders to change into her pajamas and a promise to make her macaroni and cheese with real cheese in it. After Pia departed, Anita held out a hand to Jocelyn.

"Thank you," she said as Jocelyn helped her stand. She hobbled into the kitchen and Jocelyn followed, watching as she prepared a microwaveable bowl of macaroni and cheese. Anita glanced at her. "You don't look good, Rush. You sick?"

Jocelyn shook her head. Anita stared at her for another beat, as if she didn't believe her, and then went back to mixing shredded cheddar cheese in the bowl of Easy Mac. "You making any progress on my case? I saw the news. They did that to a schoolteacher?" Anita shook her head.

Jocelyn glanced over her shoulder to make sure Pia wasn't in earshot. She licked her dry lips. "They got my sister, and the only witness we had who saw this guy's face is dead. It doesn't look good. I'm sorry, Anita."

Anita looked stricken, her eyes wide as saucers. She opened her mouth to speak but froze when Pia walked into the room wearing long, pink pajamas with cupcakes on them. Anita gave her the bowl of macaroni and cheese and sent her into the living room to watch television. She sat at the kitchen table and beckoned Jocelyn to do the same. Jocelyn continued to stand in the doorway.

"Your sister?" Anita said. "Camille, right?"

Jocelyn nodded.

"Did they—"

"Exactly what they did to you and to the other woman."

Anita stared at the table, fingering the cloth placemat in front of her. Then she shook her head quickly, as if shaking herself from a trance. She met Jocelyn's eyes. "How is she?"

Jocelyn shrugged. "I don't know. She's—"

Been gang-raped twice. How did someone survive that? Camille wanted to be done with a life of drugs and violence, and Jocelyn believed her. In all the years that their mother had tried to set Camille straight, all the years Jocelyn had made the drug and prostitution charges against her disappear, Camille had never once expressed a desire to get clean. Only tonight. Maybe she was really finished now. Jocelyn thought about Alicia Hardigan. *"But the scars on my hands—they remind me. When I think about it, all I want to do is score."* Camille wanted out, but would this make it harder for her to get straight? Or would the vicious cycle—that had started when they were teenagers and their father failed them—continue?

"Where you at, Rush?" Anita said, breaking into her thoughts. "You look like you're about to drop dead. So sit your ass down. I'll make some coffee."

Jocelyn looked back over her shoulder. Pia lay on the foldout bed, the bowl of pasta cradled in her hands, her eyes glued to the television. It cast flickering lights over her face.

"I'm on duty," Jocelyn said.

Anita's chin dropped. She eyed Jocelyn with a look only mothers give to lying children. "And I'm a victim of a crime that you're actively investigating. So sit your ass down."

Jocelyn obeyed, peeling off her coat and settling into the seat across from Anita. For the first time that night, the adrenaline that had been propelling her from the scene on Kelly Drive to Camille's hospital room to her conversation with Inez began to wear off. She felt bone tired, the way she used to feel when Olivia was a newborn and she only slept two hours a night. Anita stood, using the table to support her weight and made her way to the coffeemaker on the counter.

"You want me to do it?" Jocelyn asked.

Anita waved her off. "I have to be able to do things myself."

"But you're not even fully healed yet."

Anita turned and met Jocelyn's gaze. "I can make a pot of coffee, Rush," she said pointedly.

A few minutes later, a steaming cup of it sat in front of Jocelyn. Anita pushed cream, sugar, and a spoon across the table so Jocelyn could fix it.

"How long have we known each other, Rush?"

Jocelyn thought about it as she stirred cream and sugar into her coffee. "I don't know. It's got to be almost ten years. I think Pia was two the first time I—"

She broke off. Anita smiled. "It's okay," she said. "The first time you arrested me, yes. Not talking about it don't mean it didn't happen."

"Why do you ask?"

"Because I've seen you in a lot of different situations, and you've never looked this bad. You need to talk, Rush, so spill it."

Jocelyn closed her eyes. She couldn't bear to tell her family's deep, dark secret to one more soul, but it came out anyway. The whole sordid story: her waking up from a grievous head injury at seventeen after a car accident; finding out her sister had been gang-raped and that her father was making the whole incident disappear; Camille's descent into drug addiction; Jocelyn adopting Olivia; their parents' death; and now Camille a victim once more. Anita listened carefully, her eyes never leaving Jocelyn. When Jocelyn was finished, Anita said, "You saw it? You don't remember anything? At all?"

Jocelyn drained half her coffee cup. "Nothing. I have these nightmares about it, but I have no idea if they are memories or just something my mind made up."

Anita reached across the table, as if to touch Jocelyn's hand, but she didn't quite reach. Jocelyn stared at her bandaged hand. The blackened edge of a scab peeked out from beneath the edge of the gauze. "Rush," Anita said softly. "You need to let this go."

Jocelyn smiled grimly. "I wish it were that easy. How? How do you let it go? Every decision I've made in my life since that time has been because of what happened to Camille and what my dad did—or didn't do."

Anita pulled her hand back and regarded Jocelyn steadily. "Like what?"

"I left Princeton and joined the police academy to spite my father because of what he'd done. Because he covered it up. I stopped speaking to my parents. My mother—I kept in touch with her for a long time, but when Olivia came along . . . It's different when you have kids, you know?"

She looked at Anita, who nodded, and continued. "I kept looking at this tiny, defenseless little newborn, thinking this is how it starts with your kids—you get them when they're like this so you truly understand the gravity of your job as a parent—to protect them. Every fiber of your being is geared toward protecting them. When I looked at Olivia, I just couldn't understand how my mother could allow my father to brush the whole thing under the carpet. She could have done more. She knew it and I knew it. I didn't let her see her granddaughter because of it. I didn't go to my parents' funerals."

"Okay," Anita said. "I think I would have done the same thing if I was in your shoes. But Rush, you gotta start living your life. *Your* life. You cannot make everything about what your dad did wrong. Camille shouldn't either. I don't know what it's going to take—some rehab, some therapy, or what—but you two need to move on. For real."

Jocelyn looked into her coffee mug. She swirled the last quarter of the fluid around in the bottom of the cup. "I know you're right. But even when I'm trying to put it behind me, it rears its ugly head."

"Like how?"

"I talked to one of the rapists last week," Jocelyn told her.

"You what?" Anita exclaimed. "How did that come about?"

Jocelyn filled her in on the encounter with Zachary Whitman. Anita shook her head the whole time. When Jocelyn was finished, she said, "You sure have a fucked up past, Rush."

"I know," Jocelyn said.

"That's some Jerry Springer shit right there."

Jocelyn laughed.

"Actually," Anita said. "I think that might be too fucked up even for Jerry. Rush, go on in the living room and get the laptop off the coffee table."

Jocelyn retrieved the laptop without asking any questions. Anita popped the lid up and turned it on. She winced as she placed her hands over the keys. "Going to take me a while to get my typing back," she muttered.

"What are you doing?"

"Well, you said this kid from Society Hill that Whitman told you about was in the news, right?"

"Well, yeah, but his name was never released."

Anita raised a brow at Jocelyn. It was just visible over the top of the computer screen. She clucked her tongue. "Sometimes you cops are so smart, you're dumb. His name wasn't released, but I'll bet you fifty dollars his mom's was."

Jocelyn wanted to palm herself in the forehead. *Of course.* Why hadn't she thought of it? It was so obvious. "Are you going to Google it?"

"Nah, that many years ago? You won't find shit on Google. I'll check the *Philadelphia Inquirer* archives. All the good stuff is in there."

Jocelyn sighed as Anita clicked away, a permanent grimace on her face. A few times she had to stop using her left hand altogether and peck away with the right hand one finger at a time. "Well, you can look," Jocelyn said. "But my friend Inez thinks it's—"

"Here it is," Anita said, nearly popping out of her chair. She waved Jocelyn over to her side of the table. "A Society Hill mother crucified and killed in her home by two black drug dealers. The police thought that her teenage son had done it. He was on trial when he was exonerated with the help of his defense attorney, none other than Bruce Rush."

Jocelyn stood over Anita's shoulder and squinted at the screen. She was so tired, her eyes burned. "What was the woman's name?" she asked, still scanning the tiny print for it.

"Rosalind Finch."

FIFTY-FOUR

November 12th

The coffee that had tasted so good at Anita's burned Jocelyn's stomach as she made her way through the Thirty-Fifth District and up to Northwest Detectives. She kept darting glances around her, looking for Friendly Fire. She hoped he wasn't upstairs. She breathed a sigh of relief when she reached the top of the steps and saw only a handful of detectives, including Kevin and Chen.

Kevin sat on the edge of a desk, arms folded across his chest, eyes fixed to the small television that was on again for the second time in two months. This time it showed a building in flames, thick black smoke billowing out of its shattered windows and ascending into the night sky. It looked familiar. She pointed to the television. "Hey, isn't that—"

She stopped talking when the words "Inferno rages at Fox's Sports Bar" flashed across the bottom of the screen. She swallowed, trying to get her larynx to work again.

"That's Vince Fox's place," Chen said from two desks over without bothering to look up from the paperwork in front of him.

Kevin met Jocelyn's eyes. His whole face seemed to frown, his eyes taking on the look of sympathy he usually reserved for victims. She shook her head almost imperceptibly, her eyes pleading. *Don't bring it up*, she wanted to say. She didn't want Camille to be the hot topic of the night. Not tonight.

He seemed to get the signal. He forced a smile, pointing at the television. "Isn't that the guy you talked to a couple of weeks ago?"

"Vince Fox," Jocelyn said. "Yeah. He's retired. He had a nice place there."

A loud "puh" sound came from the direction of Chen's desk. "That guy probably set it on fire himself for the insurance money. He's dirtier than a lot full of used needles on the Stroll. Brass could never prove it, of course. Too bad Friendly Fire is such a shitty shot. Could have done us all a favor."

Jocelyn's mouth hung open. She looked at Kevin, whose brow was crinkled in confusion. Then she addressed Chen. "What did you say about Friendly Fire?"

Chen leaned back in his chair, twirling his pen between his fingers. "They were partners in the Northeast a few years back. They were out on a call—in pursuit of a suspect. Friendly Fire shot Fox in the leg. Almost took off his dick. Where do you guys think he got the nickname? Anyway, Fox had nerve damage, had to take early retirement. He opened that place right away. You've been in there—you think he could afford that place on a cop's salary?"

Kevin and Jocelyn exchanged another look. Chen went back to his paperwork, obviously not expecting an answer to his question. Kevin's gaze stayed locked on Jocelyn. "He didn't mention Friendly Fire to you when you talked to him?"

"Well, no. I only asked him about Warner and Donovan. When I asked him about retiring, he said 'accidental discharge.' He made it sound like he'd shot himself."

"Well, that certainly is interesting," Kevin said.

Jocelyn nudged his arm. "Can I talk to you in private?" she asked quietly, but not quietly enough for Chen, who missed nothing.

"Private, huh?" he heckled. "I see how you guys are."

Kevin rolled his eyes and led Jocelyn to the interrogation closet—the same one she had found Finch in attempting to flirt with a victim only a few weeks earlier. It was close and hot, and in spite of the fact that someone had recently taken the time to wipe it down with lemon-scented cleanser, the smell of cigarette smoke lingered. Jocelyn noticed someone had carved their initials into the back of the bench since the last time she had been in there.

Kevin pulled the door closed behind them and put his hands on his hips. "Look," he began. "About Camille—"

"I don't want to talk about Camille," Jocelyn said, cutting him off. She held his gaze steadily. "Kev, I think the third guy is Finch."

Kevin's face creased, then smoothed into an uncertain smile—as if he were waiting for the punch line to a joke and wasn't really sure where it was going. "Rush," he said slowly, carefully. "You've had a long night. I think you—"

She grasped his wrist. "Kevin, listen to me. Remember what I told you about my conversation with Zachary Whitman? How he said he thought the third guy was that kid from Society Hill?"

Kevin looked down at her fingers curled around his arm and back at her face, his hazel eyes sad. "Jocelyn, listen to yourself. Whitman's not a part of your investigation. He has nothing to do with the Warner–Donovan case. He's about to go down on child pornography charges. He would say anything to try to get you to help him. He has a history with you, and he's trying to exploit that."

"But, Kevin," Jocelyn said seriously. "The Society Hill victim was named Rosalind Finch."

When Kevin said nothing, she went on. "Did you hear me? Finch. As in Friendly Fire. We've always thought this guy was a cop—"

"*You've* always thought this guy was a cop," Kevin said. "Jocelyn, this is a stretch. There are lots of Finches in this area."

"But, Kevin," she implored. "The Society Hill kid was sixteen years old when it happened. That was seventeen years ago. Friendly Fire is the right age. Think about it—these guys just crucified my sister. You said it yourself, why go from women like Anita and Maisry to a street hooker like Camille? It's personal. Finch hates me."

Kevin rubbed a hand over his scalp and looked at her as if she had some kind of terrible incurable condition. Like she was terminally ill. "You two have issues, yes. That doesn't mean Friendly Fire is a sadistic rapist. You have nothing to connect him to your case except a similarity to a decades-old case involving a lady named Finch. A case you only know about because a sex offender told you about it."

"But it makes sense," she tried. "Hear me out. It starts with Vince Fox killing Warner's son. Warner does time for attacking Fox. When he gets out, he wants revenge. Somehow he hooks up with Friendly Fire—Fox's new partner. Friendly Fire uses Warner and Donovan to play out his sick little fantasy and in exchange, he helps them get revenge on Fox."

Kevin massaged his temples. "By doing what? Watching Fox open a sports bar?"

Jocelyn cracked the door open and pointed to the television, which still showed Fox's bar engulfed in flames. "By burning his place down," she said. "Maybe they were trying to kill him. Maybe that accidental discharge wasn't an accident."

Kevin sighed. "Rush, you know I've always got your back, right?"

She nodded.

"I think you've had to deal with a lot in a very short amount of time. I think you're tired and upset, and you're not thinking straight. I think you need to go home and sleep on this, and we'll talk about it tomorrow."

Jocelyn put her hands on her hips. "Don't coddle me, Kev."

He held up both hands. "I'm not coddling you. Now you hear me out. If the star witness in my big case turned up dead the same day my sister got raped, what would you tell me? For God's sake, Rush. Just go home and get some rest. Take a breath. See your daughter."

She reached out and gripped his wrist one more time. "Kevin," she said, hating the plaintive note in her voice. "This is not exhaustion talking. Please. I need someone to back me up on this—to tell me I'm not crazy."

"Rush."

"Fine. I'll go home. I'll even take a day off, but please, Kevin, just think about it. I'm right. Please."

Kevin looked at the floor, his fingers kneading his temples once more. "Are you coming at me with this because Inez thinks the third guy is Phil?"

Jocelyn's head reared back. She hadn't been expecting that. But of course he and Inez had spoken in the last couple of hours. They were her best friends. They were worried about her. She swallowed. "No, that's not why I'm bringing this up. Yes, Whitman is a coward and a criminal, even if he's not guilty of having child porn. But he's also a criminologist at an Ivy League school. That has to count for something. Can it really be a coincidence that the Society Hill crime is so similar to these crimes and that the woman's name was Finch?"

Kevin gazed at her, looking less pitying and more exhausted. "Have you shared this theory with Lover Boy?"

"Who? Vaughn?"

Kevin rolled his eyes. "No, Finch. Yes, Vaughn."

She shook her head. "We haven't talked since you and I left the scene at the Schuylkill." She slid her phone out of her pocket and looked at the screen. "But he's sent me three text messages and called once."

"That sounds serious."

"Don't change the subject."

Kevin pulled the closet door all the way open. "Okay, okay, Rush. If you promise to go home right now, I will promise to seriously consider your little theory. But for God's sake, get the hell out of here."

FIFTY-FIVE

November 13th

Kevin stared at the evidence voucher in his hand, the words blurring. He blinked, but it didn't help. His eyes burned from fatigue and the hot, dry air in the Northwest Division. He only had a few items of paperwork to put in order before he could finish his shift—which had actually ended an hour ago. He moved the voucher closer to his face, but that only made it worse. He looked around and then reached into the bottom right-hand drawer of his desk and pulled out his reading glasses. He always resisted wearing them, but more and more he needed them. With a sigh, he took another look at the voucher.

"Much better," he muttered to himself, the inevitability of age sinking like a stone into the pit of his stomach. He took a sip of cold coffee and fished the corresponding file from one of the piles on his desk, inserting the voucher into it.

He moved through his piles more quickly, until he was interrupted by a loud throat-clearing behind him. He swiveled his chair around, tucking his chin into his chest so he could peer over top of his reading glasses at Phil Delisi. Even at one a.m., the man looked perfectly pressed, and Kevin noted the chunky Michael Kors watch that Jocelyn had told him about peeking from the edge of his left shirtsleeve. He wore a suit and a long black wool coat. His brow was creased. “Where’s Jocelyn?” he asked.

Slowly, Kevin swiveled a half turn and looked at the clock on the wall, then back at Phil. “What do you need to talk to Rush about at one in the morning?”

Phil was not used to being questioned. It was all over him. The way he looked, the way he talked, the way he now stared at Kevin like he just fell off the damn turnip truck. “That’s between me and Rush,” he said.

Kevin spun his chair back to his desk and picked up another file. He adjusted his glasses and opened it in front of him.

An exasperated sigh sounded over his shoulder. Ignoring Phil, Kevin glanced up to see Finch walk up the steps and over to one of the other detectives to deposit some paperwork. The two conferred for a moment, and then Finch meandered toward the steps, glancing at each desk as he passed it.

“Sullivan,” Phil said, impatience edging his tone.

“Hey, Phil,” Kevin said loudly, without taking his eyes from Finch. “I ever tell you that story about the woman whose baby I delivered on a domestic?”

Phil’s voice went up an octave. He moved to the side of Kevin’s desk, trying to place himself in Kevin’s field of vision. “What?”

“Yeah,” Kevin went on. “I was on this domestic—drunk baby daddy versus giant pregnant lady. When I got there he had the door barricaded. I could hear her screaming in there. Finally, I talked him into letting me in. There she was on the couch bleeding from the head with this baby already crowning. So I zip tie the guy and get her to push. That baby popped right out.”

Finch, who had paused by the watercooler, began to walk back toward the steps. “So she tells me I can name the baby,” Kevin said. Phil moved around to the front of Kevin’s desk, nearly obstructing his view of Finch. Kevin glanced at him long enough to see the pulsing blue vein in his forehead. "You know what I chose?"

Phil slapped the desk, causing Finch to jump and a few of the other detectives to look over. Kevin smiled, catching Finch's gaze.

"No, I don't," Phil said through gritted teeth. "And I don't give a rat's—"

"Rosalind," Kevin said. He looked at Phil. "You know, like in Shakespeare? It's a pretty name, don't you think?"

Phil's face had a sunburned look. Kevin turned his attention back to Finch. "You ever meet someone in real life with that name? It's pretty uncommon."

Finch poured himself a small cup of water from the watercooler. He stared into it, a smile playing on his lips. He swirled the fluid around. "That was my mother's name," he said.

Phil turned to look at Finch with another exasperated sigh. "I don't know what the fuck is going on here, but—" he started, but Kevin talked over him, shutting him down.

"Was?" he asked Finch.

The smile never left his face. He tossed back the cup of water and threw the crumpled cup into the trash can. "Yeah," he said. "She's dead."

"You don't say," Kevin replied.

"She had it coming," Finch added, almost to himself.

"That's an interesting thing to say about your own mother," Kevin noted. "She any relation to the Rosalind Finch who was crucified in her Society Hill home, oh, about sixteen, seventeen years ago?"

The change in Finch's face was instantaneous. It was a complete unmaking of his smug expression—his eyes and lips drooping, the skin of his cheeks turning gray. His eyes blinked rapidly and his nose twitched—almost as though it was involuntary. He managed a smile, as if trying to take control of his face again.

"Sullivan," Phil said again, leaning over the desk so that he was practically in Kevin's face. "Where is Rush?"

Kevin wheeled his chair to the side so he could look at the top of the stairwell, but Finch was gone. He took off his glasses and stood up, facing Phil, man to man. He poked a finger in the air, inches from Phil's chest. "You leave Rush alone. There's nothing you have to say that she needs to hear, unless you're going to apologize for generally being a prick."

Phil crossed his arms over his chest and regarded Kevin, his face hardening. The blue vein bulged. "You need to remember your place, Sullivan."

Kevin laughed. He waved a hand around them. "This is my place, douche bag. You're the one who doesn't belong here, so why don't you get out of here before I punch you in your pompous face."

Phil's eyes flashed. "Are you threatening me?"

"What do you think?"

Phil pointed at Kevin as he turned to leave. "You'll be sorry."

"Talk to my supervisor," Kevin called after him.

He shook his head and eased back into his chair. Two reports later, his cell phone chirped. He smiled as he read the text from Kim Bottinger. Her shift had gone late as well. Did he want to get something to eat?

"Do I ever," he said as he typed back to her, once again needing his glasses to see the tiny letters on the screen. *Meet you in 15*, he wrote.

He whistled his way down the steps, his thoughts turning to Rush, feeling somewhat guilty that he hadn't been more receptive to her earlier. He'd have to have a longer conversation with her in the morning—especially about Friendly Fire. A few feet from his car, he pressed the Unlock button on his key fob, when, suddenly, pain exploded across the back of his head. He went down like someone had let the air out of him. His limbs felt like jelly. Only vaguely aware of his cheek scraping against the asphalt, rough hands flipped him onto his back. His eyes were open, at least he thought they were, but he couldn't see anything. He blinked, but nothing happened. Another blink, and the world reappeared in a blurry haze of inky shadows and the soft orange glow of the parking lot lights. They were directly behind the person frantically searching his pockets, relieving him of his wallet, gun, and his Nicorette. The man's face was a black smudge on Kevin's blurred view of the world.

"Wha—" Kevin tried, but his mouth wouldn't work.

"Shut up, old man," his assailant said. "I've had it with you. You and your cunt partner."

Rush.

"Don't—" he began, but the world went black.

FIFTY-SIX

November 13th

It was nearly two a.m. by the time Jocelyn got home, after checking in on Camille one more time. She tucked Olivia in and changed into a pair of sweatpants and a T-shirt. She removed the splint from her right wrist and wrapped it in a more flexible ACE bandage for sleeping. But she was wired from all the coffee and the drama of the night. She couldn't believe the night was still going on—it had to be the longest of her life. Well, besides the nights she had had to stay up with a fussy, teething Olivia. She opened her refrigerator, staring at the contents without seeing them. She did the same with her kitchen cabinets before returning to the fridge. This time she pulled out a bottle of wine. She was trying to find a clean wineglass when she heard a soft knock on her door.

"Shit," she said. She had left her gun upstairs. She snatched up her phone, trying to decide how she was going to handle a two a.m. visitor when she noticed the five additional text messages from Caleb, the last of which read, *I'm outside.*

Instantly, the tension disappeared from her shoulders. She smiled as she pulled the door open and let him in. He leaned down to kiss her as she pushed the door closed behind him and turned the lock. She let her mouth linger on his before he pulled away. He motioned toward the steps. "I won't wake Olivia, will I?"

Jocelyn beckoned him into the living room. She picked up the video monitor on her coffee table and tapped the tiny black-and-white screen. "I doubt it, but if you do, we'll have some advanced notice."

He took the handheld unit from her and studied it, turning it over in his hands. "Man," he said, "I wish they had had these when Brian was a baby—would have saved me an awful lot of trouble."

"Yeah, well that camera is staying in there until she's twenty years old," Jocelyn said wryly, returning the monitor to the coffee table. They sat side by side on the couch. "Do you have any news?" she asked.

He grimaced. "I stopped at Einstein and saw Camille," he said. "Took her statement, but I don't think it gives us anything we didn't already have."

Jocelyn nodded. The image of Camille in that bed with her hands and feet bandaged made Jocelyn's chest hurt, so she changed the subject. "What's the word on Raeann Church?"

Caleb cleared his throat. "The ME estimates that she's been dead for forty-eight to seventy-two hours—hard to tell with her being in the water."

"So, basically she was killed within a day of the press conference. Was it strangulation?"

"Yeah. Looks like whoever did it knocked her around a little before he killed her. There was no evidence of sexual assault."

Jocelyn pressed against the edge of the coffee table with the balls of her feet, pushing against it just so—enough to feel a pinch in her feet but not enough to push the table away. "So much for a composite. We're going to have to figure out how to spin this to the press. Did they get wind of the assault on Camille yet?"

"No, not that I know of. Listen, Jocelyn, these guys targeting your sister—it feels personal."

"Because it is," she replied. She sighed and leaned her head back into the couch cushions. She didn't look at him as she recounted her conversation with Inez, who believed Phil was the third man as well as what Anita had found in her search of the Philadelphia newspaper archives. She reiterated the theories she had just discussed with Kevin about Kyle Finch, ending with, "It's okay if you think I'm crazy. I got the feeling Kevin does."

He reached out and gently turned her chin to face him. He pushed a strand of her hair behind her ear and smiled. "I don't think you're crazy. Our next step would have been to look at people you've made enemies of, and by all indications, both Phil Delisi and Kyle Finch fit that designation. I will start checking alibis, and in the morning I'll make a report to Internal Affairs."

Jocelyn pulled his hand away from her face and held it. She closed her eyes for a moment to savor the immediate sense of relief she felt. It was a welcome feeling after the night she had had and the feelings she'd been grappling with right up until Caleb walked through her door—grief over what had happened to Camille and disappointment over Raeann Church's murder. She still wasn't comfortable with the idea that Phil could be the perpetrator, but it felt good to be taken seriously.

"But you know you can't work this case anymore, right?" Caleb said.

Jocelyn smiled wanly. "I don't really want to work this case anymore. I'd just love to go back to robberies, attempted murders, and domestics."

Caleb smiled back. "Done. Look, I really want to stay with you, but I've got to get back to work. I'm on till eight in the morning—and I've got three very dangerous suspects to track down."

She walked him to the door. He stopped, resting his hand on the doorknob and turned back to her. "We're still looking for Warner and Donovan. We will get these guys," he said.

"You don't have to do that," Jocelyn said.

"What's that?" he asked, gazing down at her.

"Reassure me, all cop-like. I know how these things work."

He nodded, his still hand lingering on the doorknob. "I'm sorry about Camille."

Jocelyn managed another weak smile and nodded.

His brows drew together, his forehead wrinkling. "Are you okay?"

She was surprised how quickly tears stung the backs of her eyes. Of all the people she'd spoken to today, only Caleb had asked if she was okay.

"No," she breathed, her voice trembling. "I don't think I am."

"Oh, Jocelyn," he said, his voice softening. His hand slid off the doorknob as he reached for her. He pulled her into his arms and she let him, her limbs going slack as he held her against him. She burrowed her face into the folds of his jacket, resting her head against his innermost layer of clothing. She could hear his heartbeat. He smelled like aftershave and coffee with a trace of cigarette smoke.

She sighed and closed her eyes, pushing every single thing out of her head except for the feel of him, the smell of him, and his touch. He was warm and solid, a wall keeping the world out, keeping the terrible thoughts from inundating her mind. She slid her hands beneath his jacket, around his waist and traced the hard planes of muscle up and down his back. She felt his heartbeat quicken against her cheek and smiled. Pulling one hand out from his jacket, she snaked it around the back of his neck. She only had to tug once, lightly, and his lips clamped down over hers. His tongue probed her mouth, gently and slowly. He gathered her in closer, his hands moving down over her ass. He broke from her mouth and met her eyes.

She stared back at him, unwavering. "Don't stop touching me," she whispered.

He smiled, eyes twinkling and bent his mouth to the hollow behind her ear. He kissed his way lightly across her throat to the other side of her neck, his tongue flicking against her skin. His breath caused a deep, hot flush that went from her scalp to her toes. Her heart pounded in her ears. She felt sensations in her body she couldn't remember ever feeling—and something else, something entirely new to her: need.

She put both hands in his thick brown hair, trying to pull him closer to her. His hands roamed over her, reaching under her T-shirt, tracing the length of her spine. He pulled back to look in her eyes once more, the intensity in his gaze sending a shiver through her entire body. Then his mouth crashed down on hers, hungry, searching, claiming. She peeled his jacket off his shoulders, and it fell to the floor. His hands returned immediately to her body. She let go of him and pushed her sweatpants and underwear down over her hips. She shook her legs until they fell to her ankles. Using one foot, she pushed the bunched fabric down to the floor and stepped out of it. She did the same with her other foot and kicked her pants away.

Caleb pulled his mouth from hers when she started unbuckling his belt. "I'm on the job," he murmured, even as his hands cupped her bare ass, branding her skin with their heat.

"Please don't go," she implored. "Not yet."

He gasped as she thrust her hand into his pants and wrapped it firmly around his shaft. She freed him and worked her hand up and down the length of his hardness. His face was flushed, his head tipped back. His breathing was uneven, labored. "Jocelyn," he said hoarsely.

Watching the effect she had on him turned her on even more than his touch did. Just like every other time they'd touched, it was nothing at all like things had been with Phil. She'd never had such an effect on Phil, and he'd never sent her reeling with pleasure before they even got to the act. This was new territory for her, and she didn't want to stop.

"Jocelyn," he said again.

She tipped her face up. "Kiss me," she commanded.

Their mouths met again. She let go of him and pulled on his shoulders, hooking one leg around his thigh. He took her cue and lifted her easily, his large hands curling under her upper thighs. He set her on top of him, entering her slowly. She wrapped her legs around him, hooking her ankles together behind him.

"Oh," she moaned, closing her eyes, concentrating only on the feel of him inside her and the sensation it provoked in her. There was nothing but this. For a few frantic, blissful moments, there was nothing bad. There were no heartless criminals, no rape victims, no tortured family history, no broken sister, no horrors. There was only this man making her feel good—taking her away from everything that hurt. She clasped her arms around his neck as he moved her atop him. He breathed jerkily into the hollow of her throat. She could feel herself tightening around him, pleasure starting as a slow tingle inside and spreading out in waves, encompassing her entire pelvis, making her legs quiver. He gripped her and turned so that her back pressed against the door, thrusting deeper into her, each thrust intensifying her climax. She bit her lower lip and buried her face in his neck to keep from crying out. He wasn't far behind her, finishing with a series of shudders, groaning softly into her hair. He held her against him for a few moments. She felt his heartbeat thundering against her own.

"Wow," he said as their breathing evened out.

"Yeah," she agreed. He carried her awkwardly over to the couch and set her down, going back to the door to retrieve her sweatpants. She pulled them on while he buttoned his pants and righted himself. Then he knelt in front of her, his elbows on either side of her thighs. He rested his head on her chest, and she pushed her hands through his hair again, feeling slightly drunk on his closeness.

"I want to say I'm sorry—that wasn't the way I imagined our first time—but I'm really not sorry because that was hot," he said, smiling up at her sheepishly.

She laughed. "I'm not sorry either. If you didn't have to work, I'd make you do it again."

He kissed her throat, her chin, and then her mouth. "Oh, we'll do it again," he assured her.

The sound of Olivia sighing in her sleep startled them both. Caleb pointed at the monitor. "I should get going, in case she wakes up."

Jocelyn nodded. This time she saw him to the door without incident. As she locked the door behind him, sleepiness finally overcame her. She trudged up to the bathroom to clean herself up and then to bed. She nestled her head into her pillow, pulling the collar of her T-shirt up over her mouth to smell him on her. Each time thoughts of Camille, Raeann Church, Warner, Donovan, and the third man crept into her mind, she pushed them aside and instead thought about the encounter with Caleb and the shock waves of pleasure still rolling through her lower body. She was asleep within minutes.

FIFTY-SEVEN

November 13th

She woke to the sound of glass shattering. She bolted upright in bed, sweat dripping down her back. Her heart thundered, a dull roar in her ears. She reached down to throw the covers off and gripped one of Olivia's legs. The girl snored softly beside her. Jocelyn listened for a moment and thought she heard a creak on the steps. Had she actually heard glass breaking or had it been a dream?

In the half-light of the hallway nightlight, Olivia's round face was peaceful. Beyond that, the bedside clock read 3:34 a.m.

Creeeak.

This was definitely not Caleb.

In a single motion, Jocelyn scooped Olivia up, leapt from the bed, and darted across the hall. She tucked Olivia into her bed as quickly as she could. She'd probably wake up, but Jocelyn couldn't help that. She had to keep her safe and out of the way until the threat was neutralized. Jocelyn locked Olivia's door from the inside and pulled it closed behind her. The girl didn't yet have the dexterity to unlock the door from the inside. All it would take was one good kick to get into the room. For now, it would deter Olivia from getting up and wandering around the house, at least until Jocelyn figured out what was going on.

She dashed across the hall to her bedroom, headed for her gun, which was in a lockbox in the top drawer of her dresser. The moment she was through the door, the man clotheslined her. His arm across her chest sent her flat on her back and knocked the wind out of her.

Her mouth worked to gulp air, but none would come. The dark figure tangled his hand in her hair and pulled her down the hall. Her limbs flailed, trying to keep up with him, to keep him from tearing her scalp off. Her chest burned. Panic tightened the noose around her throat. Her bowels loosened.

Olivia.

Her mouth formed the word involuntarily, but no sound came. The struggle to the bottom of the steps was largely silent. Air returned to her lungs. She pressed his hand to the top of her head with both of her palms to take the pressure off and kicked at him ineffectually. He tossed her off the landing at the bottom of the steps. She landed in the middle of her living room, inches from her coffee table. She scrambled to her feet and launched herself at him, shooting for his hips. The party wall was plaster, and he hit it hard, letting out a cry. He recovered quickly and grabbed her face, large paws covering both her ears. Jocelyn reached up and gripped his pinky fingers, peeling them all the way back until he gasped and let go of her head. She was close. She could smell his minty breath and knew at once that it was Finch.

She pushed his hands down and elbowed him hard across the face.

"Ow! You bitch!"

She elbowed him again, harder, trying to draw every last ounce of strength she had from her terrified, trembling body. She heard a crack—another cry—and brought a knee up as hard as she could, aiming for his crotch. She got his abdomen, and he issued a grunt. She was swinging elbows again when he placed a palm on her sternum and pushed hard and fast. She stumbled back and fell on her ass. He was on her before she could rise, one hand in her hair, the other socking her with a heavy fist. It was a solid hit to the right side of her face. Pinpoints of light dazzled their way across her field of vision. Her limbs flopped around uselessly for a moment. The blow dazed her, and she went down more easily than she would have liked.

He sat on her chest. "Hold still, you stupid bitch."

The full weight of his body crushed her sternum. His legs lay straight on her left side and his hands worked to pin her left palm to the floor. Jocelyn flailed with her other arm, hitting his body, straining to reach his collar. She kicked her legs, tried to buck him with her pelvis, but his crushing weight on her rib cage was too much. Her lungs screamed. He easily had one hundred pounds on her. He was forcing the air out of her. If she didn't calm down, she would pass out, and then what? She would be at his mercy. The pain in her chest and ribs was excruciating. She clenched her teeth and prayed her ribs wouldn't crack beneath his weight. She'd had broken ribs before. They were extremely painful. She couldn't imagine fighting him off with a torso full of broken ribs. She tightened her abdomen, trying to preserve what breath she had left and keep her body from crumpling.

The nail went into her palm on one uneven stroke. She didn't have the air to cry out. Her vision filled with black spots.

Hold on, a voice in her head shouted.

He would move soon, shift to the other side. She'd have a slim chance then. Jocelyn let her body go limp, her eyes fall to half-mast. She tried to think about anything besides the pain in her hand. It wasn't easy. He hammered twice more, embedding the nail into the floor beneath her hand.

Finally, he stood up, laughing softly. For a split second, the relief of having him off her eclipsed all thoughts of the pain in her hand. She sucked in air noisily. He stood over her, a hammer in his hand and an erection straining against his pants. A shaft of light from a nearby window fell across his face, giving his features an otherworldly glow. His lips curled in something between a sneer and a smile. He was leering at her, hungry like a wild animal. A shudder worked its way up her body, tugging at her pinned hand. It sent a streak of pain searing up her arm. He licked his lips and stepped closer. She worked hard to keep her body still, to discourage him from sitting on her chest again right away. She needed her breath.

"They always stop fighting after the first nail," he said, chuckling. He nudged her ribs with his foot.

Please don't kick, she prayed silently.

"You're no different," he said. "Look at you. Where's your big mouth now, you fucking cunt?"

Jocelyn turned her head and for the first time, looked at her hand. The head of the nail was small. Not as small as she would have liked but small enough for what she was about to do. A wave of nausea assailed her. Just looking at it—the silver head with the dark-red blood blooming around it—seemed to make it throb with greater intensity. She turned away from it, choking on the bile that rose in her throat.

Finch moved around to the other side and knelt beside her, his knee on the soft flesh above her right elbow, pinning her arm to the floor and cutting off her circulation. His excited smile loomed, filling up her field of vision. "How's it feel, Rush?"

She turned away from him, an involuntary groan escaping her lips. Tears burned the backs of her eyes.

Pull it together, Rush, said the voice in her head.

She had to get out of this. She didn't care what he did to her. He could cut her hands off if he wanted to, as long as he didn't hurt Olivia. She closed her eyes again and sent up a silent prayer that Olivia would not wake up.

"You know, your sister fought a lot harder."

It was meant to upset her, but it made her feel better. She opened her eyes again and rolled her head in his direction. Her right arm was numb. She tried to wiggle her fingers, but she couldn't be sure if they were moving. "What do you want?" she asked, still trying to even out her breath, to find some semblance of calm in her adrenaline-induced terror. She was only going to get one chance at this. Olivia's life depended on it.

Oh God. Olivia.

Finch laughed. "I want you to beg for it, Rush."

She coughed, spluttered, and said in a throaty voice, "Beg for what?"

He shifted, releasing her right arm and slid a hand down between her legs, cupping her. Ice filled her veins. A new wave of terror and disgust overwhelmed her. And anger. She wanted to break every one of his fingers. She had to focus. Again, she tried flexing the fingers of her right hand, relieved to feel the blood flow back into her arm.

"I want you to beg me to fuck you," he said. "And then I want you to beg me to kill you. Because, Rush, by the time I get done with you, you'll wish you were dead."

She had no doubt. She glanced all around him, trying to see if he had his gun. It didn't look like it. She remained silent, shoring up her strength.

"What? You have nothing to say? You?"

His hand fumbled beneath the waistband of her pajama pants. His fingers pried roughly inside her.

Is this what it was like? she wondered briefly, thinking of Camille and Anita.

She crossed her legs, trying to trap his hand and stop it from moving. He licked his lips again, moving his face closer to hers. "What's wrong, Rush? Don't you like it?"

A sound from upstairs froze them both in place. Then Olivia's voice, muffled but high-pitched. "Mommy?"

Finch looked down at her. "Who the fuck is that?"

"My daughter, you asshole. You leave her alone."

The cry came again. "Mommy?"

A noise. Rattling. She was trying to open the door.

"It's okay, sweetheart," Jocelyn called as loudly as she could.

The rattling stopped.

Hold on, Jocelyn said silently. *Just hold on.*

Finch's jaw was set, his brow an angry line. He obviously hadn't planned on the interruption. "How old is she?"

"Three. She's locked in her room. You don't need her. Leave her alone."

He stopped his ministrations and pulled his hand free. He looked uncertain. He didn't know what to do, she realized. The hammer hung loosely in his other hand. He glanced toward the steps, made a move toward them.

"Finch!"

He turned back toward her. She swallowed over the lump in her throat. "Gi-give it to me. I want it. Give it to me n-now."

He shifted back toward her, his face half smile, half puzzlement. "Say please," he tried.

"P-p-please."

He smiled, knelt beside her again. "Please, what?"

The words felt like razor blades over her tongue. "Please f-fuck me."

He snaked a hand under her shirt and squeezed one of her breasts.

This was it.

"Mommy!"

In one swift motion, Jocelyn brought both legs up as high as she could, capturing Finch's head between her knees and toppling him backward. She used the momentum of his falling body and tore her hand from the floor with a primal scream. The nail remained there, tufts of tissue and skin slick on its shaft. With the other hand, she fumbled for the hammer, wrestling it from his hand as she squeezed his head between her thighs.

"Mommy! Mommy! I'm scared!"

Me too, baby. Me too.

Jocelyn brought the hammer down on Finch's head as hard as she could. After three tries, his skull caved with a sickening thunk. She kept his head scissor-locked between her legs and watched him, all the while trying not to throw up in his face. Slowly, he stopped fighting, until all the life went out of him. She took the hammer and dashed up the steps.

"Hold on, baby, I'm coming," she called to Olivia. She reached the door and put her mouth to the crack. "Get back, baby. I need you to get back. I have to kick the door open."

"Mommy," came the tiny, tremulous voice. "I'm scared."

Jocelyn tried to keep the tremor from her own voice. "It's okay, baby. Everything is okay. The door is just stuck. I'm going to kick it. Are you in the bed? Get in the bed."

Jocelyn listened for footsteps, then the rustling of blankets. She stepped back to put some distance between her and the door and stumbled, falling back against the wall. Dizziness washed over her. She took a deep breath and righted herself, kicking the door heartily, right beside the doorknob. It took two tries, but finally the door splintered. Jocelyn pushed through it and found Olivia cowering in her bed, Lulu clutched to her chest.

Tears streamed down Olivia's face. Jocelyn scooped her up and held her tightly, burying her face in the girl's hair. "It's okay, baby. It's okay."

The scent of Olivia's Baby Magic shampoo filled Jocelyn's nostrils. Relief swept through her, so big that it swept everything away, leaving only shivers behind.

"I couldn't get the door open," Olivia said.

"I know. It's okay. It's okay now."

Olivia pulled away from Jocelyn and glanced at the blood streaking her pajamas. "Mommy, you have a boo-boo. A really bad one."

"I know, honey. It's okay."

Olivia's face crumpled and fat teardrops rolled down her face. "Are you going to die?"

Jocelyn smiled and kissed Olivia's forehead, gathering her in close. "No, honey. I'm not going to die. We're going to call the police right now, and they'll take us to the hospital."

Olivia said nothing, but she let Jocelyn carry her across the hall into her bedroom. Jocelyn picked up her cell phone, smearing the blood all over the screen. She dialed 911 and put the phone between her ear and shoulder as she shifted Olivia's weight in her arms.

"Nine-one-one, where's your emergency?"

Her voice was steady. "Philadelphia. I've just killed an intruder in my home."

FIFTY-EIGHT

November 13th

Jocelyn woke from a deep sleep, slowly coming to, approaching consciousness as if from a great distance. Sleep was like a heavy wet blanket, and she couldn't shrug it off. But she had to. She had to wake up. There was something she had to do. *Something important.*

"Olivia!" She woke herself with her own scream, the sound something between a shriek and the sound a dying animal makes. She thrashed before she even knew where she was, her limbs clanging off something hard and metal. Bed rails.

When she opened her eyes, the white light of the hospital room was near blinding. She blinked rapidly and squinted, trying to make sense of the figures surrounding her bed. Gentle hands pressed her arms to her side. "Hey, Jocelyn," a familiar voice murmured. "It's okay."

It was Caleb's voice, and she turned toward it, her eyes finally adjusting to the light. She looked up at him, relief chasing away the terror she'd felt upon waking. She grasped his arms, trying to pull him toward her. The heavy bundle of bandages encasing her left hand made it impossible. He leaned over the side of the bed awkwardly, sliding an arm across her back.

"It's okay now," he whispered in her ear. "You're okay. You're in the hospital. You passed out in the ambulance, and they kept you sedated so they could clean out your wound."

"Olivia," she said, tears leaking from her eyes. "Where's Olivia? Oh my God, Olivia!"

Caleb stepped back so she could look behind him, where Inez sat in a cushy bedside chair, wearing street clothes and cradling a sleeping Olivia in her arms. Olivia's face lay on her shoulder with the slackened look that came only from utter exhaustion. Her lips looked almost swollen, half-open in an O shape. Jocelyn knew that look. They could light off a hundred fireworks right next to her and she wouldn't wake up. Blankie covered her back and Lulu dangled from her left hand, a bloody fingerprint between her ears. "She's fine," Inez said, smiling.

"Thank God," Jocelyn said, falling back into her pillow. That's when she noticed Phil and Captain Ahearn standing on the other side of the bed. Phil gave her an awkward wave. She'd never seen him so unkempt. His eyes were glassy, and he had a five o'clock shadow. He had undone his tie and the top two buttons of his dress shirt. He smiled at her but didn't speak.

"Rush," Ahearn said by way of greeting.

She nodded and closed her eyes, concentrating on her breathing. The pain in her hand finally broke through her fatigue with the kind of ache she hadn't felt since she'd woken up from the accident at seventeen. "Jesus," she gasped.

"You can have more pain meds in an hour," Inez informed her.

Jocelyn opened her eyes again and scanned the room once more. "Where's Kevin?"

She didn't like the look that passed among them. "Please," she said. "Just tell me."

Phil stepped forward. "He's in the ICU with a head injury. Last night he was leaving work and someone hit him over the head and robbed him."

Her bundled hand flew to her chest. "Oh no."

"He was lucky," Caleb added, exchanging a look with Phil. "Delisi here was also leaving Northwest, and he caught the guy in the act. Chased him off. He'd probably be dead if Phil hadn't found him and gotten him help right away."

Jocelyn swallowed. She met Phil's eyes. "Thank you," she said.

He nodded. "We think it was Finch," Caleb added. "He had Kevin's wallet, badge, and gun on him when we removed his body from your living room."

"Will he—will he live?" she asked, her voice breaking on the last word.

Again the exchange of looks all around the room, as if she were a child and they were deciding how much to tell her. "Just tell me," she demanded. "Don't keep anything from me, please."

"His head injury was pretty bad, but the doctors say that the odds are in his favor," Ahearn said from the far corner of the room. "But there is always a small chance he won't pull through."

Jocelyn nodded. "Thank you."

Caleb perched on the side of the bed, near her feet. "We, uh, found Warner and Donovan," he said. "Apparently, there was some kind of shoot-out at Vince Fox's home after his bar burned down. Both Fox and Donovan were shot and killed. Warner took a bullet to the shoulder. He was picked up fleeing the scene with a bag of money. We found almost a million dollars in cash and drugs in a gun safe in Fox's basement."

"Guess he was dirty like Chen said," Jocelyn mused.

Caleb chuckled. "You could say that."

"There will be a full-scale investigation," Ahearn added.

"And Camille seems to be recovering well," Caleb said. "She'll be discharged in a day or two—to a rehab facility."

"At her request," Inez piped in. "Oh, and your Uncle Simon has called several times, but he wasn't sure if you'd want to see him, so he hasn't come by. He has, however, been stationed by Camille's bedside for the last several hours."

"Thank goodness for happy endings," Jocelyn said, somewhat sarcastically.

"It could have been a lot worse," Caleb pointed out, staring at her intently.

Inez caught Jocelyn's eye and winked. She struggled to her feet with Olivia in her arms and made her way to Phil and Ahearn. "Can I talk to you guys outside?" she said.

Once they were alone, Caleb put the bed rail down so he could sit closer to her. He lined his hips up with hers and sat on the edge of the bed facing her. He touched her cheek and then her hair, smoothing it away from her forehead. "I'm sorry," he said. "I should have stayed."

"It's not your fault," Jocelyn assured him. "But thank you."

"I'm going to be here for you."

She smiled and caught his hand with her ACE bandaged right hand, pressing it against her heart. "I would like that a lot."

He left her with a soft, slow kiss. "I'll let you get some rest," he said as Inez slipped back into the room. Once he was gone, Inez laid Olivia in the bed next to Jocelyn. Jocelyn turned on her side so she could soak in her daughter's sleeping face. Inez settled back into the bedside chair. "You know," she said after a few minutes. "You are going to need therapy after this."

Jocelyn laughed. "Yeah, I know."

A few minutes of easy silence passed between them. Then Inez spoke once more. "You know what Sullivan would say, right?"

Jocelyn looked past Olivia at her best friend. "What's that?"

"Hey, Rush. You know that time you killed Finch with a hammer after he broke into your house and threatened you and your daughter?"

Jocelyn couldn't suppress the shudder that worked its way through her, but she answered anyway. "Yeah?"

"That was pretty badass."

"Yes," Jocelyn said. "Yes, it was."

FIFTY-NINE

November 15th

For the next two days, Jocelyn drifted in and out of a heavy, hazy, painkiller-induced sleep. There was a regular parade of people, and there was always someone at her bedside when she woke up, for which she was grateful. Even Phil took a shift, tending to her when she woke with a tenderness that had been missing their entire relationship. When Caleb came to relieve him, they even shook hands. Inez and Martina had taken over caring for Olivia, and Inez brought her by as much as possible. They would stay with Inez until Jocelyn's house was habitable again. Once the crime scene unit had finished with it, Inez and Caleb got to work on removing the bloodstains. But it would be awhile before she could go back there with Olivia.

On the third day of her hospital stay, she was discharged. She was trying unsuccessfully to snap the button on her jeans with her two injured hands when a nurse wheeled Camille into her hospital room. Her bandaged feet sat atop the foot rests, her hands in her lap. She wore a thick peach-colored robe over sweatpants and a hospital gown. Her hair was freshly washed. She was still pale and thin—sickly looking—but cleaner and prettier than Jocelyn had seen her look in years.

"Nice robe," Jocelyn remarked, smiling.

Her sister smiled back. The nurse wheeled her around to where Jocelyn stood and left. "Simon is taking good care of me," Camille said. "It's kind of nice. You need a little help there?"

Jocelyn looked down at her unfastened jeans and sighed. "It took me twenty minutes just to get these damn things on." She motioned to Camille's lap. "I don't think you'll have much better luck than me."

"Hurts like hell, doesn't it?"

"Yeah," Jocelyn agreed, plopping back down onto the bed.

Camille held up a bundled hand. "We'll have scars."

"I know. I'm so—"

"I'm glad," Camille said quickly. Her chin jutted out, the sharp lines of defiance hardening her expression. It was a sight Jocelyn hadn't seen in twenty years. She felt a warmth envelop her body that had nothing to do with the drugs she was on or the temperature in the room.

"Last time," Camille continued. "There were no scars. There was nothing that people could see. Sure, I had some bruising, but it was gone in a few weeks. I was wrecked. Totally and completely wrecked, but on the outside I looked just fine. I looked the same as I always looked. Do you know what that's like? To feel like your soul has been wrenched out of your body and shit on, and have absolutely no tangible sign of it? It fucking sucks. It's like you're invisible. It's like you really died."

"Camille, I am so sorry."

Her sister's eyes narrowed. Her voice shook—not with grief, but with anger. Jocelyn recognized the emotion. It had been her constant companion for two decades now. "I'm glad I have scars this time. No one can pretend that my pain isn't real."

"No one can brush it under the carpet," Jocelyn agreed. She had never thought of it that way.

"I want to talk about it," Camille said. Her words had a quality of false bravado, her voice a little too high, as if she was expecting Jocelyn to refuse to talk about it.

Tears stung Jocelyn's eyes. "I've only been waiting twenty years to talk about it, Camille. I have these dreams where I'm standing at your bedroom door, watching them rape you. I don't know if they are memories or not."

Camille shook her head. "It wasn't in my bedroom. It was in the game room. On the pool table."

"Did I—did I see it?"

"At the time, you said that you went to the door of the game room, and you saw them all gathered around the pool table with their pants around their ankles. Then you saw my legs. You pushed on the door and one of them—the lookout—reached for you, so you ran."

Whitman. So that part had been a real memory. His eye peering through the crack in the door. His hand reaching for her. Jocelyn shivered. "Then what?"

"You called Dad. Him and Mom were at a wedding in Delaware. They were going to stay the night there, so we had a big party. He came, alone. By then the boys had left. Dad came and made everyone else leave. When you realized he wasn't going to call the police, you called Mom. She made him take me to the hospital."

"I called Dad?" Jocelyn asked, puzzled. She wished she could remember that time. "Why would I call Dad? Why didn't I call the police?"

Camille rolled her eyes. "We were teenagers, Joce. Dad was the end-all, be-all. I probably would have done the same thing."

"But it was a crime—I should have called the police. That's what I would do."

Camille shook her head again. "That's what you would do now. You were different then. You have been since the accident. You had a major head injury. The doctors said your personality might be different. But you did try to help me. You wouldn't let it go."

A tear slid down Jocelyn's cheek, and she wiped it away with the back of her ACE bandage. "Then what happened?"

Camille rested a paw on Jocelyn's knee. "Don't cry," she said. "I hate it when you cry. It's not—it's not natural."

Jocelyn laughed and wiped more tears away. She used her right hand to swipe a tissue from the bedside stand and blow her nose. "I can't make any promises. Just tell me."

"Dad said that the case would never hold up. We had invited them all over. I had exchanged suggestive notes with Daniel Blackburn. We were all skinny-dipping earlier that night. I kissed Daniel before it happened. A good defense lawyer would eat me alive."

"But I saw it," Jocelyn pointed out, poking her chest with her right hand.

"You saw the end of it. You didn't see any of them actually . . ." Camille hesitated, remembering what Jocelyn was certain were their father's words. "Penetrate me. Then you called Dad and not the police. It didn't make you credible."

Jocelyn felt sick. She knew for a fact that Phil had sent people to prison on far less. She swallowed over the lump in her throat. "Did they do a rape kit?"

Camille nodded. "Mom insisted. Dad had to buy off the hospital staff and the local police."

"What did it show?"

Camille bit her lip. Her shoulders trembled. "Four different types of semen."

Vomit rocketed up into Jocelyn's throat. She barely made it to the trash can beside the bed.

She didn't know what was worse—the rape or what her father had done in the wake of it.

"He said it wasn't a good case," Camille continued. "I was fifteen. You remember how overbearing he was—it was easier to do what he said. And I was so ashamed. I felt so disgusting and dirty. Then you had the car accident and couldn't remember anything."

Jocelyn took a sip of water from the cup on the tray table. "So after the accident when I dragged you and Dad to that meeting with the sheriff and the DA, and they asked you if you had been raped—"

Camille closed her eyes. "I said no."

Jocelyn felt as if she were having an out of body experience. She didn't remember any of it—nothing before the accident. Not even the accident itself. She couldn't remember what she was like before that. It was almost as though she had never been that seventeen-year-old girl—the one who came before all the violence and lies.

"The accident—what happened?" Jocelyn asked.

"You drove your car into a tree."

"On purpose?"

Camille shrugged. "Only you would have known that. But, yes, I think so."

Jocelyn had a strange feeling in her chest, like her heart had suddenly been inflated with helium and was trying to float away. Had she really been that desperate? That demoralized? Had she really been the kind of girl who would take that kind of out? It seemed so out of character, but like Camille said, she had been different before the accident. "Oh my God," she whispered.

"Jocelyn, I'm sorry," Camille said.

"Oh God, Camille, none of this was your fault. It's okay."

Camille gave her a rueful smile. Her hands moved in her lap, fingertips awkwardly smoothing invisible folds. She was doing phantom origami, Jocelyn realized, or trying to with her damaged hands. "No, it's really not," Camille croaked.

Jocelyn smiled back grimly. "You're right."

"That rape destroyed our family, our lives."

"Dad destroyed our family and Mom let him. People recover from violence all the time. They rise above it. He didn't give us that chance. He had to be in control of everything. Everything was about appearances, his reputation. He couldn't just do the right thing."

"He fucked up," Camille agreed.

"Yeah, but he didn't destroy our lives."

Tears filled Camille's eyes. She looked down at her battered body and back to Jocelyn. "Didn't he?"

"Camille," Jocelyn said, holding her sister's gaze. "We're still here. We're still alive. I don't know about you, but I'm not done living."

"Your optimism makes my head hurt. You've got a career, a house, a kid—it's easy for you. You already have a good life. I'm an addict. A fuckup. All that money Mom and Dad left me won't change that."

"You've got me—no, you can't live with me, at least not yet—but you've got me."

"Well, okay," Camille said without conviction.

"I'm serious."

"I know you are."

Jocelyn reached out and touched Camille's shoulder. "Let's forgive each other, Camille. For all of it—for everything. Let's start over, right here and right now."

Camille smiled through tears. "I'd like that," she said. "What about Olivia?"

Jocelyn pulled her hand back but kept her voice even. "Olivia is mine. That will never change. You can be in her life and have a relationship with her, but I am her mother."

Camille looked away but nodded. "Okay," she murmured. "That's fair."

"But, Camille," Jocelyn said. "We would like you in our lives. There's so little left of our family. Don't let what Mom and Dad did ruin our chance to be a family again."

Camille gave her a weak smile, tears still streaming down her face. "I'll think about it," she said.

SIXTY

November 22nd

One week later, Jocelyn sat in a small room at SVU watching a closed circuit video broadcast of Caleb questioning Larry Warner. It was almost as she had theorized to Kevin. Warner's son had been good friends with Angel. Dwayne, Angel, and Larry had been running numbers and prostitutes. They dabbled in the drug trade, but their main source of income was gambling—it was extremely lucrative. They were bringing in thousands of dollars a week. Vince Fox was their man on the police force, looking the other way when he caught them doing something illegal—making evidence against them in cases where other officers had arrested them disappear. All he wanted was a cut and to sample some of the girls now and then. He had been with Shasta more than once, in fact. Dwayne didn't like it, but he had no choice. Fox could hurt them as much as he helped them.

As it turned out, Shasta didn't mind Fox all that much. The two agreed to get rid of Dwayne, Angel, and Larry and take on the whole operation themselves. Dwayne found out, and everything went to shit. That was the day of the shooting that took Dwayne's and Shasta's lives, rendered Angel speechless for the rest of his life, and put Larry in prison for his first violent offense. And Fox walked away with a lot of money and a lot of drugs.

Larry and Angel didn't like that so much.

Once Larry got out of the pen, he and Angel started plotting on how they could get their revenge on Fox. He caught them following him one day, planted drugs on them, threatened to arrest them if they didn't keep their mouths shut. Finch, who was Fox's new partner, saw the whole thing. A few days later, Finch sought them out. The deal was simple. Warner and Angel would get him girls, girls with whom he could do as he pleased, and, in return, he would carry out their revenge on Fox. He would also keep them out of trouble with the police and provide them with enough drugs pilfered from the evidence unit to make them a lot of money—which of course they had to split with him.

But Finch's first effort at assassinating Fox ended in his partner taking early retirement and Finch being transferred with a new nickname: Friendly Fire.

"So what was the plan after that, Larry?" Caleb asked the man.

Larry, who had taken on the same slumped posture he'd used when Jocelyn interrogated him, shrugged, wincing immediately at the pain in his bandaged shoulder. He shifted his arm sling. "Wasn't no plan. Not really. It was the same arrangement. We got the girls and he would kill Fox and get our money back. But we kept getting girls, and he wasn't doing nothing to hold up his end of the bargain. That last one—she was supposed to be the last one."

Caleb wrote something on the legal pad in front of him. "I see," he said. "And whose idea was it to torch Fox's bar?"

Larry rubbed the side of his nose. "Angel's. He didn't think Face—I mean Finch—would ever do it. He thought we should take matters into our own hands. But Fox wasn't at the bar. So we went to his house. He shot Angel, and I shot him in self-defense."

Caleb was nodding like a metronome, writing slowly with his pen. Jocelyn would bet a lot of money that he was simply doodling while Larry lied his ass off about whose idea it finally was to go after Fox. They couldn't prove it with ballistics, but Jocelyn wondered if it was really Larry who had shot Angel—so he could have all the loot for himself.

Jocelyn's cell phone danced in her jacket pocket. She pulled it out with her right hand and answered it. "Anita?"

"Yeah. I got your message. What's up, Rush?"

Jocelyn stood and turned away from the television, staring at the dank gray wall behind her. "There was something I needed to run by you. I'm going private—opening my own private investigation firm." It hadn't taken her long to decide. She was tired of the daily violence. The horror of it all. With her inheritance, she could open her own firm, taking on cheating spouses and background checks. She'd have more time for Olivia—and Caleb too. She could also keep tabs on Camille—and give her some support during her rehab. Maybe the nightmares would go away. Plus someone had to look after Kevin once he was discharged—he had a long recovery ahead of him, and she wasn't sure if Nurse Bottinger was in for the long haul or not. "I need someone to help me get the business off the ground," she added.

Anita clucked her tongue. "And you're calling me? Rush, I ain't no private detective. Don't you have to be a cop first to be a private detective?"

Jocelyn paced the tiny room. "Yeah, that's true, but I don't really need another investigator. I need a partner, someone who can head up the administrative end of things."

Silence. Then, "Partner? Rush, are you out of your mind? I don't have money to be startin' no business."

"You don't need money," Jocelyn said. "I need someone I can trust—someone smart and savvy—who knows their way around computers. You know, someone who can maybe find the name of a victim who was killed seventeen years ago when the police, the DA, and the defense attorney can't. What do you say?"

There was more dead air as Anita considered it. Jocelyn thought she could make out Pia singing in the background. "It will pay well," Jocelyn added. "Very well. Benefits, the whole nine. Plus a one-hundred-thousand-dollar signing bonus if you agree to work with me for one year."

There was the sound of coughing, then a loud bang, as if Anita had dropped the phone. Finally, she came back on. "Now I know you're out of your damn mind," she said.

Jocelyn smiled. "So you'll do it?"

"Oh, I'll do it, but I want that in writing," she replied. Jocelyn could still detect the note of skepticism in her voice.

"Done. I'll stop by at the end of the week with a contract. Right now, I have to go see my attorney. See about the start-up funds."

SIXTY-ONE

November 22nd

The offices of Rush and Wilde hadn't changed much since Jocelyn was a child. She hadn't been there since she was about thirteen. The offices took up an entire floor of a swanky high-rise near Twentieth and Market. The elevator ride seemed to go on forever. Jocelyn hated elevators—and places with windows that didn't open. The lobby walls were dark paneling, giving it more of an old-school courtroom look than a Sheetrocked office look. Her feet sunk into the plush blue carpeting, which showed wear in the places people walked the most. Paintings of Philadelphia's biggest attractions—Boathouse Row, the art museum—hung below thick crown molding. Large potted plants sat like sentries beside the office doors. A receptionist sat at a large wraparound desk across from a seating area for clients. It looked a lot like someone's living room, only far more elegant and less used.

Simon's secretary ushered her into a conference room with a large, glass-topped table and high-backed leather seats more cushy than her couch. She didn't have to wait long to see her uncle. He looked like he had aged ten years since she had last seen him. She had refused to see him in the hospital. She stood when he entered and they hugged awkwardly, their bodies not really touching, their hands barely patting each other's backs.

He held an accordion file in his hand, which he placed on the table. "Please, sit," he said. She sat back in the chair, and he sat next to her, turning so he could face her. "I'm glad you came."

"I'd like to wrap up my parents' estate," Jocelyn said. "I am going into business for myself, and Camille will need the money—she's got a lengthy rehab stint ahead of her, and she's been talking about going to a place out in California, getting away from here."

Simon's eyes moistened. He smiled. "I think that would be lovely. We can make distribution today if you'd like. There's just one thing. Something your mother wanted done before everything was put to rest."

Her mouth was suddenly very dry. "It's about the rape, isn't it?"

He pulled the file toward him. "Your mother came to me—it was Camille's second stint in rehab. I had known for years that something had changed in your family."

Jocelyn nodded. "She wasn't the same. She was angry and bitter. They hadn't told you about the rape before that?"

Simon shook his head. "I was on trial when it happened. A big one. Lots of publicity, high stakes. It lasted four months. Your father didn't want me to be distracted. Your mother called me a few times but I—I never returned her calls."

He looked away sheepishly. When he turned back to her, his face was lined with sadness. "I'm sorry, Jocelyn. I asked your father what was going on. He said there had been a car accident, but that you were okay. He never even mentioned Camille. I didn't give it another thought."

Jocelyn sighed. "Of course you didn't."

Simon had always been every bit as driven as her father, if not more. It was that singularity of purpose that had made their firm so successful. When your cases came before everything else in your life, you were bound to win a good deal of them.

"Jocelyn," Simon said.

She waved a hand in dismissal. "It doesn't matter. What's done is done. My mother approached you. What did she want?"

"She wanted me to help her build a case that we could take to the Montgomery County DA. She thought once Camille was clean she would be strong enough to tell the truth, that she'd make a better witness."

"Camille never really got clean."

Simon hung his head. "Yes, I know. But there were other issues. Your father was criminally culpable."

"Obstruction of justice is not that big a charge," Jocelyn said.

"Bribery is," Simon countered. "He bribed the hospital staff, the sheriff's office. Think of the ramifications. The firm would be destroyed. Every case we ever won would come under scrutiny. All those people—some of them were innocent—and the people who took the bribes. The families of the boys who paid your father for his silence—"

"For my family's silence," Jocelyn corrected. She leveled a finger at Simon. "This destroyed my family. We weren't perfect, but before my father brushed this under the carpet, we were okay. My mother was happy. Camille was a normal fifteen-year-old. Who knows what she would have been?"

Simon frowned, his eyes on the glass tabletop. His fingers tapped lightly against the file. "It wasn't my decision, Jocelyn. I did as your mother asked, and once she saw the lengths your father had gone to, the extent of the cover-up, she couldn't go through with it. The number of lives and careers that would have been destroyed was just too great, especially for something Camille had already denied to the authorities. You were the only witness, and you didn't remember it. Credibility was a serious issue."

"All of those people were just as wrong as my father. They deserved whatever consequences they had coming to them."

Simon's smile was sad. He looked down at her with pinched eyes, as if he were looking at a recalcitrant child. "Jocelyn, some things in life are not that simple."

"Maybe they aren't," she agreed. "But you don't get to decide that. You don't get to decide the consequences of people's wrongdoing."

"It wasn't my decision," he repeated.

"But it was. You made a choice. So did my mother and my father and Camille. And every person along the way who turned a blind eye. None of you are God. None of you are judge and jury, and apparently none of you have an ethical bone in your body." Her next words shook in her throat, sounding tremulous and angry all at once. "Camille was fifteen years old. She was gang-raped. That is a crime. There is no way around that. What happened to her was wrong. Those boys should have been punished."

"It would have been a shaky case—"

Jocelyn slapped a palm against the tabletop, making Simon jump and sending a skewer of pain reverberating through her hand. "Stop thinking like a lawyer, and start thinking like a human being. For God's sake."

She couldn't look at him. Her body trembled with rage. The hole in her left hand ached.

"Jocelyn," Simon said, reaching for her.

"Don't," she said coldly.

Simon didn't have children. In a way, she could understand why the whole thing hadn't presented as much of an issue for him. If anyone ever hurt Olivia, Jocelyn would kill them. She *had* killed to protect Olivia. Why hadn't her parents felt the same? That was the thing that bothered her the most. The thing that kept her up nights. She couldn't remember the day Camille was raped, but she remembered well the horrific aftermath. Why hadn't they stood up for her? Damn the cost.

In her reverie, she hadn't noticed Simon creeping closer to her. He laid a palm on her shoulder. As if reading her thoughts, he said, "They thought they were protecting her."

Jocelyn stared straight ahead, past Simon, her eyes locked on the wall behind him where a framed photo of the Liberty Bell hung. It was a bitter pill to swallow. Whatever her parents' motivations, it was done, and she couldn't undo it.

You have to start from where you are. Camille said that's what a therapist at her new rehab facility had told her. It resonated for both of them.

She sighed and rubbed her right temple. Her head was starting to pound. "My mother would not have let this go. What did she ask you to do?"

He rifled through the file and pulled a large manila envelope from it. After slipping a finger beneath the flap, he opened it and handed it to her. She turned it over and glossy photos fell onto the table and into her lap. She surveyed them quickly, wanting to look away, trying to appear cool and unaffected. But each photo was like a knife twisting in her insides. They were all of Camille at fifteen, her hair mussed, her eyes glassy and vacant. She lay in a hospital bed. Her hospital gown only came to midthigh, handprint bruises showing beneath the hem. Some of the photos showed the bruising up close. Jocelyn could only imagine how hard the boys had had to grip Camille's thighs to make those marks.

"Oh my God," she gasped.

"There are lab results in there as well," Simon said. "DNA tests."

"Proof," Jocelyn said.

"Your father held on to it, in case the families of the boys who raped her didn't keep paying. Once the statute of limitations ran, he didn't need it anymore. Your mother asked me to give it to you once she was gone."

Jocelyn's stomach burned. She pressed a bandaged hand to her middle. "To me? Why not Camille? And why now?"

Simon threw his hands in the air. He stood and paced. "I don't know. Validation, maybe? She said you would know how to handle it—what to do with them. She wanted me to tell you girls that she was sorry."

"That's what she asked you to do? Give me proof that my sister was raped that I can never use? Apologize for something unforgiveable? No. She asked you to do something else. What was it, Simon?"

He grimaced and held his hands out, as if making an offering. "I think you know what she asked me to do."

Again her stomach acids roiled. "Good God."

He sat down again, leaning his elbows on his knees, his face inches from her. "Think about it. There was no touching these guys once the statute ran. Even if we went to the press with that," he pointed to the envelope in her lap, "Camille would have been humiliated in the process. What else was there? What is the worst thing that you can do to them? That even if it doesn't stick, their reputations will be forever ruined? They have to live with the shame, with the stigma forever."

"My mother asked you to frame them for child pornography?"

He pursed his lips, screwing up his face as if he had tasted something sour. He didn't answer. Of course not. He would never come out and say it. Not even to her. Because he knew that if she ever ended up on the stand testifying against him—testifying to this very conversation they were having—she would need more than his silent acquiescence to be credible. A good defense attorney would ask her, "Did Mr. Wilde actually tell you that he framed these men?" and she would have to say no. All he had done was pose a question, which he would claim was rhetorical. She was the one who said the words, not him. She made the suggestion, and that's what Simon would say—it was only a suggestion, nothing more.

"I was wondering where you would have gotten the photos," she said quietly. "Then I remembered that Caleb—Lieutenant Vaughn said that they were pretty old images, that they had been circulating for a while. Who besides the police and an actual child pornographer would have access to such things? An attorney who defended perverts in the past, of course. It's sick, what you've done."

Again he said nothing, but he had the grace to look as though she had slapped him. His eyes moistened again. In that moment, he looked very frail. Just a sad old man who had tried to remedy something horrific with something else horrific. A man trying to put a Band-Aid on a severed limb. A man who was utterly lost.

"Michael Pearce killed himself over this, Simon. He jumped off the Henry Avenue Bridge. His death is on your conscience."

Simon smiled sadly. "Are you really sorry about his death?"

This time she didn't answer. A moment passed between them. She shoved the photographs of Camille back into the envelope and snatched the file from the table, tucking both under her arm. "Framing someone for a crime they didn't commit is wrong, Simon. Whether that person is morally bankrupt or not. You think I don't want those men to suffer? I do. But not like this."

"Jocelyn," he said.

She stood up, her chair bumping the table. "You can mail me a check for my half of the estate."

He called out to her as she reached the door. She thought she heard something like panic in his voice. "What are you going to do?" he asked.

She gave him one last look before she walked out. "The right thing," she told him. "I'm going to do the right thing."

EPILOGUE

December 23rd

Jocelyn winced as pain shot through her left hand. She dropped the knife she had been using to chop vegetables, and it clanged against her dining room table.

"Shit," she said, holding her hand against her middle.

"Mommy," Olivia chided.

Jocelyn looked across the table. From where they sat, Olivia, Raquel, and Ana stared at her. Ana looked almost afraid, her eyes wide as saucers, her body unnaturally still. Jocelyn got that a lot lately. People didn't know how to act around her—even people who had known her for years. It was as if they were waiting for her to explode, to go crazy, to fly into a fit of rage so big it would incinerate everything in its wake.

Only Olivia and Raquel treated her exactly the same as they always had. Using the red crayon she had been coloring with, Olivia pointed toward the far end of the table where a small jar sat, stuffed full of dollar bills. "That's one dollar, Mommy."

Damn swear jar. There would be enough in it to buy Olivia her first home before she was even four.

"Yeah, yeah," Jocelyn muttered under her breath. She reached into the left-hand pocket of her jeans and pulled out a crumpled dollar bill. She stuffed it into the jar, and another dagger of pain shot through her left hand. "Dammit," she said before she could stop herself.

The holes had long closed up, and she'd had weeks of physical therapy to regain full function in her hand, but sometimes, if she used it a lot in a short period of time, the pain would return. Like spikes or barbs. Like the nail was being driven through all over again. She wondered if some of it was psychological.

"That's another dollar, Mommy."

Raquel's giggles broke some of the tension building in the room. Ana's body relaxed, and she walked over and stood beside Jocelyn. "You put the pasta on," she told Jocelyn. "I'll do the salad."

"Okay, thanks." Jocelyn smiled and disappeared into the kitchen.

As she filled a pot of water and put it on the stove to boil, she heard Raquel ask, "When are Mommy and Daddy coming back?"

"Not until tomorrow," Ana replied. "You know that."

Raquel's voice took on a slightly whiny quality. "What are they doing?"

"They're making you a baby brother," Ana teased.

Jocelyn moved to the doorway. Raquel's baby-smooth brow was creased with worry. "A brother? I don't want a brother!"

"They're not making a brother," Jocelyn put in, moving around the table so she could look over the girls' shoulders. She stroked Raquel's long black hair. "Your daddy has been away for a very long time, and he only gets to come home for a couple of weeks. He and your mommy need to spend some time alone. You'll stay with us until tomorrow."

Olivia looked up at Jocelyn. "What do you think, Mommy? Do you think Aunt Camille will like it?"

Jocelyn studied the card the girls had been working on for the past day—ever since she'd told Olivia she had an aunt and that

Camille would be coming to visit for Christmas. Jocelyn might as well have told her Santa Claus was spending the holidays with them, she was so excited about the prospect of a mysterious new family member. She had asked hundreds of questions, exhausting Jocelyn and testing the limits of what she was prepared to tell Olivia about Camille and why they had never met before.

Camille had been in rehab in California for several weeks. It was her idea to come home for Christmas. It was Jocelyn's idea for her to stay with them and finally meet Olivia. But now Jocelyn was a nervous wreck. She hadn't spent any meaningful time with her sister in two decades. She had no idea how Olivia and Camille would react to one another or whether or not they would hit it off. But the greater part of her couldn't wait to see her sister and spend a holiday like a real family.

Jocelyn bent and kissed her daughter's head. "I think she'll love it. Look at all those hearts and rainbows. It's very colorful and beautiful."

"I drew the unicorn," Raquel said, pointing to a purple unicorn flying over top of an array of flowers.

"I love it!" Jocelyn exclaimed.

"We both did the flowers," Olivia said. "When will Aunt Camille get here?"

Jocelyn glanced at the clock on the wall. "Hopefully in another hour or so."

A knock at her door drew their attention. "Ana, watch the pasta, will you?"

Ana nodded as Jocelyn left the girls in the dining room. She looked through the peephole on her front door and found Kevin and Nurse Kim waiting on her porch. She opened her door wide, smiling in greeting. The hair the neurosurgeon had shaved to operate on Kevin's head had grown in nicely. He still walked with a cane and had several more weeks of physical therapy before he could resume his normal routine. Nurse Kim had been looking after him quite diligently. It gave Jocelyn hope.

"Rush," Kevin said as he and Kim entered. "Good to see you." He pulled her into a bear hug. Kim said hello, then wandered into the dining room to greet the girls. Kevin released her but kept an arm around her shoulders. "You look good," he said. Leaning into her ear, he lowered his voice. "Your friend is outside. I'll distract the kids while you talk to him."

Jocelyn smiled despite the characteristic heat that rose to her face at the mere mention of Caleb. "Thanks, Kev."

As she stepped outside into the frigid December air, she could hear Olivia and Raquel's gleeful shouts of "Uncle Kevin! Uncle Kevin!"

Caleb waited in her driveway, leaning casually against her Explorer. The smile he gave her made her heart skip. She picked up her pace, nearly falling into him when she reached the driveway. He caught her in his arms, steadied her, and planted a gentle kiss on her forehead. "Hey," he breathed into her hair.

She wrapped her arms around his waist, inhaling his scent. "Hey," she replied.

He looked up at her house. "Is Camille here yet?"

"No. Soon, though."

She let go of him, putting some distance between them in case Olivia came looking for her and spied them from the front door.

"I just came to see how you were doing," Caleb said.

Jocelyn shrugged. "Great. Nervous but good."

Caleb glanced again at her front door. "I have some news. We tracked down one of your uncle Simon's old clients. A guy with more burglary arrests than this city has potholes. He admitted to pulling a job for Simon."

Jocelyn's breath caught in her throat. "Is it enough to exonerate Whitman?"

Caleb frowned. "No. He'll only admit to Simon hiring him to plant the cranes, nothing else. We think the pornography was planted remotely. We've got someone in computer crimes looking into it."

"What about clients Simon represented for cybercrimes—hacking or identity theft—that sort of thing?" she suggested.

Caleb nodded. "That's next on my list. We'll keep working it."

They stood in companionable silence for a long moment, Caleb furtively running his fingers along her forearm. "I'd invite you in," Jocelyn said, "but Olivia . . ."

Caleb grinned. "Don't sweat it. My son never met anyone I dated unless they were around for at least a year. When the time is right, Olivia and I will meet. For now, I'll settle for this." He caught her in his arms once more and planted a slow, soft kiss on her mouth, making every inch of her body hum with pleasure.

"Okay," she said breathlessly.

He let go of her and stepped away. "I'll call you later," he said, then winked at her before sauntering down the street. She stood in the cold for another minute, watching him until he reached the end of her block and turned the corner.

Back inside, everyone was gathered around Jocelyn's kitchen table, talking and laughing. The delicious smell of garlic bread filled the air. Jocelyn stood and watched them for several minutes, her heart full. A mixture of gratitude and relief washed over her—bigger and more all-encompassing than any fit of anger she had ever felt.

A second knock at her door startled her. She pulled the door open and grinned at her sister. "Camille, it's good to see you."

ACKNOWLEDGMENTS

As always I have to thank my husband, Fred, and daughter, Morgan, for their patience over the many, many hours that went into this book. I have to thank my friend, fellow author, and first reader, Michael Infinito. Thank you to my CPs who helped me shape the early drafts with their excellent insight and advice: Libby Heily, Jeff O'Handley, and, as always, my bestie and writing soul mate, Nancy S. Thompson. I'd also like to thank the many friends and family—my beta readers—who read early drafts and gave me excellent feedback: Dana Mason, Joyce Regan, Karen Hardy, Eric Gorman, Renee Crabill, and Laura Aiello. Thanks to the wonderful law enforcement people who helped me research this novel: Detective James Sloan, Detective Joe Murray, and Officer Timothy Taylor. Thanks to ADAs and fellow authors Mark Pryor and Paul Parisi for letting me run my fictional legal scenarios by them. Thanks to my unofficial "street team"—my friends, family, readers, and fans whose passion and enthusiasm always keeps me writing when I feel like giving up: my mom, Donna House; my dad, William Regan; my dad, Rusty House; my stepmom, Julie House; sister, Grace House; Melissia McKittrick; Aunt Jean Regan and Uncle Dennis Regan; my sister-in-law, Debbie Tralies; Ava and Tom McKittrick; Carol Conlen; Judy LaMay; the Delaware Valley Chapter of Sisters in Crime; my brother and sister-in-law, Sean and Cassie House;

my brothers, Andy and Kevin Brock; my sister-in-law, Christine Brock; my sister, Rebecca Brock; Tanya Fisher; Lottie Franta; Tracy Dauphin; Helen Conlen; the Dorton family; Marilyn House; Al and Kitty Funk; my aunts and uncles, Ronald and Debbie Conlen, Dennis and Mary Conlen, and Paul and Susan Conlen, who have read everything I've written and always spread the word. Thanks to all my sisters at D.A.M.N. for always being there for me and having my back. Thank you to Rob Conway for selling me a used laptop at a reasonable price so that I could actually focus on finishing this book! Thank you to Carrie Butler of Forward Authority Design, T. S. Tate, Tajare Taylor, and Dale Pease, who worked on the first edition. Thank you to Anh Schluep for taking a chance on me and the entire team at Amazon for your amazing work making this book shine. Finally, thank you to my readers—you are the absolute best.

ABOUT THE AUTHOR

Photograph by Target Studios/2012

Lisa Regan is a suspense novelist. She has a bachelor's degree in English and a master of education from Bloomsburg University. She is a member of Sisters in Crime. She lives in Philadelphia with her husband and daughter. Her debut novel, *Finding Claire Fletcher*, won Best Heroine and was runner-up in Best Novel in the eFestival of Words Best of the Independent eBook Awards for 2013. To learn more, please visit her website at www.lisaregan.com.